Melanie Milburne read her first Mills & Boon novel at the age of seventeen, in between studying for her final exams. After completing a master's degree in education, she decided to write a novel, and thus her career as a romance author was born. Melanie is an ambassador for the Australian Childhood Foundation and a keen dog-lover and trainer. She enjoys long walks in the Tasmanian bush. In 2015 Melanie won the HOLT Medallion, a prestigious award honouring outstanding literary talent.

With two university degrees and a variety of false career starts under her belt, **Michelle Conder** decided to satisfy her lifelong desire to write and finally found her dream job. She currently lives in Melbourne, Australia, with one super-indulgent husband, three self-indulgent but exquisite children, a menagerie of over-indulged pets, and the intention of doing some form of exercise daily. She loves to hear from her readers at michelleconder.com.

BILLIONAIRE'S WIFE ON PAPER

MELANIE MILBURNE

THEIR ROYAL WEDDING BARGAIN

MICHELLE CONDER

MILLS & BOON

First Published in Great Britain 2019
by Mills & Boon, an imprint of HarperCollins*Publishers*
1 London Bridge Street, London, SE1 9GF

Billionaire's Wife on Paper © 2019 by Melanie Milburne

Their Royal Wedding Bargain © 2019 by Michelle Conder

ISBN: 978-0-263-27799-9

BILLIONAIRE'S WIFE ON PAPER

MELANIE MILBURNE

To my darling little black poodle, Gonzo,
who sadly passed away during the writing of this novel.
I miss you sleeping on the sofa behind me in my office
while I write. I miss your ebullient nature and zest for
life—as if you always knew, like us, that it wasn't going
to be a long one. Your life may have been short
but you have left love footprints all over our hearts.
Rest in peace. No more seizures now.

CHAPTER ONE

LAYLA CAMPBELL WAS placing dust sheets on the furniture in the now deserted northern wing of Bellbrae Castle when she heard the sound of a firm footfall on the stairs. Goosebumps peppered her skin like Braille and a cold draught of air circled her ankles like the ghost of a long-dead cat.

No such things as ghosts. No such things as ghosts.

Her old childhood chant wasn't working any better than when she had first come to live in the Scottish Highlands castle as a frightened and lonely twelve-year-old orphan. Taken in by her great-aunt, who had worked as housekeeper for the super-wealthy aristocratic McLaughlin family, Layla had been raised in the kitchen and corridors of the castle. In the early days, downstairs had been her only domain, upstairs out of bounds. And not just because of her limp. Upstairs had been another world—a world in which she did not and could not ever belong.

'Is anyone th-there?' Her voice echoed in the silence, her heart thumping so loudly she could hear it booming in her ears. Who would be coming up to the north tower at this time of day? Logan, the new heir to the estate, was working abroad in Italy, and last time Layla had heard, Logan's younger brother Robbie was doing a casino crawl in the US. Fear crept up her spine with ice-cube-clad feet, her breathing coming to a halt when a tall figure materialised out of the shadows.

'Layla?' Logan McLaughlin said, with a heavy frown. 'What are you doing up here?'

Layla clasped her hand against her pounding chest, sure her heart was going to punch its way out of her body and land at his Italian-leather-covered feet. 'You didn't half give me a fright. Aunt Elsie told me you wouldn't be back until November. Aren't you supposed to be working in Tuscany this month?'

She hadn't seen him since his grandfather's funeral in September. And she figured he hadn't seen *her* even then. Layla had tried to offer her condolences a couple of times before and after his grandfather's service and at the wake, but she'd been busy helping her great-aunt with the catering and Logan had left before she could get a chance to speak to him in private.

But the upstairs-downstairs thing had always coloured her relationship with the McLaughlins. Logan and his brother and grandfather were landed gentry, privileged from birth, coming from a long line of aristocratic ancestors. Layla's great-aunt and her, by default, were downstairs. The staff who were meant to stay in the background and go about their work with quiet dedication, not share intimate chit-chats with their employers.

Layla could never quite forget she was the interloper, the charity case—only living there out of Logan's grandfather's pity for a homeless orphan. It made her keep a prickly and prideful rather than polite distance.

Logan scraped a hand through his hair as if his scalp was feeling too tight for his head. 'I postponed my trip. I have some business to see to here first.' His dark blue gaze swept over the dust-sheeted furniture, the crease in his forehead deepening. 'Why are you doing this? I thought Robbie was going to hire someone to see to it?'

Layla turned to pick up one of the folded dust sheets, flapping it open and then laying it over a mahogany table with cabriole legs. Hundreds of disturbed dust motes rose in the air in a galaxy of activity. 'He did see to it—by hiring me. Not that I want to be paid or anything.' She leaned down to tuck the edge of the dust sheet closer around the legs of the table and flicked him a glance. 'You do realise this is my job now? Cleaning, sorting, organising. I have a small team of people working for me and all. Didn't your grandfather tell you? He gave me a loan to get my business started.'

One brow came up in a perfect arc. 'A loan?' There was a note of surprise—or was it cynicism?—in his tone.

Layla pursed her lips and planted her hands on her hips like she was channelling a starchy nineteenth-century governess. 'A loan I paid back, with interest.' What did he think she was? An elder abuser? Exploiting an old man dying of cancer with requests for money she had no intention of paying back? She might share the genes of people like that but she didn't share their morals. 'I wouldn't have agreed to the loan otherwise.'

His navy-blue eyes narrowed. 'Seriously? He offered you a loan?'

Layla moved past him to pack up her cleaning basket. 'For your information, I have never taken your grandfather's largesse for granted.'

Feather duster. *Tick*. Soft polishing cloths. *Tick*.

'He allowed me to live here with my great-aunt rent-free and for that I will be grateful for ever.'

She shoved the furniture polish bottle in amongst the other cleaning products in her basket. She had become closer to the old man in his last months of life, coming to understand the gruff exterior of a proud man who had done his best to keep his family together after repeated tragedy.

Logan let out a long breath, still frowning like he didn't know any other way to look at her. Story of her life. One look at her scarred leg and her limp and that's what most people did—frowned. Or asked intrusive questions she refused on principle to answer. Layla never talked about what had happened to her leg, not in any detail that is. 'A car crash' was her stripped-down answer. She never said who was driving or why they were driving the way they were, or who else had been injured or killed.

Who wanted to be reminded of the day that had changed her life for ever?

'Why didn't he just give you the money?' Logan asked.

Layla's old friend pride steeled her gaze and tightened her mouth. 'Oh, you mean because he felt sorry for me?'

Logan's covert glance at her left leg told her all she needed to know. Just like everyone else, he saw her damaged leg first and her later—if at all. Layla was fiercely proud of how she had made something of herself in spite of impossible odds. She didn't want to be seen as the orphaned girl with the limp, but the gutsy woman with gumption, drive, ambition and resourcefulness.

'No.' His tone was weighted. 'Because he was a wealthy man and you're practically family.' He moved away to look at some of the boxes she'd packed earlier. He peeled back the cardboard flaps of one box and took out a leather-bound book, fanning through the pages, his features set in lines of deep thought.

Practically family? Was *that* how he saw her? As a surrogate sister or distant cousin? At six feet four with a lean and rangy build, dark brown loosely styled wavy hair, a chiselled Lord Byron jaw and deep blue eyes the colour of a Highland tarn, it would be a crying waste if Logan McLaughlin were her brother or cousin.

It was a crying waste to women the world over that he hadn't dated since the tragic death of his fiancée Susannah.

Not that he would ever date Layla. No one had ever dated her…well, not since she was a teenager. And she deliberately tried *not* to think of that one and only date and the excruciating embarrassment it had entailed. From that day on, she had decided her career plans would always be more important. More important than trying to go to parties or nightclubs in short dresses and heels that drew even more attention to her leg. More important than being told by a guy she wasn't good enough. Could never be good enough.

Logan closed the book with a little snap and placed it back on top of the others. He turned to look at her.

Yep, with a frown.

'Where will you and your aunt go if this place is sold?'

Layla's eyes widened and her chest developed a tight, can't-take-another-breath ache. '*Sold?* You're selling Bellbrae?' She could think of no bigger tragedy…well, she could because she'd lived through one big hell of a tragedy, but still. Selling Bellbrae was way up there on the list. Who would she be without the shelter of Bellbrae watching over her? Her identity had been formed here, her sense of security and safety honed within the fortress-like walls of the centuries-old castle. 'How could you do that, Logan? Your grandfather left it to you as his eldest male heir. Your dad is buried here along with your grandparents and generations of ancestors. You surely don't need to sell it for the money?'

His expression went as blank as one of the dust sheets on the furniture, but his tone was jaded. 'It's not about money. I am unwilling to fulfil the terms of my grandfather's will.'

Layla frowned like she was in competition with him for Best Frown in Show. 'Terms? What terms?'

He stuffed his hands into his trouser pockets and moved to look out of one of the mullioned windows, his back turned to her. Layla could see the tension in his shoulders even through his clothes. The breadth of his shoulders had always secretly fascinated her.

She had often seen him rowing and swimming in summer on the lake on the Bellbrae estate when he'd come home to visit. Tall and lean-hipped with abdomen muscles ridged with strength and endurance, she had been fascinated by his athleticism as it had been in such stark contrast to her young broken body. And when he'd brought Susannah home for visits, Layla had watched them both. Susannah had been supermodel stunning, slim and glamourous. Never had Layla seen two people more perfect for each other or more devotedly in love. It had set a benchmark for her to aspire to. An impossible benchmark perhaps, but a girl could dream, couldn't she?

Logan turned to look at her, his jaw set in a taut line. 'Unless I marry within three months, the entire estate will pass to Robbie.'

Layla licked her carpet-dry lips, her heart suddenly flapping like a loose window shutter in a stiff Highland breeze. 'Oh...'

He drew in a breath and released it in a gust of frustration. 'Yes. Oh. And we both know what he will do when he gets his hands on this place.'

Layla couldn't allow her mind to even go there. No two brothers could ever be more disparate. Logan was the strong, silent type—hard-working and responsible. Robbie was a loud party boy with a streak of recklessness who had already brought shame on the family too many times to count. 'You think he'd sell it?'

He gave a grim movement of his lips that wasn't anywhere near a smile. 'Or—worse—turn it into party central for irresponsible playboys like himself.'

Layla chewed her lower lip, her thoughts in a tangled knot. If Bellbrae was sold, what would happen to her great-aunt? Where would Aunt Elsie live if not here? Her great-aunt lived in a little cottage on the estate where she had spent the last forty years. Like Layla, it was the only home she knew. And what would happen to

Logan's grandfather's elderly dog, Flossie? The dog was almost blind and would find a move to another place even more distressing than Aunt Elsie would. 'There must be something you can do to challenge the terms of your grandfather's will.'

'The will is ironclad.' He turned away to look at the view from the windows, even the sound of his feet moving across the carpet conveyed his disgust.

'Why did your grandfather write it in such a way?' Layla asked into the echoing silence. 'Did he talk to you about it before he…?' She still found it hard to believe the old man was gone.

Packing up Angus McLaughlin's things had made her realise how different Bellbrae would be without him. Picky and pedantic, he hadn't been the easiest person to get along with, but over the last few months Layla had made a point of ignoring his bad points and had found him to have a softer side he'd been at great pains to keep hidden.

Logan rubbed a hand over the back of his neck and partially turned from the window to look at her. 'He's been telling me for years to settle down and do my duty. Marry and provide a couple of heirs to continue the family line.'

'But you don't want to get married.' It was a statement, not a question.

A shadow passed through his gaze like a background figure moving across a stage. He turned back to face the view from the windows; there might as well have been a 'Keep Away' sign printed on his back. It seemed a decade before he spoke. 'No.' His tone had a note of finality that made something in Layla's chest tighten.

The thought of him marrying someone one day had always niggled at her like a mild toothache. She could ignore it mostly but now and again a sharp jab would catch her off guard. But how could he ever find some-one as perfect for him as Susannah? No wonder he was a little reluctant to date seriously these days. If only Layla could find someone to love her with such last-ing loyalty. *Sigh*.

'What about a marriage of convenience? You could find someone who would agree to marry you just long enough to fulfil the terms of the will.'

One of his dark eyebrows rose in a cynical arc above his left eye. 'Are you volunteering for the role as my paper bride?'

Eek! Why had she even mentioned such a thing? Maybe it was time to stop reading paperback romances and start reading thriller or horror novels instead. Layla could feel a hot flush of colour flooding her cheeks and bent down to straighten the items in her basket to disguise it. 'No. Of course not.' Her voice was part laugh, part gasp and came out shamefully high and tight. Her? His bride of convenience? Ha-di-ha-ha-ha. She wouldn't be a convenient bride for anyone, much less Logan McLaughlin.

A strange silence crept from the far corners of the room, stealing oxygen particles, stilling dust motes, stirring possibilities…

Logan walked back to where she was hovering over her cleaning basket, his footsteps steady and sure. Step. Step. Step. Step. Layla slowly raised her gaze to his in-scrutable one, her heart doing a crazy tap dance in her chest. She drank in the landscape of his face—the ink-black prominent eyebrows over impossibly blue eyes, the patrician nose, the sensually sculpted mouth, the steely determined jaw. The lines of grief etched into his skin that made him seem older than he was. At thirty-three, he was in the prime of his life. Wealthy, talented, a world-renowned landscape architect—you could not find a more eligible bachelor…or one so determined to avoid commitment.

'Think about it, Layla.' His tone was deep with a side note of roughness that made a faint shiver course through her body. A shiver of awareness. A shiver of longing that could no longer be restrained in its secret home.

Layla picked up her basket from the floor and held it in front of her body like a shield. Was he teasing her? Making fun of her? He must surely know she wasn't marriage material—certainly not for someone like him. She was about as far away from Susannah as you could get. 'Don't be ridiculous.'

His hand came down to touch her on the forearm, and even through two layers of clothing her skin tingled. She looked down at his long strong fingers and disguised a swallow. She could count on one hand the number of times he had touched her over the years and still have fingers left over. His touch was unfamiliar and strange, alien almost, and yet her body reacted like a crocus bulb to spring sunshine.

'I'm serious,' he said, looking at her with watchful intensity. 'I need a temporary wife to save Bellbrae from being sold or destroyed and who better than someone who loves this place as much as I do?'

But you don't love me.

The words came into her head at random but she had no way of getting rid of them. They were like gate-crashers at a party, unwelcome, intrusive. Forbidden. Yep, she definitely had to switch reading genres. Layla slipped out of his hold and moved a couple of steps back, still holding her basket in front of her body. 'I'm sure you can find someone much more suitable to be your wife than me.'

Someone beautiful.

Someone glamourous.

Someone perfect.

'Layla, I'm not talking about a real marriage here.' His frown was back, his voice as steady and calm as a patient teacher speaking to a slow student. 'It would be a marriage on paper and would only last a year, max. We wouldn't even have to go through the charade of a big wedding. We could marry privately with only the minimum witnesses required to make it legal.'

Layla rolled her lips together, her gaze slipping away from his. Her mind was wheeling round and round like a hamster on performance-enhancing drugs. A short-term marriage to Logan McLaughlin to save Bellbrae. To save her great-aunt and Flossie the geriatric dog. Layla would wear Logan's ring but not be a real bride. Given her dating record, it might be her only chance to be anyone's bride. Could she agree to spend the year being 'married' to Logan? Living with him for all intents and purposes as if they had married for all the right reasons?

But who would ever believe *she* was the love of his life?

Layla brought her gaze back up to meet his. 'Aren't

you worried what people might say? I mean, the up-stairs-downstairs thing? I'm the housekeeper's or-phaned great-niece. You're the Laird of the castle. I'm hardly what anyone would consider a suitable bride for you.'

His frown carved a trench between his midnight-blue eyes. 'Why are you so hard on yourself? You're a beau-tiful young woman. You have nothing to be ashamed of.'

Wow. A compliment.

A warm glow flooded through her body, her self-esteem waking from a coma. Beautiful, huh? That cer-tainly wasn't what her mirror told her, but then Logan had never seen the full extent of her scars. But a com-pliment was a compliment and she was going to take it at face value for once. She brought her gaze back to his, keeping her tone even. 'And what happens when the year is up?'

'We have the marriage annulled and get on with our lives as before.'

Layla put down the cleaning basket and wiped her suddenly damp palms on her thighs. She had suffered temptation before and mostly resisted. Mostly. But walking past a bowl of her great-aunt's Belgian choco-late mousse was clearly not in the same league as agree-ing to be Logan's temporary bride. She would be in close contact with him, not sleeping with him but liv-ing with him.

Sharing his life for a Whole Year.

How was she going to stop herself from develop-ing feelings for him? Feelings that were already lurk-ing in the background like a secret smouldering coal that only needed a tiny whiff of oxygen to leap into a

scorching hot flame. She could feel it now—the slow
burn of attraction that made her aware of every movement he made. Every time he took a breath, every time
he frowned, every time his gaze meshed with hers.

'I don't expect you to do this for nothing, Layla. I'll
make sure you are financially well compensated.' He
named a figure that made her eyebrows shoot up so
high they nearly flew off her face.

Now was probably not the time to tell him she would
have done it free. There was probably never going to be
that time. Logan had loved and loved deeply and had
tragically lost that love. No woman would ever take the
place of his fiancée and any woman who thought she
could would be a silly romantic fool.

But the amount of money he was offering would
allow Layla to expand her cleaning business into a
household concierge service as well. She could take
on more staff so she didn't have to do so much of the
physical work, which increasingly tired her. It would
mean she could be at the helm of her business playing
to her strengths instead of her weakness.

Layla raised her chin, keen to portray a cool and
steady composure she was nowhere near feeling. 'I'd
like a day or two to think about it.' She was proud of
the evenness of her tone given the pitty-pat, pitty-pat
hammering of her pulse.

His expression barely changed but she sensed a restrained relief sweeping through him. 'Of course. It's
a big decision and not without its risks, which brings
me to a difficult but necessary discussion.'

Layla knew where he was going with this and it annoyed her that he thought her so gauche for it to even

be a possibility for her to fall in love with him. She was definitely no Jane Eyre. She might find him ridiculously attractive and her pulse might go a little crazy when he was around but that's as far as it could ever go. As far as she would *let* it go. She had willpower, didn't she? She would send it to boot camp ASAP.

She raised her brows in twin arcs of derision. 'Oh, the one about me not getting any silly ideas about falling head over heels in love with you?'

Heels? Now *that* was the stuff of fantasy.

If he was taken aback by her bluntness, he didn't show it. 'I would hate you to get hurt in the process of helping me save Bellbrae. We both love this place but it doesn't mean we have to fall in love with each other.'

Layla painted a stiff smile on her lips but something inside her shrivelled. Of course, he would never fall in love with her. Why would he? She was more or less invisible to him and had been for the past fourteen years. But for him to rule the possibility out at the get-go was still a slap in the face to her feminine ego. 'Message received loud and clear.'

He gave a slight nod, the quiet intensity of his gaze unsettling her already shaky equilibrium. 'Here—I'll carry your basket downstairs for you.'

He stepped forward to pick up her basket at the same time she bent down to get it. Their hands met on the handle and a jolt of electricity shot up Layla's arm and straight to her core, fizzing like the ignited wick of a firework. She pulled hers out away and straightened but in her haste, she lost her balance and would have fallen if it hadn't been for the quick action of Logan grabbing her arm to hold her steady. His fingers overlapped on the slim bones of her wrist and another wave of heat coursed through her body. Heat that simmered and sizzled in all her secret places.

His gaze locked with hers and she got the strangest sense he was seeing her for the first time. The slight flare of his pupils, the gentling of his fingers around her wrist less of a steadying hold, more like that of a caress. She could smell the cool fresh lime top notes of his aftershave and the base notes of cool forest wood and country leather. She could see the various shades of blue flecks in his eyes, reminding her of flickering shadows over a deep mountain lake. His lean jaw was lightly sprinkled with regrowth; the dark pinpricks a reminder of the potent male hormones surging around his body.

His mouth...

Her heart skipped a beat. Her stomach flip-flopped. Her female hormones started a party. She should *not* have looked at his mouth. But she was drawn by an impulse she had zero control over. His lips were more or less even in volume with well-defined contours that hinted at his determined, goal-achieving personality. She wondered what his mouth would feel like pressed to her own. Wondered and wanted and wished for it to happen.

'Are you okay?' His voice was husky and low—as low as an intimate lover's voice.

Layla stretched her lips into a polite smile that felt shaky around the edges. 'I'm fine. Thanks.' She stepped out of his hold to create some distance between them but she couldn't help noticing he was opening and closing his fingers as if to remove the same tingling sensation she had felt. Or maybe he hadn't felt tingles. Maybe he was disgusted…as disgusted as her teenage date all those years ago when he'd seen her damaged body.

'I'll go and see to your room.' Layla injected house-keeper briskness into her tone. 'I assume you're stay-ing for a night or two?'

'It depends.'

'On?'

His unwavering gaze held hers. 'On your decision.'

'And if I say no?'

A fault line of tension rippled along his jaw and an embittered light came into his eyes. 'You and your great-aunt will no longer have a home here. Not if my brother Robbie has his way.'

Logan waited until Layla had left before he let out a breath he hadn't realised he'd been holding. But truth be told, he felt like he'd been holding his breath ever since he'd found out the contents of his grandfather's will. Nothing could have come as more of a shock than finding the survival of the Bellbrae estate was depen-dent on him finding a wife. A wife, he had resolutely decided seven years ago, he would never have.

Not after the suicide of his fiancée Susannah.

Logan went back to the windows that overlooked the estate. His chest ached and burned with the thought of losing his family's ancestral home. Generations of McLaughlins had lived and loved and died here. Every Highland slope and crag, every bubbling burn had watched him grow from baby to boy to man. Every tree was like an old friend. There were trees on the estate his great-great-grandfather had planted. There were gardens his own father had designed before he had been taken by pancreatic cancer when Logan was eighteen. Logan had learned the skills of landscape design from his father and developed it into a global career that gave him more money than he needed and fame he didn't want.

He drew in a breath as rough and uneven as Highland scree. There was no other way but to marry if he was to save the estate from his reckless and foolish younger brother.

And who better to marry than Layla Campbell, who had lived here since she was a child?

Logan would be lying if he said he hadn't noticed how beautiful she was. Perhaps not in a classical sense, but with her waist-length chestnut hair and creamy complexion and grey-green eyes, she had an ethereal quality about her that was just as captivating—maybe even more so. For years she'd just been a cute but somewhat annoying child lurking around the estate, spying on him and his brother.

But it was impossible not to notice her now.

But he would have to, because he wasn't entering into a long-term relationship.

Not now.

Not again.

Not ever.

Logan walked back over to the boxes Layla had packed and opened the lid of one that contained his grandfather's clothes. It didn't seem real that his grandfather was no longer here. He lifted out a Shetland island sweater and held it against his face, breathing in the faint smell of his grandfather's old-fashioned spicy aftershave.

If the estate was sold, there would be no trace left of his grandfather or his father. They would be gone. Lost. Erased.

For years, Logan had spent hours in his father's study at Bellbrae, sitting at his father's desk, reading the books his father had read, writing with the pens he had used—just so he could feel close to his dad. To hold onto the memory of his dad for as long as possible.

Logan put the sweater back in the box and closed the cardboard flaps, wishing he could close a lid on his guilt and regret. He hadn't been as close to his grandfather as he should have been. But losing his father on the threshold of his own adulthood had made Logan resentful of his grandfather's old-school parenting style. He hadn't wanted his grandfather to be a stand-in dad. He'd wanted his father to still be alive. He'd resented the way his grandfather had tried to control every decision he made, everything he did and who he did it with. It had been suffocating and had only made him miss his father more.

It had hit Robbie even harder and Logan blamed himself for the way his younger brother had rebelled. Logan had been too lenient with him, allowing the pendulum to swing too far back the other way to compensate for his grandfather's strict authoritarian style. But hadn't he always been too lenient with Robbie? Ever since their mother had left, Logan had tried to fill the gaping hole she'd left in their lives. But, of course, he had failed.

What was with him and relationships? Why was he destined to screw up each and every one?

But maybe he could repair some of that damage by saving Bellbrae.

He had been straight with Layla on the terms of the deal. Brutally straight, but he was unapologetic for it. He had no intention of hurting her by giving her false hope. A marriage of convenience was the only way he could save his family's home. A home Layla had loved from the moment she'd arrived to live with her great-aunt Elsie. If Logan thought his brother would do the right thing by Bellbrae he wouldn't have bothered with the messy business of fulfilling the terms of the will.

But lately he'd become aware of Robbie's gambling habit. A disturbing habit that had run up some eye-watering debt. Robbie saw Bellbrae differently from him. He didn't have the same deep-in-the-DNA connection with the estate Logan had. Once his brother got hold of Bellbrae he would sell it to the highest bidder and walk away from the estate that had been in their family for centuries.

But selling Bellbrae wasn't going to happen if Logan could help it. He would enter a short-term marriage to protect a long-term estate. To protect the legacy his father had handed to him on his deathbed.

'Always do the right thing by Bellbrae.'

And he would do the right thing by Layla by making sure she had no illusions about their marriage from the get-go. He would pay her generously for her time as his wife. They would marry as friends and part as friends. He knew how much this place meant to her—how much she used it as a base when she wasn't in Edinburgh, where she ran her small business. Any niggling of his conscience he settled with the conviction he was helping her in the long run. He was offering her a staggering amount of money to be his temporary wife.

How could she possibly say no?

CHAPTER TWO

'BUT YOU HAVE to say no,' Layla's best friend Isla said on the phone later that evening. 'You'll get your heart broken for sure.'

'But it will break my heart to see Bellbrae sold,' Layla said. 'This is the first real home I've ever had. I've spent the last fourteen years here—it's made me who I am today. I can't bear the thought of it going out of the McLaughlin family. It belongs to Logan. It was wrong of Angus to make his will in such a way.'

'Do you know why Angus did it that way?'

Layla sighed so heavily her shoulders slumped. 'Logan has made it pretty clear over the years that he has no intention of settling down again. Losing Susannah was such a terrible shock to him—as it would be to anyone. I've overheard a few conversations where Angus insisted Logan move on with his life but Logan isn't someone you can tell what to do. Once his mind is made up, that's it.'

'So, he's made up his mind to marry you in a marriage of convenience?'

Layla pulled at her top lip with her finger and thumb as she thought about her conversation with Logan in the north tower. 'Yes, well, I think I kind of planted the idea in his head. But we both love Bellbrae and we both know how impulsive Robbie can be. He doesn't love the place the same way we do. He thinks it's boring and cold and too isolated. We have to stop him inheriting the estate even if it means giving up a year of our lives in a paper marriage.'

'Are you sure it's going to be on paper? Logan's a full-blooded man. You're a young and beautiful woman. Living together is going to test the boundaries surely?'

Layla affected a laugh. 'Calling me beautiful is a bit of a stretch. Anyway, can you imagine him being attracted to me? I'm hardly what you'd call his type. I'm not anyone's type.'

'You're way too hard on yourself,' Isla said, echoing Logan's words. 'You shouldn't let what happened in your teens colour how you see yourself now. But the whole friends-to-lovers thing can happen, you know. It doesn't just happen in romance novels.'

'I'm not sure how to describe our relationship,' Layla said. 'Friends is probably too generous a description. We're distant and polite to each other. I sometimes think he doesn't even register I'm around now that I'm an adult. I'm like part of the furniture.'

'I just hope you don't get hurt in the long run,' Isla said. 'I want you to be as happy as I am. I still can't believe how wonderful it is to be married to Rafe, knowing he loves me more than anything. We're both so excited about our Christmas baby.'

'I'm excited about your baby too.'

It was hard not to feel envious of her best friend's happiness. After a rough start, Isla and Rafe had finally come together again and were eagerly awaiting the birth of their 'accidental' baby. But would Layla's marriage to Logan have an equally happy ending?

The odds were stacked against it and the sooner she got that straight and clear in her mind, the better.

Logan walked through the south garden at Bellbrae, the scattered leaves of the ancient deciduous trees crunching under his feet. The vivid reds and golds and bronze and yellows were like wild splashes of paint. The autumn air was crisp and redolent of the smell of cooling earth and leaf litter with a hint of the harsh winter to come. Each season at Bellbrae held its magic for him. The gardens and fields and Highlands beyond could be blanketed in white as thick as a pile of duvets and still stir him to the marrow. But unless Layla agreed to a marriage of convenience, he would have to say goodbye to this place. The land and home of his ancestors, the place where he felt deeply rooted to the estate as surely and securely as the ancient trees around him.

Logan waited for Flossie, his grandfather's old Border collie, to keep up. She was sniffing around the tendon-like roots of an old oak tree. 'Come on, Floss.' He patted his hand against his thigh and the dog slowly waddled over to him, her tail wagging, her tongue hanging out of her mouth in spite of the chill in the air. He leaned down to scratch behind her ears, a pang jabbing him deep in his gut at the thought of what would happen to her if Robbie inherited the estate. The old dog would not cope with a move to another home and Robbie wouldn't want to keep her.

Logan straightened from petting the dog and caught

a glimpse of a slim figure walking through the archway of trees in the distance. With her wild chestnut hair and creamy skin and irregular gait, Layla looked as much a part of this landscape as heather on the Highlands. For years he had seen her moving about on the estate, reminding him of a faery or other mythic person. Touching her on the arm the day before had sent a shockwave of awareness through him—an awareness he found faintly disturbing. He would have to try harder not to touch her unless absolutely necessary.

The boundaries were not to be blurred and especially not by him.

Layla turned her head as if she had suddenly sensed him nearby. She clutched the front of her jacket around the front of her body and began to walk in his direction. 'I was looking for Flossie,' she called out to him, sweeping the cloud of her hair back over one slim shoulder. 'I thought she might have gone out alone and got lost.'

Logan met her more than halfway across the wooded garden to save her from negotiating the treacherous tree roots. 'I took her out with me earlier. Sorry to worry you.' He turned back to look at the lumbering Border collie. 'She's slowed down a lot, hasn't she?'

Layla bent down to ruffle the dog's ears just where his hand had been moments earlier, her hair tumbling from behind her shoulders. He suddenly had an urge to run his fingers through her hair—to see if it was as soft and silky as it looked.

He curled his hands into tight fists and gave his willpower a pep talk. *No touching. Hands off. Paper relationship only.*

'Yes, I noticed a big change after your grandfather

passed,' she said. 'She misses him, don't you, sweetie?' She addressed the dog affectionately and was rewarded by an enthusiastic tail wag. Layla straightened and met his gaze. 'We all miss him.'

For a moment, Logan wondered if his grandfather had planned this all along—a marriage between him and Layla. The old man had spent a lot of time with her over the last months of his life. And his grandfather had given her that loan she'd mentioned. After all, she had been the one to suggest he enter a marriage of convenience when they'd spoken in his grandfather's suite in the north tower. Had that been deliberate on her part or just a throwaway line borne out of her love for Bellbrae?

And why the hell was he suddenly so cynical about her? She was part of the family—or close enough to being so. He couldn't imagine Bellbrae without her.

Logan had taken it a step further by suggesting she offer herself as his paper bride. He still didn't quite believe he had done that, but it had seemed a solution he could live with at the time. The *only* solution he could live with. 'Did you ever speak to my grandfather about his intentions regarding the will?'

Her grey-green eyes widened in affront and her chin came up at a proud angle. 'What are you suggesting? That I somehow put him up to changing his original will?'

Logan shrugged one shoulder with a nonchalance he didn't feel. 'You stand to gain quite a lot if you marry me. You said it yourself—the upstairs-downstairs thing.'

She coughed out a derisive laugh. 'Newsflash, Logan. I'm not going to marry you. It would be beneath my dignity to marry someone who's such an appalling snob.' She swung away to walk back the way she had come but Logan caught up in one or two strides and clasped her by the wrist and turned her to face him.

'No, wait,' he said, suddenly aware of how tiny her wrist was, tiny enough for his fingers to overlap. Aware too, of the bergamot and geranium fragrance of her hair. Her eyes sparked with chips of ice, her rose-pink lips tightly pursed. It was a mistake to look too closely at her mouth. For years he had avoided doing so. It was soft and plump with her top lip shaped in a perfect cupid's bow, with dimples either side when she smiled, which she was not currently doing.

'I'm sorry, Layla. That was crass of me.' He sighed and released her wrist, his fingers feeling strangely restless and empty when she stepped back.

She rubbed at her wrist as if he had given her a Chinese burn, her eyes still flashing. 'I find your accusation deeply insulting. The last thing I want is for you to lose Bellbrae but I refuse to marry a man who is so deeply distrustful of my motives.'

Logan had always secretly admired her stubborn streak of pride. She hadn't had the easiest start in life but she had made the most of the opportunities that had come her way after coming to live on the estate. She was a hard worker—too hard, he thought, given her leg—but it was a brave person indeed who took it upon themselves to tell her to slow down.

'I can only apologise again. It was a stupid thing to say.' He held her gaze, watching for any softening of her expression.

She appeared to be slightly mollified. Slightly, not

fully. Her lips were still tightly compressed but the daggers in her eyes had been sheathed. For now. 'Apology accepted.' Her voice sounded a little gruff and she delicately cleared her throat and added, 'But there's another thing I find annoying. You're assuming I don't already have a partner.'

An invisible punch hit him in the chest and for a moment he couldn't take a breath. He'd heard nothing about her love life recently…in fact, he couldn't remember hearing anything about a boyfriend for years. But she spent heaps of time in Edinburgh these days with her cleaning business. She could have any number of lovers. And why shouldn't she?

'Do you?' he asked, not sure he really wanted to know. But a current partner would be a problem. A big problem in more ways than he wanted to think about.

Her eyes fell away from his and twin spots of colour darkened on her cheeks. 'Not at the moment.'

There was a small silence broken only by the rustling of the leaves at their feet as a cool breeze passed through the copse of trees. Some remaining leaves fell from the craggy branches overhead, floating down like over-sized confetti. *What was it with the wedding imagery?* Weddings were something he never thought of. He never even attended them, not if he could help it.

Layla's gaze went to the elderly dog who was now lying down at Logan's feet. 'What do you think will happen to Flossie if Robbie inherits Bellbrae?' Her tone contained a chord of disquiet, the same disquiet he felt about his ruthless younger brother's intentions. 'Would you take her to live with you?'

'She's too old to travel and I'm on the road too much

in any case.' He exhaled a long breath. 'He'll probably have her put down.'

She gave an audible swallow and her wide eyes met his. 'We can't let that happen. She might be old and mostly blind but she still enjoys life. Your grandfather would spin in his grave if—'

'If my grandfather was so concerned about Flossie, then why the hell did he write his will like that?' Logan couldn't strip back the frustration in his voice. His grandfather's will had put him in an impossible situation. He felt cornered, compromised, blackmailed.

Layla's teeth sank into her lower lip. 'If I were to marry you, what would we tell people about us? I mean, are we going to pretend it's a real marriage, or—?'

Logan rubbed a hand along the side of his jaw before dropping his hand back by his side. 'I would prefer people to think it's a genuine love match. I'm not sure who's going to buy it, but still.'

Her chin came back up and the daggers were back glinting in her eyes. 'Thank you.' Her tone was distinctly wry.

Logan could have thumped himself for being so insensitive. 'That came out wrong. I was thinking more about in terms of myself.'

A small frown appeared on her smooth-as-cream forehead. 'Because of what you felt for Susannah?' She paused for a beat and added, 'What you *still* feel for her?'

Logan had never discussed with anyone the complicated relationship he'd had with Susannah. He didn't even like thinking about how badly he had handled things. It was better to let people think he was still grieving the loss of his fiancée, but in truth he felt guilt rather than grief. Gut-shredding guilt that gnawed and clawed at him with savage teeth and talons.

So many mistakes he had made, costly mistakes that had ended in tragedy.

'It's pretty common knowledge I never intended to settle down with anyone after Susannah's death,' he said. 'I guess my grandfather decided to take the matter into his own hands and force me to face my responsibilities as the eldest McLaughlin heir.'

The frown on her brow deepened. 'So, who will your heir be? Or will you eventually leave Bellbrae to a nephew or niece if Robbie has children at some point?'

Logan hadn't got to thinking that far ahead. His sole goal had been rescuing Bellbrae from being auctioned off to settle his brother's gambling debts. Marrying to save the estate was a big enough step, siring an heir was a giant leap he wasn't sure he was ready to even consider. Yet. He gave one of his carefully rationed smiles. 'I don't suppose you'd like to help me with that?'

Her cheeks burned a fire-engine red and her plump rosy lips flattened to a thin disapproving line. 'No.' Her tone was as starchy as a prim Victorian Sunday schoolteacher's.

'Only joking.' It was no joking matter but he refused to think about having a child. Hadn't he done enough damage with his brother?

Layla shifted her gaze, but he noticed her small white teeth resumed their savaging of her lower lip. 'I need to get back to help Aunt Elsie with something.' Her voice was not much more than a mumble.

'I need your final answer, Layla. Tonight, if possible. There are legal documents to arrange before we—'

'I'll see you tonight. At dinner.'

Logan nodded in agreement. 'It's a date.'

It had been a heck of a long time since he'd had one of those.

Layla sat with her great-aunt at the Bellbrae kitchen table half an hour later with a pot of tea and freshly baked cupcakes.

'You're not eating,' Aunt Elsie said, pushing the tiered cake stand closer. 'Is something on your mind?'

Layla took a cake from the stand and peeled the polka-dotted paper case off the cupcake. 'I'm not sure how to tell you this…' she began.

Her great-aunt paused in the action of sipping her tea, her light blue gaze wide with interest. 'You've met someone?'

Layla only just resisted the impulse to roll her eyes. 'No. It's a little more complicated than that.' She took a deep breath and added, 'Logan's asked me to marry him.'

Her great-aunt's cup gave a tiny rattle as she placed it back in its saucer. 'And what was your answer?'

Layla wasn't sure what to make of her great-aunt's mild expression. 'Aren't you surprised he proposed to me?'

Aunt Elsie reached for the teapot and topped up both of their cups with the rich brew. She placed the teapot back on its heat protector before responding. 'Not one bit surprised. He's known you since you were a wee child. He's watched you grow up into a fine young woman. You'll be a good wife for him. Loyal and steady and stable.' She peered at Layla over the top of her bi-focals. 'You said yes, didn't you?'

Layla nibbled at one side of her mouth. 'I'm still deciding…'

Aunt Elsie sat back in her chair, lifted the little milk jug to pour some into her tea and then set the jug back down on the table. 'You'd be mad to refuse, my girl. He's a good man. A bit on the quiet side but you don't want a husband who talks more than he listens. He'll take good care of you.'

Layla broke off a piece of cupcake with her fingers. 'He only wants to stay married for a year to secure the estate. If he doesn't marry within three months, Bell-brae will automatically pass to Robbie.' She put the small portion of cake in her mouth, chewed and swallowed, continuing to gauge her great-aunt's reaction.

Aunt Elsie stirred her tea into a small whirlpool, glancing at her again. 'I know about Angus's will. He told me before he died.'

Layla frowned. 'And you didn't try and change his mind?'

Aunt Elsie sighed and picked up her cup again. 'There isn't a person alive or dead who could change that man's mind. Angus was frustrated Logan hadn't moved on from losing Susannah. Sure, he has casual lovers occasionally but his grandfather wanted him to settle down and do the right thing by Bellbrae. If marrying you is the only way Logan can see fit to do it, then so be it. You love this place and you love him.' She made a toast of her last words by taking a sip of her tea.

'Excuse me.' Layla gave a choked laugh. 'Not like *that*!'

Aunt Elsie arched her eyebrows. 'Are you sure?'

Growing up, Layla had idolised Logan from afar. He had been a romantic fantasy any teenage girl would have drooled over. But it was a bit of a leap to describe her feelings now as love, or at least *that* sort of love. Although…that tiny secret smouldering coal inside her was still there waiting, waiting, waiting for enough oxygen to fan it into life.

Layla looked down at the cake crumbs on her plate and expelled a long breath. 'It wouldn't matter how I felt about him. It's not going to be a proper marriage.' She pushed the crumbs into a neat pile and then glanced back at her great-aunt. 'It will be on paper only.'

Aunt Elsie's eyes began to twinkle like they were auditioning for a new constellation in the northern hemisphere. 'Of course it will.'

Layla gave an eye roll and stood to take her plate and cup and saucer to the sink. Her great-aunt was suffering a massive delusion if she thought Logan would be remotely interested in sleeping with *her*. She had seen photos of Logan's casual lovers. She had seen his fiancée Susannah in the stunningly beautiful and unscarred flesh.

How could she ever hope to compete with that?

CHAPTER THREE

LATER THAT EVENING Layla fed Flossie and let her out for a comfort walk. When she got back, the old dog began to snore almost as soon as she settled back in her wicker basket in front of the fire in Angus's study a few doors away from the kitchen. There was a pet door in one of the back doors off the kitchen, but Flossie was too arthritic these days to get through it.

It was sad to see the old girl's decline. Layla had only been at Bellbrae a couple of weeks when Angus McLaughlin had brought Flossie home as a playful and needle-toothed puppy. She had often wondered if he had bought the dog to help her settle in. She had asked him once but he'd dismissed the suggestion in his gruff and off-hand way.

Layla had spent many a happy time playing with Flossie, brushing her silky coat and taking her on walks about the estate, which had seemed so huge and terrifying when she had first arrived. But with the company of the ebullient puppy it had suddenly become a home. A home she could not imagine losing. Her happiest memories—the *only* happy memories she possessed—had been crafted and laid down here at Bellbrae.

Layla was putting the finishing touches to dinner shortly after when Logan strode into the kitchen. She glanced over her shoulder and turned back to the pot she was stirring on the cooktop. 'Dinner won't be long.'

'Where's Elsie?'

Layla put the cooking spoon down on the ceramic spoon rest and turned and faced him, wiping her hands on her apron. 'I gave her the night off. She hasn't been doing so much cooking now your grandfather's no longer with us.' She waited a beat and added, 'She knew about the change to his will.'

Logan frowned. 'Thoughtful of him to share it with the household help but not with me.'

Layla pursed her lips. 'You might think of Aunt Elsie as little more than a humble housekeeper but she has supported your family through every high and low of the last three decades.' She whipped off her apron and flung it on the benchtop.

'When your mother left when you and Robbie were little, when your father died, when Robbie went off the rails that first time in his teens. And when your grandmother died when you were away at university. Aunt Elsie has cooked and cleaned and consoled everyone, working long hours and forsaking a normal life of her own. Don't you dare refer to her as just the help.' Her chest was heaving like she had just run up one of the Bellbrae turrets. Three turrets. Possibly all twelve of them.

He closed his eyes in a slow blink and sighed. 'All I seem to do lately around you is open my mouth and change feet.' He twisted his lips into a rueful grimace. 'I meant no offence. My only excuse is that I'm still reeling from being so much in the dark about my grand-father's intentions. I hate surprises at the best of times and this was one hell of a surprise.'

There were surprises and there were surprises. Layla could only imagine the surprises Logan had received over the course of his life were not the pleasant type. His mother abandoning him and his brother as small children to go and live with her lover abroad, the sudden death of his father from pancreatic cancer, the terrible shock of his fiancée's suicide and now his grandfather's odd conditions on his will. She could hardly blame him for wanting a little more predictability in his life. 'I hope you don't mind but I told Aunt Elsie about your proposal.'

Logan's gaze was steady and watchful. 'And?'

'She told me I'd be a fool not to accept.'

'And have you accepted?'

'Just to be clear—I don't want you to lose Bellbrae much more than I want to be your wife. Think of my acceptance as an act of charity, if you will.'

If he was relieved by her answer he gave no sign of it on his features. They might as well have been dis-cussing the weather. 'I appreciate your honesty. Neither of us want this but we have a common goal in saving Bellbrae.'

Layla kept her chin high, her gaze level, her pride on active duty. 'She also thinks it won't be a paper mar-riage for very long.'

One side of his mouth came up in a vestige of a smile. It took years off his face and made something in her stomach slip sideways. It had been years, seven years at least, since she had seen him give anything close to a smile.

He approached the island bench on the opposite side from where she was standing.

'Why would she think that?' His voice had gone down to a rough deep burr.

Her gaze flicked away from his, her cheeks warming like she'd been standing too close to the oven. She gave a little shrug. 'Who knows? Perhaps she thinks you'll be overcome with uncontrollable lust and won't be able to resist me.'

There was a loaded silence. A silence with an undercurrent of unusual energy vibrating through every particle of air. Energy that made the fine hairs on the back of her neck and along her arms tingle at the roots.

Layla sneaked a glance at him and found him looking at her with a contemplative frown.

After a moment, he appeared to give himself a mental shake and then raked his splayed fingers through his hair, dropping his hand back by his side. 'I would hope you know me well enough to be reassured I am a man of my word. If I say our marriage will not be consummated, then you can count on it that it won't be.'

Why? Because she was so undesirable? So repugnant to him as she had been to her first and only boyfriend when she was sixteen? So unlike the gorgeous supermodel types Logan had occasional casual flings with?

'Right now, I don't know whether I should be reassured or insulted.' The words slipped out before her wounded ego could check in with her brain.

Logan's gaze dipped to her mouth, lingering there a fraction longer than was necessary. His eyes came back to mesh with hers and her heart gave an odd little thumpity-thump. She had to summon every bit of willpower she possessed and then some not to glance at his mouth. She wondered if he kissed hard or soft or somewhere in between. Her mind suddenly filled with images of them making love, her limbs entangled with his, her senses singing from his touch, his mouth clamped to hers in passion. A passion she could only imagine because she had never experienced it herself.

'It would only complicate things if we were to have a normal relationship.' His voice had a rough edge as if something was clogging his throat. 'It wouldn't be fair to you.'

Layla turned and went back to the pot simmering on the cooktop behind her. Her body was simmering too. Smouldering with new sensations and longings she had no idea how to control. Had his 'proposal' unlocked something in her? Made her aware of herself in a way she hadn't been before? Aware of her needs, the needs she had ignored and denied, always telling herself no one would ever want to marry her.

She took the lid off the pot, picked up the spoon and gave the casserole a couple of stirs. 'Will you continue to have casual lovers during our marriage?'

'No. That's something else that wouldn't be fair to you. And I would hope you would refrain from any dalliances yourself.'

Layla put the spoon down again and placed the lid back on the pot with a clang. 'You don't have to worry on that score. I haven't had a casual lover my entire adult life.'

Why did you tell him that?

There was another pulsing silence.

Logan came to her side of the island bench and stood next to her near the cooktop. Her body went on high alert, every nerve and cell aware of his closeness. Not touching, but close enough to do so if either of them moved half a step.

'But you've had lovers, right?'

Layla turned her head to glance at him, hoping he would put her flaming cheeks down to her proximity to the simmering pot in front of her. 'Not as many as you might think.' No way was she going to announce she was a twenty-six-year-old virgin. She moved from the cooktop to gather the serving utensils. 'I haven't opened any wine for dinner. Do you want to grab a bottle? We'll be eating in the small green dining room since it's just the two of us.'

'I'll bring something up from the cellar.'

Just the two of us.

How cosy and intimate that sounded, but it wasn't true. He would never have asked her to marry him if it hadn't been for the strange conditions on his grandfather's will. She had to remember that at all costs. This was a business deal. Nothing personal. Nothing lasting. Nothing.

Logan spent longer than he needed to choosing a wine from the well-stocked Bellbrae cellar. He remembered the bottle of vintage champagne he'd selected when he'd got engaged to Susannah. How excited he'd felt, how ready he'd felt for the commitment he'd made. How he had imagined himself to be in love and Susannah in love with him. He had been Layla's age—twenty-six. Susannah had been two years younger with a host of issues he had been completely oblivious to until it was too late.

Losing his father after a devastatingly brief battle with cancer had compelled him to settle down as soon as he could. With hindsight, he could see now how many signs he'd missed about the suitability of Susannah, even his own readiness for such a permanent commitment. He'd had no way of knowing how that night of celebrating his engagement would end less than a year later in Susannah's death. How could he have been so ignorant of the demons she'd battled on a daily basis?

What did that say about *him*?

It said he wasn't relationship material, that's what it said. Or at least, not *that* sort of relationship. Promising to love someone no matter what, making a long-term commitment were things he could no longer do. Would never do.

But a paper marriage to save his beloved home was something he could do and do it willingly.

Logan selected a bottle of champagne from the wine fridge in the cellar next to the racks of vintage wine. His upcoming marriage to Layla might not be a real one in every sense of the word but it was surely worth celebrating their joint commitment to save Bellbrae.

Layla wheeled the serving trolley into the green dining room rather than risk carrying plates and dishes. Because of the muscle grafts performed to keep her leg functioning as best as it could, it was often weaker and more painful at the end of the day. And the last thing she wanted to do was make a fool of herself by losing her balance again and needing Logan's assistance. She was already feeling a little nervous about having dinner with him.

In the early days, Aunt Elsie had been very old-school about dining with the family upstairs and had always insisted Layla eat in the kitchen with her. But since the death of Logan's grandmother the rules had been relaxed as Angus McLaughlin had appreciated the company at dinner to get him through the long lonely evenings.

But she had never dined alone with Logan.

The green dining room was one Layla's favourite rooms in the castle. It had windows that overlooked the loch on the estate and the Highlands beyond. She left the curtains open as the moon had risen and was shining a bolt of shimmering silver across the crushed silk surface of the water.

Logan came back from the cellar just as Layla was straightening the settings on the table. He was carrying a bottle of French champagne in one hand and holding two crystal glasses by the stems in the other.

'I seem to recall you like champagne. But if you'd prefer wine...'

'No, I love champagne. It's my favourite drink.' She raised her brows when she saw the label. 'Gosh, that's a good one. But should we be wasting it on an everyday dinner?'

He placed the glasses on the table and began to remove the foil covering and wire from the cork. 'This isn't an everyday dinner. Tonight, we're celebrating our success in saving Bellbrae. That's worth ten thousand bottles of this drop.'

Layla watched as he deftly removed the cork and

poured the champagne into the two crystal glasses. He handed her a glass and raised his own glass in a toast. 'To saving Bellbrae.'

She sipped the champagne, savouring the honey and lavender notes as they burst on her tongue. 'Mmm... lovely.'

Logan put his glass down and reached for something inside his trouser pocket. 'I have something for you.' He took out a vintage emerald-green velvet ring box and handed it to her.

Layla knew exactly what was inside the box. She'd helped Aunt Elsie pack away Logan's grandmother's things when Margaret McLaughlin had died from complications after routine surgery. The collection of beautiful heirloom jewellery had fascinated Layla so much she had secretly looked at it on many occasions when no one had been around. She knew the code to the safe where it was kept, and had even tried various pieces on, looking at herself in the mirror, pretending she was a princess about to be married to the handsome prince of her dreams.

Layla put her champagne glass down and prised open the lid of the box and stared at the gorgeous Art Deco setting with its array of glittering diamonds. 'Oh, my... I'd forgotten how beautiful your grandmother's ring is.' She met his gaze. 'But surely you don't want me to wear it? I mean, given the circumstances of our... um...marriage?'

His expression was largely unreadable...all except for the way his eyes dipped to her mouth before going back to mesh with hers. 'My grandmother would want you to have it. She was fond of you. Try it on. See if it fits. We can have it resized if not.'

Layla already knew how well it fitted but didn't want to reveal her guilty secret. She took the ring out of the box, a part of her disappointed he wasn't the one slipping it over her finger for her, just as a man deeply in love with his fiancée would do. But nothing about their engagement was normal, so how silly of her to wish for things she couldn't have.

But as if Logan had suddenly read her mind, he held out his palm for the ring. 'Here—let me do that. I believe it's my job.' There was a strange quality to his voice, a low deep chord of some unidentifiable emotion.

Layla placed the ring in the middle of his palm and held her breath as he took her hand in his. Her fingers were so white against the tan of his, her skin alive with sensations—tingly, fizzing sensations—that sent tiny zaps of electricity to the far reaches of her body.

He slid the ring over the knuckles of her ring finger and smiled when it met no resistance. 'It's like it was made for you.'

She was so captivated by his smile she forgot to look down at the ring on her finger. It had been years since she had seen him give a genuine smile. Not one of those half-baked twists of his mouth but a real smile that involved his eyes, making them crinkle attractively at the corners. He looked younger, less stressed, more approachable. The grief-damaged landscape of his face restored to one of hope instead of quiet despair. He was still holding her hand, his fingers warm and gentle as if he was holding a kitten.

The atmosphere changed as if there was a sudden

rent in time. A stillness. A silence waiting with bated breath for something to happen…

Layla couldn't tear her gaze away from his mouth, couldn't stop wondering what it would be like to feel his lips against her own. She moistened her own lips with a darting movement of her tongue, her heart giving an extra beat like a musician misreading a musical score. 'I—I don't know what to say…'

'Don't say anything.' The pitch of his voice went down another notch and he slid his other hand under the curtain of her hair, his eyes locked on hers.

Every nerve tingled at his touch, every cell in her body throbbing with awareness. His eyes were the deepest blue she had ever seen them—bluer than the Bellbrae loch at midnight, bluer than a midnight winter sky. He was still holding her left hand, the heat from his hand seeping into her body with the potency of a powerful narcotic. She was aware of every part of his hand where it touched hers—the pads of his fingertips, the latent strength of his fingers, the protective warmth of his palm.

Layla forgot to breathe. She was transfixed by the slow descent of his mouth towards hers, spellbound by the clean fresh scent of his warm breath, mesmerised by the magnetic force drawing her inexorably closer, closer, closer to his lips. It was as if she had been waiting her entire life for this to happen. She hadn't been truly alive until now. She had been a formless ghost wandering through life until this moment when she had morphed into a live and vibrant female body with urgent needs and desires. Her heart sped up, her pulse leapt, her anticipation for the touchdown of his lips so acute it was almost unbearable.

Kiss me. Kiss me. Kiss me.

It was a silent chant keeping time with the pounding beat of her heart.

But suddenly Logan dropped his hold and stepped back, opening and closing his fingers as if to rid himself of the taint of touching her. 'Forgive me. That wasn't meant to happen.' His tone was brusque, his expression masked.

Layla was so overcome with disappointment she couldn't find her voice. She couldn't bear to look at his face in case she saw his disgust for her written on his features. The cruel taunts of her teenage boyfriend echoed out of the past in her head.

'You're ugly. You're a cripple. Who would ever want you?'

She looked down at her left hand where the ring was mockingly glinting, her stomach plummeting in despair. Such a beautiful ring for a girl who couldn't even attract a man enough for him to kiss her. What a mockery that ring was. A glittering, glaring, gut-wrenching reminder of everything Layla was not and never could be.

'It's okay,' she said at last, forcing herself to meet his gaze. 'I understand completely.'

He sucked in a deep breath, sending his hand through his hair so roughly it left deep crooked finger trails. 'I don't think you do.'

Layla turned and got down to the business of serving their meal onto the plates where she had left them on the sideboard, next to the serving trolley. She placed the plates on the dining table and glanced his way. 'I think I do understand, Logan. This engagement is nothing like your last. You loved Susannah.' She released a painful breath. 'You still love her. That's why getting engaged to me makes you feel so uncomfortable, because you feel you're betraying her memory.'

A muscle in his jaw flickered as if he was grinding down on his molars. 'I don't wish to discuss Susannah with you or anyone.' His eyes were like closed windows. Curtains drawn. Shutters down.

Layla sat down at the table and spread her napkin over her lap. 'I realise you're still grieving. I'm sorry things have worked out the way they have—for her and for you. It was the saddest thing, especially since you've had so many other tragic losses in your life. But I think your grandfather was right in encouraging you to move on with your life.'

'Oh, so you quite like the way he went about it, do you?' His tone was as caustic as flesh-eating acid.

Layla pressed her lips together, fighting to control her see-sawing emotions. One second she was furious with him, the next she felt sad he couldn't let go of the past. 'Please sit down and have dinner. I'm getting a crick in my neck looking up at you.'

Logan strode over to the table and pulled out the chair and sat down, his knees bumping hers under the table. She shifted back a bit, trying to ignore the rush of heat that shot through her legs and straight to her core. Why couldn't she be immune to him? Why was she so acutely aware of him?

They began eating in a stiff silence, only the clanging discordant music of cutlery scraping against crockery puncturing the air.

Layla drank her glass of champagne and Logan re-filled her glass as if he were a robotic waiter, but she noticed he didn't drink from his. His untouched champagne glass stood in front of his place setting, releasing bubble after bubble in a series of tiny vertical towers.

She picked up her glass with her left hand and the diamonds on the ring winked at her under the chandelier light coming from overhead. Something was niggling at the back of her brain... Why hadn't Logan given Susannah his grandmother's ring? Layla remembered Susannah's engagement ring as being ultra-modern and flashy. It was a look-at-me ring that was not to Layla's taste at all. 'Logan?'

He looked up from the mechanical task of relaying food from his plate to his mouth. 'What?' His curt tone wasn't exactly encouraging, neither was the heavy frown between his eyes.

Layla toyed with the ring on her left hand. 'Why didn't you give your grandmother's ring to Susannah when you became engaged?'

Something passed through his gaze with camera shutter speed. 'She didn't like vintage jewellery.' He put his cutlery down and shifted his water glass an infinitesimal distance. 'I didn't take it personally. I was happy to buy her what she wanted.' He picked up his cutlery again and stabbed a piece of parsnip as if it had personally offended him.

Layla waited until he had finished his mouthful before asking, 'How are her parents and siblings coping? Do you hear from them or contact them yourself?'

A shadow moved across his face like clouds scudding across a troubled autumn sky. 'I used to call them or drop in on them in the early days but not lately. It only upset them to be reminded.' He put his cutlery down in the finished position on his plate and rested his arms on the table, his frown a roadmap of lines.

Layla reached for his forearm and gave it a gentle squeeze. 'I can only imagine how awful it must have been to have come home and found her...like that...'

He pulled his arm away and sat stiffly upright in his chair, his expression as blank as the white table-cloth. But after a long moment he relaxed his posture as if something tightly bound within him had loosened slightly. 'When someone takes their own life it's not like any other death.' His gaze was haunted, his tone bleak. 'The guilt, the what-ifs, the if-onlys, the what-could-I-have-done-to-prevent-this are unbearable.' He expelled a heavy breath and continued, 'I blame myself for not seeing the signs.'

'You mustn't blame yourself but I understand how you and most people do,' Layla said. 'But I read some-where that sixteen percent of suicides are completely unheralded. It's a snap in the moment decision borne out of some hidden anguish.'

Logan picked up his champagne and drained it in a couple of swallows, placing the glass back down with a savage little thump. 'There were signs but I ignored them.' He waited a beat or two before continuing in a ragged voice. 'She had an eating disorder. Bulimia. I don't know how I missed it.' His mouth twisted in a gri-mace and his tone became tortured with self-loathing. 'How can you live with someone for months and not know that about her?'

Layla reached for his hand but this time he didn't pull

away. 'Shame makes people hide lots of stuff. Bulimia is mostly a secret disease and much harder to pick up on than anorexia, where the physical effect is so obvious.'

Logan looked down at their joined hands and turned his over to anchor hers to the table. He began to absently stroke the back of her hand with his thumb, the caress only light, lazy almost, but no less magical. Nerves she hadn't known she possessed reacted as if touched by a live electrode, zinging, singing, tingling.

He lifted his gaze to hers and something toppled over in her stomach. His thumb stilled on the back of her hand but he didn't release her. His gaze moved over her face as if he were memorising her features one by one. When he got to her mouth she couldn't stop herself from sweeping the tip of her tongue across her lips—it was an impulse she had zero control over.

Logan gave her hand another quick squeeze in time with the on-off movement of his lips, in a blink-and-you'd-miss-it smile. A smile that didn't reach high enough to take the shadows out of his eyes. But then he let go of her hand and sat back in his chair and picked up his water glass and drained it, placing it back down with a definitive thud.

'Finish your dinner. We have a busy day tomorrow meeting with the lawyer to organise the legal paperwork. Rather than drive, I've taken the liberty of organising a flight from Inverness to Edinburgh.' His business-like tone and abrupt change of subject was disquieting and left her with far too many questions unanswered.

'Okay…' Layla wanted to know more about his relationship with Susannah. She had idolised them as a couple, seeing them as a match made in heaven. Feeling jealous of the love they'd shared, hoping one day someone would love her in the same way. But finding out their relationship might not have been as open and wonderful as she had imagined made her understand why Logan was so reluctant to commit to anyone else.

But Layla had personal experience of the tricky question of how well could you know anyone, even someone you had lived with for years. Didn't her childhood circumstances prove that? Her father had always been a difficult man; prone to angry outbursts, regular violence—especially when on drugs or drunk, but who would have thought he was capable of the crime he'd eventually committed—driving into a tree at full speed to kill the family he'd purported to love?

'The legal stuff…' She chewed her lip for a moment, desperate to get her mind off the accident that had killed her mother and changed her own life for ever. 'You mean a pre-nup, right?'

'Pre-nups are commonplace these days. Please don't be offended by my desire for one. You have your own assets to consider—your cleaning business, for example.'

Layla gave a self-deprecating snort and picked up her champagne glass. 'Yeah, right. My assets hardly compare to yours. You have offices all over the UK and Europe. My office is basically on my phone. I decided to give up my Edinburgh office after your grandfather died to come back and help Aunt Elsie. It seemed easier to work from here until everything is settled with the estate.'

'I'm sorry you've been so inconvenienced,' he said,

looking at her with a concerned frown. 'I had no idea you'd given up your office.'

She waved a dismissive hand. 'I was glad to come home. Flossie was missing your grandfather and Aunt Elsie was finding it hard to do everything on her own.'

'Your business is doing well, though, isn't it? You're running at a decent profit?'

Layla was not going to admit to him or to anyone how close to the wind she sailed at times with her business. Failure was not an option. A nightmare that haunted her, yes, but *not* an option. Failure would prove she was nothing but a product of her chaotic child-hood—a child of addicts. Her parents had had no am-bition beyond the goal of sourcing enough alcohol and drugs for their next binge.

Owning her own cleaning business gave Layla power and control, and God alone knew how little of that she'd had in her childhood. 'I do okay.' She put her glass back down again.

'How okay?' His gaze was as direct as a laser pointer.

Layla shifted in her seat and lowered her eyes to the remains of her meal on her plate. 'It's not always easy to get reliable workers. It takes time to build up trust, to know they're always going to do the right thing by me and the people I get them to clean for.' She met his gaze and continued. 'They're cleaning people's homes where valuables and personal effects are not always under lock and key, and often the clients are not at home when my staff are there.'

A frown brought his ink-black eyebrows together. 'Don't you do background checks on them first?'

'Some of the young people I employ wouldn't pass

a background check,' Layla said. 'They need someone to give them a break for once. To not always be expecting them to slip up or fail. I believe in showing trust first and teaching them some skills, hoping it triggers the desire in them to make better choices.' The sort of choices she wished her parents had made.

'Admirable of you, but you're setting yourself up for guaranteed disappointment.' His tone matched his cynical expression.

Layla hoisted her chin a fraction. 'My vision for my business is not just about making a big profit. It's about making a difference in people's lives. Lives that others have judged and found wanting. But I know how powerful it can be when someone believes in you. Someone who sees something in you that no one else does. It's… it's transformative.'

His eyes moved over her face like a searchlight for a long moment and she had to fight not to shift her gaze.

'Is that because of what happened in your childhood?' His tone had lost its cynical edge. 'My grandparents giving permission for you to come and live here with your great-aunt?'

'It's getting late.' Layla pushed back her chair and rose from the table and began to gather the plates. Next he'd be asking her to spill all about her miserable childhood and that she was determined *not* to do. Thankfully, privacy laws had prevented the McLaughlins from hearing too many of the gory details about her early years—details Layla dearly wished she could forget. 'I think I can hear Flossie asking to be let out.'

Logan placed a hand over her forearm as she reached for his plate. 'I don't want you to wait on me, Layla.

I want you to talk to me. There's a lot we don't know about each other, and we need to know it if we're going to make our relationship appear genuine.'

She glanced at his hand on her arm and gave him a pointed look. 'Do you mind?'

He released her hand, his tone and expression softening. 'I don't know all the details but I know your background was difficult. It must have been, otherwise you wouldn't have ended up living here. I think it's great how you've taken charge and started your own business. But don't be too proud to ask for help if you need it.' He rose to his feet and pushed in his chair, adding, 'There's one other thing I think I should tell you. We'll have to get married abroad and soon. According to Scottish law, there's a twenty-eight-day waiting period before we can get a marriage licence, and I don't want to lose any more valuable time.'

'Married abroad?' Layla opened and closed her mouth. 'Please tell me you're not thinking Vegas and an Elvis impersonator?'

He gave a crooked smile that made something in her chest ping like a latch springing open. 'No. But if you're not keen on an impersonal register office, how about a small and simple ceremony on a beach in Hawaii?'

Hawaii. The land of bikinis and beaches and beautiful bodies.

Oh, joy.

CHAPTER FOUR

A COUPLE OF days after the legal work was completed in Edinburgh, Layla flew business class with Logan to the island of Maui in Hawaii. The luxury villa he'd organised for their short stay was situated at Kapalua Bay beach, a gorgeous crescent of blindingly white sand and turquoise water and palm trees. Layla felt as if she was living in a dream sequence—swept away to an exotic location by a handsome billionaire who was intent on marrying her as quickly as he could.

But not for the romantic reasons her girlhood dreams had envisaged.

The speed and efficiency with which Logan set about achieving a goal was nothing less than breathtaking. Layla barely had time to get her head around the idea of a beach wedding, let alone buy the appropriate attire for it, when she found herself standing on the balcony of the beautiful villa overlooking the ocean with just minutes to spare before the ceremony.

Her wedding day.

It was strange to think that this time last week she had been a single woman with a simple goal of keeping her business on track. Now she was about to be married to a man she had known for most of her life who didn't love her the way a husband should love his bride.

But Logan did love his family's home and so did she, so it would have to be a good enough reason to marry. The *only* reason to marry, because the last thing she needed was to get silly ideas in her head about their relationship lasting beyond the year, as set down in the document his lawyer had drawn up.

One year and one year only.

The money Logan had transferred to her account on signing the document would guarantee Layla's business success. It was exactly the windfall she needed to expand her business from a scribbled sticky-note vision into a profit-making reality.

Logan came out to the balcony where she was standing looking at the view. She turned to face him with an attempt at a smile. Their wedding ceremony was minutes away but if he was uncomfortable or uneasy about what they were about to do, he wasn't showing it on his face. They might as well have been heading down the beach for an afternoon stroll.

He pushed back his shirt sleeve to glance at the silver watch on his strong tanned wrist. 'The celebrant will be here in ten minutes.'

'Okay…' Layla took a deep breath and smoothed her hand down over her churning stomach. 'Isn't it meant to be bad luck for you to see me in my dress before the ceremony?'

His eyes ran over the Bohemian-style white dress she had bought in a boutique in Edinburgh. It was enough like a wedding dress for her to feel like a bride, even if she wasn't a real one, and long enough to cover the scars on her leg. And—even more important—she could wear flat sandals or bare feet rather than struggle with heels.

'I can safely say I've already had more than my fair share of bad luck. You too, I imagine.' His tone was wry. 'You look beautiful, by the way.' His gaze held hers in a lock that did strange things to her insides. Tingling things, thrilling things. Forbidden things.

Layla was the first to look away, worried he would see things she didn't want him to see. Things she didn't even want to admit to herself. 'I don't have a bouquet or anything. I hope that's not bad luck too.'

He walked over to a box that was sitting on the coffee table in the large open-plan room off the balcony. She hadn't noticed it earlier as she'd been preoccupied with getting ready so soon after their arrival. Or it had been delivered while she was in the shower. He took the lid off and the sweet tropical scent of frangipanis filled the air. He took out a simple but beautiful bouquet and handed it to her.

'I hope this will do?'

'It's perfect.' Layla took the bouquet from him and bent her face to the creamy blooms with their egg-yolk-yellow hearts, the glorious fragrance drugging her senses. Not to mention Logan's intoxicating closeness doing exactly the same thing. He was dressed in an open-necked white shirt and mid-blue jacket and trousers that brought out the intense blue in his eyes and the deep olive tan of his skin. She could smell his aftershave—could even pick up the clean fruity smell of his shampoo from his recent shower. His jaw was freshly shaven and her fingers itched to touch his face to trace where the razor had glided over his tanned skin. She was aware of every inch of his body standing within touching distance of hers. Aware of every breath he took, every flare of his nostrils, every rustle of his clothes when he moved.

Within a few minutes they would be husband and wife.

On paper.

She had to keep reminding herself of that pesky little detail.

Logan held out his hand, his expression inscrutable. 'Ready to head down?'

Layla put her hand in his, holding the bouquet in the other, her heart thumping, her pulse racing. 'I'm ready.'

I think...

When they got down to the beach, Layla took off her sandals and Logan his shoes so they could walk on the sand. They walked together towards the celebrant, who was waiting for them on the beach with two witnesses— a couple, Makani and Ken, whose award-winning landscape design Logan had done for them at their main home in the Hamptons in the US a few years ago. They spent part of the year on Maui, where Makani had family. Logan had informed Layla earlier that he had told Makani and Ken nothing about the reason behind his sudden marriage to Layla, allowing them to draw the conclusion it was a genuine love match.

If only it was...

Then Layla wouldn't be feeling so conflicted about making promises that were essentially meaningless. Entering a marriage that after a year would be terminated.

The rhythm of the ocean lapping the shore was the

only music to accompany them to their position in front of the male celebrant, who was holding two colourful leis. He gave the traditional Hawaiian welcome, placed the leis over their heads and began the simple service. 'We are gathered here today to join this man and this woman in marriage...'

Layla repeated the vows as instructed, intensely aware of Logan's warm blue gaze and the feel of his hand holding hers as he slid the wedding ring home on her finger. His voice as he said his vows was strong and steady and assured—no one would ever think he didn't mean a word he'd said. Apart from her, that is. But it was an act and good actors, the best actors, made themselves *feel* the emotion so they could bring authenticity to the scene.

'You may kiss the bride.'

Layla had fooled herself that Logan might skip this part of the service, especially since he had pulled away from kissing her the other day. But as soon as the celebrant spoke the words, Logan drew her closer and his head came down, down, down until his lips touched hers. She was expecting him to lift them straight off, to be satisfied with a perfunctory kiss for the sake of appearances, but the pressure of his lips changed, warmed, heated, hardened. Burned and branded.

Her lips moved with the sensual rhythm of his, opening to his, welcoming the slow sexy stroke of his tongue meeting hers for the first time. It wasn't a deep kiss— no tangling or thrusting of tongues—but gentle nudges and playful touches of lips and tongue tips that sent a shiver coursing through her body from the top of her sun-warmed head to the soles of her sand-caressed bare feet. There was a swooping sensation deep in her belly, an ache spreading in a river of heat, simmering, smouldering, sizzling in her core.

His lips were gentle and yet firm, purposeful, passionate and utterly addictive. Layla nudged his lips with her own, sweeping the tip of her tongue over his lower lip, delighting in the way his breath hitched and his hold on her tightened.

His hand glided down to the base of her spine, drawing her closer to the hard ridge of his stirring arousal. It was both shocking and exhilarating to feel the intimate pulse of his blood. Shocking, because she hadn't dared hope he would be attracted to her in such a way.

Layla slid her hands to the hard plane of his chest, feeling the thumpity-thump, thump-thump of his heart beneath her palm. She forgot about everything but the sensation of his lips moving with such exquisite expertise on hers, drawing from her a passionate response, a clawing and desperate need building in her body with such force it was overwhelming. Every nerve in her body seemed to be attuned to his mouth, to the warmth and potency of it, to the eroticism it boldly, blatantly promised.

She was so consumed by his kiss she no longer heard the swish and slap and sigh of the waves as they lapped and sucked at the shore. No longer aware of the ocean breeze stirring the fronds on the palm trees, no longer aware of the fine grains of sand beneath her feet or the sun shining down on her head.

The sound of the witnesses clapping seemed to snap Logan out of the moment. He lifted his mouth off hers and gave a crooked smile that said everything and yet nothing.

Layla licked her lips and tasted him, wanted him with a deep ache that vibrated in her core like a plucked cello string. Her heart was still racing, her pulse off the charts, her legs trembling. Now, *that* was a kiss. She felt dazed, stunned, spinning with lingering sensations. Her mouth still felt sensitive, her lips slightly swollen. She searched his gaze for any sign he was as affected by their kiss as she was but his gaze was like the ocean beside them with its mysterious depths and shifting shadows.

They were soon swept up in the hearty congratulations of Makani and Ken, followed by the official signing of the register. Logan had organised refreshments back at the villa but things had to be cut short when Makani got a call from her mother, who was babysitting their children, that the youngest was running a temperature.

'Sorry to leave so soon,' Makani said, and added with a twinkling smile, 'But just you wait until you have kids. Life will never be the same, but in a totally good way.'

'Now, now, honey,' Ken said, looping an arm around his wife's waist. 'Don't go putting baby ideas in their heads just yet. Let them enjoy their honeymoon.'

Honeymoon.

The word was enough to send another shiver shooting through Layla's body.

Logan saw his guests out and came back to where Layla was sipping a glass of champagne on one of the sofas overlooking the ocean view. If he closed his eyes, he could take himself back to the moment of their kiss at the ceremony. Damn it—he didn't even need to close his eyes. He could still taste the milk and honey sweetness of her mouth—could still feel the thrum of lust deep in his body.

He was relieved he was good at concealing his emotions because that kiss had rocked him to the core. He hadn't wanted it to end. He had lost track of where they were and why they were there. All he'd cared about, all he'd craved was the smooth, soft, sweet delicacy of her mouth moving against his. The shy playfulness of her tongue had sent a rocket blast of need to his groin. Triggering a need that was still humming in the background—a low, persistent hum he was doing his level best to ignore.

Their marriage was on paper. That was the deal. It was for one year and one year only and then it would be over.

No damage done.

But that kiss had already done damage because he wanted to kiss her again. Their kiss had made him think about taking things further, doing things he had no business doing with her. Things he had no business doing with anyone. He didn't do long-term intimate relationships.

Not again.

But that kiss had stirred something inside him— something that until now had been lying dormant, in a coma, dead. The touch of Layla's pillow-soft lips had sent electrodes of awareness to every part of his body, jolting it awake, making his flesh hungry, greedy for sensual satiation. Not for the quick-fix, hook-up type sex he had indulged in during the last seven years. He would be fooling himself if he said he had enjoyed those encounters beyond the brief physical relief they had provided.

But he suspected making love with Layla would be entirely different, which was why he couldn't allow himself to go there. Couldn't allow himself permission to even *think* about the possibility. There would be too many complications when it came to ending their arrangement. The sort of complications he could well do without.

Layla turned her head to look at him, still cradling her champagne, her expression bland. 'So, here we are, then.'

Logan fought to keep a frown off his face and tried a crooked smile instead but wasn't sure it was too convincing. 'Yes...' He picked up the bottle of champagne in the ice bucket and brought it over to where she was sitting to refill her glass. 'More?'

She placed her hand over the top of the glass. 'Better not. I might start saying things I wouldn't normally say.' She gave a twisted smile and added, '*In vino veritas* and all that.'

'In the wine lies the truth.' Logan grunted in agreement, topping up his own glass, and then put the champagne bottle back in the ice bucket with a rattle against the ice cubes and continued, 'Drunk words, sober thoughts.' He wondered what she would say if he told her what he was thinking. What he'd been thinking ever since he'd kissed her. No, even before that—when he'd encountered her in the north tower at Bellbrae. Something had happened, something had changed between them and he wasn't sure how to change it back.

There was a beat or two of silence.

Logan turned back to look at her. 'Feel free to speak your mind with me, Layla. I don't expect you to have to drink to excess in order to do it.'

She leaned forward to put her glass on the coffee table, her eyes slipping out of reach of his. She sat back and smoothed a crease out of her dress before returning her gaze to his with disquieting intensity. 'Why did you kiss me like that at the ceremony?'

Logan took a sip of his champagne before responding. Not because he needed alcohol but because he didn't know how to answer without betraying himself. He wanted to kiss her again. Now. And not just kiss her but explore her beautiful body with the same thoroughness. He wanted to run his hands through the silk cloud of her hair. He wanted to kiss the soft creamy skin at the base of her throat, to trail his tongue along the contours of her collarbones, to breathe in the flowery scent of her until he was drunk with it.

'It seemed the right thing to do at the time.' Logan's tone held no trace of the battle going on inside him. 'Malaki and Ken, and indeed the celebrant, would have thought it strange if we hadn't kissed.'

A tiny frown wrinkled her brow. 'True. But you kissed me as if you didn't want to stop.' Her teeth snagged her bottom lip and she added, 'Was that…just acting?' Her voice had a note of uncertainty that was strangely touching.

Logan put his champagne glass down and released a long breath. 'No. It wasn't just acting.' He closed his eyes in a slow blink and dragged a hand down his face. 'It was a moment of foolishness that won't be repeated.'

Must not be repeated. Must not. Must not. Must not. He drummed it into his head but his body was offline. Off-script.

There was a silence broken only by the sound of waves pulsing against the shore.

Layla rose from the sofa and wandered over to look out of the open balcony doors to the beach below. Her arms were around her mid-section, her posture stiff and guarded as if she was shielding herself from an expected insult. 'So, you didn't enjoy it, then?' Her voice still echoed with self-doubt.

Logan told himself to stay where he was—to keep his distance. To not tempt himself beyond his endurance by crossing the floor to her. But step by step he went, programmed by a force he had no way of countering. He placed his hands on the tops of her shoulders, turning her to face him. Her grey-green gaze assiduously avoided his so he tipped up her chin with one of his fingers so she had no choice but to meet his eyes. 'I enjoyed it way too much and therein lies our problem.'

She moistened her lips with the tip of her tongue, making them even more unbearably tempting. 'Why is that a problem?' Her voice was as low and husky as a whispered secret and it sent shivers racing down his spine.

Logan stroked his thumb across her cheek, marvelling at the creamy softness of her skin. 'You know why.' His tone was so low and rough it sounded like he'd been filing his tonsils with a blacksmith's rasp.

'Because of our paper marriage?' Her eyes reminded him of cloudy sea glass.

He couldn't seem to stop his thumb from stroking her cheek, couldn't stop his gaze from drinking in every nuance of her features. Couldn't stop the thrum of lust that assailed his body like an invisible invader. Marching through every inch of his flesh, aching, wanting, needing. 'We have to be sensible about this, Layla.'

I have to be sensible. I have to be in control.

She reached up with her hand and stroked his jaw from his cheekbone to his chin, her eyes luminous. 'I think I must have already had too much champagne because right now I want you to kiss me again. I want to know if the first time was a fluke or…or something else.'

It was the 'something else' that most worried Logan. He fought every aroused cell in his body but it was a battle he was worried he might not win, or at least not in the long run. One year of this level of temptation and he would be a certifiable mess. How much temptation could a man endure? Especially for a man who had actively avoided contact as intimate as this.

Kissing a hook-up date was one thing, kissing someone he had known for years and was currently married to was another. Their paper marriage would be incinerated, obliterated if he gave in to the temptation to kiss her again. One taste of her mouth had already unleashed something feral inside him, something he wasn't sure he could control for too much longer.

Calling on every bit of willpower he possessed, Logan dropped his hand from her face and took a step back. 'I'm sorry, Layla, but this can't happen. I made the rules for a reason.'

Her gaze reminded him of the still surface of a lake. Calm. Controlled. But there was a faint ripple of disappointment around the edges. 'Okey-dokey.' Her words and tone were flippant given the topic under discussion. So too her overly bright, breezy smile. 'We'll leave it at that, then.' She moved across the room to where the champagne bottle was and topped up her glass. She turned and held her glass up in a toast, her expression faintly mocking. 'Long live the rules.'

Logan ground his teeth so hard he mentally apologised to his dentist. 'Listen—I'm not doing this to insult you. It's not personal.'

'Isn't it?' Her eyes were glittering as brightly as the diamonds on her left hand next to her wedding ring. Not glittering with tears but with anger.

He let out a slowly controlled breath, anchoring his hands on his hips like he was about to deliver an important lecture. Which he was, but he suspected he was the one who needed to hear it most. 'Think about it. If we were to have a normal relationship, it would be much more complicated to end it when the year was up. This way we can get an annulment and leave it at that. No harm done.' He dropped his hands from his hips. 'I'm not saying it will be an easy year. But we're both mature adults, and I want us to remain friends at the end of it.'

She rolled her lips together, her arms crossed, with her champagne glass tilted at a threatening-to-spill angle. 'What have you told your brother about us? Does he know it's just a paper marriage?'

Logan folded back the cuffs of his shirt for something to do with his hands. 'I haven't spoken to him yet. He hasn't answered any of my calls or texts or emails.' Which, unfortunately, wasn't unusual when Robbie was on one of his gambling sprees.

'But what will you tell him?'

It was a question Logan had been asking himself for the last few days. He hadn't been able to contact his younger brother to talk about anything, much less his sudden marriage to Layla Campbell, the housekeeper's great-niece. 'He will have seen the will by now but I'm hoping he'll accept our marriage as the real deal. It's not as if you and I are complete strangers and he knows my grandfather always had a soft spot for you.'

'It might be tricky convincing Robbie we're a genuine couple when he comes home to Bellbrae sometime. You know what he's like—he often arrives unannounced. If we're sleeping on opposite sides of the castle it will look kind of odd.'

Logan could see her point. His brother might be immature and reckless but he wasn't a total fool. It wouldn't take Robbie long to pick up on any irregularities in Logan's relationship with Layla, and their living arrangements in particular. 'We could move into the west tower. The large suite that has the connecting bedrooms.' He would be far closer to her than he'd intended—sleeping with just a door between them.

A door he would keep locked—literally and mentally.

'Fine,' Layla said, draining her glass. 'But can I make a request?'

'Sure.'

She put her glass down and faced him squarely.

'When we're pretending to be happily married to Robbie and anyone else, will you use terms of endearment or just call me Layla?'

'What would you prefer?'

'You can call me anything but babe.' She gave a faint shudder as if even saying the word upset her.

'Why not babe?'

A hard light came into her eyes and her expression set like fast-acting glue. 'Someone I used to know used it a lot. I've loathed it ever since.'

Before Logan could ask her to elaborate, she turned and walked out of the room, leaving him with just the lingering fragrance of her perfume.

CHAPTER FIVE

ARGH! WHY HAD she drunk that second glass of champagne? Their beach wedding had got to her, that was why. She had been swept away by the romantic setting, swept away by Logan's kiss. The kiss that had sent shivers up and down her spine and driven silly ideas into her head. Ideas of him wanting things to go further, him wanting *her.* Not just physically but intellectually and emotionally.

But he had drawn a line in the sand. *Do Not Cross.*

Layla plonked herself down on the bed in her room with a despondent sigh. She'd made a class-A fool of herself, practically begging Logan to kiss her. Shame washed through her at how gauche she had been—how unworldly and foolish to think he might want to tweak the rules on their relationship.

But his kiss had been so…so genuine. So authentic. So powerfully passionate she could feel it on her lips even now. She only had to close her eyes and she was back there on the warm grainy sand, with the waves washing against the shore with their fringe of white lace, and Logan's mouth clamped to hers as if he never wanted to let her go. The need he had stirred in her was still humming in her body—a faint background ache she couldn't ignore.

Layla hitched up the hem of her dress and wriggled her feet and curled her toes. The white jagged scars on her left leg a jarring reminder of her past. The past that contained memories she wished she could forget. Painful memories that were embedded so deeply into her brain she still had nightmares.

Babe. The word she loathed because her father had used it to address her mother in love and hate and everything in between. The word her father had said in the moments before the car had slammed into the tree.

Layla pushed herself off the bed and walked over to the windows overlooking the beach. She hugged her arms around her body, trying to contain the disturbing images that flashed into her brain every time she thought of the accident. Accident? What a misnomer that was. It had been no accident. Her father had wanted to kill them all and had just about succeeded in doing so. He and her mother had died at the scene but Layla had been saved by a passing motorist—an off-duty nurse who had controlled the bleeding until the paramedics had arrived. *Lucky Layla.* That was what she'd heard the medical staff call her at the hospital.

Why, then, didn't she feel it?

Layla blinked away the past and focussed on the beach below. The turquoise water beckoned but she hadn't swum since rehab after the accident. And you could hardly call *that* swimming. She wasn't sure she could even do it anymore. And she couldn't imagine doing it without a body suit on, because going out in public with her scars on show drew too many stares, too many pitying looks, too many intrusive questions.

But on a whim she still couldn't explain, she had bought a swimsuit when she'd bought her wedding dress. It was a strapless emerald-green one-piece with a ruched panel in the front and a matching sarong. It was still in her suitcase—she hadn't bothered unpacking it—because taking it out would be admitting she longed to swim, to feel the cool caress of ocean around her body, to be lifted weightless in its embrace. Free to move with perfect symmetry instead of her syncopated gait.

Layla narrowed her gaze when she saw a tall figure walking to the water. Logan had changed into a black hipster swimming costume, which showcased his athletic physique to perfection. Lean and taut with well-trained muscles, his skin tanned from numerous trips abroad, he turned every female head on the beach but seemed completely unaware of it. He waded through the waves until he got to deeper water and began striking out beyond the breakers in an effortless freestyle that was both graceful and powerful.

She turned away from the window with another sigh. She was on beautiful Maui in Hawaii with her brand-new husband who didn't want her other than as a means to an end.

Where was Lucky Layla now?

Logan towelled off on the beach after his swim, but the restlessness in him hadn't gone away in spite of the punishing exercise. He'd considered asking Layla to join him for a swim but had decided against it. This was not a honeymoon. They didn't have to spend every minute of the day together—even if he wanted to a lot more than he should.

He walked back to the villa and found Layla sitting on one of the sun lounge chairs on the terrace over-looking the beach. She was wearing blue denim jeans and ballet flats and an untucked white cotton shirt. Her head was shaded by a wide-brimmed hat and her eyes screened behind a pair of sunglasses. She looked up from the magazine she was flicking through and low-ered her sunglasses a fraction to look at him. 'How was the water?'

'Wet.'

She pushed her sunglasses back up to the bridge of her nose. 'Funny, ha-ha.'

Logan took the sun lounge seat beside hers and hooked one arm around one of his bent knees. 'Did you bring a swimming costume with you?'

'Yes, but I don't want to swim.' Her tone was brusque to the point of rudeness, her gaze staring out in front of her rather than facing him. 'Please don't ask me again.'

'If you're worried about your leg, then let me as-sure you—'

Her gaze whipped around to his with such speed it dislodged her hat and she had to steady it with one of her hands. 'You laid down some rules so I'm going to do the same. I don't like swimming. I don't like wearing bikinis or shorts or skirts that are above the knee. And if you *do* want me to wear them, then you've married the wrong person.' She removed her hand from holding her hat in place and turned back to stare out at the ocean.

Logan swung his legs over the side of the sun lounge

seat and leaned his arms on his knees, studying her rigid features. Her mouth was set, her chin at a haughty height, her eyes fixed on a view he could tell she wasn't even registering.

'Layla.' He kept his voice low and gentle. 'Look at me.'

Her fingers began to pick at a frayed patch on her jeans, her mouth still set in a stubborn line. 'I know what you're going to say, so don't bother saying it.'

'Tell me what you think I'm going to say.'

She pulled a thread out of the patch on her jeans and played tug-of-war with a series of sharp little tugs until it snapped. 'You're going to tell me I'm being silly about being self-conscious about my leg. That I should try and live a normal life and not care what anyone says or if they stare and ask rude questions.' She rolled the broken pieces of thread into a ball and dropped them onto the table beside her chair. 'But you're you. You're not me.'

Logan took one of her hands and anchored it against his thigh close to his bent knee. 'You're not silly to be self-conscious. It's tough having anything that draws unwelcome attention. But it concerns me you're limiting your enjoyment of life because of other people's reaction or judgement.'

She went to pull her hand out from under his but he countered it with a little more pressure. Her palm was soft against his thigh—warm and soft—and he couldn't stop imagining how it would feel on other parts of his body. His groin stirred, his blood rushed, his self-control went AWOL. Before he could stop himself, he brought her hand up to his mouth, pressing a light kiss to her bent knuckles. She gave a little whole-body shiver as if his touch was having the same effect on her as hers was on him. The tip of her tongue darted out to sweep a layer of moisture over her lips, her throat rising and falling in an audible swallow.

He took her sunglasses off her nose and laid them aside so he could mesh his gaze with hers. 'You don't have to be self-conscious around me. If we're going to convince Robbie and others that this is the real deal, then we're both going to have to feel more relaxed around each other. And even if we don't feel it we'll have to act it.'

Her pupils were like black ink spots, her eyelashes miniature fans. Her gaze dipped to his mouth, her in-drawn breath sounding ragged. 'Relaxed...in what way?'

Logan turned her hand over and stroked his thumb over her palm in a rhythmic fashion. 'There will be occasions when we'll be required to show some af-fection. Holding hands, a kiss on the cheek or a quick peck on the lips for appearances' sake. It would look odd if we didn't.'

'Okay...' Her voice was as soft as the whisper of the afternoon breeze. 'But earlier today you were pretty de-termined we weren't going to kiss again.'

'Unless absolutely necessary.'

Her eyebrows lifted in a wry manner. 'And who gets to decide whether it's necessary or not?'

'Me.' Logan released her hand and stood. He was un-apologetic for being so adamant. He wanted no blurry boundaries. He wanted control at all times. He wanted to keep his wanting under lock and key.

She anchored her hat and tilted her head to look up at him. 'Is that fair?'

'Probably not but that's the way it's going to be.' He scooped up his towel and flung it around his shoulders. 'I'm heading in for a shower. I've booked a restaurant for dinner at eight. It's a short walk from here but we can get a taxi if you'd prefer.'

Pride shone in her eyes and rang in her voice. 'That won't be necessary.'

Layla dressed for dinner later that evening with her mind still replaying their conversation out on the terrace. When he'd come to join her still dressed in nothing but his close-fitting swimming briefs, she had almost fainted on the spot with lust. And when he'd placed her hand on his bare thigh, it had been all she could do not to move it up higher. Her hand had tingled the whole time he'd held it.

When he'd repeatedly stroked his thumb across her palm, a fluttery sensation had gone through her belly and her female hormones went crazy. They were still going crazy. Her body was awake to needs it hadn't been conscious of before. Needs that made her long to have his hands stroking other places on her body. Places where no one had ever touched her.

Layla smoothed down the black all-in-one, spaghetti-strapped pantsuit that clung to her slim frame and widened at the legs in an elegant flare. It was a shame she couldn't wear high heels but the small kitten-heeled shoes were about as glamourous as she was prepared to go. She had lived her life since the car crash living safely and she didn't want to change. *Couldn't* change when it came to it. She had spent months and months in hospital and then more in a rehabilitation clinic. Long lonely bewildering months trying to get used to her new circumstances.

Adjusting to the presence of a new friend—survivor guilt.

Feeling guilty about her pretence of grieving for the loss of her parents, when what she had really felt was relief. She had felt far more relief over not losing her leg than grief over losing her parents. What did that say about her? Her scars reminded her every day of the conflict of her emotions. To this day, she felt relieved to be finally free of the chaotic family life both her parents had been responsible for, although she held her father to most of the blame.

A crazy, unpredictable life where alcohol and drugs had been on the table instead of food. A life where violence and shouting insults and smashing plates and glasses had been commonplace. Where there had been no peace even when it was quiet because you knew there was a storm brewing that could erupt at any moment. Without warning. Without any recognisable trigger. It just happened and you had to take shelter if you could and pray like crazy if you couldn't.

Layla sighed and swept her hair up in a makeshift bun, blocking her thoughts of the past like a shutter coming down. She refused to be a victim these days. She was strong and resilient and was fiercely proud of what she had achieved so far. And this temporary marriage with Logan would help her achieve even more. The money he had deposited into her bank account had already turned her financial situation around. Her business expansion plans could go ahead without fear of failure. She would focus on the positives of their marriage arrangement, not the niggling negatives.

She opened her cosmetics bag and touched up her make-up, spritzing perfume on her pulse points and applying lip-gloss to her lips. She gave herself a quick appraisal by turning this way and that in front of the mirror, deciding that even if she wasn't perfect, at least she was passable.

Logan had just ended a call dealing with a work issue on a large project he had going on in Tuscany when Layla came into the sitting room. Her all-in-one black outfit skimmed her slim figure in all the right places. Places he couldn't stop thinking about touching, caressing, exploring. Her make-up highlighted the regal elegance of her finely drawn features—the smoky eyeshadow and mascara on her lashes making her eyes stand out. Her chestnut hair was on top of her head in a loosely casual knot, leaving her swan-like neck and creamy shoulders exposed.

He imagined kissing a trail of light kisses along her smooth skin, down to her collarbones, down to the slight swell of her breasts. He imagined himself unclipping her hair from its knot and running his fingers through it to see if it was as silky as it looked. Her lips were shimmering with a layer of pink-toned lip-gloss and all he could think about was pressing his lips to hers to remove it with a kiss. He could still recall the sweet vanilla and honey taste of her mouth, could still feel the texture of her lips—soft…impossibly soft and responsive. Could still feel the background beat of desire ticking in his blood.

Oh, boy, he had some work to do on his willpower. Some big work.

If he was fantasising like this on day one of their marriage, what would he be like at the end of it?

'You look beautiful,' he said, slipping his phone into his trouser pocket.

A light tinge of pink pooled high in her cheeks and she lowered her gaze a fraction. 'Thank you.'

'Shall we go?' Logan led the way outside so they could walk to the restaurant, which was only a short stroll further along the bay. The night air had a salty tang from the ocean and there was a gibbous moon. Layla walked beside him in silence but he was increasingly aware of her limp. She was wearing small heels but they clearly weren't giving her the stability she needed. After she gave a precarious wobble, he reached for her hand and enveloped it in his. 'The pathway is a little uneven here.'

She glanced up at him with a brief smile of thanks and looked away again. They walked the rest of the way in silence but Logan was aware of every whorl of her skin where it touched his. Aware of the light flowery fragrance she was wearing, aware of how her head only came to just below his shoulders.

They came to the restaurant and were soon led to their table overlooking Kapalua Bay. The waiter took their drinks orders and left them with menus. Logan gave the menu a cursory glance because he could barely take his eyes off Layla. He had never spent so much concentrated time with her before. But when it came to that, he hadn't spent much time with anyone over the last seven years. He had preferred to be alone with his thoughts, with his regrets, with his guilt. Not just his guilt over Susannah.

Robbie caused him more guilt than he could handle and had done so for more years than he cared to count. His worry about his younger brother stretched back as far as childhood when their mother had left. Logan had done everything he could to shield Robbie from the sudden loss of their mother but he hadn't succeeded.

But when had he ever succeeded in a relationship of any kind?

Spending time with Layla opened up a new world of connection and emotional intimacy—that thing he had so assiduously avoided even in his relationship with his fiancée. Getting to know Layla on a deeper level had made him realise what his relationship with Susannah had been missing.

It was hard to get his head around the fact they were now officially married. It didn't seem real but it was—he had the marriage certificate to prove it. It was there in black and white.

On paper.

Layla looked up from examining the menu and frowned. 'Is something wrong?'

Logan rearranged his features into an impassive mask. 'No. Why?'

She closed the menu. 'You keep staring at me and frowning.'

He gave an on-off smile. 'Sorry. I was thinking.'

'About what?'

'About us.' Even saying the word 'us' made something in him sit up like a meerkat and take notice.

She lowered her gaze to focus on the candle flickering on the table between them. 'It's kind of weird, isn't it? I mean, us being married.' Her gaze came back to his. 'But at least we've saved Bellbrae. That's what matters most.'

'It's not the only thing that matters,' Logan said. 'It's important you aren't too badly inconvenienced by our arrangement. I know a year is a long time but once we annul our marriage, you'll be free to move on with your life.'

The waiter approached with their drinks to take their meal order at that point. Logan tried not to think about Layla's life after their marriage ended. It would be strange seeing her marry someone else one day, perhaps even have a family. And if she moved away, she might not even be a part of Bellbrae any more. He couldn't imagine the Highland estate without her. The place would seem empty and colourless. Bleak.

Once the waiter had left, Layla picked up her wineglass and gently twirled the contents. 'My life is my business. That's all I care about. I want to be successful and self-sufficient.'

'Do you want a family as well one day?' Why was he asking when he didn't want to know? He didn't want to think about her as a mother of some other man's babies. It was none of his business what she did with her life after their 'marriage' came to an end. No business at all.

Layla lifted one slim shoulder in a tiny shrug, a frown forming between her downcast eyes. 'I'm not sure about that... Sometimes I think it would be wonderful to have a family. But other times I worry I could end up like my mother.' She flicked him a veiled glance. 'She married the wrong person. It not only ruined her life, it cut it short.'

Logan suspected there was a lot more to Layla's background than she had let on. Her guardedness around the subject of her childhood was testament to that. He knew she had been in a car accident that had claimed her parents' lives and caused her to be severely injured but he had a sense she hadn't had an easy life even before that terrible tragedy. 'Do you feel comfortable telling me what happened?'

Layla took a sip of wine and then placed her glass back on the table. Her features were a battleground of conflicting emotions as if she was deciding whether to reveal or conceal. But after a long moment, she started speaking in a voice that throbbed with conviction.

'My mother made a series of choices she might not have made if she'd been better supported. She came from a difficult background herself and then got caught up in a downward spiral of petty crime to lift herself out of poverty. One job would have broken the cycle, I'm sure of it. It would have given her independence and a sense of worth.'

'Is that why you're so keen to employ people from disadvantaged backgrounds?' Logan asked.

'Absolutely. They sometimes just need someone to believe in them.' She tapped her hand on the table for emphasis. 'To give them a fighting chance. My mother didn't have anyone in her life who believed in her potential.'

'What was your father like?'

A flash of anger lit her grey-green gaze and her mouth tightened. 'He was a brute and a bully but my mother got completely taken in by him because he promised to give her a better life. He said all the charming things she wanted to hear but they were empty promises. She thought because he called her "babe" that he actually loved her. But when he started to show his true colours, she didn't have the strength or self-esteem to stand up to him. The worst part was she drank and used drugs to escape his behaviour but in doing so became more like him.'

She released a ragged sigh and looked back at the candle flickering on the table, a hot flare of anger still smouldering in her gaze. 'If I can save one woman from what happened to my mother, then all the hard work and sacrifice will be worth it.'

Logan reached for her hand across the table and gave it a gentle squeeze. 'I think it's amazing what you're doing with your business. It's an honourable and compassionate approach that is innovative and enterprising. If you'd like me to help you with a business expansion plan, I can do that.'

She pulled her hand away and placed it on her lap, her expression defensive. Wary. 'I'm not completely incompetent. I've run my business for the last couple of years without going bankrupt.'

'I meant no offence, Layla. Good structure is vital in business expansion. A lot of small businesses fold when they try to expand too quickly. I have some skills in that area so the offer is on the table. Take it or leave it.'

Something softened in her tight expression. 'I'll think about it.'

A small silence passed.

'What was your mother like?' Layla asked.

The question blindsided Logan. He was so used to not thinking about his mother that it took him a moment to even bring her features to mind. Thinking about his mother made him think about himself and his brother as distraught children who didn't understand why Mummy wasn't coming back home. Why she never came back or never wanted to see them or even talk to them on the phone. It had been a brutal abandonment that had all but destroyed his father and changed Logan's and Robbie's lives for ever.

'She was beautiful and charming,' Logan said, stripping his voice of emotion. 'If my father hadn't destroyed all the photos of her, I could've shown you how beautiful she was.'

'Aunt Elsie told me how gorgeous she was,' Layla said. 'And that your father fell madly in love with her the moment he met her.'

'My father was completely captivated by her. They had a whirlwind courtship and I was born a few months after their wedding. I don't think it was ever a happy marriage but when Robbie came four years after me, things really started to come unstuck.' He picked up his wineglass. 'One day, I came home from school to find she had left.' He drank from his glass and put it back down on the table with an audible thud. 'That morning we'd had a mother. That afternoon we didn't. No goodbye. No note. Not even a phone call. She'd gone to live with her lover in America. I haven't seen her or heard from her since.'

Layla frowned in concern. 'It must have been devastating for you both. You were so terribly young—what? Both under ten?'

'Seven and four.' Logan's tone was flat. 'We didn't understand why she left. We both thought we must have done something to make her leave us.'

'I guess a lot of kids would think like that but surely you realise it wasn't anything to do with you or Robbie?'

He shifted the base of his wineglass a quarter-turn. 'It took me years to realise it wasn't us. It was her. She didn't have the capacity to bond. I heard she's been married three or four times since then.' He paused for a moment before adding, 'It was harder on Robbie. He was only four and missed her badly. He cried for weeks, months really. I did what I could to compensate but it wasn't enough—nowhere near enough. He needed his mother and no one else was going to fill the hole she left behind. Not even our father, who was struggling himself to cope.'

A frown pulled at her brow. 'You can't possibly blame yourself for Robbie's problems. You were left by your mother too and you didn't go off the rails.'

Logan gave her a grim look. 'I do blame myself. I was too lenient with him then and after our father died. Robbie was only fourteen and full of raging hormones and risk-taking behaviour, which was part puberty and part acting out his grief. My grandfather was too controlling with him and I tried to make up for it in other ways. It was a mistake to swing back too far the other way. I should've tried a more balanced approach.' He made a self-deprecating sound and added, 'I'm definitely not cut out for parenthood. Not with all the mistakes I've made with my brother.'

Layla leaned forward in her chair, her expression etched with concern. 'Logan, you're not to blame. I think you've been an amazing older brother. And you would make an amazing father. Robbie hasn't made great choices along the way but you've done nothing but support him and encourage him to make better ones. Even the way you've put your own life on hold to save Bellbrae is proof of that. It's not just your heritage that would've been lost but his as well. I know how your mind works—by marrying me you're ultimately protecting him from the shame of losing his family's ancestral home in a poker game.' She picked up her wineglass and sat back in her chair. 'And I admire you for it.'

Logan gave a twisted smile. 'Let's hope you still admire me after you've lived with me for a year.'

Something passed over her features—a shadow in her quickly averted gaze, the flicker of a tiny muscle near her cheek, a flattening of her mouth. 'That works both ways.' Her voice dropped half a semitone in pitch. 'Let's hope we remain friends.'

Logan raised his glass in a toast. 'To staying friends.'

CHAPTER SIX

LATER THAT NIGHT back at the villa after dinner, Layla joined Logan for a nightcap in the sitting room before going to bed. She found herself reluctant to allow the evening to end. She had learned so much about Logan over dinner—what motivated him, what drove him, what tortured him. She had revealed things about herself too, and hadn't felt as uncomfortable about doing so as she'd thought she would. There were still some things she didn't feel comfortable revealing— she couldn't imagine a time when she ever would. To anyone.

'Here we go,' Logan said, handing her a small glass with Cointreau on ice. 'One nightcap.'

'I really don't need any more alcohol,' Layla said. 'But since this is kind of a holiday…'

One side of his mouth tipped up in a half-smile. 'I bet you haven't had one of those in a while.'

'Like you can talk, Mr Workaholic.' Layla took a sip of her drink, giving him a wry look over the rim of her glass.

He sat on the sofa opposite hers and crossed one ankle over his other knee, one arm draped over the back of the sofa, the other holding his brandy and dry. 'Yes, well, I've never been much good at relaxing.' He took a sip of his drink, held it in his mouth for a brief moment before swallowing.

Layla kicked off her shoes and tucked her good leg underneath her, making sure her scars on her other leg were covered by her pantsuit trousers. 'When was your last holiday?'

A small frown carved into his forehead and he stared at the contents of his glass. 'I sometimes take an afternoon off when I'm away on a project.'

'An afternoon?' Layla snorted. 'Even I've managed better than that. I had a couple of weekends off in a row three months back.'

His lazy half-smile was back and it made something in her stomach slip. 'Go, you.' His voice was low and husky, his sapphire-blue eyes as dark as a midnight sky. 'Did you do anything special on those weekends off?'

Layla gave a laugh. 'Okay, you've got your *gotcha* moment. I did paperwork while I watched movies and ate pizza.'

His gaze was unwavering, his smile mesmerising. 'Looks like we both need lessons in how to relax.'

There was a sudden change in the atmosphere and Layla was the first to look away. Or maybe it was where her mind was taking her—to long, sleepy, relaxing lie-ins after making love. Her head resting on Logan's chest, his fingers playing with her hair, their legs entwined. That would be a good way to relax, surely? She sipped some more of her drink and hoped her cheeks weren't looking as hot as they felt.

'How about we stay on a few extras days here?' Logan said. 'We could explore some of the other islands. That is, if you can juggle your work commitments.'

Layla kept looking at the ice cubes in her glass rather than meet his gaze. An extended holiday in Hawaii would surely involve wearing a swimsuit, swimming, being surrounded by beautiful unscarred bodies on the beach. She could hardly relax under those circumstances. She would be waiting in dread for the whispered comments, the sideways glances, the *What happened to you?* questions. She leaned forward to put her glass on the coaster on the table in front of her. 'I don't know... Don't you have to check out your project in Tuscany?'

'It can wait a few more days.'

Layla could have used her work commitments as an excuse to get back to Scotland but the temptation to spend more time here with Logan was too hard to resist. She only had to send a couple of emails or make a few calls to make sure everything was ticking along efficiently with her cleaning business. She had some reliable staff who were more than capable of standing in for her. Why shouldn't she relax and enjoy herself for once? 'I guess it would be nice to see a bit more of Hawaii before we go home.'

'I'll make the arrangements.'

Layla tried but failed to disguise a yawn. 'Who knew eating and drinking could be so exhausting?' She carefully unfolded her leg from beneath her and rose from the sofa. 'I think I'll turn in. Thanks for a lovely dinner and...everything.'

He gave one of his rare smiles. 'You're welcome.'

* * *

Logan sat back and finished his drink once Layla had gone off to bed, wondering if he'd done the right thing in suggesting they extend their stay. He had originally planned to fly in and fly out once they were officially married. But he'd thought a few extra days might help both of them get used to their new circumstances before they went back to Bellbrae. Living together as man and wife, even on paper, was going to take some considerable adjustment, especially if they were to do it as authentically as they could by sharing the west tower suite. Besides, they were both hard workers who rarely took a break.

But her initial reluctance to stay on for a few extra days made him wonder if it was not so much about spending time with him that troubled her but something else. The beach environment? Or maybe it was both. Not everyone enjoyed the beach, especially those with fair complexions like Layla, but he had seen her looking at other swimmers and sunbathers with a wistful look on her face.

His memory snagged on something…a memory from way back to when she had been a young teenager, not long after she had come to live with his family. He seen her watching him swim on the loch at Bellbrae. He'd pretended not to notice as he hadn't wanted to make her feel uncomfortable, but he'd been aware of her hiding in the shadows of the trees. When he'd brought his fiancée home, Layla had spied on them both. It had made Susannah annoyed but he'd forbidden her to say anything to Layla. And thankfully she hadn't. But he realised now he had never seen Layla swimming, not even in the indoor pool his grandfather had installed a few years ago after he'd had a hip replacement.

If Logan did nothing else on their 'honeymoon' he would help her overcome her reluctance to wear a swimsuit. Although just thinking about her in a swimsuit was enough to make his imagination run wild and his blood run hot. And the last thing his imagination needed was any encouragement. His willpower was having enough trouble as it was.

He had to remember—this wasn't a real honeymoon and it wasn't a real marriage.

Neither could it ever become one.

The following morning Layla woke to bright sunshine pouring through the windows of her bedroom. *Her* bedroom. Not *their* bedroom. Her first night as a married woman and she had spent it alone.

She heard sounds of Logan moving about in the suite outside her room and wondered if he too had found it odd to have spent their first night as a married couple in separate beds. Probably not. He was the one who had made the rules and was so determined to stick to them. And she had agreed to them, so why was she even mulling over their situation?

It was a sensible plan to keep their emotions out of the arrangement. It was wise for both of them to refrain from developing feelings that demanded more permanency. Her dream of finding someone to love her was just that—a dream. A fanciful dream that had little hope of being realised. And that secret little smouldering coal inside her? It needed a bucket of ice-cold reality thrown over it.

The fragrant smell of freshly brewed coffee tantalised Layla's nostrils and she threw off the bedcovers and slipped on a bathrobe to cover her satin pyjama set. She came out to the dining area of the luxury villa to find a colourful fruit platter and fresh croissants and rolls with butter and preserves laid out ready for breakfast.

Logan was pouring coffee into a cup and glanced up when she came in. 'Ah, Sleeping Beauty awakes. Coffee? Or would you prefer tea?'

'That coffee smells delicious,' Layla said, thinking he looked and smelled pretty damn delicious too.

His hair was still damp from a shower, his jaw was cleanly shaven and she could pick up a trace of the lemon and lime notes of his aftershave. He was dressed casually in white cotton shorts that set off the deep tan of his legs, his light blue T-shirt showcasing his well-toned chest. He looked rested, relaxed and ridiculously sexy, and her female hormones swooned.

He handed her a cup of steaming coffee. 'How did you sleep?'

Layla took the cup from him and breathed in the delicious aroma. 'Not bad...considering.' She took a sip of coffee, conscious of his unwavering gaze.

'Considering what?' He leaned one hip against the counter, holding his cup by the base.

Seemed she didn't need alcohol to get her tongue out of control. Some inner demon was goading her to point out the weirdness of their situation. A honeymoon with separate bedrooms. If that wasn't weird, what was? Layla put the cup down on the table and, pulling out a chair, sat and reached for a piece of golden pineapple.

'Considering it was the first night of my honeymoon.' She raised her fingers in air quotes over the word 'honeymoon', sending him an ironic look. 'It's not the way I imagined it as a child. Just saying…'

A ripple of tension crossed his features like sand blown by a breeze. 'You know my reasons for insisting our relationship stays on paper only.' His tone was schoolmaster stern, his gaze determined. 'I couldn't have made it any clearer.'

Layla took a bite of the juicy pineapple and chewed and swallowed. 'Yes, you've made it perfectly clear. And I'm totally fine with it.' *Was she?* Or was she just paying lip service? 'But I can't help wondering if it's not me you're trying to protect but yourself.'

He placed his cup on the table with a thud and frowned. 'Protect myself from what?'

She kept her gaze trained on his. 'From getting too close to someone. To feeling something for someone other than transient lust. You keep people at a distance. You've had plenty of casual lovers but you haven't had a live-in lover since you lost Susannah.'

He picked up the coffee pot and refilled his cup. 'You seem to know a lot about my love life.'

'But it's not a love life, is it? It's a lust life.'

He gave a rough laugh that held not a shred of humour. 'Works for me, sweetheart.' He raised his cup to his mouth and took a mouthful of coffee.

'It will work until one day it won't,' Layla said, picking up another piece of fruit—a wedge of pink watermelon this time—and placing it on her plate.

Logan pulled out the chair opposite hers and sat down and placed his coffee cup on the table, his forehead creased in a frown. 'Why is it so important to you how I live my life?'

Layla found it hard to hold his gaze. 'I've known you since I was a twelve-year-old kid. How could I not care about how you live your life?'

He gave a brief movement of his lips that fell short of a smile. 'I know you mean well, Layla, but, believe me, it's best if you don't care too much. Now, finish your breakfast. We have some serious sightseeing to do.'

Over the next couple of days Layla was left in no doubt about Logan's skill as a tour guide. He organised a tour of Haleakala National Park, located on Maui's inactive volcano, as well as visits to the Seven Sacred Pools of the Oheo Ravine and Makahika and Waimoko waterfalls. The lush rainforests with their towering, tumbling waterfalls were breathtaking, and Logan organised a private helicopter tour of the summit of the volcano, which gave stunning views over the crater and the whole island. He was sensitive without being patronising over the walks they took through the rainforest, and he always had a steadying hand at the ready if she gave any hint of losing her footing.

In the evenings they dined out at various restaurants, chatting over the day's sights, and then returned to the villa and retired to their separate quarters. It was clear Logan was doing everything he could to ensure their relationship remained platonic, but every now and again when he touched her as he helped her out of the car or took her hand over a rough part of a walk, her senses went into a frenzy.

The morning after their trip to the volcano Layla

joined Logan at breakfast but instead of a day of touring, he suggested they stay at the villa for the day.

'It's going to be quite warm today and I thought you might appreciate a quieter day, relaxing around the pool,' he said, refilling her glass with fruit juice.

Layla had been pointedly ignoring the sparkling blue infinity saltwater lap pool on the seaboard terrace. Just like she ignored the beautiful indoor pool Angus McLaughlin had installed at Bellbrae to help him recover from a hip replacement a few years ago. 'I don't really enjoy swimming that much,' she said, picking up the glass of orange juice. 'But I'm happy to watch you do laps.' More than happy if she were to be perfectly honest. Hadn't she found secret pleasure in watching him for years?

Logan's gaze searched hers. 'Does it hurt your leg to swim?'

'No, it's just I...' She lowered her gaze back to the frothy juice in her glass. 'I'm a bit self-conscious about my scars.'

And I feel weirdly grateful I have them instead of my parents.

Of course she could never tell him. She couldn't tell anyone. It was too shameful to admit out loud.

'It will only be us here and you don't need to be shy around me.' His tone had a gentle note that ambushed her emotions. Could she do it? Could she reveal the marks on her body that signified the biggest turning point in her life?

Layla brought her gaze back up to his. 'It's been a long time since I've been in the water.'

Warmth shone in his eyes and his smile made her stomach do a somersault. 'I'll be there to help you.'

A short time later Layla came out to the pool area dressed in her green swimming costume with her sarong wrapped around her body and her hair tied back in a high ponytail. Logan was already in the pool, doing laps, and she stood in the shade of the shrubbery, watching him carve through the water with effortless grace and efficiency. He performed fluid tumble turns at each end, the water glistening on his tanned back and shoulders.

He stopped at the end closest to where she was standing and scraped his hair back away from his forehead. 'Hang on—I'll help you down the steps.' He placed his hands on the edge of the pool and launched himself out in one athletic movement that showcased his powerful biceps. He held out his hand, an encouraging smile tilting his mouth. 'You can do it, Layla. I won't let you slip.'

Wasn't she already slipping? Slipping into the dangerous waters of developing feelings she had promised she wouldn't feel. For anyone. How could she dare hope to be loved when even her own parents hadn't truly loved her? Their first love had been their addictions. But the more time she spent with Logan, the deeper her feelings grew. How could they not? It was like asking a flower not to bloom under healing, restorative sunshine.

Layla took a deep breath and let go of her sarong. It slipped to the pool deck at her feet, leaving her in nothing but the green costume. Her leg was criss-crossed with vivid white scars with dents where muscle had been grafted from her thigh to her calf. Her leg had been through a long hard battle to avoid being amputated and had only just won. And it showed.

She waited for the look of distaste, for the screwed-up expression of horror she had seen too many times to count. But Logan didn't show any of that. His eyes did an appraising scan of her body, lingering a little longer on the upthrust of her breasts and the cleavage its design highlighted, but there was no disgust in his gaze. There was desire. Desire that made her feel more of a woman than she had ever felt.

Layla took his outstretched hand and drew comfort and courage from the warm press of his fingers around hers. 'Okay...let's do this...' She walked with him down the slab steps of the pool into the silky embrace of the water. She was conscious of his strong male body right beside her, conscious of the fact he was wearing even less than she was. Conscious of the way her body responded to him in secret—the subtle increase in her heart rate, the little flickers of lust between her thighs.

Logan let go of her hand once she was standing waist deep in the water. 'Let the water support you. Don't fight it. Go with it.'

Layla bounced her feet off the bottom of the pool to put herself in a floating position, allowing the water to carry her weight. It was nothing short of bliss to be supported and she starting swimming a slow freestyle, because the gentle kicking motion was a little easier to manage with her leg. Tumble turns were beyond her capability, so she stopped at the end instead, caught her breath and then turned around and came back.

The sun was warm and the water shimmering as she passed through it. She was aware of every inch of her body the water touched, her muscles enjoying the pull and tug of exercise, her skin enjoying the caress of water.

She stopped at the end where Logan was waiting for her. She stood upright and smiled, flicking wet hair out of her face. 'I'm not quite up to your standard but thank you for encouraging me.'

'You look very at home in the water. Like a mermaid.' His tone had a husky edge and his dark blue eyes did another slow appraisal of her cleavage.

Layla knew she should turn around and keep swimming but something kept her frozen in place. Well, perhaps not quite frozen, for smouldering heat was travelling to every part of her body. Logan's gaze met hers and suddenly there wasn't a foot of space between them anymore. They were practically pelvis to pelvis with only a millimetre or two of water separating them. The magnetic pull of his body drew her inexorably closer until her breasts met the hard wall of his chest. His hands settled on each of her hips, his taut abdomen close enough for her to feel the jut of his growing erection.

Time stood still for an infinitesimal moment as if an invisible hand had blocked the ticking hand of a clock. Tick. Tock. Stop.

Logan's head came down and his mouth met hers in a kiss that tasted of salt water, sun and male sensuality. Her mouth flowered open under the passionate pressure, her tongue meeting his in a sexy tangle that made shivers course down her spine. He moved against her and the hard nudge of his aroused body made her legs almost fold beneath her. He brought a hand to the small of her back, pressing her even closer to the throb of his flesh, his kiss deepening with a thrust of his tongue that was blatantly erotic.

Layla made a whimpering sound of encouragement, one of her hands sliding up to caress the back of his neck, the other his lean jaw. Escalating need pulsated through her entire body, her legs trembling with the sheer force of its unstoppable tide.

Logan's hand came to her swimsuit-clad breast, cupping it through the ruched fabric, but his touch still sent a shockwave of longing through her flesh. His arousal jutted against her feminine mound and he gave a deep rough-sounding groan against her mouth before finally lifting off.

He kept hold of her by the upper arms, his breathing heavy, his gaze hooded. 'I'm sorry.' His tone was full of self-reproach and he released her from his hold and stepped back with a brooding frown between his dark brows.

Layla licked her lips, relishing the taste of him still lingering there. 'You don't have to apologise. I—'

'I don't want to give you the wrong impression.' He dragged a hand over his face as if wanting to reset his features. 'It's not fair to confuse you by saying one thing and then doing another.'

'The impression I got was that you wanted to kiss me and enjoyed it as much as I did,' Layla said, challenging him to deny it with her unwavering gaze.

His gaze slipped to her mouth and he drew in a harsh-sounding breath, releasing it a whoosh of self-recrimination. 'I enjoyed it too damn much but it doesn't mean it's going to happen again.' He turned and launched himself out of the pool, spraying water droplets in an arc around him. 'I'm going to go for a run. I'll see you later.'

Layla sighed and sank under the water and began swimming again. Maybe a few punishing laps of the pool would tame her own frustrated desire.

Logan ran along the shoreline oblivious to the protestation of overused muscles. He was determined to beat this obsession with kissing Layla. He was the one who had made the rules—why was he finding it so damn hard to stick to them? Her mouth was a drug he had suddenly developed a hunger for and it was taking every bit of willpower he possessed to resist. What was it about her that made him so tempted to step over every boundary he had laid down?

But then a thought strayed into his mind...maybe he shouldn't resist. Maybe he could tweak the rules and see what happened. The thought sat down like an uninvited guest, put its feet up and got comfortable but Logan frogmarched it out of his head. He knew what would happen and he had to avoid it at all costs. He increased his pace along the sand, ignoring the burning sensations in his legs. Ignoring the heaving of his chest as he dragged in each gulping breath.

He hadn't forgiven himself for his last relationship disaster.

He couldn't—*wouldn't*—go there again.

CHAPTER SEVEN

LAYLA WAS TIRED after her swimming session and after a shower lay down on the bed to rest with one ear out to listen for when Logan returned from his run. But he must have been doing a marathon because every time she glanced at the clock by the bed, it had gone around another half an hour until finally she closed her eyes and drifted off to sleep...

Layla hadn't had the dream in years. She was in the back of the car, her parents were arguing in the front, with her father in the driving seat. The trees on the roadside were blurred by the speed her father was going. The car swerved and spun but her father corrected it, laughing manically and asking if they were wetting their pants yet. Her mother had stopped shouting back and was now shrunk into her seat, begging him to slow down in a whimpering voice, one side of her face already blackened by her husband's fist from the day before.

Layla saw the tree coming towards them, looming, looming. She screamed but it was too late. Too late. Too late...

Someone was trying to revive her. She could feel

their hands on her shoulders and hear them calling her name. 'Layla. Wake up. You're having a bad dream. Wake up.'

But it wasn't the off-duty nurse or the paramedics who had been first on the scene that day. Layla opened her eyes to see Logan perched on the edge of her bed, his hands stroking back the hair that had fallen across her face.

'It's all right, I'm here. It was just a nightmare.' His voice was gentle and his touch soothing, anchoring her in the present, not the past.

Layla blinked away the terrifying images lingering in her head. She pushed herself upright into a sitting position, wincing against the light of the bedside lamp he had switched on. How long had she been sleeping? Hours and hours for it was now dark outside.

'Sorry. Gosh, I didn't realise it was night already. Did I wake you up?'

He took one of her hands and held it in his, stroking the back of it with slow, rhythmic movements. 'In bed but not asleep. I was going through some emails on my phone when I heard you call out.'

Layla peered at the bedside clock to find it was close to midnight. 'Oh, I must have wrecked your dinner booking. Sorry. I didn't realise how tired I would be after swimming.'

'Can I get you something to eat or a drink of milk or something?'

She screwed up her face. 'Eww. I hate milk.'

His crooked smile transformed his features and made her heart do a little flip turn. 'I should have remembered that. What about fruit juice or herbal tea?'

'You don't have to fuss over me like I'm a little kid.' She plucked at the hem of the sheet with her fingers. 'I'm not hungry and I'm perfectly able to get myself back to sleep.' She kept her gaze lowered, conscious of his hair-roughened thigh so close to hers on the bed. Conscious of his stroking fingers on her hand, conscious of her body secretly reacting to his touch. Warmth spreading through her lower body, flickers of heat smouldering in her core.

He was dressed in boxer shorts but naked from the waist up. His lean and athletic build could have been no better advertisement for regular exercise. His pectoral muscles were toned and carved on his broad chest and the neat washboard ridges of the muscles on his abdomen spoke of man who was not afraid of pushing himself to the limit. It was all she could do to keep her hands to herself. Her fingers tingled with the desire to explore those toned ridges, to trace every hard contour.

'Do you want to talk about it? Your dream?' Logan's baritone voice was deep, calm and even and as soothing as his stroking fingers on the back of her hand.

Layla fixed her gaze on her hand encased in the shelter of his. Her skin was so pale against his tan, a reminder of all the essential differences between them. She hadn't been in a gym since rehab. She felt sick to her stomach at the thought. Too many reminders of the pain of trying to walk again, trying to be normal when normal was something other people took for granted and never had to question.

'I haven't had a nightmare in ages...' She chanced a glance at him to find him watching her with concern etched on his features. She lowered her eyes again and asked, 'Did I say anything while I was asleep?'

'You were calling out "Stop" repeatedly. I was worried we might've had an intruder. I came rushing in to find you thrashing on the bed in the throes of a nightmare.' His eyes were haunted with the stress of finding her so distressed. 'You were dreaming about the accident?'

Layla gave a small nod, her gaze still focussed on their joined hands. For years she had heard everyone refer to it as an accident. A chance thing, a driver error that had gone horribly wrong. Her memory might have been patchy for months after the crash but one thing she had always known was that it hadn't been a simple driver error. 'It wasn't an accident.' She brought her gaze back to his, her voice tight, her throat tighter. 'It was a deliberate car crash.'

Logan's hand stilled on hers, his eyes widening in alarm. 'What do you mean?' His tone was hollowed out, echoing with shock.

'My father wanted to kill us all. He drove the car into the tree because my mother told him she wanted to leave him.'

'Oh, Layla…' Logan's hand gripped hers as if he was trying to anchor her to him. To stop her being swept away by a tide of distressing memories. 'I can't imagine the panic and fear and pain you must have gone through. What a cowardly act. A disgustingly cowardly act.' His voice was full of cutting contempt for her father and deep concern for her.

Layla rolled her eyes in a tell-me-about-it manner. 'I certainly didn't win the father lottery, that's for sure.

Or the mother one, although I think she would've had a much better chance of being a better mother if she hadn't married my father. His influence was destructive and damaging but by the time she got the courage to leave him, it was too late.'

Logan brushed back some imaginary hair off her forehead, his gaze steady and compassionate. 'The more I hear about your childhood, the more I admire you. You've done an amazing job of overcoming those terrible experiences.'

'I wouldn't have been able to do it without Aunt Elsie and your family's help,' Layla said. 'I know your grandparents were old-school Scots but their hearts were in the right place. I'm not sure how my life would've turned out if I'd stayed too much longer in foster care. I was there for a few weeks after I came out of rehab until Aunt Elsie got official guardianship of me. Some of those group homes were pretty terrifying. Damaged kids damaging other kids.'

She shook her head, trying to shake away the memories of the past.

'I know not all foster homes are awful but it's not the same as belonging to your own family.' She twisted her mouth and added, 'Not that my family was anything to crow about. My father was an angel in public but a bullying devil behind closed doors. He claimed to love us but he didn't know the meaning of the word.' She flopped back down against the pillows with a heavy sigh. 'Now I'm going to shut up about my childhood. I'm probably boring you.'

Logan turned her hand over and traced a slow line across her palm. 'You're not boring me at all.' He locked his gaze on hers. 'In fact, I find you one of the most interesting and intriguing people I've ever met.' He drew a circle on her palm this time, the lazy movement of his finger sending shivers shooting up and down her spine.

Layla sucked in an uneven breath, her insides coiling with desire. She could see the same desire reflected in his sapphire-blue gaze. Desire that sent a current through the air like high-voltage electricity. She disguised a swallow, her heart picking up its pace, her pulse sprinting.

'Will you stay with me until I go back to sleep?' The question popped out almost before she knew she was going to say it. Her cheeks grew warm and she lowered her gaze and bit down on her lower lip, pulling her hand out of his and burying it under the sheet covering her lower body. 'Forget I said that. I'm old enough to get myself back to sleep.'

A silence ticked past. Tick. Tick. Tick.

Logan stood from where he was perched on the side of the bed, but he didn't leave. 'Scoot over,' he said, gesturing with his hand. 'I'll lie on top of the covers, though.'

Layla gave him a wry look. 'Don't you trust me?'

His expression was grim. 'I don't trust myself.'

It was a while before Layla fell back to sleep, but when she did it was deep and peaceful and dreamless. She woke as dawn was breaking, the sun stealing into the room, casting the bed in a golden beam of light as direct as a spotlight. She was lying on her side with the warm band of Logan's arm wrapped around her middle and one of his strong muscular legs flung over hers.

Sometime during the night, he must have joined her

under the bedcovers but she had no clear memory of it. But now she was acutely aware of every part of his body where it was in contact with hers—his hard chest against her back, his strong thighs against her bottom, his arm across her waist. His head was resting on the top of hers, his breathing deep and even, each of his expelled breaths gently feathering her cheek.

He shifted position slightly, his arm tightening around her middle to draw her closer, his other hand skating over one of her breasts. Even through the light barrier of her silk pyjama top she could feel the outline of his broad male hand. Could feel the erratic leap of her pulse at his intimate touch. Could feel one of his hair-roughened thighs coming between hers, triggering a firestorm in her female flesh.

He gave a low sleepy murmur. 'Mmm...you feel nice.'

Layla knew she should wake him but she couldn't quite bring herself to do it. No one had ever held her like this. She had never experienced the warmth and comfort of a lover's touch. Was it wrong of her to want to break the rules he had laid down? She moved her legs experimentally against his, enjoying the feel of hard muscle and rough masculine hair against her smoother skin. His hand came back to her breast, cradling it with exquisite gentleness, his thumb rolling back and forth across her tightening nipple. Tingling sensations rioted through her body from her breast to her feminine core. Her breathing stalled, her belly swooped, her senses reeled.

Layla turned in his arms and he opened his eyes and swore not quite under his breath and released her and sat upright.

'Sorry.' His apology was brief, brusque and bruising to her ego.

'It's okay, Logan,' Layla said. 'You didn't do anything.'

He rubbed a hand down his face, the sound of his palm scratching across his morning stubble loud in the echoing silence. 'You should have woken me.' His tone was gruff, his eyes haunted with guilt and self-loathing.

Layla rolled her eyes. 'Oh, for goodness' sake. Why are you making such a big deal out of this? I enjoyed sleeping next to you. I enjoyed you holding me.'

His mouth was set in a taut line. 'This has to stop.' He sprang off the bed as if it had just poked him. '*I* have to stop.' He said it not quite under his breath, as if he was reminding himself, not her.

Layla pulled her knees up to her chest and wrapped her arms around them. 'Why do you have to stop?'

Whoa! What did you just say?

But her conscience wasn't listening and neither was her traitorous body. It was awake and wanting. Why shouldn't they explore the chemistry they shared? She could be casual about the time limit on their relationship, couldn't she? And maybe, just maybe the time limit would become irrelevant…

'You know why.'

'Because you feel you'd be betraying Susannah's memory?'

He frowned as if she had started speaking in a foreign language. 'No. Of course not. It's not about Susannah.'

'So it's me then. It's because it's me.' Layla couldn't quite remove the note of despondency in her tone.

He speared a hand through his hair and gave a rough sigh. 'It's me. Me not wanting to hurt you in the long run. Sex can be casual and God knows I've had plenty of it. But it wouldn't be casual between us. You know it wouldn't. It couldn't be. We already have an existing relationship and building sex onto that would make things way more complicated when the year is up on our marriage.'

Layla straightened her legs, crossed her ankles and folded her arms across her chest. 'But what if we decided not to end it after a year? We might decide to extend it for a bit long—'

'No.' His sharply delivered word was as stinging as a slap. 'We're not doing that, Layla. The rules are there for a reason.'

'I think the rules are there because deep down you want more than you'd like everyone to believe,' Layla said. 'You're still punishing yourself because of Susannah's death. It's understandable—it was a terrible tragedy to lose the love of your life. But you're entitled to have a life, even though hers has gone. You deserve to have some measure of happiness, even if it won't be on the same level as before.'

Logan muttered a thick curse and speared her gaze with his hard and glittering one.

'She wasn't the love of my life. There, that's shocked you, hasn't it? I thought I loved her at the start but then I started to feel less certain. I knew something wasn't right between us but I put it down to my preoccupation with work. I had a few big projects going on and I travelled a lot, and, to tell you the truth, I enjoyed coming home to someone who always seemed happy to see me.

I think because I was away so much it took me longer to realise how unsuited we actually were. But when I finally realised, I *should* have ended it then and there, but her emotional fragility had started to worry me. I stupidly let our relationship limp along for the rest of the year but, as it turned out, I was right to be worried.'

Layla couldn't hope to conceal her shock at his embittered words. Her mouth was open, her eyes wide, her heart heavy for what he'd been through and the guilt that still plagued him. He had told her a few days ago that things hadn't been as perfect between him and Susanna as she had believed but she had still assumed he had loved his fiancée. Dearly loved her. Layla had always seen them as the ideal couple. They'd looked so good together, they had seemed to treat each other with the utmost respect, they came from the same world of wealth and privilege.

But had she *wanted* to see them that way? To fulfil her own girlhood romantic fantasy. Ignoring the subtle clues that things weren't quite as rosy and romantic as she'd wanted to believe.

But who knew how any relationship worked from the inside? Hadn't her childhood more than proved that? Happy Families was a game her father had played and played extremely well. Only those on the inside, behind the door closed to the public, knew what the true dynamics were.

Layla unfolded her arms and pushed the bedcovers off and got off the bed. It didn't matter that she was only dressed in cream silk pyjamas that draped her body contours rather too closely. He had seen her in far less in the pool the previous day. All that mattered was going to him, to offer some support and understanding, some compassion. She stood in front of him, never more conscious of their difference in height—she had to tilt her head right back to gain eye contact.

She touched him lightly on the arm, his masculine hairs tickling her palm, reminding her of yet another difference between them. 'I don't know what to say other than I'm so sorry things were so…so difficult…'

The tense lines around his mouth slackened on a heavily released breath and he took her hand from his arm and held it in his. His thumb moved across the back of her hand in an almost absent fashion, his eyes meshing with hers. 'The thing that haunts me is—' he winced, as if recalling the memory pained him '—I think she knew I was going to call off our engagement eventually. I was waiting for the right time, when I thought she could handle it better emotionally. But I didn't know about her eating disorder—apparently, she had it before we met. I still can't forgive myself for not realising how ill she was. I probably made her illness worse by not being fully present in the relationship for all those months.'

Layla moved closer without even realising she was doing it. It seemed natural to be standing so close to him, natural to put her arms around him and even more natural to hug him. His arms came around her—warm, strong, male arms that made everything feminine in her body shiver in delight.

'We're all good at hiding things we're ashamed of, and unfortunately eating disorders are high on the list,' she said, resting her head against his chest. 'I know it's useless me telling you not to blame yourself, but you did what you could based on the information you had at the time. You stayed with her and supported her as best you could for far longer than most men would've done.'

Logan began a gentle stroking of the back of her head, each downward movement of his hand making the base of her spine melt. Her breasts were pressed against the broad wall of his chest, her pelvis so close to his, a sensation spread through her lower body like a slow flow of warm treacle. The stirring of his male flesh against her sent a dart of lust between her legs, her inner core pulsating, contracting with a tender ache.

He eased back to look down at her, his eyes so dark it was hard to tell his pupils from the deep blue of his irises. The haunting shadows in his gaze had faded and now his eyes contained a new energy—an intense energy that spoke of attraction, desire, need.

Logan framed her face with his hands, his touch so gentle it made a closed space inside her chest suddenly flare open. 'I told myself this wasn't going to happen.' His voice was as rough as gravel, deep as a base chord with a side note of longing. His gaze dipped to her mouth, lingering, smouldering. 'You deserve better than what I can offer. Much better.'

'But what if I'm happy with what you're offering?' Layla laid one of her hands on the hard plane of his chest, the other on his richly stubbled jaw. 'What if I want you to kiss me and make love to me, even if it's only for the duration of our marriage?' She could scarcely believe she was offering herself on such stripped-down terms. What had happened to her dream of lifelong love? What had happened to her secret belief in the happy-ever-after fairy-tale?

Logan had happened, that was what. Her need for him overrode every other thought.

He closed his eyes in a tight blink as if calling on whatever internal willpower he possessed but finding it missing. 'I don't want to hurt you. I seem to have a particular talent for hurting people I care about. I don't want you to be one of them.'

Layla linked her arms around his neck, her fingers playing with the dark brown ends of hair that brushed against his neck. 'The way you'll hurt me is to not kiss me, to not want me the way I want you. But you do want me, don't you? Or am I just imagining it?'

He placed a hand at the base of her spine and drew her against the evidence of his arousal, his eyes glinting. 'You're not imagining it. I want you so badly it's making me crazy. Ever since I saw you packing up my grandfather's things in the north tower, it was like a switch turned on inside me. I can't seem to turn it off.'

Layla stepped up on tiptoe, bringing her mouth closer to the slow descent of his. 'I don't want you to turn it off. Not now. Not yet.' *Not ever.*

His head came down, a deep groan coming from the back of his throat as their lips met in an explosive kiss. Heat flared, flames of lust licking along Layla's flesh like wildfire in a tinder-dry forest. His tongue met hers, playing, duelling, teasing, dancing. His fingers splayed through her hair, his head tilting so he could deepen the kiss, his lower body pressed to hers in passionate desperation. She instinctively moved against his hot hard heat, her body delighting in the potency and power of his body. It was erotic, it was exciting, it was exhilarating to feel the throb and pound of his blood in such an intimate manner. She had never been so close to a man before. Her teenage date that ended so humiliatingly hadn't been anything like this.

This was adult attraction in full flare—mutual attraction that sent fizzing sensations to every secret corner of her body. Her spine loosened like molten candlewax, her legs trembled, the backs of her knees tingled, her pulse raced.

Logan placed his hands on her hips and raised his mouth off hers, his breathing ragged. 'It's not too late to stop this. You have to be sure—*I* have to be sure you really want this.'

Layla stroked the side of his face with her palm. 'I want you, Logan.' Her voice was whisper-soft but no less determined. 'You turned a switch on in me too. I want you to make love to me.'

His hands tightened on her hips and for a sinking moment she thought he was going to put her from him, but then he brought her closer again—close enough for her to feel the imprint of his erection against her belly. His head came back down and his mouth met hers in a drugging kiss that made the hairs on the back of her neck pirouette.

He tore his mouth away after a long moment. 'Wait. Condom.' He left her briefly to go to the other bedroom where his things were stored.

Layla held her breath the whole time he was away, fearful he would change his mind about making love to her. But he came back carrying the tiny foil packet, his eyes smouldering as soon as they met hers. 'Still okay about this?'

'More than okay.'

Somehow, they made it back to the bed in a series of stop-starts where the kiss deepened, intensified, electrified. Where their breathing became laboured, their need escalating. Where his hands skated over her aching flesh in a voyage of discovery, and hers did the same, with boldness she hadn't known she possessed.

A distant part of Layla's mind told her she should tell him she was a virgin but she couldn't bring herself to do it. She didn't want to risk him changing his mind—she suspected he would call an immediate halt to their lovemaking. He would see her lack of experience as yet another reason to keep their marriage on paper. But she wanted him to be her first lover. Why shouldn't it be him? Someone who had known her for many years, who had seen her grow from girl to woman.

Someone she trusted, cared about, respected. *Loved.*

Of course she loved him. She wasn't sure when it had started. It had been a gradual awakening, a slow burn of interest and attraction that had morphed into a persistent and powerful emotion.

Logan laid her down on the bed and came down beside her. He slowly undid the buttons on the front of her pyjama jacket, the feel of his fingers against her bare skin making her shiver in anticipation. He peeled the silky jacket from her shoulders and his breath audibly hitched. 'You're so perfect, so beautiful…' he said, his hand cupping her right breast, his touch sending tingles shooting through her body.

Perfect? That was a word Layla wasn't used to associating with herself. Neither was the word beautiful, but right then she felt like a beautiful woman. A beautiful desirable woman who was embracing her sexual power for the first time.

She explored the toned muscles of his chest, her fingers finding his hard, flat male nipples. His chest was lightly dusted with dark hair that narrowed down to a tantalising trail that disappeared below the waistband of his boxer shorts.

Logan brought his mouth to her breast, closing his lips over her budded nipple, his tongue flicking the sensitised nub. It was a pleasurable torture, the sensation of his warm mouth and raspy tongue sending her into raptures of delight.

Until now her breasts had been nothing but breasts. On the small side, occasionally a little tender around period time, but just breasts. No more, no less.

Now they were an erogenous zone—an intense pleasure spot that made her proud to be a woman.

Layla shuddered when he took her other breast in his mouth, the same riotous sensations shooting through her body from chest to core and back again. A hollow ache began spreading in her lower limbs, a heavy dragging sense of need.

'I want you...' Her voice was a breathless plea, her hands instinctively reaching between them for the jut of his erection.

'Same goes.' He groaned and brought his mouth back to hers in a kiss that spoke of burning, building, blatant passion.

One of his hands began to slide her pyjama trousers down but Layla suddenly froze, placing her hand over his. 'Wait.' The room was brightly lit now with morning sunshine. The water in the pool yesterday had provided a bit of a cover, not much but a bit. But now there was nowhere to hide. Even with the blinds and curtains drawn, her scars would be clearly visible.

He frowned at her in concern. 'Did I go too fast? Do you want to stop?'

She swallowed and pressed her lips together, not quite able to hold his gaze. 'I don't want to stop but I'm worried you will want to when you see my scars up close.'

'Oh, sweetheart...' His breath came out on a jagged sigh. 'Do you really think I would be so insensitive?'

She gave a half-shrug. 'My scars have turned off men before.' Only one, but it had been enough to stop her dating since.

His frown deepened. 'Then you've been dating the wrong men. You're a beautiful young woman who's survived a terrible car crash. No one should judge or shame you for bearing the scars of a tragedy you were caught up in. If they do, then it says more about them than it does you.'

Layla knew what he said was intellectually sound but she had lived experience of being judged and shamed by people who couldn't stomach her scars. There were times when she couldn't stomach them herself. She had spent years of her life avoiding intimacy, making excuses not to get into the dating scene—she was always too busy with work, too tired to indulge in late nights at clubs or parties.

But the real reason was what her scars represented. Not just the culmination of years of abuse and neglect now worn on her body like an indelible brand. Those scars represented her guilty secret—the secret relief that she had lost her parents and not her leg.

How could she ever tell anyone?

'It's just hard...you know?' Layla blinked away the sting of tears. 'Everywhere I look I see perfect bodies, especially in a place like Hawaii. Before yesterday, I hadn't been in a swimsuit since I was at the rehab clinic. I used to love swimming, but even at the clinic therapy pool, other patients stared at me like I was some sort of freak show.'

Logan brushed some strands of hair off her face, his gaze grave and yet tender. 'Your scars are a part of you, but they aren't *you*. You are so much more than that. So much more.'

Layla touched his mouth with her fingers. 'Kiss me. Make love to me. Please?'

His mouth tilted in a slow sexy smile. 'With pleasure.'

CHAPTER EIGHT

LOGAN'S MOUTH CAME back to hers in a kiss that melted away Layla's lingering doubts and fears. It was almost worth the long years of celibacy to have Logan be the first one to introduce her to the delights of the flesh. He moved from her mouth back to her breasts, caressing each one until her back was arching off the bed. He drew her pyjama trousers down, leaving a trail of kisses on each part of her exposed flesh. When he came to the jagged scars that were carved like runnels in her flesh, he was especially tender and it made tears spout in her eyes and her throat tighten with emotion.

He traced the feminine seam of her body with a lazy finger, his eyes glittering darkly with lust. 'Tell me if I do anything you don't like or don't feel comfortable doing.'

'I love what you're doing.' Layla could barely speak for the sensations rippling through her.

He kissed his way down her body from her breasts to the swell of her mound. She sucked in a breath, her legs turning to water as his lips gently parted her tender folds. Layla was in two minds—one to stop him out of her shyness at such an intimate caress and the other to just lie back and enjoy every pulse-racing moment. She chose the latter. His lips and tongue sending her on a sensual roller-coaster that catapulted her into a vortex of dizzying sensations. Sensations that coursed through her body in waves and pulses and delicious flickers, finally leaving her in a state of utter bliss and relaxation.

Never had she felt so in tune with herself, so free of the burdensome worry of how her broken body looked. Her body felt amazing, beautiful and sexy and capable of giving and receiving pleasure.

How could she not be thrilled it was Logan who had transformed her, awakened her to her sensual potential?

'Oh, wow...' Layla said on a breathless sigh.

Logan planted a soft kiss on her lips and then lifted off to mesh his gaze with hers. 'It will only get better once we get used to each other.' He kissed his way from her neck to her breasts, stroking her with his tongue, grazing her with the gentle tug of his teeth, sending her senses into another rapturous tailspin.

Layla explored him with her hands, shyly at first but becoming more comfortable with the hard contours of his body that were so exotically, erotically different from her own. His arousal was thickened with the same need she could feel throbbing in her own body.

His breathing became more hectic under her touch, his eyes dark and lustrous with desire. He positioned himself between her legs, taking his own weight on his elbows, his body poised to possess her. 'It's not too late for second thoughts. We can stop if you don't want to go any—'

Layla pushed her finger against his lips to stop him speaking. To stop him talking himself out of making love to her. 'I don't want to stop. I want you to make love to me. You *want* to, don't you?'

His mouth came up in a rueful half-smile. 'You surely don't doubt it? Can't you feel what you do to me?'

She could and she loved feeling it. Loved feeling desirable and feminine and sensually powerful for the first time in her life. 'Don't leave me hanging like this,' she whispered against his mouth. 'I need you.'

Logan made a sound deep in his throat and captured her mouth with his in a kiss that spoke of the feral rumble of passion throbbing in his blood. The same passionate throb she could feel in her lower body, the ache and drag of tender muscles crying out for intimate friction. His body nudged her entrance, gently parting her, and she opened herself to him, her shyness falling away, replaced by her escalating need to feel him inside her. His first thrust was shallow, restrained, careful, as if he was reluctant to allow his desire too much freedom.

Layla arched her spine, welcoming him deeper into her body by placing her hands on his toned buttocks. He thrust into her with a guttural groan, his pelvis moving in primal motion with hers. She felt a tiny sting of pain, a slight tug of resistance when he went deeper and she suppressed a gasp, hoping he hadn't noticed.

He suddenly stilled his movements. 'Did I hurt you?' His voice contained a deep chord of concern, his gaze searching hers.

'Of course not.' Layla smiled and stroked the side of his face with her hand. 'I'm just getting used to the feel of you.' She held her breath, hoping he wouldn't see through her little white lie. She didn't want him to stop making love to her, not while her body was aching and throbbing for more stimulation.

His eyes moved between each of hers, dipping every now and again to her mouth, his breathing still uneven, his body still encased in hers. 'I'll take it a little more slowly. But tell me if you're not comfortable at any time.'

'I'm perfectly comfortable.' Layla moved beneath him, rocking her body to encourage him to keep moving. Her body was used to him now, her intimate muscles wrapping around him, welcoming him, delighting in his strength and potency.

He slowly began to thrust, his movements measured and controlled. Layla's excitement grew as his body within hers triggered flickers of heat through her female flesh. The erotic motion of their bodies working together in perfect harmony was like a complicated but beautiful dance she hadn't realised she had known the steps to until now. The choreography of their movements was instinctive, intuitive, intensely arousing. Her senses soared, her desire leapt, her blood hummed and thrummed like the rhythmic backbeat of a musical score.

His mouth came back to hers in a long, drugging kiss that ramped up her passion for him like fuel flung on a naked flame. Their tongues met, tangled, mated, moved with the same perfect symmetry as their bodies. His hands caressed the swell of her breast, the curve of her waist, her thigh and then he found the slippery secret heart of her. The soft stroking of his fingers on her most intimate flesh made her gasp and writhe and shudder as the orgasm swept over her in pulsating waves.

Waves that fanned out from her core to the far reaches of her body, making every cell of her body vibrate with aftershocks of pleasure.

Logan's release followed hers with a series of deep urgent thrusts, his face buried into the side of her neck, his breathing as erratic as hers. He groaned and the tension in his body left him, making him slump against her.

Layla held him to her, not wanting him to pull away, wanting, needing to feel the warm embrace of his body for as long as possible. Their breathing came back to normal almost in unison, their entwined limbs rearranging themselves as if they had been doing it since time began.

After a long moment, Logan raised himself on one elbow to look down at her, his fingers idly playing with some tendrils of her hair. His features were cast in relaxation and the afterglow of pleasure and she had never seen him look more heart-stoppingly attractive.

'I'm having my own *Oh, wow* moment here.' His eyes were dark and warm, his voice pitched low, a lazy smile tilting his mouth. 'Make that *oh, wow* to the power of ten.'

An internal glow radiated through Layla's body at his words. She drew a line from the bridge of his nose to the well-defined philtrum ridge below and then traced his mouth. 'It was pretty amazing, wasn't it? Or maybe it's always amazing for you?'

He coiled a tendril of her hair around his finger, releasing it so it bounced against her cheek. He tucked the curl behind her ear, his expression undergoing a subtle change like the slow drift of clouds across the sky.

'I'm not the sort of man to kiss and tell, but sometimes sex works well and other times...' he twisted his mouth '...it's best left as a one-off.' He eased away to dispose of the condom in the bathroom, and Layla rolled onto her side, her eyes drinking in the long lean line of his back and taut buttocks and strong thighs.

She sighed and stretched like a sleepy cat, her limbs feeling so relaxed it was as if her bones had been removed. But then she happened to notice a mark on the bedlinen where she had been lying and her heart came to a screeching halt. She scrambled into a sitting position, hauling the bedcovers up to cover the bloodstain and her nakedness just as Logan came back into the bedroom.

'Is something wrong?' he asked, frowning.

'Um...no, I—I just feel a bit embarrassed about being...naked.' Layla bit her lip and couldn't hold his gaze.

Logan came over to the bed and sat down beside her. He pushed the fall of her hair back behind her shoulders, his hand going to the small of her back in a warm circular caress. 'I saw the blood on the condom. You don't have to be embarrassed about having your period.'

Layla swallowed, her heart beating so loudly she could feel it in her ears. 'I'm not having my period.' The words fell into the room like a loaded grenade, fizzing in the sudden silence.

Logan's hand stilled on her back, his body stiffening as if snap-frozen, his expression etched in shock as realisation slowly dawned. 'You were a...a *virgin*?' His voice was so hoarse it came out like the screech of tyres on gravel. He shot off the bed and shoved a hand through his hair, looking at her in alarm. 'Why didn't you say so?'

Layla pulled the bedcovers closer. 'It's not like it's a disease.'

He let out a short sharp swearword. 'I *hurt* you. You should have told me so I could've—'

'Could've what?' Layla shot back. 'Stopped? Not made love at all? Go on, admit it—you would never have made love with me if I'd told you I was a virgin.'

He closed his eyes in a slow blink and swore again. He turned away and snatched up his trousers from where they were lying on the floor and stepped into them with such force she was sure they would rip. The sound of his zipper going up was as savage as another bitter curse.

'You made me believe you were experienced,' he said, reaching for his shirt and shoving his arms through the sleeves. 'You lied to me, if not outright then by omission.'

'Stop making such a big issue out of it. It was just sex.'

'It was damn well not just sex.' His tone was gruff, his gaze diamond-hard. 'You knew I was uneasy about making our marriage a real one because we don't fit the criteria for a one-night stand.' He tucked his shirt into his trousers with rough movements. 'I can't believe how screwed up this is. I hurt you enough to make you bleed.' He rubbed a hand down his face, dragging and distorting his features.

'You didn't hurt me,' Layla said. 'It was the tiniest sting—I hardly even noticed it and everything was fine after that. More than fine—wonderful.'

Logan came over to the bed and sat beside her but

he clamped his hands to his thighs as if he was worried they might touch her of their own accord. 'Why were you still a virgin? Was it a deliberate choice or something else?' His tone lost its sharp edge, his expression softening from its harsh lines of self-recrimination.

Layla looked down at her hands clasped around her bent knees. 'I came close once to having sex when I was a teenager but the guy got cold feet when he saw my leg. He made me feel terrible about my body. I've avoided any sort of intimacy ever since.'

Logan scrunched up his face as if suffering from an internal pain. He let out a sigh and took one of her hands in his, the gentle press of his fingers against hers making her eyes well with tears. 'I'm sorry you've had such an awful experience. That kid was a jerk for making you feel that way. You're beautiful and desirable and deserve to be treated with nothing but respect. But don't you see how what happened just now makes *me* feel like a jerk? I hurt you and that's the last thing I wanted to do to you or to anyone.'

Layla looked into his frowning gaze and sighed. 'I'm sorry. I was embarrassed, that's all. I mean, what girl these days gets to the age of twenty-six without having had sex? It made me feel like a pariah. Completely out of step.'

He gave her hand another squeeze. 'One day you'll find what you're looking for. Someone who can give you the security and longevity that enriches a physical relationship.' He rose from the bed and moved some distance away, his expression still wrought with lines of tension.

'What if I'm not looking for that right now?' Layla

asked. 'What if I only want a fling to get some experience under my belt? What would be wrong with you being the person who helps me with that?'

He turned back to look at her, his fisted hands clenching and unclenching by his sides as if he was fighting the urge to come back and haul her into his arms. 'I'm trying to do the right thing by you, Layla. I try to do the right thing by everyone I care about and yet I always seem to screw up.'

'I'm sorry for not telling you…'

He approached her again, his expression wistful, the gentle stroke of his finger down the slope of her cheek making her heart swell to twice its size. 'None of this is your fault, sweetheart. None of it.'

Layla grasped his wrist and turned his hand over so she could plant a soft kiss to the middle of his palm. 'I'm glad it was you. I mean, that you were my first lover.'

His eyes smouldered for a long moment, his fingers entwining with hers. 'It was pretty damn good, wasn't it?' His voice had a side note of gravel that made her inner core tingle.

'Does that mean you're going to tweak the rules?'

A shadow drifted through his gaze and he let out a sigh and released her hand. 'Let's not get too far ahead of ourselves.' He softened it with a crooked smile. 'I couldn't have asked for a more generous and responsive lover. But there are consequences to factor in if we take this any further.'

'I know,' Layla said. 'But I'm prepared to accept the consequences if you are.'

He traced the line of her lower lip with his finger, his expression sobering once more. 'Thing is…it's kind of scary how little I care about the consequences right now, which is why I'm going to sleep in the spare room. We both need some space to think clearly.'

Layla flopped back down on the pillows once he left the room. She didn't need space. She needed him.

Logan gave up on any notion of sleeping for the rest of the night. He paced one of the spare bedrooms with his thoughts as tangled as fishing line. He could not forgive himself for not realising Layla's lack of experience. How could he have been so blind? In hindsight, all the clues were there. He had never heard any mention of a boyfriend, he had never seen her bring anyone home to Bellbrae, and although he knew little of her life in Edinburgh, she had given him the impression she was experienced with her misleading and ambiguous comments about her past love life. And he'd fallen for it, because he'd *wanted* an excuse to sleep with her. That was the part of his conscience he was struggling with the most. He had broken his own rules—the rules he had instated to protect her from unnecessary hurt.

And he had gone and done it anyway.

He sucked in a jagged breath and released it in a rush. He had done it because ever since that day in the north tower, he had felt something shift in their relationship. A tectonic shift. He couldn't be in the same room as her without feeling the subtle change in energy. Sensual energy that tingled and tightened his skin and made him want and want and want with an ache that wouldn't go away, no matter how hard he tried to ignore it.

And that was another tripwire in his conscience— he'd enjoyed every pulse-racing minute of their lovemaking. It had been off the scale in terms of pleasure. Satisfying in a way sex hadn't been for him for years. The intuitive connection of their bodies, the rhythm and timing of every movement had felt so natural, so fluid and free and phenomenal it still rang in his flesh like a struck tuning fork.

Logan walked to the windows overlooking the ocean, trying to distract himself with the view, but it was no good.

How could you have not known? What were you thinking? You hurt her.

He wanted to blank them out but a perverse part of him relished in the self-flagellation. It was no more than he deserved. He had once thought he was pretty good at reading people but not now. His disastrous and tragic relationship with his fiancée had taught him otherwise. And now this situation with Layla had only reinforced it.

He was rubbish at relationships. How could he hope to change that abysmal track record? Was there any point even trying?

The journey back to Scotland was painfully silent. Layla tried once or twice to engage Logan in conversation on the flight but he only answered in monosyllables and seemed preoccupied with his thoughts. He rarely touched her. In fact, he seemed to be avoiding all contact, even eye contact. Was he still regretting their lovemaking? He had been so tender and considerate afterwards that a hope had sprouted in her chest that maybe he would agree to deepening their relationship.

Had he weighed up the potential consequences and decided it wasn't worth it?

That *she* wasn't worth it?

On the drive back to Bellbrae from Inverness airport, Logan drove with clenched hands and jaw, his forehead creased in a perpetual frown, which didn't nurture her fledgling hope one little bit.

'You know, we're not going to be very convincing as a married couple if we don't even exchange a few polite words now and again,' Layla said.

He flicked her a glance. 'Sorry. Did you say something?'

She gave a humourless laugh. 'I've been trying to make conversation with you ever since we left Honolulu. You've barely spoken four or five words to me. I guess the honeymoon is definitely over, then?'

He flinched at the word 'honeymoon' and his hands tightened like clamps on the steering wheel. 'I can't tell you how much I regret what happened. I hate myself for hurting you.'

'I wish you'd stop making such an enormous deal about it. So what if we had sex? Even perfect strangers have sex with each other. Besides, no harm has been done.'

His gaze swung her way again. 'Hasn't it?'

'Of course not.' Layla surreptitiously squeezed her legs together, secretly enjoying the pull of still tender muscles that his intimate presence had caused. She had relived their lovemaking numerous times, remembering each touch, each caress, each kiss that had set her flesh on fire and left it thrumming with pleasure. Her body ached to feel his presence again, to experi-

ence more of his magical lovemaking. To explore the
sensuality that had erupted so naturally between them
and shown her a world of heady and erotic delights she
hadn't known existed. She kept her hands planted on
her lap but she longed to place her hand on his thigh
like a lover would do.

The rest of the journey continued in mutual silence
but just as they approached the long driveway leading
to the Bellbrae estate, Logan let out a stiff curse, not
quite under his breath.

'What's wrong?' Layla asked.

'That's Robbie's new car,' he said, indicating the
flashy red sports car ahead of them on the driveway.
'God only knows how he's paying for it. It's worth five
hundred thousand euros at least.'

Layla looked ahead to see the sports car's wheels
spinning over the gravel, spraying stones out to each
side and it reminded her yet again of the stark differences between the two brothers. Logan was steady, reliable and cautious, someone who thought before he
acted. Robbie, on the other hand, leapt before he looked,
reacted rather than reflected, took risks and suffered
little or no remorse for his reckless actions.

'Have you spoken to him since we…got married?'
Layla asked. The word was still a novelty to her, even
though she wore his ring on her left hand.

'I sent an email. I gave up on the phone—he hardly
ever gets back to me when I call or text.' The weariness
in Logan's tone spoke of a long and frustrating history
between him and his younger brother. 'I told him we'd
formed a relationship and decided to get married.'

Nerves in Layla's stomach unfurled and fluttered

their razor-sharp wings. It was going to be difficult to convince his brother their marriage was genuine when Logan was so determined to keep his distance from her. 'But he would have seen the will, surely? Won't he have already put two and two together?'

'It's immaterial what he thinks. It doesn't change the fact our marriage is legal.'

Layla bit down on her lower lip. 'I'll try not to let you down.'

He flashed her the briefest of rueful smiles but it didn't take the shadows out of his eyes. 'That seems to be my job. Letting people down.'

Logan helped Layla out of the car a short time later, placing his arm around her waist as his brother sauntered over to them. She nestled against his side and he caught a whiff of the flowery fragrance of her hair, stirring his senses, making him long to bury his head in those silky chestnut tresses as he had when they had made love. He tried to block the images of that night but they flashed up in his mind, causing his blood to pound and thicken, dragging at his lower body with a tight primal ache.

Robbie swept his gaze over them with an elevation of his eyebrows. 'Well, well, well, what have we here? Congratulations, Layla. You've landed yourself quite a catch. For a simple charwoman, that is.'

Logan felt Layla stiffen beside him and he wanted to thump his brother for being such a snobbish jerk. He drew her closer to his side and sent his brother a warning look. 'If you don't treat my wife with respect you won't be welcome here, Robert. Got that?'

'Your wife?' Robbie threw his head back and laughed. 'You expect me to believe you two are the real deal?'

'We have the documentation to prove it,' Logan said. 'Now, if you'll excuse us. Layla is tired from travelling and—'

'I bet you put the old man up to it,' Robbie said, addressing Layla with a curl of his lip. 'You've always had the hots for my big brother. But he would never have looked at you without some serious arm twisting. And it doesn't get more serious than his precious Bellbrae hanging in the balance.'

Logan was ashamed to hear his brother voice his own earlier thoughts over his grandfather's changes to his will. And as to Layla's interest in him, well, it was more than reciprocated. And if he were to be honest with himself, that spark of attraction had started way earlier than the afternoon in the north tower. Way, way earlier.

'Layla had nothing to do with Grandad's will being changed. If anyone is to blame for that it's me. I've taken way too long to get on with my life after losing Susannah. But the time is right now and I can't think of a better person to marry than Layla, who loves this place as much as I do.'

'Personally, I don't get what either of you see in this place,' Robbie said, throwing the castle a look of distaste. 'It's old and cold and too far away from any action. You're welcome to it. And to each other.'

Layla's cheeks were a bright shade of pink and yet he was proud of the way her chin came up and her grey-green gaze stared his brother down. 'I know our marriage must've come as a complete surprise to you,

Robbie, but Logan and I have always been friends. I hope, in time, you can be happy for us.'

Robbie's smile was cynical. 'I've seen the will. I know what this is—a marriage of convenience to secure Bellbrae. My brother will never love you, Layla. He's not capable of it.'

'You're wrong,' Layla said. 'He's capable of much more than you give him credit for.'

'I think it might be time for you to leave,' Logan said to his brother. 'We're still on our honeymoon and three's a crowd and all that.'

Robbie tossed his car keys in the air and deftly caught them, his expression mocking. 'I give you guys a year, tops.'

That's all I want, Logan thought.

And Logan led Layla into the castle without a backward glance as his brother roared down the driveway with a squeal of tyres over the gravel.

CHAPTER NINE

LAYLA LOOKED AT Logan once the door was closed on their entry into the castle. His expression was thunderous and a muscle kept flicking in his cheek.

'Are you okay?' she asked.

He let out a rough-edged sigh and shrugged himself out of his jacket and hung it on the coat rack near the entrance. 'I'm sorry about that. My brother can be a prize jerk sometimes. Most of the time, actually.'

'It's okay.' She began to unbutton her own coat. 'Our relationship must've come as a bit of a shock. I mean, you and me? It's a bit of a stretch to think you would ever be—'

His hand came down in a gentle press on the top of her shoulder, his expression softening. 'Don't keep doing that. You're a beautiful and desirable woman and if things were different, I would…' He pressed his lips together as if determined not to voice the words out loud.

'Would what?' Layla's voice was barely more than a whisper.

His navy-blue eyes darkened and his other hand came down on her other shoulder. She wasn't sure who moved first but suddenly they were standing almost chest to chest and hip to hip. The quality of the air changed—a tension was building, crackling, fizzing like a current of electricity singing along a wire. His gaze dipped to her mouth and she heard the intake of his breath. Held her own breath as his head lowered as if in slow motion, down…down…down…

'Oh, sorry to be a gooseberry!' Aunt Elsie's cheery lilt sounded from the right of the foyer. 'How did the wedding and honeymoon go?'

Logan stepped back but kept one of Layla's hands in his. 'It was short but wonderful.'

Aunt Elsie beamed like she was intent on solving an energy crisis for the whole of Scotland. 'Well, it wasn't long enough to my way of thinking, which is why I'm going to go on a wee holiday of my own to give you two lovebirds some space.'

Lovebirds? If only. And since when had her great-aunt ever left Bellbrae?

Layla looked at her great-aunt as if she had just said she was going to tap dance on the castle roof. Naked. 'But where will you go? You haven't been on a holiday since I don't know when.'

'Which is why I'm going now,' Aunt Elsie said. 'I've booked myself a few days in the Outer Hebrides—on the Isle of Harris to start with. I've an old pen-pal from school who lives there. Her husband passed away recently so she could do with some company. You'll be right with looking after Flossie for a few days?'

'Of course,' Logan said. 'We're not going anywhere.'

That was news to Layla. What about his big landscaping project in Tuscany that he'd put on hold? Surely he couldn't postpone it too much longer. She had ex-

pected him to deliver her back to Bellbrae and fly out
again as soon as he could to put even more distance between them. Had he changed his mind? And if so, why?

'Do you need transport? A lift anywhere?' Logan
continued.

'Och, no, I've got it all sorted,' Aunt Elsie said. 'I'm
being picked up in half an hour by my friend's daughter.
I thought that was her just now but I saw it was Robbie. He didn't stay?'

'No,' Logan said, his mouth pulled into a grim line.
'He had other plans.'

'Good.' Aunt Elsie smiled as if she'd just received
the best news of the day. 'You'll be all alone.'

Logan left Layla to say her goodbyes to her great-aunt
and saw to some business in his grandfather's study. It
was strange to think of it now as *his* study. Strange but
deeply satisfying. He cast his gaze around the room,
from the wall-to-wall bookshelves, the leather-topped
desk that both his father and grandfather had used, at
the Aubusson carpet that generations of McLaughlins
had walked on. He looked out of the windows that overlooked the estate—the loch, the forest, the Highlands
that were currently shrouded by clouds.

The whole of Bellbrae now belonged to him, thanks
to Layla's willingness to be his bride. His *paper* bride.
He had to keep reminding himself of that simple fact.
Not so simple when she made him feel things he didn't
want to feel. Things he had forbidden himself to feel.
He had been so close to kissing her before her great-
aunt had interrupted them. So close to once again disregarding the rules he had set down. The rules he was

having trouble obeying because of the aching need their lovemaking had awakened.

By making love with her, he had crossed a threshold and he couldn't find a way back. The door had slammed behind him and no matter how hard he tried to prise it open, it wouldn't budge. His body had been reprogrammed, finely tuned to notice every one of her movements, to respond to every smile or velvet-like touch.

He suppressed a whole-body tremor. It was her touch he craved. The glide of her small hands over his flesh, the press of her soft lips to his mouth, the playful teasing of her tongue, the hot wet tight cocoon of her body.

He wanted it all, hungered for it like he would starve without it. It consumed him like a fever, it occupied his every thought, it kept him from sleep.

Logan walked back to the desk and sent the leather chair into a slow spin, his forehead tight with a frown. He had planned to fly to Italy to check in on his project but he didn't feel comfortable leaving Layla alone now her great-aunt wouldn't be at Bellbrae. There were ground staff who came and went on the estate but the castle was a big place to stay in alone. And these days Flossie was hardly what anyone could describe as a guard dog.

There was a tap at the door. 'Logan?' Layla's voice called out.

'Come in.'

She opened the door and entered the study with the old dog padding slowly behind her. She had changed from her travelling outfit into black leggings and an oversized dove-grey boyfriend sweater that had slipped off one creamy shoulder, revealing the thin white strap of her bra. 'Am I interrupting you?'

'No.' He walked from behind the desk and bent down to scratch Flossie behind the ears. He glanced up at Layla. 'What's up?'

She hitched her sweater back over her shoulder. 'I was wondering what you wanted me to do about…um… our sleeping arrangements.' Her cheeks were stained a faint shade of pink. 'Now that Aunt Elsie is going away and Robbie's not around, we don't have to share the west tower suite. For appearances' sake, I mean.'

Logan rose to his full height, only just resisting the urge to put his arms around her and draw her closer. She licked her lower lip and a lightning bolt of lust zapped him in the groin. 'Are you worried I might not stick to the rules?' he asked. Damn it. *He* was worried. Right at that moment he couldn't think of a single reason why he should stick to the rules.

Her gaze skittered away from his, concentrating on the open neck of his shirt instead. She began to pluck at the overly long sleeve of her sweater as if she needed something to do with her hands. 'No, of course not. I just thought you'd prefer it if I was in my own quarters. Away from you. Or at least, that's the message I've been getting since we left Hawaii.'

Logan inched up her chin with the end of his finger, meshing his gaze with hers. Every rational cell in his body told him to stop. Do not pass go. Do not go any further. But right then his body was programmed to follow instinct, not rationality. A primal instinct that demanded contact. Physical contact.

Intimate contact.

'The problem is, I don't want you away from me.' He slid a hand behind her head to the nape of her neck under the silky curtain of her hair. 'I want you close to me. Closer than is probably wise.' He breathed in the fresh flowery scent of her perfume, his senses going haywire, his blood thickening with each thunderous beat of his pulse.

She closed her eyes in a slow blink, like a sensuous cat enjoying a caress. Her lips softly parting, her breath hitching, her slim throat rising and falling over a swallow. 'Why is that a problem when I want the same thing?' Her voice was husky and it sent another punch of lust into his lower body.

Logan slowly brought his mouth down to hers, promising himself one taste, one reminder of how sweet and soft her lips were. But as soon as their lips met, a wave of intense heat swept through him and he deepened the kiss with a gliding thrust of his tongue that made her moan and press herself closer. His arms went around her, holding her to the length of his hardening body, desire hot and strong rippling through him in an unstoppable tide.

He buried one hand in the thick tresses of her hair, the other pressed into the small of her back to keep her pressed against him, his mouth locked on hers in a kiss that sent shivers across his scalp and down the entire length of his spine. He lifted his mouth off hers to graze her neck with his teeth, breathing in the scent of her skin. 'I can't tell you how hard I've fought with myself not to do this.'

'But I want you to do it.' Layla moved against him,

sending a whiplash of longing through his body. 'I want you.'

'I want you so much it's driving me nuts.' He groaned and clamped his mouth back down on hers, their lips moving in perfect motion as if they had been kissing for years. Her tongue touched his and the backs of his knees tingled, his blood pounding through his veins like a tribal drum.

He lifted her sweater so he could access her breasts, desperate to feel her soft creamy skin against his palm. He unclipped her bra to find her nipples were already tightly budded and he lowered his mouth to each one in turn, lavishing them with strokes and licks of his tongue, teasing them with the gentle press of his teeth. She made soft murmurs of approval, her breathing rate increasing, her hands reaching for the waistband of his trousers.

Logan hauled her sweater over her head, tossing it to the floor and only just missing Flossie, who was lying on her side, snoring. It was enough to break his stride and he took a deep steadying breath and grasped Layla by the upper arms. 'Let's take this upstairs. I want you to be comfortable and I'd rather not have an audience.' He jerked his head towards the sleeping dog.

A shadow of worry passed through Layla's gaze. 'What if you change your mind before we get upstairs? I thought you were okay with taking our relationship further the other night but then you seemed to change your mind and could barely look at me, much less talk to me.'

He took one of her hands and brought it up to his mouth, pressing a kiss to the backs of her knuckles, his eyes locked on hers. 'If I was a better man—a stronger man—then that's exactly what I would do. I would reinstate the rules. But apparently I'm not as strong as I thought.' He released her hand and bent down to retrieve her sweater, helping her put it back on like she was a small child.

She smiled as her head came out of the top of the sweater and something near his heart split open, leaking warmth into every cold and closed-off cavity of his chest. His breath hitched, his heart stuttered, his desire throbbed and pounded. He had never wanted anyone with such fervour, with such ferocity, with such frightening intensity. It was a clawing need inside him that he was worried would get out of control. Making him want her longer than the year they had agreed on. Making him want things he had sworn he would never want again. Closeness, commitment, connection beyond the physical. A lasting connection that would only get deeper, more abiding and bonding each and every year.

But it was a risk he was prepared to take because he couldn't go another day—another moment—without experiencing the heart-stopping thrill of their intimate union.

Logan framed her face in his hands, lowering his mouth to hers in a lingering kiss, closing down his conscience, shutting away his fears, slamming the door on his damn rules.

He wanted her.

She wanted him.

That's all that mattered for now.

Their journey to Logan's room upstairs was a stop-start affair with kisses and caresses at various points along the way. Finally, they made it to the bed and he laid Layla down and leaned over her, kissing her lingeringly with his hands propped either side of her head, one of his knees resting on the bed near her legs. He raised his head to look down at her. 'I can't tell you how much I want you,' he said, breathing as heavily as her.

'Then don't tell me. Show me.' Layla wound her arms around his neck and brought his head back down so his mouth met hers.

His kiss was deep and thrilling, his tongue dancing with hers in a sexy salsa that made her spine loosen vertebra by vertebra. Her heart picked up its pace, her pulse pounding with the need to have him closer, to feel him skin on skin.

He lifted his mouth off hers to blaze a fiery trail of kisses along the sensitive skin of her neck, down lower to the shallow dish between her collarbones. She shivered in reaction, tingling from head to foot as desire swept through her in hot spreading waves. How could she have spent so many years of her life without experiencing this incredible passion? How could she experience it with anyone else? He was the one who evoked such powerful responses from her. Responses that travelled through her body with the force of a tumultuous storm. A tornado of lust that left her senses spinning in its wake.

Logan helped her out of her clothes and she did the same for him, but with nowhere near the same efficiency. Her fingers fumbled in her haste and he eventually took over the task and stripped off the last of his clothes. He applied a condom and came back down on the bed beside her, gliding his hands over her naked breasts, and her spine arched when his mouth came down to kiss around her achingly tight nipple. Layla made a moaning sound as pleasure shot through her. A dragging ache tugged deep and low in her womanhood—a need that begged to be assuaged.

He took her nipple into his mouth, his lips and tongue caressing it with such exquisite expertise she whimpered and writhed, impatient, greedy, desperate for more. He kissed the gentle slopes of each breast, paying particular attention to the sensitive undersides. She was almost breathless with excitement when his teeth softly grazed each nipple in turn, and her hips rose against him in a wordless plea for him to tame the raging desire barrelling through her body.

'I'll take things slowly. I don't want to hurt you again.' His voice was deep and low and husky.

Layla stroked her finger along the contour of his bottom lip. 'You didn't hurt me the first time and I don't want you to go slowly. I need you inside me.' She placed her hands on his buttocks and pushed him down towards her.

He drew in a sharp breath and entered her slickly, visibly fighting for control, his features contorted in a mixture of agony and ecstasy. He began to move with gentle thrusts, each one getting deeper and deeper until he was up to the hilt.

He gave a guttural groan and increased his pace and Layla was with him all the way, swept up in the primal rhythm that made her flesh sing. The need spiralled through every part of her body, building to a crescendo.

She hovered at the edge, needing more, straining to reach the final tipping point but not quite able to get there. She whimpered and moved her body against his, desperately seeking more friction. But then his hand slipped down between their rocking bodies to touch her, sending her over the edge into the throes of a powerful orgasm, intensified by his continued thrusting. She shattered into a thousand pieces, her body racked by tingling waves of sensation that went on and on and on, finally leaving her spent and limbless and breathless in his arms.

His release followed on the tail of hers and she drew vicarious pleasure from holding him through each shuddering thrust, riding out the storm with him as he tensed at the point of no return and then finally let go.

Logan lifted his head and, leaning his weight on his elbows, pressed a soft kiss to her mouth. His expression was bathed in lines of relaxation, his gaze warm and heart-stoppingly tender.

'No regrets?' His tone was low as a bass chord and it sent a tingly shiver cascading down her spine.

'None from me,' Layla said, tracing his upper lip with her finger. 'You?'

He took her finger into his mouth and sucked on it, his gaze glinting. He released her finger and tucked a strand of hair behind her ear, his mouth twisting into a rueful line. 'No. Not one. It was—*you were*—wonderful.'

Layla stroked her hand along his jaw from below his ear to the base of his chin. 'Thank you for making it so good for me. I feel so at ease with you. I can't explain why other than you seem to read my body like it's an extension of your own. How do you *do* that?'

He gave a lopsided smile and leaned down to kiss

the tip of her nose. 'It doesn't happen often but some-times it just works from the start with some partners. The chemistry is right.' He rolled away to dispose of the condom and came back to lie beside her with his elbow bent, his head propped against his hand. His other hand began a lazy journey from her breast to her thigh and back again. Slow, sensual, setting her flesh alight all over again.

Layla rolled towards him, her mouth meeting his in a scorching kiss that sent a hot wave of need shoot-ing through her body. Her legs entwined with his, the roughness of his sending another shiver coursing down her spine. He took a handful of her hair and bunched it against her scalp, his kiss deepening, his tongue play-ing, teasing, tangling with hers.

He dragged his mouth away and gazed down at her with a rueful expression. 'I'd better stop before I can't stop. You need to get used to this gradually otherwise you could get sore.'

His tender consideration towards her was so touch-ing it made her breath catch. She stroked his jaw again, raising her head to brush his lips with hers. 'You've cre-ated a bit of an addiction in me. I don't want to wait. I want you again…but is it too soon for you?'

He gave a low deep laugh and rolled her beneath him, his eyes dark and gleaming with lust. 'What do you think?' And then his mouth came down on hers and she stopped thinking altogether.

CHAPTER TEN

LOGAN HAD MOSTLY travelled abroad during the month of November, so he could escape the all too often grey and dismal progression of the Highlands' final month of autumn into winter. But spending the time with Layla at Bellbrae had turned the normally cold and bleak time into something else entirely. The shorter days and longer nights were no longer an inconvenience but an excellent excuse to relax over a drink in front of a roaring fire. Or to spend long hours in bed, making love, then snuggling up in a cocoon of cosy warmth. And with winter and plenty of snowbound days heading their way, instead of feeling trapped and contained, he felt...*free*.

More open, more relaxed. More human and less of an emotionless workhorse machine.

The days at Bellbrae belonged to Layla and him, no one else. Well, apart from Flossie but the old dog spent most of the time snoozing by the fire, only stirring for meals and comfort breaks. Aunt Elsie had extended her holiday and, apart from the occasional ground staff going about their business on the estate, Logan and Layla were entirely, blissfully alone.

They each juggled their work commitments but he

was increasingly worried about monopolising her time. Her generous and giving nature often had her putting her needs aside for others'. Hadn't her closing her Edinburgh office when his grandfather had gone into his final decline been proof of that? He knew he should be encouraging her to find another office off site but he couldn't bring himself to do it. He was enjoying their time together too much. He had even put another delay on his visit to Tuscany to check the progress on his project. It was out of character for him but he had competent people working for him and knew they would call him instantly if there was anything that only he could fix.

Logan left Layla sleeping while he rose early to let Flossie out downstairs. He slipped on tracksuit bottoms and slip-on shoes in case the old dog went further into the garden and got disoriented in the darkness. It had happened before and it had taken him half an hour to find her—not ideal in only boxers or less and bare feet.

The sun wasn't up yet and the frost was as thick as a carpet on the ground, the air so cold it burned his face. An owl hooted from a nearby tree and then Logan heard the swish of its wings as the bird flew off into the misty darkness. The distinctive call of a vixen looking for a mate would once have made Flossie's ears prick and her tail rise, but the old dog barely seemed to notice. She squatted on a frosty patch of ground and sighed with relief and then came plodding back to where Logan was standing, her feathery tail wagging back and forth.

'Good girl.' He bent down and ruffled her ears. 'Back to bed for you, hey?'

'Sounds good to me,' Layla's voice sounded from behind him. 'Gosh, it's freezing, isn't it?'

Logan turned, saw her framed in the doorway and something in his chest slipped. Funny, but he didn't feel cold at all. He felt warm. Hot. Hotter than hot—for her. She was dressed in his bathrobe, which was far too big for her. It swamped her petite frame and made her look like a child who had been playing with a dress-up box.

'I was about to wake you up with a cup of tea,' he said with a smile.

She rubbed her crossed-over hands up and down her arms and shivered but a smile played about her mouth. And her eyes contained a light that made his lower body sit up and take notice. 'Stop spoiling me. I'll be hell to live with if you keep treating me like a princess.'

'I'll take the risk.' He came over to her and leaned down to drop a kiss to the end of her upturned nose and then led her back inside to the warmth of the castle kitchen.

Thing was, she wasn't hell to live with. She was heaven. He had only lived with one other lover—his late fiancée—and it had definitely not been anything like this. His time with Layla worked so seamlessly, so easily, so naturally. He didn't have to second-guess or play games or have games played on him. Layla was a complex person but not a difficult one. He could relax around her, be more open and share things he hadn't shared with anyone before.

There was a growing part of him that didn't want their 'married fling' to end, which was a deeply troubling thought. The locked no long-term-commitment vault inside his mind had somehow allowed a sliver of light in under the door. A beam of light he wasn't sure he wanted illuminating the darkly shadowed corners of his mind.

One month had already passed on their one-year marriage. It was ticking away like a clock set on fast forward. Christmas would be here soon, then Hogmanay and then before he knew it, the year would be up.

Their marriage would come to its inevitable end. The end he had insisted on. That he *still* insisted on— didn't he?

So why did that seem far more of a problem than it had before?

They were in the kitchen, waiting for the kettle to boil on the stove, and Layla put her arms around his waist and rested her head on his chest. 'What do you have planned for today?'

He tipped up her face with his hand so she was looking up at him. 'You mean apart from going back to bed and making mad passionate love to you and then serving you breakfast in bed, and after that showering together?' His eyes were glinting and his lower body already stirring against her.

Layla lifted her hand to his stubbly jaw, tracing the line of his smiling mouth with her fingertip, her insides twisting and coiling with desire. 'I don't think I've ever spent so much time in bed before, not even when I've been sick.'

'Neither have I.' His voice had a husky quality that made her feel weak at the knees.

He lowered his head and covered her mouth with his in a kiss that made the ache inside her body go to fever pitch. His hands went to the small of her back, drawing her closer to his body—closer to the potency of his erection. His tongue played with hers in an erotic dance that made something swoop and dive in her belly. His mouth moved from her lips to the side of her neck, his tongue leaving a hot trail along her sensitive flesh. He used his teeth to gently nip her earlobe and a shiver shot down her spine at rocket speed.

He pulled apart the dark blue bathrobe she was wearing and uncovered her naked breasts. He caressed each breast with his lips and tongue until her inner core was melting and flowing like scorching-hot lava. His teeth grazed her nipple, his tongue rolling over its tight point, and desire drummed a primitive beat between her legs.

'Why didn't I think to leave a supply of condoms in every room?' he said, with a rueful grin.

Layla rummaged in the pocket of the bathrobe, which was hanging around her hips with just the waist tie keeping it in place. She took out a tiny foil packet and handed it to him.

He took the condom from her, his eyes darkening to a glittering blue-black. 'I just love your organisational and planning skills. You really do think of everything.'

'Glad to be of service.'

A shadow flickered across his face and he drew in a breath and pulled the edges of the bathrobe back around her shoulders, slipping the condom back in the pocket. 'Layla.' There was a guarded quality to his voice, his expression losing its earlier teasing playfulness and changing into a frown.

A cold ghost hand pressed against the back of her neck, sending a flow of ice over her scalp. 'What's wrong? What did I say to make you frown at me like that?' It had been a flippant comment, sure, but why had it upset him so much?

Logan let out a long breath. 'I don't want you to feel like you're just here to service my needs. It's important to me that you feel equal in our relationship.'

Did she feel it was an equal relationship? In some ways, yes. In others, no. How could it be truly equal when he was the one who insisted their marriage end at a specific point? 'It was just a throwaway line. I didn't mean anything by it.'

'This past month has been good, better than good, but it's not always going to be like this,' he said, still frowning in a brooding manner. 'We can't live in a bubble at Bellbrae for ever. You have work commitments and so do I.'

Now it was Layla's turn to frown, her mood soured by the sudden change in his. 'Have I stopped you from doing your work? I haven't exactly chained you to my side. You're perfectly free to fly off to wherever you need to, whenever you need to.' She spun away to lift the whistling kettle off the hob and place it on a heat protector, all but steaming herself. Why did he have to remind her this last month together wasn't going to last? She didn't need reminding. It was front and centre in her head every single day.

'I don't want to argue with—' he began.

'Then stop blaming me for you feeling guilty about taking time off,' Layla shot back, turning to face him. 'You're a human being, Logan, not a flipping robot.'

He moved across the floor to place his hands on the tops of her shoulders, giving them a light squeeze. His eyes were troubled, his frown still in place. 'But what about your work? I'm concerned you haven't got an office away from here yet.'

Layla pulled out of his hold and folded her arms across her body, her glower hotter than the hotplate the kettle had just come off. 'Oh, so that's what this is about? You're worried I'm going to get too comfortable working from here once the time is up on our marriage? Well, here's some news for you. I've already been looking online at potential rentals in Edinburgh. There's one in the Old Town that looks promising. It's a bit expensive but I want the position to attract good clientele. It's got a tiny bedsit upstairs so I can stay there if I don't feel up to driving back here. And I can live there once our marriage ends.'

His frown deepened. 'You're surely not thinking of commuting between here and Edinburgh over the winter? The roads are treacherous with black ice and snow and—'

'Make up your mind, Logan,' Layla mock-laughed. 'You either want me to prioritise my work over you or you don't.'

He came back to her and placed his hands on her hips, pulling her back against him. 'That's the whole damn problem.' His tone was a low rumbling growl, his expression still set in brooding lines. 'I don't want to share you with your work or with anyone and it scares the hell out of me.' And then his mouth came down heavily, explosively on hers.

It was a kiss of lust and anger and frustration and scorching need racing out of control. But she relished every heart-stopping second of it. His mouth was a fire on hers, his tongue a flame teasing hers into a combative dance with bone-melting expertise.

Layla thought her legs were folding beneath her but he had picked her up and sat her on the kitchen bench in front of him. Her legs parted and he stepped between her open thighs, his mouth still locked on hers. The closeness of his erection, the molten heat building in her body, the escalating need communicated by their mouths was a potent combination.

Logan untied the waistband of the bathrobe and stripped it off her shoulders, leaving her naked and exposed to his smouldering gaze. His eyes travelled over her breasts, his hands cradling them before placing his mouth on each in turn, subjecting them to a spine-tingling array of licks and strokes and circles of his tongue. Darts of pleasure shot through her and she shuffled as close to him as she possibly could.

Logan rummaged in the pocket of her discarded bathrobe for the condom, swiftly tugging down his trousers and applying it. He surged into her with a primal groan of satisfaction, thrusting deeply and rhythmically, making her senses spin out of control. The delicious pressure built and built to bursting point and then, with the added caress of his fingers against her most sensitive female flesh, she was tossed into the maelstrom of a powerful orgasm. She cried, she gasped, she shook, she shuddered and quaked and still it went on in ripples and waves that were only intensified by his release, which coincided with hers.

Logan framed her face in his hands, his breathing still laboured. 'I've always wanted to do that.'

Layla brushed his hair back from his forehead, gazing into his intensely blue eyes. 'Do what? Kitchen bench sex?'

His mouth tilted in a crooked smile. 'Yeah.' He brushed her lips with his and added, 'I was a kitchen bench sex virgin. You're so damn hot I can barely keep control of myself no matter what room we're in.'

His words thrilled her as much as his red-hot passion had moments earlier. She pressed her lips against his, once, twice, three times, pulling back to meet his gaze. 'What you said before... About it scaring you how much you want to spend time with me? I feel like that too.' Her voice was as soft as a whisper and for a moment she wondered if he'd even heard.

Flickers of deliberation passed through his gaze— thoughts and considerations, worries and balances being carefully weighed. 'We don't have to think too far ahead, sweetheart.' His tone was as rusty as the lych-gate hinge in the garden. 'We can just enjoy what we have for now.'

For now.

Layla wanted more than 'for now', but how could she be sure she would get it?

Later that evening, Logan put some more wood on the fire and then came back to sit with Layla on the sofa. She was dressed in a baby-blue cashmere sweater and black yoga pants that clung to her shapely legs like a velvet evening glove. Her hair was in a loosely tied knot at the back of her head, highlighting her finely boned features and elegant neck. He had always considered her beautiful, but lately he couldn't look at her without his breathing catching and a warm flow of heat spreading in his chest.

Layla looked up from the magazine she was idly flicking through. 'It will soon be time to put up the Christmas tree. Will you get a real one from the forest like before or a fake one?'

'It wouldn't be Christmas without the smell of pine needles,' Logan said, playing with a loose curl dangling below her ear. But, then, it wouldn't be Christmas without her bustling about the castle, helping her great-aunt get ready for the festive season. It wouldn't be Christmas without the delicious cooking smells coming from the kitchen. So many of his memories had snapshots of Layla in them. She had become an essential part of Bellbrae and he couldn't imagine the place without her. And—even more disturbing to his carefully guarded emotions—he couldn't imagine his life without her.

'True.' Layla closed the magazine and leaned forward to put it on the coffee table in front of the sofa. She sat back next to him, her gaze meeting his. 'But will you invite anyone? Will Robbie come home for it, do you think?'

'I have no idea what his plans are,' Logan said with an all-too-familiar knot of tension in his stomach whenever his younger brother was mentioned. 'You know what he's like—he'll just show up unannounced and expect everyone to dance around him like some overgrown overly indulged teenager.' He leaned his head back against the back of the sofa and released a frustrated sigh. 'I wish I could go back in time and do things differently. I thought I was doing the right thing by being easy on him but...' He left the sentence hanging with all the unspoken things he wished now he had done.

'You did what you thought was right at the time,' Layla said. 'We all have a PhD in hindsight. I think he'll wake up to himself one day. He's just taking a little longer than you hoped.'

Logan took her hand and brought it up to rest on his thigh. 'I can't help comparing you to him. Unlike Robbie, you weren't born to privilege. You've had such a rough time of it and yet you're a kind and compassionate person who is always giving your time and attention to others. I feel ashamed that Robbie hasn't made the most of the opportunities he's been given. Deeply ashamed and frustrated. He could have done so much more with his life but he's throwing it away, along with the trust fund our father left him.'

He sighed again and added in a weighted tone, 'I feel like I've failed Robbie *and* my father. That I've let them both down. And the guilt that comes with that churns my guts.'

Layla touched his face with the soft palm of her hand, her expression full of concern. 'Oh, Logan, you really mustn't blame yourself for how Robbie chooses to live his life. You and Robbie have had terrible tragedy in your lives. It must have been awful to have your mother walk out like that when you were both so young. But she didn't just walk out on Robbie and your father. She abandoned you as well. But it seems like you've had to be strong for everyone else. And then when your dad died…well, you did the same. It's in your nature to take control, to make sure everyone is okay before you see to your own needs. But your needs are important too. You can't put them on hold for ever.'

Logan cradled one side of her face with his hand, his other hand still holding her hand anchored to his thigh. 'How'd you get to be so wise and wonderful?'

Something passed through her gaze and she lowered her eyes to focus on the region of his collar. 'I'm not that wonderful...' She bit her lip and a frown pleated her smooth brow.

He lifted her chin so her gaze came back to his. 'Hey. Why do you think that?'

Her expression faltered as if she was in two minds over answering. But then she gave a jagged sigh and spoke in a muted and flat tone. 'When my parents died in the car crash... I didn't grieve for them. Not the way other kids would have grieved. I pretended to grieve, because that's what everyone expected. But I was a fraud because I was secretly relieved I didn't have to live that chaotic life with them anymore.'

Her mouth tightened as if the memories were almost too painful to speak out loud.

'The drugs, the drink binges, the violence—I hated my life and I hated being first-row witness to what my mother's life had become. But I couldn't do anything to make it better for her. But the "accident—"' she did the air quote gesture with her fingers '—changed my life for ever and I was *glad*. I was actually more relieved I didn't have to have my leg amputated than I grieved for my parents. How sick and screwed up is that? I think that makes me a bad person. A terrible person.'

Logan hugged her tightly against his chest, resting his chin on the top of her head. 'You're not any such thing, sweetheart. You were a neglected and maltreated little girl who deserved a much better start in life. My heart aches for what you went through. But you should be proud of how you've coped. For what you've done with your life.' He eased back to blot the tears from beneath her eyes with his thumbs. 'What you're doing for others in your mother's situation is a wonderful way of breaking the cycle. It's your legacy for her memory and I'm sure she would be so very proud of you.'

Her lips flickered with a wry smile. 'Gosh, this sofa has become confession central lately, hasn't it? What is it about a roaring fire and a cosy atmosphere that gets under one's guard?'

It hadn't just lowered her guard—Logan had never been so open with anyone before. It was a strange feeling—a feeling he wasn't sure he could or wanted to name. He framed her face in his hands and brought his lips within a breath of hers. 'I don't know but it sure feels pretty damn good.' And he covered her mouth with his.

CHAPTER ELEVEN

PREPARING FOR CHRISTMAS at Bellbrae had always been one of Layla's favourite pastimes, but with Logan there to offer his assistance, it took her enjoyment to a whole new level. He helped her select a tree from the forest on the estate and with two of the grounds staff's help, it was transported to the largest sitting room in the castle.

In the past, Layla and her great-aunt had done the decorating of the tree, especially in later years when Logan and his brother had often been abroad and Logan's grandfather had been too infirm to do much more than sit and watch and offer suggestions about where a bauble or strip of tinsel should be placed.

They were in the sitting room, putting the last touches to the tree, Logan standing on a ladder while she held it steady so he could place the porcelain angel, which had been in the McLaughlin family for six decades, at the top of the tree.

'There,' he said with a note of satisfaction in his voice. 'Let's hope she makes it through one more festive season, but I seriously think we might have to get a new one for next year.' He climbed down the ladder and began tidying up the boxes in which the decorations had been stored.

Next year? Layla mentally gulped. *We?*

There would be no 'we' next year. Their marriage would have ended in October, as Logan had planned from the start. Or would it? He had been so wonderful to her over the last few weeks. Attentive and loving… yes, *loving.* Surely it wasn't just an act? There was nobody around to witness it, as Aunt Elsie had extended her holiday, and the other Bellbrae staff were mostly casual and weren't in the castle much but working in the outbuildings or grounds.

Logan turned with two empty boxes in his arms and frowned at her expression. 'Hey, what's wrong, sweetie?'

'Nothing…' Layla bent down to pick up a tiny strip of silver tinsel off the carpet.

He put the boxes down and came over to where she was standing and brushed his finger across her lower lip. 'If you keep chewing your lip like that it will bleed and then I won't be able to kiss you.'

Layla forced a quick no-teeth smile. 'I guess I'm just a bit tired…'

He tucked a loose strand of her hair behind her ear, his gaze so dark it was hard to tell where his pupils began and ended. 'Is your leg hurting you? You've been doing way too much and that walk to the forest to get the tree was a bit rough in places.'

'My leg is okay, mostly,' Layla said. The chronic neural pain she suffered from was still there but she was less conscious of it. She still limped, because one leg was shorter than the other, but she realised she had become almost oblivious to the slight awkwardness of her gait. 'I think you've helped distract me from the discomfort.' She put her arms around his waist and smiled, properly this time. 'Now, we need to find some mistletoe to hang over the doorway.'

Logan's eyes twinkled. 'Who needs mistletoe?' He lowered his mouth to hers in a long drugging kiss that made Layla's senses sing. It was silly of her to keep filling her head with doubts over the future. Silly of her to listen to alarm bells ringing in her head…except they weren't in her head.

Logan lifted his mouth off hers and cocked his head. 'Is that your phone or mine?'

'Mine.' Layla slipped out of his loose hold and picked up her phone from one of the lamp tables where she'd left it earlier. She glanced at the caller ID and smiled and answered the phone. 'Hi, Isla. How are you? I was going to call you and—'

'Guess what?' Excitement and joy sounded in Isla's voice.

Layla's heart skipped a beat 'Oh, my God, you've had the baby?'

'Yes, a little girl,' Isla said. 'She was in a big hurry to get here—almost three weeks early—and I was only in labour two hours. Rafe was beside himself, trying to get me to the hospital in time. We've called her Gabriella Marietta Layla. I can't wait for you to meet her. She's adorable. Rafe is completely and utterly smitten.'

Tears came to Layla's eyes and her chest swelled with love for her friend. 'You named her after me? Oh, my goodness, I don't know what to say.'

'Say you'll be her godmother,' Isla said. 'And we'd

like Logan to be her godfather. We would be so honoured to have you both as Gabriella's godparents.'

Layla pictured Logan standing with her at the christening font, agreeing to spiritually sponsor their godchild. It was such an honour for any couple. And since they had become more of a connected couple than before, it seemed the perfect cementing of their relationship. Didn't their increasing closeness signify a more promising future together? There were times when she was almost certain he loved her. He hadn't said it but his body, his gaze, his touch said it for him. And didn't hers tell him much the same?

'We would be delighted to,' Layla said. 'I can't wait to meet her in person. Can you put the face camera feature on so I can see her now?'

'Here we go...' Isla did the necessary button-pressing and the real-time camera showed a tiny pink bundle cradled in her adoring father's arms.

Layla was so overcome with emotion once she got off the phone that she could barely speak. Happy joyful emotion. Jubilation for her friend and for the love and security she had found in Rafe. That was what she wanted with Logan. Lasting love, a family. Building a harmonious home life together. 'Gosh, I can't believe I'm a sort of aunty. And a godmother.' She turned to Logan and smiled. 'Did you hear? We've been invited to be Gabriella's godparents. I've never been a godparent before, have you?'

Logan's expression and posture were so still he could have been snap-frozen while she'd been on the phone. 'No. I have not.' His voice was flat, almost toneless, except for a fine thread of anger running underneath.

Layla frowned, her heart missing a beat. Why was he looking so cold and distant? 'What's wrong?'

He drew in a sharp breath and moved a few paces away, released the breath and then turned back to face her. 'Do you not think it might have been appropriate to ask me first before accepting an invitation like that?'

Layla swallowed a bauble-sized lump in her throat. 'But I thought you'd be honoured to—'

'You thought wrong,' he said, brows drawn down heavily in a brooding frown.

'Logan...' She tried for a conciliatory tone but missed the mark. 'Why are you so upset? Being asked to be a godparent is such a lovely thing. It's mostly symbolic these days but, still, it's wonderful to be asked. I would feel awful saying no. And besides, they want both of us.'

'You've seen the rubbish job I've done of being responsible for my brother. And don't get me started on what a mess I made with Susannah. I'm not signing up for any more responsibility, especially when we're not really a couple. Or at least not for the long term.'

Not really a couple. Not for the long term.

The words hit her like slaps. Cold hard stinging slaps of truth. A truth she had been hiding from for weeks and weeks, fooling herself her relationship with Logan was something else. Something like Isla had with Rafe. But it wasn't. It never had been and never could be.

Why had she fooled herself it could?

Layla took a steadying breath, trying to control her spiralling emotions. 'So, what you're saying is you don't want to be Gabriella's godfather?'

'I don't want to be any child's godfather.' His eyes

were as hard as his tone. Diamond hard. Don't-ask-me-twice hard. 'You had no right to answer for me. We might be having a good time but it doesn't mean you get to sign me up for things I have no interest in.'

'A good time?' Layla gasped. 'Is that all this is to you? Is that all *I* am to you?' Pain ripped through her chest as if her ribcage was being wrenched apart with steel claws. But she wouldn't allow herself to cry. Not now. Not in front of him. How could she have been so gullible, so foolish as to think their physical closeness meant emotional closeness? He was as far away from her as he had ever been. She had fooled herself that his touch meant he loved her. That his passionate kisses meant he cared. That his lovemaking was *lovemaking*, not just sex.

Logan shoved his hands into his trouser pockets, glaring at her like she was an intruder he had never seen before and not the woman he had spent the last two months making passionate love to. 'Don't put words in my mouth. I told you right at the start how things were going to be. You accepted my terms.'

'Your terms are completely ridiculous,' Layla said. 'They're your insurance scheme against getting hurt, that's what they really are. And here I was thinking my limp was holding me back, stopping me doing all the things other people do. But at the end of the day it's just a physical limp. Your emotional limp is far worse. It completely disables you and yet you can't see it.'

He gave a mocking laugh that grated on her already shredded emotions. 'Thanks for the free psychoanalysis but I don't need you to tell me how I think.'

'You don't need me at all,' Layla said. 'You don't

need anyone. You won't allow yourself to. Which is why
I can't stay here any longer. I can't be in a relationship
that has limits set on it. I spent my childhood trying to
fit in with impossible standards. Standards that didn't
factor in my needs or aspirations. Standards that didn't
include love. I want more than that now. I deserve more
than that and you do too.'

His expression was masked but she sensed a simmering anger behind the dark screen of his gaze. 'You're
free to come and go as you please. I can't make you
stay.'

Yes, you can, Layla wanted to say. *Just three little
words would make me stay.*

But those three little words had never been a part of
their arrangement. Neither had a future together ever
been part of the deal. Logan had always been blatantly
honest about that. 'I don't think it will help either of
us if I were to stay on in this relationship. Of course,
I won't jeopardise your inheritance of Bellbrae. I will
be your wife on paper, as you first suggested, to fulfil
the terms of your grandfather's will.'

'Magnanimous of you.' His coolly delivered comment was as cutting as a switchblade.

Layla pressed her lips together to stop them from
trembling. She couldn't fall apart now. He was making
it perfectly clear there was no hope for their marriage.
No hope at all. 'I think it's best if I leave straight away.
I will pack a few things and come for the rest later.'

'There's no need to be so dramatic, Layla,' Logan
said. 'I'm sure we can be perfectly civil to each other
until tomorrow morning. It'll be dark in a couple of

hours. I don't like the thought of you driving all the way to Edinburgh at this time of day.'

And risk having him try and change her mind? No. It was better she leave now while she still had the strength and courage and self-respect to do so. Layla raised her chin to a determined height, her gaze steady on his unreadable one. 'I appreciate your concern, but my mind is made up.'

Anger flared in his gaze and his mouth went into a flat line and he began a caged-tiger-like pacing of the floor. 'This all seems rather sudden and impulsive.' He stopped pacing to spear her with a look. 'A few minutes ago, we were kissing. Now you say you want out?'

Layla smoothed her sweaty palms down her thighs, wishing she could smooth away the heartache she was feeling. 'It's not as sudden as you might think. I've been worried from the start—you know I have. I didn't want you to lose Bellbrae. But I can't lose myself in the process of you gaining your inheritance. And that's what's already happening. I can't be who I'm meant to be if I'm tailoring my needs to suit your plans. I have my own plans and they don't include a short-term loveless marriage.'

He rolled his eyes heavenwards and let out a not-quite-inaudible curse. 'Oh, I thought you'd mention the L word eventually. You think I don't care about you? Is that what you think?'

Layla forced herself to hold his embittered gaze. 'I know you care. You care about lots of people. But you don't love me.'

He sucked in a harsh breath and strode to stand in front of the waist-height bookcase. 'You're suddenly such an expert on my feelings.' He pushed a hand through his hair and then dropped it back by his side. 'Love?' He shook his head and let out another breath and continued, 'I don't trust that emotion. I don't trust the word when people say it to me. My mother said it so frequently and look how that turned out.' His gaze narrowed. 'Are you saying you love me?'

Layla ran the tip of her tongue over her parchment-dry lips. 'It wouldn't matter if I did or not. You don't love me the way I want to be loved.'

He closed his eyes and pinched the bridge of his nose. After a moment, he lowered his hand from his face to look at her. 'No one can love anyone the way they want to be loved. The standard is set too high, fed by romantic fantasies encouraged by popular culture. It's not real, Layla. What you feel for me is not real, it's just a fantasy.'

How like him to intellectualise everything. How like him to dismiss her feelings as simple fantasy. What hope was there to ever change his mind? She had seen her mother try desperately to get her father to love her and it hadn't happened. Layla had tried to get both her parents to love her and yet the drugs and drink had triumphed over her. Lucky Layla wasn't so lucky after all.

She was unlucky in love.

'I'm going upstairs to pack. I'll text you when I arrive in Edinburgh.'

'Fine.'

Layla took off the engagement ring and held it out to him. 'I think you should have this back. It's a family heirloom and I'm not family.' Or ever will be.

His eyes hardened to ice, his jaw set in stone. 'Keep it. I don't want it.'

Layla curled her fingers around the ring and slipped it into her pocket and silently left the room.

His words could just as easily be referring to her love for him.

Keep it. I don't want it.

Logan forced himself to watch Layla's tail-lights fading into the distance. Forced himself to stand there at the window, watching her leave, instead of racing to his own car and driving after her, begging her to come back. But he was not the sort of man to beg. To plead. To humiliate himself over a relationship that was never going to work. It had all the odds stacked against it from the start and wasn't he the biggest odds of them?

He was the last person to be anyone's godparent. What sort of spiritual guardian would he be? He had messed up big time with his younger brother, keeping the reins too loose, and now he couldn't pull back on them. It was painful to watch his brother self-destruct, knowing he was partly, if not wholly, responsible. He had done an even worse job of taking care of his fiancée. Taking on any more responsibility was asking for another monumental screw-up.

And now he had another one for his personal failure board—his relationship with Layla. It had been doomed from the outset because *he* was the common denominator in all his failed relationships. There was no escaping the uncomfortable truth that he was unable to care for someone without letting them down.

The tail-lights were finally swallowed by the cloaking darkness and he closed the curtains. Hadn't he stood at this very window as a seven-year-old boy, looking for the lights of his mother's car? Every night for a year he had waited, hoping, praying she would return. But, of course, she never had. His mother had told him she loved him every day of his life and yet those words had not brought her back. Her love had not brought her back. It had vanished with her. Or—even more likely—it hadn't been there in the first place.

Layla fancied herself in love with him and he blamed himself for not sticking to his rules. He had blurred the boundaries by taking their relationship from on paper to passion and now he had to pay the price.

But he still had Bellbrae.

Layla had promised not to do anything that would compromise his inheritance and for that he was grateful. To lose Bellbrae would be to lose a big part of himself. He glanced at the Christmas tree that only a short time ago they had decorated together. The porcelain angel on the top of the tree had slipped sideways and looked in danger of falling. He deliberated on whether to climb back up the ladder or leave the angel to its fate. It had been repaired a few times—once Flossie as a puppy had run off with it during the tree-decorating process. Another time Robbie had thrown it in a tantrum not long after their mother had left. It had taken Logan ages to glue it back together before anyone noticed.

Flossie pushed the sitting-room door open with her nose and padded over to him, her tail low, her brown eyes so woebegone it made something in Logan's gut tighten. 'Don't look at me like that,' he said, frowning. 'I didn't ask her to leave.'

But you didn't convince her to stay either.

He pushed aside the intrusive thought and went over to where he had propped the stepladder against the wall. He unfolded the ladder and began climbing but he had only got up three rungs when the angel toppled from the top of the tree and fell to the floor, her porcelain face smashing into pieces no amount of superglue was ever going to fix.

Layla booked herself into a bed and breakfast in Haymarket in the west end of Edinburgh and fell into bed but not into sleep. She lay on her back, eyes streaming with tears, her chest aching with emptiness. What a fool she had been to admit she loved Logan. A gauche fool who should have known better than to think he would ever return her feelings. He had locked away his heart and she had been crazy to think she of all people held the key. She didn't. And never would.

She looked at her bare ring finger and sighed. She'd left his grandmother's engagement ring and her wedding ring on Logan's bedside table. There was no way she could keep his family heirloom. The ring would just have been a painful reminder of how she had failed to win his heart—of how her dreams had been shattered like a robin's egg on concrete.

She picked up her phone and checked if he'd replied to her text informing him she had arrived safely. He had, but in characteristic fashion had kept it brief.

Okay.

No words asking her to reconsider. No words of love. Just 'Okay'.

Layla put the phone back down and flopped back against the pillows with another sigh. More fool her for wanting more than was possible.

But wasn't that the pitiful story of her life?

CHAPTER TWELVE

A WEEK WENT past and Logan swore he could still smell Layla's perfume lingering in the castle. Even when he walked outside to go on one of his long walks over the estate, he thought he could hear the sound of her laugh in the air. And every time the sun peeped out from behind the brooding clouds, he thought of her breath-snatching smile.

Bellbrae was just a deserted old castle without her here. A deserted Highland retreat that was no longer a retreat but more like a prison. He was imprisoned by his thoughts—the thoughts that plagued him day and night, but mostly at night. He would wake from a restless sleep and realised with a jolt that Layla was not sleeping beside him. That her cloud of chestnut hair wasn't splayed out over the pillow, her arms not wrapped around him, her legs not curled close to his.

He'd had to stop using the bedroom he'd shared with her as it contained too many memories. He had even left the engagement and wedding rings on the bedside table where she'd left them. He couldn't bring himself to lock them in the safe because it seemed too…final. Out of sight, out of mind. Except Layla was indeed out of sight but not out of his mind. She was there all the time. He couldn't go through a single minute of the day without thinking of her.

And that's when the pain would start. Pain that spread through his chest like a poison, seeping into his blood and even into his bones. He *ached* with it. He couldn't escape the torment of his body missing hers. But the physical torment he could handle, it was the mental torment he couldn't. The *emotional* torment. Yes, the E word he had scrubbed from his vocabulary a long time ago. Emotions were things he didn't trust, in others but also in himself.

But the emotion he felt now was different. The emptiness he felt was different. The ache inside his chest seemed to be getting worse each day.

Logan had just brought Flossie back in after a comfort walk when he saw his brother's car coming up the driveway. Great. Just what he needed—an uninvited guest at his private pity party.

Robbie parked the car under one of the trees near the old stables. The bare branches waving in the icy wind looked like arthritic fingers.

'God, this place is freezing,' Robbie said, dashing towards Logan with his hand pulling the collar of his coat against his neck.

Logan hadn't noticed the cold. He'd been too preoccupied with missing Layla. 'You didn't tell me you were coming. I would have cranked up the heating.'

Robbie grimaced and followed Logan inside. 'Yeah, sorry about that. But I had my mind on stuff.'

Tell me about it.

Logan led the way to the small sitting room where

he had been spending most of his time. Flossie was already in front of the fire with her head on her paws. She wagged her tail across the carpet but didn't go over to greet Robbie.

Robbie pulled one side of his lip into his mouth and shifted his weight from foot to foot. 'Is Layla around? I think it's important she hears what I have to say too, given you guys are married and all. I want to apologise for my behaviour last time. I was unforgivably rude to her.'

Logan walked over to the fireplace and gave the burning coals a poke with the poker. The mention of Layla's name was as painful as if the hot poker had been driven into his chest. 'She's not here.'

'Oh, where is she?'

Logan put the poker back on the fireplace tools rack and faced his brother. 'She left a week ago.'

Robbie frowned. 'Left? Why?'

Logan rubbed a hand down his face and mentally reminded himself to shave sometime. It had been three days at least. 'I suck at relationships, that's why. I hurt people I care about even when I think I'm doing the right thing by them.'

Robbie swallowed a couple of times and sat on the sofa as if his legs were not capable of keeping him upright. He leaned forward and rested his elbows on his thighs and placed his head into his hands.

'Oh, God, this is my fault.' He lifted his head and looked at Logan with a harrowed expression. 'The reason I came here today… I've been to see someone. A psychologist.' He swallowed again and continued, 'I'm not coping with stuff. I haven't been coping for a long time but I've been using other things to take my mind off it. Drinking, the occasional party drug, sex with strangers, so many strangers I've lost count. Gambling.' He groaned and placed his head back in his hands. 'I've lost everything, Logan. Please don't hate me for it. I have nothing left of my trust fund—I've gambled it all away.'

Logan went over to his brother, sat beside him and laid an arm around his quaking shoulders. 'You have me, Robbie. You'll always have me, no matter what.'

Flossie hauled herself up off the carpet in front of the fire and came plodding over to nudge Robbie's thigh, whining as if to say she was there for him too.

Robbie lifted his head out of his hands, his face wet with tears. His hand reached down and scratched behind the dog's ears. 'I want to be a better man. I want to be like you—steady, reliable, responsible. I've been blaming everyone but myself for how I behave, for the stupid choices I've made. But I'm determined to make better choices now. I want to go to rehab. I want to get control of my destructive habits before they hurt the people I love.'

'I'll support you in every way I can,' Logan said.

Robbie leaned back and met Logan's gaze. 'You've always been there for me. I couldn't have asked for a better older brother. You've always had my back and knowing that has kept me from the edge more times than I want to admit. I've let you down so much but I'm determined to change my habits. But what about you and Layla? I can't help thinking I've caused you guys to break up.'

Logan had his own destructive habits to address.

The habit of not recognising love, for instance. For not allowing himself to feel it, or receive it. Not trusting love when it was the only thing that kept him going.

Love for his brother, love for Bellbrae and most of all—love for Layla.

Maybe there was hope for him after all. Robbie had said Logan's love for him had kept him from going over the edge. It gave him hope he might be a better godparent than he'd thought. And who better to be a godparent with than with Layla? The woman he loved with all his heart and soul.

And why stop at godparenting? He started to picture Bellbrae with children sitting around the Christmas tree. The sound of their laughter echoing in the castle and in the gardens and beyond. He and Layla would make an awesome team as parents of their own children. He had loved Layla for so long he had no idea when it had started. It felt like it had always been there inside his heart. Hidden away. Locked away. But he could lock it away no longer.

'No, it wasn't you,' Logan said. 'It was me. I didn't realise how much I loved her until I lost her. I guess it's a bit like you with having to lose everything, having to reach rock bottom before you can resurface, to be reborn.'

Robbie frowned in puzzlement. 'If you love her, then why are you brooding up here all alone?'

Logan sprang from the sofa. 'You're right. I need to go and see her. To tell her I love her exactly the way she wants to be loved. And to bring her back home. Will you be okay looking after Flossie overnight?'

Robbie's face was wreathed in a smile and he turned

to look at the dog sitting beside him. 'How about it, Floss? Do you trust me to take care of you while Logan brings back his bride?'

Flossie gave an answering bark and wagged her plumy tail.

Layla was in her office-cum-bedsit in the Old Town of Edinburgh, putting the last touches to the small reception area with a pot plant and new business cards for the counter. Her business name, 'Leave it to Layla and Co', was on a black and gold plaque on the door and another one over the counter. She stepped back to admire her brand-new office space when the door tinkled open behind her.

She turned with a welcoming smile on her face. 'Welcome to…' Her heart jerked sideways in her chest. 'Oh, Logan. Hello…' She licked her lips, a little shocked at his appearance. It looked like he hadn't shaven or slept in days. And his clothes were rumpled as if he'd slept in them—if indeed he had slept. 'Are you okay?'

He closed the door and came over to where she was standing. 'I'm not okay and I'll never be okay without you.' He took her hands in his. 'I love you. I can't tell you when I started loving you. It feels like I've always loved you in one way or another. But it's the way I love you now that's most important.'

Layla's heart began to feel too big for her chest cavity. It swelled and swelled and she could hardly take a breath or speak. 'You really love me?'

He smiled and hugged her to his chest, resting his chin on top of her head. 'I love you so much I can't find the words to describe it. I would give anything up if it meant I could have you by my side. Even Bellbrae.'

'Oh, Logan,' Layla said, happy tears spilling from her eyes. 'Even Bellbrae?'

He eased back to look down at her with love shining in his gaze. He blotted her tears with the pads of his fingers. 'Even Bellbrae. It's just an isolated and draughty old cold castle without you there. You make it a home. Come back with me and make it a home for both of us. And for any children we might have if we're so lucky.'

'Children?' Layla's eyes widened and her heart just about exploded with joy. 'You want a family?'

'You once pointed out I might need an heir in the future, remember? I can think of no one I'd rather have to be the mother of my children than you. Oh, and by the way, is the invitation to be godfather to little Gabriella still open? I would be honoured to be a godparent with you.'

Layla wound her arms around his neck. 'I can't believe this is happening. I've been so miserable without you. I love you so much.'

He held her close, his arms a strong band around her back. 'When you said I had an emotional limp, that really resonated with me later. I was too angry to really understand what you meant at the time. But it's true. I've been disabled for years by my fear of failure in a relationship—any relationship. It was as destructive as Robbie's drinking and gambling. He's getting help, by the way. I'm so proud of how he's taking that step. He's minding Flossie while I'm down here sweeping you off your feet.'

'You are very definitely doing that,' Layla laughed. 'I don't think my feet will ever touch the ground again.'

He kissed her long and lovingly, finally raising his mouth off hers to say, 'Forgive me for hurting you. For not begging you to stay, and most of all for not telling you how much I love you.'

Layla stroked his prickly jaw with her hand. 'You've told me now, that's the main thing.'

Logan kissed her hand and then reached into his coat pocket. 'I was halfway down the driveway at Bellbrae when I realised I'd forgotten to get your rings. I had to dash back to get them.' He took out the wedding and engagement rings and placed them on her left hand. 'There. Back where they belong.'

Layla's smile threatened to split her face in two. 'I'm so happy I think I'm going to burst. What do you think of my office? It's a bit on the small side but it's a start.'

'It looks great. I'm so proud of you, even if I have to confess I'm worried how we're going to juggle our careers. But I'll always support you, no matter what.'

'I've already hired a receptionist to manage the bookings,' Layla said. 'I realise I can't do everything myself. It's not healthy. Besides, I quite like the idea of sleeping in now and again as long as you're there too.'

His eyes glinted and he drew her even closer. 'Come home with me for Christmas?'

Layla lifted her mouth to his. 'Just try and stop me.'

EPILOGUE

Christmas the following year

LOGAN BROUGHT THE tray of mulled wine in for their guests in the sitting room where the Christmas tree was twinkling and the fire roaring in the grate. Rafe and Isla and their adorable twelve-month-old toddler Gabriella were staying for the festive season. Gabby was at the cute cruising around the furniture stage, and every now and again would lose her balance and plonk down on her nappy-clad bottom and smile, showing off her brand new little white teeth.

Aunt Elsie was spending Christmas on a cruise with her pen pal after developing quite a penchant for travelling, but she assured them she would be back when the worst of winter was over.

Robbie was sitting on the opposite sofa with his arm around his new partner Meg, who he'd met in rehab. Logan couldn't believe the difference in his brother. The maturity and acceptance of responsibility had been slow in coming but now it was here, he couldn't have been prouder of the way his brother had addressed his issues.

And then Logan's gaze went to Layla, who was sitting on the third sofa with her feet up on a footstool, cradling their new puppy Rafferty on her lap. Flossie had sadly passed away in her sleep a few months ago and the only way Logan could think to fill the gap the old dog left was to buy Layla a puppy for her birthday. The new angel on the top of the tree already had Raffy's teeth marks on it but thankfully Logan had rescued it in time before more serious damage had been done.

Layla smiled at Logan and his chest filled with warmth. 'Is that the non-alcoholic one?' she asked with a twinkle in her eye that rivalled the Christmas-tree lights.

'I made it specially for you, darling,' Logan said, feeling a rush of love so deep and intense it took his breath away.

'You're not drinking alcohol?' Isla's eyes widened to the size of the baubles on the tree. 'Does this mean…?'

Logan put the drinks tray down and sat beside Layla and placed his arm around her waist. 'Yes, it does. We're expecting a special arrival in June next year.'

'Congratulations!' Rafe and Isla spoke at once and Robbie and Meg soon followed with hugs and kisses. Even little Gabby wanted to be part of the action and gave them both a sloppy open-mouthed kiss.

'But wait, there's more,' Layla said with a beaming smile that made his heart swell with love. 'We need two sets of godparents. So, will you guys do the honours? Rafe and Isla and Robbie and Meg?'

Robbie's eyebrows shot up. 'You're having twins?'

Logan grinned and hugged Layla close to his side. 'I did say a special arrival, didn't I? Yes, we're having twins.'

* * * * *

THEIR ROYAL
WEDDING
BARGAIN

MICHELLE CONDER

To Heather—
for years of love and friendship and for always
being in my corner. I'll always be in yours too.

And to my dad. There just wasn't enough time
in the end. I miss you.

CHAPTER ONE

TONIGHT WAS GOING to be a total disaster. Alexa could *feel* it.

The Annual Santarian Children's Charity ball, one of the most prestigious events on the international calendar, would commence in under an hour, and she felt sick with apprehension.

'He's here, Your Highness,' Nasrin, her assistant-cum-lady's-maid-cum-devoted-companion, murmured as she closed the bedroom door, a ripple of excitement evident in her quick steps as she returned to Alexa. 'One of the chambermaids confirmed that the Prince of Santara has just entered the Summer Palace.'

Retrieving the hairbrush from the old-fashioned vanity unit, Nasrin picked up a skein of Alexa's long dark hair and met her wide-eyed gaze in the mirror. 'This is so exciting. I can't believe you're actually going to do it.'

Alexa couldn't either; releasing a measured breath at the thought of what she intended to do, followed swiftly by the seizing of her stomach.

Known for her cool, unflappable poise under pressure, she felt as if she was about to throw up the grilled cheese sandwich she'd had for lunch all over her custom-made designer gown.

He was here. He was really here.

Prince Rafaele of Santara, the King's younger brother,

had actually arrived. There had been whispers that he might not attend tonight, given that he'd created a scandal at this very event last year, embarrassing the King. But apparently nothing stopped the Rebel Prince of Santara from following his own path, and that was a trait that could work in her favour tonight so she should see it as a positive. Being a determined rule follower, she found that somewhat difficult, adding to her massive sense of self-doubt.

How was she going to do it? How was she going to ask a prince with the reputation as a consummate playboy to marry her, even if she was a princess herself? Because that was what she intended to do. What she *had* to do if she wanted to appease her father.

She and Nasrin had hatched the crazy eleventh-hour plan to propose a fake marriage—or engagement because, as she would explain to the Prince, she had no intention of actually going through with the wedding—two weeks ago when she had realised that her father was deadly serious about seeing her married as soon as possible.

Of course she'd tried to argue with him. Tell him that she wasn't ready, that she needed more time, but he had shaken his head and informed her that nothing she said would change his mind. As the Crown Princess of Berenia, and only remaining heir, he would not rest until she was settled.

To be fair he had given her six months to create a list of possible marriageable contenders, but Alexa had dragged her feet, hoping he would forget all about it. On the night he'd told her he hadn't forgotten at all, she and Nasrin had sat down to commiserate over a glass of Sauterne and a completely unrealistic rom-com at the end of a long working day.

According to Nasrin the main actor looked like the dreamy Santarian Prince, his character replete with arrogant, bad boy tendencies and a super-hot body, and the idea had been born. In the film the hero had not wanted to marry the heroine, but love had won out in the end.

Alexa knew from past experience that love rarely won out in the end, but fortunately that wasn't what she required from the Prince.

'It's going to be fine, Princess Alexa; he'll do it,' Nasrin murmured, accurately reading the panic in her eyes for what it was. 'Then you'll have everything your heart desires.'

Everything her heart desired?

What she desired the most was time to make her own marriage match, and for her older brother to still be alive.

Sol had been the true heir to the Berenian throne but since his tragic death three years ago that duty had fallen to her. And she wasn't up to it, not yet anyway, and deep down she wondered if her father believed that she wasn't up to it either, especially after the serious lapse in judgement she'd made when she was seventeen. Perhaps that was one of the reasons he was pushing so hard for her to marry right now. Why he was so determined to have it done.

That, and to remove the stink of shame that still hovered over her after the King of Santara had abruptly ended their betrothal twelve months earlier. The ink hadn't even dried on their marriage contract before he had pulled out and immediately married another woman—an outsider, no less—his actions stirring up centuries-old animosity between their nations and giving the BLF—the Berenian Liberation Front—just the excuse they needed to re-engage in hostilities with Santara.

Her and King Jaeger's brief, ill-fated betrothal hadn't been a love-match by any stretch, but his rejection had still felt like yet another kick in the teeth for Alexa because she had *liked* him. She'd developed a massive crush on King

Jaeger when he had saved her from an embarrassing experience on her first official engagement as her father's consort. At thirteen, she'd been so nervous, decked out in a white tulle gown that had made her feel like a beautiful fairy, that she'd accidentally upended a full jug of cranberry juice all over herself. She'd frozen to the spot as the cold, sticky red liquid had drenched the front of her beautiful gown and chilled her skin. Before she'd been able to respond the newly crowned King of Santara had stepped in behind her and enveloped her in his jacket and whispered that everything would be okay.

Mortified, Alexa had buried her scalding cheeks against his chest, allowing him to draw her from the room without anyone really noticing them. He'd instructed a servant to find her lady's maid and then melted back into the party. Alexa hadn't drunk cranberry juice since, and nor had she forgotten the King's kindness. As she'd matured he'd become the epitome of her dream man: kind, loyal, compassionate and strong.

His brother, by contrast, couldn't be more different. The consummate good-time guy, Prince Rafaele moved from one lissom blonde to the next as if he was doing nothing more important than choosing a new tie to wear with his suit.

'Having your hair up was a good choice,' Nasrin said as she twisted the last of Alexa's waist-length tresses into place. 'It shows off the sheer panelling at the back of your dress to perfection.'

'It's not too revealing, is it?' Alexa murmured, twisting on her padded stool to get a better view. She'd chosen her nude-coloured off-the-shoulder gown to attract as much attention as she dared, but she wasn't used to wearing clothing that revealed so much skin.

'Not at all. It's perfect.'

Alexa stared at her carefully made-up face with critical indifference. Perfect would be to have the task ahead of her put behind her and sorted to her satisfaction.

'And you're sure he doesn't want to get married?' she asked, her outward calm slipping ever so slightly. One of the things that made the Prince so perfect was his reported disinclination to marry. If he didn't want to marry he would never want to make their union permanent and interfere with her chance to do things her way.

'Absolutely.' Nasrin nodded. 'He's been on record as saying he never intends to marry. Not that the women seem to be listening. They throw themselves at him like lemmings off a cliff, hoping to be the one to change his mind.'

So why did she feel so sick?

Probably because actually attracting the attention of a man like the Prince was completely foreign to her, thanks to her father's strict rules and regulations, and her own sense of inadequacy with men. Not that she'd always felt that way. Once, when she was seventeen, she'd believed a man—Stefano—had found her beautiful. But what he'd really found was that she was gullible. Gullible enough to be seduced by a man who was more interested in her title than her as a woman. The mistake had hit her budding confidence hard, pushing her to focus on her degree in business management, and her royal duties, to the exclusion of all else.

Not that she wanted to *attract* Prince Rafaele. No, she only wanted his cooperation in a scheme that, in the end, would serve him as equally as it would her by restoring cordial relations between their two nations. A scheme that had seemed a lot easier to follow through on when she'd gone over it late at night in her bed than in the cold light of day.

Trying to remain positive, Alexa slipped on her heels

and smoothed her hands down her bespoke gown, ignoring how the clever creation made her feel both elegant *and* naked—which, according to her exuberant assistant, was the whole point of the design.

'You will feel sexy and alluring,' Nasrin had assured her when she'd first set eyes on the dress. 'And every man in the room will look at you and want you.'

Right now she felt as sexy and alluring as a tree. And she didn't want *every* man in the room looking at her. She was nervous enough thinking about *one* man looking at her.

She picked up the dossier Nasrin had put together on Prince Rafaele last week, rifling through photo after photo of him attending parties and movie premieres every other week. Vastly wealthy in his own right, he owned an empire of nightclubs and bars across Europe that, once opened, became the only place to be seen. *'Dens of iniquity',* her father had once disparaged.

An unwanted shiver shot through her as she gazed at a shirtless photo of the Prince holding onto a sail line on the deck of a yacht. His white trousers were flattened against his muscular thighs by the breeze, his dark shoulder-length hair streaming out behind him, his broad chest deeply tanned to the colour of the teak deck. His face was turned towards the camera and the lens had lovingly captured his perfect wide smile, hawkish features and startling blue eyes as he laughed at something in the distance.

The caption underneath read: *The Rebel Prince in search of sun, fun and adventure.*

Alexa studied his image. Despite his relaxed pose there was something about the way he held himself that said *Danger…beware.* A jaded slant to his lips that indicated that he had seen everything there was to see in life, and was surprised by none of it. Which would be a good thing if he went along with her plan because their break-up would seem inevitable: the Playboy Prince and the shrinking violet could never have lasted. Not that she *was* a shrinking violet. She just chose not to make waves if she didn't have to.

'Hot, isn't he?' Nasrin said as she glanced at the photo before running a practised eye over Alexa. 'You look stunning, Your Highness. The Prince won't be able to resist you.'

While Alexa appreciated Nasrin's optimism, she knew from personal experience that men found her all too easy to resist. 'More likely he'll laugh in my face.' She closed the file. 'And if he's that opposed to marriage he might not even go for a temporary engagement.'

'But you have an ace up your sleeve. If he agrees, it could help settle all the bad blood between our nations. Of course he'll go for that. And the engagement would only be temporary. Unless...' Nasrin's pretty eyes sparkled mischievously '...you fall in love with each other.'

Alexa shook her head. Nasrin had a romantic nature that no amount of rational conversation could extinguish. And while Alexa might have once craved love and a happy-ever-after too, she'd been disappointed enough in the past not to wait around for it.

Love wasn't as important as dignity. Self-respect. Objectivity. And imagining the Prince of Santara falling in love with her, or her with him, was frankly hilarious.

'That's as likely to happen as the moon is to turn blue,' she said dryly.

'If you wish hard enough, Your Highness, you'll get whatever you ask for.'

Alexa knew that rarely happened either.

'Fortunately, I don't want the Prince's love. Just his co-operation.'

'Then go get it,' Nasrin urged with a flourish.

Alexa smiled. Nasrin had been like a gift when she'd come to work for her after Sol had died, organising her life and making her smile again with her chatty, easy nature. Everything else had felt so oppressive at the time, oppressive and overwhelming, during those dark days.

Not that she begrudged her role as the future Queen of Berenia. She didn't because she loved her country, and her countrymen, and she wanted to do the best job for them in Sol's stead. She wanted to make her father proud. And if the Prince went along with her plan she could do that. She could help rebuild relations between Berenia and Santara, and buy herself the necessary time to make a marriage that not only pleased her father but herself as well.

The decider would be whether or not she could implement a plan that had seemed perfectly logical at inception, but now felt desperately naive.

But if the Prince turned her down she'd just have to find someone else. Because the alternative—marrying the man who was on top of her father's list of eligible suitors—didn't bear thinking about.

Rafe gazed around the ballroom of the Santarian Summer Palace, a place he'd spent many formative years, with mixed emotions. As a general rule he tried not to return here very often, not only because it didn't hold the best memories, but because when he'd left Santara as a disaffected teenager he'd cut all ties with his nation.

And he wasn't sorry that he had. He didn't miss the life here. He didn't miss the sun that was hot enough most of the year to blister paint, and he didn't miss the endless round of lacklustre royal duties his father had expected him to carry out as the second son of Santara. The less important son. He didn't miss having his ideas shot down in flames by a man who had never understood his drive and ambition to forge his own path in life.

'It's lucky you're a prince, sibi,' his father had often snarled. *'You'd amount to nothing if you weren't.'*

Hard-nosed and narrow-minded, his father had treated opposing opinions as little more than ripples on a quiet pond.

Rafe had learned not to care, disconnecting from his father, and rubbing his nose in it any chance that he got. And despite—or perhaps because of—his father's convictions that he wouldn't amount to anything he'd made a success of his life.

He'd broken free of the constraints of royal duty and lived life on his own terms. Not that his father was around to see it. His death when Rafe had been eighteen was the very thing that had set him free. Or rather his brother had set him free when he'd stepped into the role of King at nineteen and given Rafe permission to spread his wings.

Returning from studying in the US at the time, Rafe knew that Jag could have used his insider knowledge and support, and it was only now, looking back, that he understood the sacrifice his brother had made for him, shouldering the burden of a troubled nation on his own and never asking anything of Rafe in return.

Once sharing what he would have said was an unbreakable bond, their relationship had grown strained with distance and Rafe was never sure how to bridge the gulf without losing himself in the process. Still, he owed Jag a debt of gratitude, even if his brother didn't think so.

Catching the direction of his thoughts before they progressed any further, Rafe shook them off with well-practised ease. This was partly the reason he hated returning home. The memories, the choked feeling of constraint and the heaviness that came over him that wasn't a part of the

life that he lived now. A life based on unsurpassed pleasure, beauty and freedom. A life he lived predominantly
in England, where he'd used a stellar investment in tech-
nology while attending Cambridge to purchase his first
bar and nightclub. He had 'the touch' some said, an innate
ability to tap into what his clientele wanted and to trans-
form any venue he took over into the hottest place in town.

Which often made *him* the hottest *property* in town,
pursued again and again by women looking to change his
mind about remaining single. Something he had no intention of doing. Ever. In his experience the novelty factor
rarely lasted beyond the bedroom and, even if it did, his
parents' tumultuous relationship had cured him of ever
thinking marriage was an institution he wanted to be part
of.

Much better to have fun while it lasted, and move on
before anyone got hurt. And if the tabloids wanted to paint
him as a playboy prince to get foot traffic on their web-
sites, that was hardly his problem. Something Jag didn't
understand.

But then Jag was still a little aggrieved about the whole
French heiress debacle at this event last year. Having
grown bored early on in the night, Rafe had taken her to
his hot tub upstairs, only to have her post photos of the
two of them to her social media account. If he'd known
Jag was in the middle of important negotiations with her
father at the time he would have insisted that she leave her
phone downstairs.

An oversight that had led him to promise his brother
that he would stay out of trouble this evening. Which
wasn't exactly fair because Rafe rarely went looking for
trouble any more. More often than not it found him.

As if on cue, he saw his sister making a beeline for him

as she wound her way through the throng of impeccably groomed guests at the ball.

'I take it the ostrich lost?' he teased, his eyes going to the brightly coloured feathers covering her skirt. 'Or do you have plans to return the outfit to the poor creature at the end of the night?'

'Laugh all you want,' Milena challenged with narrowed eyes. 'But I love the dress and every feather had already been shed before it was collected. Is that what you were grinning at before? Or was it something else? I swear you had that glint in your eye that said you were up to no good.'

'Just remembering a certain French heiress I met at about this time last year.'

'Oh, please.' Milena rolled her eyes. 'Don't let Jag hear you say the words "French" and "heiress" together in a sentence; he'll blow a gasket.'

'He needs to loosen up. He got the deal with her father through in the end so it was a win-win for both of us.'

'No thanks to you,' she retorted. 'When are you going to start dating women you respect *and* want to—'

'Don't say it.' Rafe shuddered. 'I like to imagine that you're still innocent of such matters. And anyway, I promised our esteemed brother that I'd be on my best behaviour tonight, so don't worry.'

He gave his sister his trademark grin, knowing that it wouldn't work one bit. She might be six years younger than his thirty years but she'd always had his measure.

'That only makes me worry more.' She groaned. 'And, speaking of Jag, you need to cut him some slack. He's got a lot on his plate right now.'

'Like?'

'The Berenian thing.'

'Still?' Rafe arched a brow. He knew Berenia was causing problems but he'd thought that would have died down by now. 'So he didn't marry their revered Princess last year. They need to move on and get over it.'

'There's more to it than that. Santara has advanced much further on the world stage than Berenia, which brings its own set of resentments.'

'Yes, but still their incompetence can hardly be our problem.'

'I don't know the ins and outs of it but… Oh, there's Jag, looking for us. I was supposed to find you so we can get the official photos out of the way.'

'Lead on,' Rafe said with amusement. He'd smile and play nice so his brother would have nothing to grumble about at the end of the night. Then tomorrow he'd fly home and resume his normal life, which wasn't dictated by pomp or protocol.

'Rafa.' Jag greeted him with a hint of stiffness. 'I wasn't sure you were going to make it this year.'

'Never miss it. Especially if there's a French heiress to be had.'

'Rafa!' Milena scolded under her breath. 'You promised.'

Rafe laughed. 'Don't worry. Jag knows I'm joking.'

'Jag hopes you're joking,' his brother muttered. 'And just because you made a career out of annoying our father don't feel that you have to carry the tradition on with me because I'm King.'

'Wouldn't dream of it.' Rafe grinned. 'I hear you're having some issues with the Berenians.'

'Don't mention that word. I swear they're the most stubborn people on earth.'

A photographer stopped in front of them. 'The lighting is probably better over by the far column, Your Majesty; do you mind moving in that direction?'

'Not at all,' Jag said, casting his eyes across the sea of

chattering guests until he spotted what he was looking for. He crooked his finger, a small smile playing at the edges of his mouth, softening his face in a way Rafe had rarely seen before. Following his line of sight, he watched as Jag's new wife made her way towards them. Clearly pregnant, in a slim-fitting gown, she looked beautiful and only had eyes for his brother.

When she reached his side, Rafe could have sworn the rest of the room dissolved for both of them. Bemused, he wondered what it felt like to want someone that much, and then decided he didn't want to know.

'Good evening, Your Majesty,' Rafe greeted his new Queen. 'You're looking as beautiful as ever.' He took her hand and raised it to his lips. 'Should you ever tire of my stiff-necked brother, you only have to—'

'Rafa—' Jag began warningly.

Queen Regan laughed softy and placed her hand on his brother's arm. 'Always the devil, Rafaele.' She smiled at him. 'It's a skill to make a pregnant woman blush. But where is your date tonight? I understand you're seeing a Spanish supermodel. Ella? Or Esme?'

'Estela,' Rafe corrected.

'My apologies.' She glanced around curiously. 'Did you bring her with you?'

'Unfortunately, we had a difference in priorities and parted ways.'

'And you're clearly crestfallen.' Regan arched a brow, a playful glow in her eyes. 'Do I want to know what those priorities were?'

'If you two are quite finished flirting,' Jag said with an edge of menace in his voice, 'the photographer is waiting.'

'Sorry.' Regan threaded her arm through his. 'But I'm a married woman now. I have to live vicariously and Rafaele always has such *interesting* stories.'

'I'll give you an interesting story later on,' Jag promised throatily. 'For now just smile and imagine it.'

'Whatever they have, I don't want it,' Rafe grouched, lining up on the other side of his sister.

'It's called love,' Milena said impishly. 'And I can't wait to experience it.'

'Just don't fall in love with anyone I haven't checked out first,' Rafe warned sternly.

'Oh, fiddle.' She waved him away. 'You and Jag are as bad as each other. You're more alike than you might think.'

She was wrong. It had always been easier to be the bad to Jag's good. But he didn't offer an objection. Instead he pasted a smile on his face and pinched his sister's side just as the photographer clicked the shutter. Milena kicked his ankle in return and it was their usual game on to see who could make the other break first.

Two hours later, bored to the bone, Rafe thought about heading to his hot tub—alone—when he saw her. A vision who appeared to be nude at first glance but who, unfortunately, wasn't. But she was breathtaking, with her dark hair, smooth caramel skin and elegant cameo-like profile. Her delicate features were complemented by slender curves and long legs.

They'd fit, he realised with a jolt, somehow already knowing just how good they would be together though he'd never even spoken to her. Instantly intrigued by the notion that he wanted to know the colour of her eyes and the taste of her lips under his. He wanted to feel her warm silken skin and feast his eyes on her sweet curves as he stripped that clever gown from her body with aching slowness for the very first time.

As if sensing the heat of his thoughts, she turned her head, her eyes instantly finding his.

She blinked, as if she felt the caress of the erotic images coursing through his brain, a flush touching her high cheekbones. Or was that just his imagination going overboard? It certainly couldn't be because of the fool standing in front of her. Count Kushnir wouldn't know what to do with a woman like that if he had a set of instructions and an accompanying magnifying glass.

Rafe let a slow grin curve the corners of his lips, noting the way her eyes widened with alarm as if she too already knew that they were destined to become lovers.

Because they would become lovers. Tonight, tomorrow night—for Rafe it was already a forgone conclusion. He only hoped she wasn't one of those women who liked to play hard to get, imagining that if he had to work for it he'd be more interested. He wouldn't. Because he couldn't be more interested in this woman if he tried.

CHAPTER TWO

ALEXA FELT PRINCE RAFAELE'S gaze on her as if it were a tractor beam.

This was it. The moment she'd been waiting for. The moment he'd notice her so that they would meet and she could introduce herself. Not that she'd probably need to do that because he would surely know who she was but still, it was the polite thing to do. She'd introduce herself, make small talk and…and…

'Choo-choo…choo-choo!'

'I'm sorry?' Forcing her attention back to the man in front of her, with a noble Russian lineage dating back before Peter the Great, she tried to smile. 'I don't think I heard you right?'

At least she hoped she hadn't. But no…there it was again. An obnoxious, high-pitched noise as he mimicked the sound his toy steam engine made as it trundled around an apparently life-sized track. It reminded her of the stories of sybaritic kings of old who set up lifelike warships in large lakes and watched them battle for supremacy. If she had thought this man might be a possible candidate for a fake engagement should Prince Rafaele turn her down, he'd just convinced her to look elsewhere. The only thing she could fake in this man's company was a smile. And even that was growing old.

'May I interrupt?' A smooth deep voice beside her thankfully broke off the man's description of yet another steam engine.

Expecting the voice to belong to Prince Rafaele, she breathed a heavy sigh of relief intermingled with disappointment when it wasn't. Immediately her eyes cut to the place she had last seen him but he wasn't there any more.

'Your Royal Highness?'

Somewhat perplexed that the Prince had simply walked away after staring at her so openly, Alexa smiled at the newcomer beside her. What had he asked her? To dance? 'Yes. Thank you.'

She didn't actually want to dance but maybe movement would help settle her suddenly jangled nerves.

It had been the look the Prince had given her. That all-encompassing male glance that had raked her from head to toe and then pierced her with heat. It had completely thrown her. Of course she'd known he was good-looking. The mouth-watering photos Nasrin had dredged up on the Internet were demonstration enough of that, but in the flesh... In the flesh he was something more. More charismatic. More powerful. More sensual. More *physical*.

Taller than those around him, he'd been wide-shouldered and lean-hipped, his body exuding the kind of animal grace that drew the eye of anyone in his vicinity and held it. His dark brown hair was cut in longer layers, framing his chiselled jaw and well-shaped lips to perfection.

In many ways he'd reminded her of King Jaeger but this man had a laconic, laidback sense to him that was powerfully sexy, and strangely she'd never once thought of the King as sexy.

Powerful, yes. Intimidating and regal, yes. But she'd never looked at him and felt her blood pump faster through her veins, as had happened from one long, wicked look from Prince Rafaele.

Feeling guilty that she was completely ignoring the man who was currently holding her at a respectful distance on the dance floor, she tried to dredge up something interesting to say to break the silence between them. God knew she had years of banal small talk rolling around inside her head but, for the life of her, she couldn't seem to recall any of it, her brain stuck on the strange lethargy that had entered her body at Prince Rafaele's heated stare.

'I hate to cut in, Lord Stanton, but you need to contact your office. Something about a paternity test being carried out with your name on it.'

'Pardon?' Her dance partner instantly dropped her hand and frowned at the man she'd been waiting all night to 'run into' with horror. 'That can't be true.'

Prince Rafaele gave an indolent shrug of one wide shoulder. 'Don't shoot the messenger.'

Alexa frowned as Lord Stanton mumbled an apology and carved a purposeful path through the crowded dance floor as if the devil was on his trail.

'Allow me,' the Prince said, taking her into his arms and holding her much closer than Lord Stanton had done.

It took her only a moment to realise that he'd done that deliberately, and that there was probably no paternity test in the works at all.

'Was any of that true?'

'Not a word.'

Alexa didn't know whether to laugh or frown at his candour. 'That wasn't very nice. I think you really scared poor Lord Stanton.'

'Only because it's happened to *poor* Lord Stanton before.'

'It has?' She blinked at him. 'How do you know that? Is he a friend of yours?'

'I know everything. But no, he isn't a friend. Not even close.'

'He's not going to be happy when he finds out you lied.'

'Probably not.' The Prince raised an eyebrow as if to say he couldn't care less, his gaze skimming her face. 'But first things first. That soft accent I can hear in your voice isn't French, is it?'

'No.'

'Good.' Before she could think too much about his question he manoeuvred her closer, distracting her. 'Now I can just enjoy how good you feel in my arms.'

Incredibly aware of the warm male chest mere inches from hers, Alexa's breath caught. One of his hard thighs was pressed ever so slightly between her legs, keeping her slightly off balance, so that she had to grip onto his hand to stay upright. Aware that she'd never felt such a powerful response to anyone like this before, she automatically drew back, her reaction causing a slow masculine grin to curve his lips. 'Too fast for you?'

'I...' Completely unprepared to be meeting him like this, let alone be plastered up against his hard body, Alexa frowned. 'Yes. I don't like being crowded.'

Truth be told, she wasn't used to being touched like this. Her father had never been overly tactile and, as her mother had died giving birth to her, she'd been raised by a procession of nannies, each one leaving before she or Sol could become attached to them. It had been her father's way of training any neediness out of them, his methods intended to instil in them both a sense of objectivity and distance befitting a monarch of their realm.

She still remembered the day her beloved Mrs Halstead had left. At five, Alexa had cried herself into a stupor, thus proving her father's point. After a while she had stopped crying when people left but, given the mistake she'd made with Stefano, the lesson in objectivity had taken much longer to master. And sometimes she worried that she still hadn't got it. Especially now, when she was struggling to remain objective in this man's arms.

'By all means I can do slow,' he said with a grin, his mesmerising eyes flicking over her with sensual intent.

Even though she had dressed to attract attention she was so unused to men flirting with her it took Alexa a moment to assimilate his meaning. When she did, heat curved up the side of her neck. She hadn't fully worked out what she was going to say to him when they finally met so she found herself at a loss for words. It was only her love for her country, and a desire to placate her father, that had her still considering going ahead with her plan.

Because ordinarily she wouldn't go near a man like the Prince. And not just because of his bad boy reputation but because he was too big and too male—his level of testosterone swamping her and making her way too aware of him. It was like being confronted by an enormous, sated wolf; even though you knew it was well fed you still couldn't relax in its presence for fear that it might pounce just for the fun of it.

The orchestra music changed tempo and she realised that the Prince danced very well, his movements fluid and graceful as he moved her in time with the beat. Wondering how to gain control of the situation and suggest a place for them to sit down and talk, she was completely unprepared for his enticing all-male scent to swamp her as he leaned in closer.

'You're exceptionally beautiful,' he murmured, bringing her left hand up to his lips in one smooth move, smiling against her fingertips. 'And unmarried. Two of my favourite attributes in a woman.'

His earlier question about her being French came back to her and she pulled back to stare up at him.

Did he not know who she was?

She'd received so many sympathetic glances during the night from those who knew her to be the jilted Princess of Berenia that her teeth had wanted to grind together.

For him not to recognise her... It didn't seem possible but...perhaps it was. After all, he'd been off doing his own thing for a decade now, where her life had remained incredibly small by comparison. A bolt of inspiration shot through her. If he didn't know who she was it would give her a chance to find out how amenable he would be to her plan without having to embarrass herself by asking outright.

His eyes watched her, confident and direct. Sapphire blue surrounded by inky black lashes, they drew her in with the promise of delights she had probably never even dreamed of, drew her in as if he could read every one of her secret wishes and desires and had the power to answer them all. The notion was both terrifying and utterly irresistible.

The prince's heavy-lidded gaze held an amused glint as if he knew exactly how he was affecting her. Only she didn't plan to become one of his worshippers so it was best to set the scene early.

'Are you always this direct?' she asked, meeting fire with fire.

'I'm not one to waste time on trivialities.' His fingers brushed the inside of her wrist, sending an unexpected trail of goosebumps along her arm. She fought off another tremor as she thought about what those fingers would feel like stroking other, more intimate, parts of her body. 'State what you want and go after it has always been my motto.'

She didn't doubt it.

But ever since her brother had died her life had been mapped out for her and stripped of any real choice so she rarely, if ever, stated what she wanted, or went after it.

He swung her in a tight circle, the hand at the base of her spine covering the small of her back. 'It hasn't failed me yet.' The smile he gave her was one hundred per cent lupine in nature. 'I hope it's not about to.'

'Are you propositioning me?'

The words were out before she could stop them and she only just managed to stop herself from cringing. No doubt none of the sophisticated beauties he was frequently photographed with would need to ask such a gauche question.

Even white teeth were revealed by a frankly amused smile. 'I do believe I am.'

'But you don't even know me.'

'I don't need to know you to know that I want you.' His tone lowered to a sexual purr. 'But if names make you feel more at ease I am Prince Rafaele al-Hadrid. Rafe to my intimates, Rafa to my family.'

'I know who you are,' she said, blinking hard to defuse the sensual spell he was effortlessly weaving around her. 'And I also know of your reputation.'

His smile widened. 'Which one?'

Not sure how to handle the fact that he seemed completely unperturbed by her revelation, Alexa pushed on with her plan to gain information about him. 'The one that says that you're not marriage material.'

'Very true,' he drawled. 'I am good at many things but being a husband would not be one of them. And I believe in playing to my strengths.'

So did she. 'Why wouldn't you be a good husband?'

'According to many of the women I've seen, I'm emotionally stunted, closed off from genuine affection, afraid of true intimacy and utterly selfish.' His eyes twinkled down at her with amusement. 'I did take exception to the "closed off from genuine affection" comment as I happen to think I'm very affectionate when the mood strikes.'

'I'm sure she was way off base.' Alexa laughed despite herself.

'I'm glad you agree.' He grinned charmingly. 'But you haven't introduced yourself,' he reminded her softly.

'No, I haven't.'

His dark brow arched with quicksilver interest. 'And you're not going to,' he surmised accurately. 'Do you want me to guess?' His gaze roamed her face, heating her up as it went. 'You do seem vaguely familiar. Should I know you?'

'I would say so.'

'Have we ever—'

'No.' She stumbled as his meaning became clear, causing him to bring her into direct contact with his warm body again. Heat that had been simmering away inside her exploded low in her pelvis.

Sensual amusement curved his lips as if he had her right where he wanted her.

Danger, her brain signalled once more, only stronger this time, with the added instruction to retreat. Only she couldn't because she couldn't remember why she should. Not with those intense blue eyes lingering on her lips and turning her mouth so dry she had to fight not to moisten it. Her heart felt like a trapped bird trying to break out of its cage, her whole body assailed with a kind of sweet lethargy she'd never felt before.

The drawn-out notes from a violin signalled the end of the musical score they'd been dancing to, and then someone on the end of a microphone announced that the silent auction was about to take place.

Clusters of murmuring guests started making their way

towards one of the anterooms, and Alexa was startled to find that she hadn't moved an inch out of the Prince's arms. Scrambling to get her brain back on line, it took her a moment to realise that he had taken her hand and was leading her in the opposite direction to everyone else.

'Where are you taking me?' She pulled up, digging her spindly heels into the marble floor and gaining no traction at all.

'Somewhere we can talk.' The Prince's enigmatic gaze swept her from head to toe. 'I made a promise that I wouldn't cause any scandals this evening and I'm very close to breaking it.'

He steered her through a set of open doors and along a wide corridor before she had the wherewithal to stop him once more. 'Wait.'

Instantly coming to a halt, he looked back at her.

Alexa blinked as she tried to regulate her thoughts—and her breathing. At some point she would need to get him alone to go over her proposition with him but, with her body sending a whole host of mixed messages to her brain, she knew she wasn't ready for that now. Plus, he wasn't taking her anywhere for them to talk. She might be relatively inexperienced when it came to men, but she already knew that they could be unscrupulous when it came to getting what they wanted.

He looked down at her, amusement lighting his eyes as she gently tugged her hand free of his.

'I'm not going to kiss you.' The bold statement slipped out before it had fully formed in her mind and she knew she'd never felt as tempted to do exactly what she said she wouldn't in her life before.

His sinful lips curved into that devilish smile and a blush stained her cheeks. 'You don't like kissing?'

Not particularly, but that wasn't the point, was it? 'I don't kiss strangers.'

'But I'm not the stranger here; you are,' he pointed out. 'And fortunately I have no such reservations.'

His tone was teasing but she sensed his hunger in the coiled strength of his body and the heat that radiated from every pore. The earlier image of a wolf about to pounce returned. This time it was definitely hungry and she was in its crosshairs. Rather than scare her as it probably should, it sent another thrill of sensation down her spine. She shuddered with unexpected anticipation and of course he noticed, his blue eyes darkening, his nostrils flaring slightly with his next breath.

Something exciting and wickedly enticing wound between them.

'Come with me,' he invited huskily. 'I get the impression that your life could do with a little excitement in it.'

She wanted to deny it but his assessment was so accurate she couldn't. Every hour of her day was usually accounted for with paperwork or meetings and she rarely took time out to just have fun. A roar of laughter from nearby guests broke into her reverie as if to drive the point home.

Those serious doubts she'd had about going ahead with her plan returned tenfold.

Prince Rafaele was much more lethally male and charismatic than she had anticipated, and the blatantly sexual way he looked at her awoke every one of her senses. She hadn't expected him to have such an uncontrollable edge beneath the civility of his custom-made tuxedo but it was there—primal and dangerous and totally untameable.

'Come,' he coaxed once more, his hand raised towards her. 'Take my hand.'

It was more command than invitation, the silken gravel

of his tone making her forget that her future was on the line this weekend. Making her forget how much she had at stake: the ability to fulfil her royal duty to Berenia *her* way.

Against all rational thought, Alexa gave into temptation and placed her hand in his, allowing him to lead her through a solid door and into a beautiful, softly lit reading room. Glancing around, she noted that it was empty, the soft furnishings and gauzy curtains in the windows giving the room an odd sense of intimacy that was heightened when she heard the door click closed behind her.

'I'm not sure this is wise,' she said, knowing by the wild hammering of her heart that it definitely wasn't.

He grinned with mischievous intent. 'Probably not.'

Completely absorbed by the animal grace of his stride as he pushed away from the door and came towards her, Alexa was unprepared for him to invade her personal space and bumped the low table behind her as she unconsciously retreated.

Fortunately, he caught her around the waist, his fingertips spanning her hipbones with blatant possession.

'Your Highness!' Alexa exclaimed on a breathless rush, her mind as unbalanced as her body. 'I told you I'm not—'

'Kissing me. I know.' His head lowered to hers, the warmth of his lips ghosting across the line of her jaw as he inhaled her scent deep into his lungs.

A shiver of awareness bolted down Alexa's spine, turning her knees to water. Her hands flattened against his hard chest as if to hold herself steady, her senses logging the hard heat of his body and the strong beat of his heart through the thick fabric of his jacket.

Despite her four-inch heels, their height difference put her only at eye level with his chiselled mouth and she couldn't look away, her fingers curling of their own accord into his dinner jacket.

The prince's hands firmed on her hips. 'You've got exactly three seconds to step out of my arms before I kiss you properly.'

His tone was low and husky with need and Alexa flushed as an answering need flooded her lower body with silken heat. Completely out of her depth, her knees almost too weak to hold her upright, she leant against him in a move that perfectly signalled her desires to a man well versed in reading the play.

'I'm pretty sure that's five,' he murmured, his head bending as his mouth found hers. This kiss was firm, warm, his lips capturing hers with consummate skill and drawing a response from her she didn't even know she had in her to give.

When she didn't resist a soft groan left his mouth and one of his hands rose to cup the nape of her neck, his body moulding to hers as he took control of her very will.

Alexa knew she shouldn't be doing this but she couldn't seem to organise her thoughts when the desire to taste him was so strong. The prince's heat and scent surrounded her and soaked into her, his mouth driving out any thought of resisting.

'That's it, sweetheart,' he whispered, 'open for me.'

Having never been kissed with such carnal expertise, Alexa felt a rush of burning heat as his tongue entered her mouth and licked at her own. The unexpected eroticism of the move made her hands grip his shoulders, her body arching towards his, seeking more. Craving more.

The sensations were so wickedly enticing that when his fingers curved around one of her breasts she moaned, no longer concerned with what she was here to do. This was all that mattered. This man's mouth fused with hers, his hands caressing her all over and making her burn.

She slid her fingers into his hair, tugging him closer,

and he groaned again, his hands moving lower to cup her bottom and bring her in closer against his body, his callused palms snagging on the tiny crystals covering her dress.

'You taste like honey and nectar,' he murmured, his lips trailing a heated line along her jaw towards her ear.

'You taste like heat and mint,' she panted, her neck arching to accommodate his lips, her nipples painfully tight against the fabric of her dress.

He laughed huskily as if she delighted him. It was quite the aphrodisiac after her previous sexual encounter had obliterated her burgeoning self-confidence.

'Come upstairs with me.' The Prince's kisses continued down her neck and she felt him shudder as he gently bit down on the tendons that joined her shoulder. 'I can't take you here; we'll get caught.'

Alexa didn't know which part of that statement permeated her stunned senses more, but suddenly her hands were firm on the hard balls of his biceps as she pushed him back. Memories of her teenage mistake tumbled into the space between them, tripping up her thoughts as she fought to draw oxygen into her lungs and clear the haze from her brain. 'We can't... I'm not... Let me go!'

As soon as the words were out he released her, his chest heaving like bellows as his breath rasped in and out of his lungs.

His dark hair was in disarray around his shoulders and she realised with a mortified groan that her fingers must have done that.

'What's wrong?'

'What's wrong?' Her eyes widened at his ridiculous question. 'We nearly... I just... I didn't come in here for that.'

Struggling to even out his breathing as much as she

was, the Prince's brows drew together. 'Why did you come in here then?'

Still experiencing the drugging after-effects of being in his arms, Alexa blurted out the first thing that came into her head. 'I came in here to ask you to marry me.'

CHAPTER THREE

'You should have gone with that as your opening line, sweetheart,' Prince Rafaele drawled. 'It would have smothered the chemistry between us faster than a Santarian sandstorm.'

Unsure how to handle him as well as her rioting emotions, Alexa frowned. 'I didn't expect you to pounce on me as soon as we got here.'

'Pounce?' He gave an amused look. 'I gave you a chance to pull back.'

'Three seconds?'

His grin deepened. 'It ended up being five.'

'You don't even know my name,' she said, flabbergasted that he could so quickly switch from arousal to amusement when she was still struggling for composure.

'I've never found that to be all that important when I want a woman.'

Well, that stung. No woman wanted to be just another notch on a man's bedpost. But what had she expected? This was the exalted Rebel Prince who had attempted to seduce her. Attempted and nearly succeeded! 'Why?' she felt compelled to ask. 'Because you don't plan on seeing the woman again?' she challenged.

'Now that depends on the night. And the woman.' His eyes narrowed on her face as if he was trying to work

something out. 'So who are you? Because I have to admit
you're damned familiar, although I know I've never
touched you before.'

She didn't know whether to be flattered by that statement or not and went with not. 'My name is Alexa, Crown
Princess of the House of Berenia.' She gave her tone just
the right amount of haughtiness to signal her displeasure
with him, and was pleased when his eyes widened.

He raked a hand through his hair. 'You might have mentioned that sooner as well.'

'I did plan to when we got inside the room, but you
kissed me before I could come out with it.'

Rafe's gaze dropped to her lips and he cursed under his
breath. She was right. He'd never acted on his attraction
for a woman faster. His only excuse being that he'd felt
her hunger run as deep as his own and he'd been unable to
resist testing that hunger when they were alone. And he'd
been right. She'd gone off like a firecracker in his arms.
Another few minutes and they both would have been naked
and horizontal.

Thank God he'd had enough sense to suggest they go
to his room, and the restraint to release her when she'd
asked. But he hadn't wanted to. The inferno that she had
lit inside him had been ready to explode. It still was, but
this time partly with recrimination. He should probably
apologise for pouncing on her as she had accused him of
doing. It wasn't his usual style, which leant itself to more
finesse and a small measure of self-control!

And she was his brother's cast-off, dammit, the daughter of the man who was currently making his brother's life
hell. Jag would just love it if he had witnessed this near
blunder. It had been one thing to piss his father off deliberately, but he'd never do that to his brother.

'Well, I'm not kissing you now, Princess, so I suggest we leave and forget this ever happened.'

If he could. He had a feeling he'd be dreaming about the taste of her mouth and those soft kittenish sounds she'd made as he'd cupped her bottom in his hands for a few nights yet. Even now he wanted to reach for her again.

'But I was serious about what I said before.' She drew in a long breath, her lovely breasts straining against the fabric of her gown. 'And I'd really like to make a time to speak with you about it.'

Rafe sent his mind back and focused on what she'd said that had halted him in his tracks. 'Marriage?'

'Well, engaged more than married.'

He shook his head gently, unable to believe that she was actually serious. 'I don't do marriage. You'll have to find someone else to fulfil that fantasy.'

'I know you don't do marriage. That's the point. I don't either.'

He frowned at her earnest expression. She was either crazy or... 'How much have you had to drink, Princess, because you're not making any sense?'

'I've hardly had anything to drink,' she retorted as if he'd insulted her. 'I'm perfectly sober.'

'Then that response before was all you?' He gave her a lazy smile as her cheeks coloured. 'Good to know.'

'I'd rather not talk about that.' Her lips pinched together. 'And, given what just happened, now probably isn't the best time to discuss my proposal. Could we meet tomorrow?'

'Tomorrow isn't going to change my mind. Neither will the day after.'

'Look...' she held her hands up as if to placate him '... I'm not talking about a real marriage. I'm talking about a temporary engagement that works for us both. We won't even have to spend that much time together. We just need to put out a joint statement, go to a couple of events together and break up amicably at a time that suits us both.'

'As far as proposals go, this one is definitely novel, but marriage—sorry, *engagement*—doesn't work for me at all. Temporary or not.'

'I know.' She gave a heavy sigh, tucking a strand of thick silky hair that had come loose back behind her ear. She looked gloriously mussed from where his hands had been and that reminded him of how much he'd like to put them there again. Unwind all that magnificent hair and find out how long it was.

As if they had a will of their own, his eyes followed her as she paced the mahogany-decked reading room, her gown hugging her heavenly curves as she moved. 'That's why I chose you.'

'Chose me?' He blinked to get his brain back on line.

'Yes,' she said with the patience of a mother speaking to a recalcitrant child. 'I need to get married—or at least engaged—and you have all the attributes I want in a fiancé.'

Curious, Rafe found himself extending the conversation, if only for the amusement factor. 'Such as?'

'You follow your own rules, you're completely disinterested in marriage, and your values in life are questionable.'

'Questionable?'

'According to everything that's said about you, you're quite the hedonist.'

Rafe leant against the back of a sofa. 'Really?'

'I'm paraphrasing. But the point is we're completely incompatible so it won't surprise anyone when we don't go through with the marriage, and no one will be blamed for it not working out.' Unlike when his brother had called off their engagement and everyone had thought it was her fault. That she hadn't been woman enough for the King of Santara. 'It will just seem obvious.'

'I have to confess,' Rafe drawled, 'I've never had those reasons put forward by a woman wanting me to put a ring on her finger before. Usually it's more along the lines of: *You're rich, powerful and a prince.*'

'Oh, the prince part is important to me too. At least that you're from Santara.' She frowned as she perched on the edge of the sofa. 'Women actually say that to you?'

'I was paraphrasing.' His eyes glinted mockingly. 'So why is my being a Santarian prince important to you? I would have thought it was the last thing you would want.'

'My father is convinced that seeing me happily settled will ease the current tension between Santara and Berenia and help our people move forward from your brother breaking our betrothal. He gave me six months to find someone, but I didn't realise he was serious. Now he's planning to take matters into his own hands and arrange a marriage that I don't want.'

'Ah, I'm beginning to see the picture.'

She let out a slow breath, her narrow shoulders slumping slightly forward. 'When my father is like this he's immovable, and I need more time.'

'Hmm…' Feeling a little sorry for her, Rafe offered up the only solution he could think of. 'You know you could always say no.'

'No isn't a word my father understands.'

'Is doormat a word *you* understand?'

Her eyes flashed up at him like deep pools of jade backlit by fire. 'Are you implying that I'm a doormat?'

Rafe shrugged, enjoying her display of defiance. 'If the shoe fits.'

'The shoe does not fit,' she said a little too vehemently. 'The fact is my father has been through a lot in recent years and I'm not going to add to his problems. And this is partly your brother's fault. If he had gone ahead with our marriage as he had agreed to do then none of this would be an issue right now.'

'But nor would you have got to kiss me quite so passionately, so there is that.'

Her feathers well and truly ruffled, the Princess pushed to her feet. 'You either have a colossal ego or you're making fun of me.'

'Let's go with the ego theory. A lot less volatile.' Rafe crossed to the booze cabinet between two arched bookcases and poured himself a whisky. 'Drink?' he asked, holding the crystal decanter up for her to see.

She set her top teeth into her plush bottom lip, reminding him of how exquisite her mouth had felt under his, and surprised him with a terse nod.

'Dutiful does not equal doormat, you know.' She moved towards him, careful not to touch his fingers as she took the glass. He gave her a small smile that said he knew exactly how nervous he made her and watched her chin come up in response. 'Not that I expect you to understand that.'

'I understand it,' he said curtly. 'I just don't adhere to it.'

'Well, you're lucky. I don't have that choice.'

Rafe clinked the ice in his glass, wondering what it was about her he found so enthralling. Because he did find her enthralling—from the way she moved to the feminine lilt in her voice, and definitely in the sexy lines of her body. He suspected that she took life far too seriously, and for some reason he wanted to change that.

'You're an intelligent, beautiful woman,' he began, watching her closely. 'And a future queen. How hard can it be to find a husband?'

'It's not hard at all.' She sighed. 'But finding the *right* husband is.'

'Do I even want to know what the right husband looks like?'

'Someone kind, compassionate, caring.' She took a delicate sip of his brother's hundred-year-old Scotch, shuddering delicately as it hit the back of her throat. 'Someone I can respect and who will put Berenia first. Someone who has a similar outlook to me.'

'Not looking for someone with a sense of humour?' he enquired lightly.

Alexa frowned. 'That would go under "similar outlook to me".'

'So none then.' He grinned as her eyes widened. 'What about love?'

'I have a sense of humour, thank you very much,' she defended hotly. 'And love is not essential.'

Rafe's eyes widened at that. 'I think you're the first woman I've ever heard admit that.'

'Love complicates things and who even knows if it exists? I think it's made up by Hollywood executives and songwriters trying to make money.'

'And I thought I was cynical.' Her brow furrowed and his grin widened. 'That was a compliment, by the way. But what about passion? Surely that's on your list.'

She wrinkled her nose. 'Not essential either. I'm not the most passionate person on the planet, and respect far outweighs passion.'

Contemplating what had put her off passion when his body still throbbed at the memory of her mouth opening under his, Rafe gave her a smile that was pure sex. 'You felt pretty passionate to me before.'

She moved to sit again on the sofa, unable to meet his gaze. 'That wasn't me. I don't know who that person was.'

'Whoever she was, she was intoxicating.'

She wrinkled her nose. 'So will you consider it? I'm not sure how long I have before my father takes the decision completely out of my hands. And, frankly, I'm desperate.'

'I can see that.' He was actually sorry he had to turn her offer down. If life hadn't taught him that he needed to steer clear of matrimonial entanglements at all costs he might even have considered it. But marriage had the potential to inflict pain on the unwary and the innocent. Why would any man deliberately buy into that? Temporary or not. 'Sorry, Princess, but I'm not that desperate.'

'You won't even consider it to help improve relations between our nations?'

Rafe blinked away the dark memories of his past and found himself pinned by a pair of gorgeous green eyes that, if he wasn't careful, had the potential to suck him in deep and never let him go. 'See, the problem with that part of your argument is that I don't care about the issues between Santara and Berenia.'

She blinked as if he'd just said *Down with world peace*. 'But how can you not?'

'I live in London and have done for a decade. I have as little to do with Santara as I can.'

'Then what about to improve your reputation? Being engaged to me would stop some of the gossip. For a while at least.'

Princess Alexa, he realised, was a real fighter. He liked that. Not enough to agree with her hare-brained scheme, but enough to find that he was enjoying her company. A lot.

'Who said I wanted the gossip to stop?'

'But surely some of the things written about you must bother you.'

'Not particularly.'

'Why is that?' Her brow pleated as if his attitude was something she couldn't contemplate. 'Because it's all true?'

Rafe wondered which particular piece of gossip had widened her eyes to the size of dinner plates. Hardly any of it was true but denying the many claims made about him would only give them energy so he rarely bothered. Still, he knew that Alexa didn't think much of his supposedly 'hedonistic' lifestyle and he couldn't help teasing her a little. 'Only the really bad ones.'

Watching the wings of colour heat her cheeks almost made him want to rescind his words so that she'd think better of him. Then he wondered why he cared and remained silent. He didn't like that he'd already delayed this conversation for the pure pleasure of listening to her speak. Adding to his uncharacteristic behaviour would only make things worse.

'So your answer is no?'

'My answer is no.'

She blew out a breath and set her glass on the table abutting the sofa. 'Then there's nothing more to say.'

There was plenty more to say, starting with enquiring which room she had been allocated so they could revisit that kiss, the sensations of which were still echoing inside his veins. But instead he said, 'What are you going to do now?'

She raised her chin and gave him a look he imagined she gave international dignitaries she had no further use for. 'Find someone else, of course.'

Find someone else? Rafe scowled at his fogged-up reflection as he stepped from the shower the following morning. *Just how many men did she plan to approach with her absurd proposal? And, more importantly, had she found someone who had taken her up on her offer last night?*

He didn't want that question running through his head but he was unable to banish it. After she had walked away from him he'd spent another hour at the party looking for her, to no avail. Presumably she'd gone to bed, so he had done the same, thinking about her all night as he'd known he would.

Even though he had no intention of countenancing her proposal himself, he knew that someone would eventually agree to it. What sane man wouldn't? With that face and body…

Rafe dropped his towel on the floor and padded back to his room to dress. *He'd* turned her down, hadn't he, and he was a sane man.

Yes, but he was sane and *smart*. Smart enough to know that her problems were none of his business and that he should let it go.

And he would. As of now.

His jet was waiting to fly him back to London and he planned to stop downstairs long enough to grab an espresso, wish his sister-in-law well in her pregnancy and tell his siblings he'd see them some time in the future.

What he wouldn't do was think about the beguiling Alexa any more today.

Pleased to be back on track, he pulled a clean shirt over his head, stepped into his jeans and shoved his feet into his boots.

Women just shouldn't go around proposing to men who were basically strangers and expect that it would all work out exactly as they wanted it to. Especially not future queens who looked like cover girls. Alexa was asking for trouble.

Trouble that had nothing to do with him.

And why was she back in his head again? So she'd surprised him when so few people did any more—so what? At the end of the day she was just a beautiful woman he'd wanted to take to bed. And she'd wanted to be there too. The way she'd caught fire in his arms…her response to his touch… Grinding his teeth, he zipped his overnight bag closed. What she'd done was drive all rational thought from his head, and kept him up way too long last night.

But it wasn't just the chemistry that had kept him awake. It was the puzzle she represented. She'd gone up like a flame in his arms but then claimed that she didn't have a passionate nature, dismissing the desire between them as an anomaly. And what about her belief that love might not exist? Presumably something, or someone, had put that in her head and he'd like to know who or what. Not that he disagreed with her. He didn't. He didn't believe in love either, but something about the way she'd said it made him think that she was either lying to him, or lying to herself. And yet she'd seemed so honest...so sincere...

Scowling at the procession of questions that wouldn't say die, Rafe grabbed his phone. Time to push Princess Alexa from his mind and think about something else. Because thinking about her made no sense. She wasn't someone he planned to pursue—not with marriage on her mind—and added to that she was his brother's ex, for God's sake.

Assailed by a sudden wave of jealousy he'd never before felt for his brother, Rafe nearly put a hole in his pocket shoving his phone into it. He didn't share his women. Ever.

And since when is a woman yours after one kiss?

Leaving that ridiculous question unanswered, he slammed out of his room and made his way to breakfast. He needed coffee before his mood deteriorated any further.

Refusing to wonder if he'd meet up with the beguiling Alexa, he heard a message arrive on his phone and homed in on it like a drowning man reaching for a life vest. Unfortunately, it was only a stock commodity update and he was in the process of closing it when he nearly barrelled into Jag as he rounded the corner of his private hallway.

Instantly alerted by his brother's taut, exhausted expression, Rafe frowned. 'What is it? Is there something wrong with Regan?'

Rafe might not have much to do with his brother any more but he could still read him and he couldn't think of anything else that might put that ragged look on his brother's face other than his wife, or all-out war.

'No, Regan's fine. I've just come from a meeting with King Ronan and Princess Alexa.'

Rafe felt himself instantly tense. 'They haven't declared war, have they?'

'Not yet.' Jag's scowl deepened. 'But last night a fire-bomb was thrown into a building site near the border in a show of protest at King Ronan and Princess Alexa attending the charity ball last night. Two of our workers were injured.'

'That's insane,' Rafe growled. 'Why did the King even attend if things are that volatile?'

'We believed it would be a display of unity between us but the Berenians didn't take it that way. They see my slight of their Princess as the highest insult.' He smiled faintly. 'Sorry to burden you with my problems. It was nice seeing you mucking around with Milena. It's a pity we don't see each other more often. I know Regan would like it if we did. I would too.'

Rafe swallowed the lump that suddenly lodged in his throat. He loved his siblings but he wasn't like either of them; he was a loner. He didn't require the same level of closeness, or connection, that drove others to forge unbreakable bonds. He didn't need someone, or something, special and neither Jag nor Milena understood that about him.

'Let's focus on one thing at a time. What can I do to help sort out the Berenia thing?'

Alexa's proposal of the previous night came into his head and he instantly shelved it. Marriage—or becoming engaged—was not the answer here.

'I thought you needed to head back to London?'

'I do. But if there's something I can assist you with while I'm here then I will. I'm not so obtuse that I can't see how much you have on your plate right now.' Not that he expected that Jag would need him. Their father never had. The important issues he'd gone to Jag for counsel. Rafe had been relegated to the lesser duties of opening flower shows or attending state dinners where he was expected to be on his best behaviour to prove what a great parent and leader his father was. Rafe was pretty sure they hadn't fooled anyone on that score.

'I appreciate the offer but, as I said, I've just had a meeting with King Ronan and Princess Alexa. We've come up with a diplomatic response to ease the tension.'

Rafe had a feeling he wasn't going to like the response. 'What was decided?'

'You really want to know?'

Yes, for once he really did.

'Why not? I'm here and I am still a Santarian.'

'Princess Alexa has agreed to a union with Lord Alec Richton of Urbana. I'm not sure when the wedding will take place, but the plan is for Lord Richton to fly into Berenia later in the week for a formal announcement.'

Rafe's whole body went still. 'You've got to be kidding me?'

'No, why would I do that?'

'Because it's barbaric and I can't believe you'd allow Alexa to be bandied around like a box of chocolates everyone can take a pick at.'

Jag frowned at his harsh tone. 'That's hardly what's happening here.'

'Isn't it?' Rafe felt unreasonably livid. 'You were betrothed to her.'

'When King Ronan approached me early last year I said I'd consider the idea,' Jag said evenly. 'It was never a done deal, and it should not have been made public.'

'So now Richton gets a go at her?' Rafe swore under his breath. 'What if he pulls out? Do you and Ronan have someone else up your sleeve for her?'

Jag's gaze sharpened. 'Someone else...?' His tone turned thoughtful. 'That's the kind of question a jealous lover might ask.'

'Hardly.' Unable to remain still under his brother's perceptive gaze, Rafe paced the floor.

'Richton won't pull out,' Jag said. 'Apparently he's been in talks with King Ronan for some months about a union, but regardless, the Princess is an incredibly lovely and intelligent woman. Most men would jump at the chance to marry her.'

Rafe knew how lovely she was, and having his brother notice only made his aggravation deepen. 'But what about what she wants?'

Jag sighed. 'I really don't understand what's got you so het-up about this but she does want it. We all want to end the hostilities between Berenia and Santara so we can move forward. If Alexa's marriage is able to promote peace in the minds of the Berenians, then I'm all for it.' He frowned as Rafe continued to pace. 'Come on, Rafa. You know that arranged marriages have been happening here for centuries. They've worked out in the past, and they'll work for a while to come yet.'

Too agitated to argue with his brother any further, Rafe headed for the door. 'We'll see,' he said, slamming it closed behind him.

* * *

He found Alexa in the breakfast room, speaking to another of the guests who had stayed overnight at the palace.

The smell of coffee made his saliva glands go into overdrive but he bypassed the silver pot on the sideboard and headed straight for Alexa.

As he neared he realised she was speaking to Lord Graham, the son of an English earl. Had he been another one of her candidates?

Not that it mattered any more.

'Princess Alexa?' He stopped beside her, completely ignoring Lord Graham. 'We need to talk.'

Clearly startled by his abrupt tone, her green eyes widened. 'Your Highness?'

'I told you last night, it's Rafe. I rarely use my title.'

'Prince Rafaele…' Lord Graham frowned at him. 'Princess Alexa and I are in the middle of—'

'Nothing.' Rafe turned his most cutting gaze on Graham. He knew he could be intimidating; he owned nightclubs and had been called upon to throw more than one drunken patron out onto the pavement, so he wasn't surprised when the other man's eyes flickered warily. 'The Princess and I have…unfinished business to settle.'

Not at all as intimidated by him as Graham, Alexa frowned. 'What unfinished business?'

Unprepared to stand around explaining himself in the middle of a room full of people, Rafe raised a brow. 'Have you forgotten the proposal you made last night? Perhaps you were drunk after all.'

'I was not!'

'Then you haven't forgotten.' He cut his gaze back to Graham, who had foolishly remained rooted to the spot. 'And unless you want Lord Graham here to be privy to our chat I suggest we take this somewhere private.'

Clearly unimpressed with his high-handed tactics, Alexa's mouth tightened. 'Fine. Please accept my apologies, Lord Graham. Prince Rafaele obviously has a bee in his bonnet about something.'

A bee in his bonnet?

Rafe shook his head and reached for her elbow. 'You don't have to be nice to everyone, you know. Graham will survive without your company for a while.'

Rafe directed Alexa through a nearby door to a small private terrace, which was thankfully empty.

'You need to stop doing that,' she complained, glaring up at him. 'I am not a horse to be led around at will.'

She brushed past him as she moved out of the direct line of the sun and the subtle scent of her perfume drew his muscles tight.

Irritated that he was affected by a woman who wasn't even trying to win his favour, Rafe met her icy stare with one of his own. 'All evidence to the contrary.'

'What does that mean?'

'It means I've just spoken with my brother, who informed me about your impending nuptials with Lord Richton.'

'He had no right to do that.'

'Why not? He didn't reveal anything I wouldn't know in a week or two anyway.'

'Then you also know why we reached the decision.'

'Because a group of hot-headed Berenians went about a hundred steps too far? Yes, I heard. Did you ever think of just calling in the army for protection?'

'Oh, that would really work,' she scoffed. 'Make a show of aggression and give the BLF even more of an excuse to start a war. Maybe you could lend us a few of the bouncers who work the doors at your nightclubs for extra muscle.'

'It seems a damn sight better than marrying someone to reach an outcome it might not even achieve.'

Her eyes narrowed at his disparaging comment. 'Diplomacy is always better than might.'

Not in his view. 'I take it this marriage isn't of the fake variety,' he said, an edge in his voice he was struggling to control.

'No.' She paused, as if what she was about to say was distasteful, staring out over the expanse of green lawn surrounded by potted roses and gardenia bushes. 'It won't be fake.'

Silent fury made his voice gruff. 'Is that what you want? To marry Richton?'

She gave him a fulminating look. 'You know it isn't.'

'But you'll do it anyway.'

'If my country needs me to do it.' Her chin lifted, as if daring him to contradict her. 'Then yes, I'll do it.'

'The dutiful little mouse.'

Jade fire flashed from her eyes at his mocking tone but what did she expect, that he'd ignore the obvious?

'I am no more a mouse than a doormat,' she said icily.

'You're doing something you don't want to do. I'd say that makes you one or the other.'

'Sometimes sacrifices have to be made,' she said with regal fortitude. 'Why do you care?'

'I don't like injustice. And I know how it feels to be trapped by circumstance.' He knew how it felt to be bullied into doing something you didn't want to do. His father had made an art form out of it, and it seemed her father was doing the same to her. 'It's why I left Santara.'

'So you're trying to help me? Very chivalrous, Prince Rafaele,' she mocked softly. 'But I don't have the luxury of choice. I have to marry at some point.' She swallowed heavily and turned her gaze out over the elaborate garden once more. 'It might as well be Lord Richton.'

Watching how controlled and closed-up she was only made Rafe's temper hit a new high. 'Richton might seem like an upstanding citizen, but word is that he has a dark side. One you don't want to meet.'

'How would you know that?'

'Because he's been blacklisted from at least seven clubs that I'm aware of, including mine.'

A grimace crossed her face as she shook her head. 'I'd prefer not to know that.'

'Dammit, Alexa. That's not even the point here.' He stepped closer, deliberately crowding her. 'Stop being a martyr.'

'My, you have a lot of names for me, don't you?' she mocked, her eyes cool enough to freeze lava.

Yes, he did have a lot of names for her, utterly beautiful being one of them.

'My brother died three years ago,' she said, a note of sadness replacing the iciness of moments ago, 'leaving all of us utterly devastated and me the only heir to the throne. When you add in the problems with Santara, combined with the corruption my father has just weeded out of our government, that has set back our modernisation plans and given the BLF even more to gripe about, you can see that something has to be done. And quickly.'

'I'm sorry you lost your brother, and I'm sorry you're facing political challenges, but that doesn't mean you just give up.'

'I'm not a quitter!' she denied hotly. 'I'm not giving up. I'm giving in. There's a difference.'

'I don't see that.'

'You don't have to. And I'm sorry if asking you to marry me last night made you think that you have the right to question me. In hindsight, the whole fake engagement idea was a mistake. It probably wouldn't have worked anyway. I was desperate for an alternative but now I don't need one. If by marrying Lord Richton I can ease the political tension between our two countries, and prevent more violence, then I'll consider that a win.'

He saw the line of her throat move as she swallowed. She was putting on a brave face but he'd bet that she wanted to marry Richton about as much as a person wanted a root canal. She was just too nice to say it. Too nice to demand her due. And that bothered him. Almost as much as it bothered him to imagine Alec Richton putting his hands on her. His mouth.

'Have you even met Richton?' he grated.

'Of course.'

'Have you kissed him?'

'That's none of your business.'

It wasn't difficult to read that she was furious with his question. As she had a right to be. He was behaving entirely out of character, getting involved with a woman beyond the bedroom, especially with a woman he had already made off-limits. He didn't bed women who were looking for marriage—either temporary or permanent. Especially not princesses from politically hostile neighbouring countries.

And yet thinking of her married to some other man when she'd kissed him as she had the night before left a nasty taste in his mouth. And that was strange in itself. He'd kissed—hell, he'd made love to—plenty of women and never given a thought to who they might end up with. The notion had never entered his head before.

But then he'd never been as attracted to a woman as he was to this one. It was something he wasn't sure how to handle. Because he still wanted her. In fact right now he wanted to take her into his arms, press her back against the wall and challenge her to ignore the sexual chemistry that pulsed between them.

'I'm making it my business,' he said, noting how her eyes widened at his tone.

'You can't.' She made to move past him and her body brushed his. Raw, unparalleled desire arced between them, making a mockery of her words. Frowning in consternation, he knew she would have put more space between them if she hadn't found herself neatly trapped between him and an outdoor table. 'Marriages in our part of the world have been arranged for centuries,' she continued, raising irritated eyes to his. 'It's a tradition.'

'That's what my brother said. But I'm a bit of an anti-traditionalist unless both parties are in agreement.'

'Not all of us have the freedom that you do. And I have a duty to uphold.'

'A duty that will lead you into a worse situation than you're already in.'

'That's your opinion, not mine. An opinion you have no right to offer since you very clearly turned down my proposal last night.'

'And the chemistry between us?' He hadn't realised he'd moved closer to her until she made to move away from him again. Irritated, he reached out and clasped her wrist in his hand. It was fine-boned, delicate, so small. His body hardened as memories of how she had felt in his arms coursed through his veins. Of how her nails had dug into his shoulders through his clothing. He wanted that again, but directly on his skin this time. 'You're just going to walk away from it? You're going to pretend that you didn't dream about me last night?'

Her breath left her in a soft rush. 'I did not dream about you last night.'

'I dreamt about you.'

Her eyes widened at the admission, her sharp inhalation setting every one of his nerve-endings on fire.

'What would you have me do?' She shot him a wary look, as well she might, given the nature of the questions and the answering thoughts currently running through his head.

What a pity that he couldn't give into any of them.

'I'd have you stand up for what you want,' he bit out. Which was true enough. Being dutiful was one thing, being foolish another thing entirely.

She shook her head as if that wasn't even a possibility. 'Sometimes the only way to win is to retreat. It's called strategy.'

'It's called insanity.'

'To you,' she said curtly. 'To me it's my duty. But I still don't understand why you're so interested in all this. Apart from wanting to play the white knight, that is.'

'I don't play the white knight,' Rafe growled. He'd done that as a boy, stepping in between his parents during their more vitriolic arguments to protect his mother from his father's rages. Neither parent had appreciated the conciliatory gesture—his father thinking him insubordinate, and therefore worthless, and his mother too caught up in her own pain to notice his.

The memory was a timely reminder as to why he steered clear of emotional entanglements. Entanglements like this.

'And you're right. This isn't my business. If you want to marry Richton and commit to a life of unhappiness then have it.'

'I didn't say I *wanted* that.'

'Then what do you want?'

Already charged with emotions he was unused to feeling, Rafe's jaw clenched. She must have read his tension accurately because her gaze dropped to his mouth, her tongue darting out to moisten her lips. The air between them went from volatile to explosive. The pulse in her neck throbbed and her eyes widened as if she sensed danger. But she didn't move away.

Instead she went still, her whole body taut as if she was waiting for something. As if she was *wanting* something...

Rafe told himself not to do it. Not to reach for her. Not to touch her. But he might as well have told himself to cut off his own foot while he was at it.

'Ah, to hell with it.' Without giving either of them a chance to think, and completely disregarding any consequences, Rafe lowered his mouth to hers.

If she'd shown any form or resistance or hesitation he might have stopped, he might have pulled back and reminded himself that she was not only 'off-limits', but that he didn't go around kissing women just to prove a point. But she didn't resist. Instead she gave a low moan of assent, wound her arms around his neck and pulled him in closer.

This. *This* was what he'd woken up craving today. The soft velvet feel of her mouth under his again, the sweet taste of her on his tongue and the long length of her warm curves moulded to the hard planes of his body.

Shock waves of pleasure shot through him as her fingers gripped his hair, her tongue caressing along his, filling his mouth as she shyly tasted him in return. Rafe groaned, curving his fingers around the slender nape of her neck, his thumbs firm against her cheeks as he deepened the kiss. He couldn't seem to get enough of her. Her taste, her touch. He wanted more, he needed—

'What the devil is the meaning of this?'

Rafe knew instantly that the deep voice that thundered behind Alexa was her father, and from the way her body instantly stiffened so did she.

He could have kicked himself. Never before had he become so lost in a woman, so lost in his own senses, that he'd forgotten his surroundings the way he just had. The way he nearly had the night before.

Cursing softly, he raised his head to see the shocked fury on her father's face, followed by the shocked disbelief on his brother's.

Alexa's stricken gaze rose to his. 'Please tell me it's not as bad as I think,' she whispered unevenly.

'Worse,' he murmured, his gaze firmly fixed on her father.

'Well? Are you just going to stand there and ignore me?' the King thundered. 'I want to know the meaning of this! Alexa? Explain yourself.'

Straightening her shoulders, Alexa moistened her kiss-swollen lips and turned to face her father's wrath, smoothing her hands down over her hips. 'Father... Your Majesty...' Her face flamed anew as her gaze landed on his brother, a fresh wave of mortification turning her cheeks rosy. 'I was... That is to say we were...'

'Celebrating,' Rafe said, knowing that there was only one way out of this mess and taking it.

'Celebrating?' King Ronan's face became almost mottled.

'Rafe—' Alexa's worried gaze met his as if she had already guessed what he was about to say, but Rafe ignored the look.

Taking her hand in his, he raised it to his lips. 'That's right,' he confirmed, his eyes never leaving hers. 'Alexa and I were celebrating our betrothal.'

CHAPTER FOUR

'BETROTHAL?'

Her father's voice was imbued with such a note of incredulity that Alexa knew immediately what he was thinking—that this man would never do as her future consort. It was only Rafe's rank as second in line to the throne of Santara that kept complete scorn from his voice.

'That's right,' the Prince drawled lazily.

Alexa nearly groaned out loud at the Prince's antagonistic tone.

'Is this true, Alexa?' Her father's voice sliced like a filleting knife. 'Did you accept Prince Rafaele's hand in marriage?'

No, *she* had asked *him*. And he'd said no. But, that aside, how was she to answer his question diplomatically when she had no idea *how* to answer it at all? Rafe had thrown her in at the deep end with his charged announcement and she wasn't at all sure why he had done it. An outright denial seemed implausible given that she'd been caught with her arms wrapped around the Prince like a vine, but agreeing seemed just as problematic.

Fortunately her father was too incensed to notice that she was struggling to come up with an answer and didn't have the patience for her to formulate one. 'After we had already agreed that you would marry Lord Richton this morning?'

Oh, dear. Lord Richton. She had completely forgotten about him. If the floor were to open up and swallow her whole right now, she wouldn't mind.

'Lord Richton is no longer in the picture,' the Prince declared, his hard-packed body lethally tense beside her.

Alexa frowned at the way he took control of the situation, at the way he took control of her, as if he had every right to do so.

Just then a flutter of movement caught her eye and Alexa was appalled to note that they were no longer alone. Some of the King's other overnight guests had also come out to the terrace to view the stunning gardens.

'Why don't we take this discussion inside?' King Jaeger offered smoothly. 'The terrace is hardly the place to discuss something of this magnitude.'

Her father looked like he wanted to argue but gave a curt nod.

Rafe settled his hand in the small of her back, causing a jolt of fresh awareness to race through her.

'After you,' he said politely.

Hanging back from her father and his brother, Alexa glanced up at him from beneath the fringe of her lashes. 'Why on earth did you tell them we were betrothed?' she whispered hoarsely, absently noting that Rafe had matched his stride to hers.

'Because I could hardly tell your father that I wanted to take you to bed, and that you wanted to be there. I do value my life,' he countered.

Not nearly enough, she fumed silently at his cavalier answer.

'Just because I kissed you does not mean that I want to sleep with you!' she hissed, wondering if she would have had the wherewithal to deny him this time if it had come to that.

'My apologies, Princess. I assumed you wouldn't want a scandal any more than I do, and you did ask me to marry you. I thought it was what you wanted.'

It had been. Last night. Last night, before he had kissed her and brought forth a whole host of emotions she didn't want to feel. Before she had dreamt about the two of them in bed together. Naked.

Easing out a choked breath, Alexa nodded at King Jaeger as he held a door open. She reluctantly followed her father inside, with Rafe so close behind her she could feel his body heat through her clothing.

At least she understood his thinking now. He'd promised his brother that he wouldn't create a scandal and so he'd improvised by taking up her proposal. Something she should feel much better about, given that it *was* her idea and it *had* been what she wanted.

Only the purpose of asking the Prince to marry her was to *gain* control of her life, and she somehow felt that she was about to lose it altogether.

She surreptitiously placed a finger against her temple, which had started to throb. She supposed there was no other option but to go along with it now because Rafe was right; she didn't want to marry Lord Richton, and she had always viewed a fake engagement as a better option.

King Jaeger offered her father a seat but he refused, choosing to stand beside an oak dresser, his arms folded across his corpulent chest.

Rafe planted himself in the middle of the room, his legs braced wide on the silk rug, facing his brother. Not wanting to be the only person in the room seated, Alexa chose to remain beside him, even though her legs felt as capable of holding her up as matchsticks.

'Well, now that we're all standing,' King Jaeger began

with a resigned note in his voice, 'would someone mind explaining what's going on here?'

'There's nothing to explain,' Rafe began. 'Alexa and I share a certain *chemistry*, and have decided to take things further.'

Wondering why he hadn't led with the political advantages their union would bring, Alexa was only grateful that he hadn't chosen to reveal how she had approached him the night before.

'When did this happen?' her father asked suspiciously.

'We spoke about it last night,' Rafe answered, throwing her a heated glance that told her exactly which part of last night he was thinking about. 'At length.'

'If you spoke about it last night, Alexa—' her father's gaze pierced hers '—why did you agree to marry Lord Richton during the meeting this morning?'

'Last night I got cold feet,' Rafe interjected smoothly, placing his arm around her waist. 'It put Alexa in an awkward position. After thinking things through however, I now know what I want. Do you think we could ring for coffee? I'm parched.'

'I was addressing my daughter,' her father snapped impatiently. 'Alexa can speak for herself.'

Yes, but nowhere near as eloquently. She was almost in awe of how the Prince could reveal so much and yet so little at the same time.

'Prince Rafaele is correct, Father,' she said, trying to ignore the heavy warmth of Rafe's hand against her hip. 'We did speak about it last night and I'm… I'm still coming to terms with his change of heart.' She glanced at the Prince with a look just short of panic, hoping that King Jaeger had indeed rung for coffee—or perhaps something stronger.

'Sometimes a man doesn't know what's important until it's about to be taken away.' Prince Rafaele gave her an indulgent smile. 'When Alexa informed me of your plan to marry her off to Lord Richton, I couldn't let that happen. If Alexa marries anyone, she'll marry me.'

Alexa swallowed at the possessive note in his voice. What would it be like if he truly meant those words? If he actually wanted to marry her for real? And why had that thought even entered her head? She wasn't looking to turn this into a love story. No matter how well he could kiss, Prince Rafaele was completely the wrong kind of man for her.

'This is all very surprising,' King Jacger said reasonably. 'Why don't we take some time to think about it and agree to meet next week to—?'

'No.' Her father cut the King's offer off before it was fully formed. 'If your brother wants to marry my daughter then the wedding will be held at the end of the month.'

In three weeks!

Her father's words sounded like a death knell in the quiet room. Alexa swallowed hard. This was only meant to be a temporary engagement, not an actual marriage.

'That's not possible,' she choked out. 'I...that is to say, we...'

'This isn't a game, Alexa,' her father interrupted tersely. 'Of his own admission, Prince Rafaele has already experienced cold feet and I will not have another Santarian royal make a fool of you by pulling out at the last minute.' He turned to square off against the Prince. 'If you want my daughter, those are the terms.'

Fully expecting Rafe to run from the room like a man with the devil after him, Alexa wasn't surprised to hear him say, 'The end of the month doesn't work for me. I have a new club opening on that weekend and I have to be there.'

'There you go,' she said, breathing a sigh of relief. 'Now why don't we—?'

'The weekend before then,' her father challenged.

Alexa felt Rafe go dangerously still beside her. Her father didn't move either; his chin jutted out at an angle she knew meant that nothing would get him to back down. They were like two stags facing off against each other over unclaimed territory. Only she was the piece of precious veld they were fighting over.

Deciding she had to do something to defuse the tension in the room, Alexa stepped towards her father, only to have Rafe's hand firm on her hip to hold her in place beside him.

'Tight,' he murmured, his hard gaze flicking from her father's to hers. 'But so be it.'

'So be it? *So be it?*'

Somehow Alexa had convinced her father that she needed a moment alone with her *fiancé*. She moved out of his arms now, and rounded on him.

'Are you completely mad? Why did you say that to him? Why did you agree with his terms?'

'Breathe, Princess,' the Prince ordered curtly, 'before you pass out.'

She wasn't going to pass out. She was going to… Alexa groped for the edge of the sofa behind her and all but fell onto the cushioned seat. She was going to pass out.

'Here.' A glass with amber liquid in it, not unlike the horrible Scotch she'd sipped the night before, was thrust in front of her face. 'Drink this.'

'It's too early for alcohol.'

'It's five o clock somewhere in the world. If you don't drink it, I will.'

'Have it.' Alexa took a deep breath, her palms against her belly to settle the pitching sensation inside. 'I'm too much in shock to drink it.'

'Why are you so shocked? You're the one who asked me to marry you in the first place.'

'I asked you to cooperate in a fake engagement, not enter into a real marriage.'

'And why *was* that?' His eyes were like blue granite when they met hers. 'You weren't surprised when your father initially disapproved of you marrying me. Was this just an act of rebellion on your part? The perfect, pampered little princess, lashing out against authority by becoming engaged to the Rebel Prince?'

'No!'

Rafe gave a mocking stare. 'Your face gives you away, Princess. Don't ever play poker. You'll lose the bank.'

'Okay, yes, in some small way I was rebelling, but not because I'm perfect, or pampered. Far from it. I don't want to marry anyone right now, and because I knew my father didn't approve of you I never imagined he would push us both to the altar the way that he has.'

'Appears you were wrong.' He paced away from her to stare out of the window. 'It seems the bad brother is just as good for his Princess as the good one.'

Alexa frowned. 'You mean King Jaeger?'

He turned back, his brow lifted in a cynical arch. 'I do only have one brother.'

'I… I've never compared the two of you like that.'

'Like I said, don't play poker.'

'Okay, fine,' Alexa conceded. 'But you can't deny that you're totally different from each other. By your own admission you're not interested in duty and commitment, and you don't care about Santara or politics. Honestly, your life is completely alien to me.'

'Because it's based on pleasure?'

'Because it's hedonistic.' Her face flamed as his eyebrow arched again. 'What I mean is, you do what you want, whenever you want, regardless of what others think of you. You live by your own rules, and I don't know anyone else who does that. Frankly, I envy it.'

For a moment he didn't say anything. Then he sighed and dragged a hand through his overlong hair. Alexa didn't want to remember how thick and soft it had felt beneath her fingertips but she couldn't help it. Her gaze drifted over his unshaven jaw and paused on his well-shaped lips. Lips that were skilled and warm.

Suddenly aware that he was watching her just as closely, she lifted her chin and forced her gaze to remain steady even though she was quaking inside.

'Well, regardless of how this all came about, your father has effectively checkmated us both.'

'So it would seem.' Unable to sit still with so much energy coursing through her body, Alexa rose from the sofa, her mind in a whirl. 'And now we have to un-checkmate ourselves.' Not that she had any idea how to do that. Her father was more stubborn than a mule when he chose to be.

'That won't be possible.'

Alexa frowned as the Prince stared moodily into the glass he was holding.

'It has to be.'

'Not without seriously angering and embarrassing both our Kings.'

Feeling trapped, Alexa absently reached for the glass in his hand, taking a fortifying gulp before handing it back with a grimace. 'So what do we do now?'

'We do what your father wants. We marry. You get to appease your father and help your country and, if you're right, the violence between our countries ceases. I get to pay off a long-standing debt I owe to my brother and ease his load.' He tossed back the remaining contents of the glass and placed it on a low table. 'But nothing else changes. You live in Berenia. I live in London. At a time that is convenient to us both we'll agree that the marriage isn't working and end it.' His gaze sharpened. 'Six months should be long enough.'

'I don't know if that will work. My people will expect you to move to Berenia.'

'I expect billion-dollar deals to fall into my lap every day but unfortunately that doesn't happen either.'

Ignoring his sarcasm, Alexa paced away from him. 'You really think this will work?'

'Why not? I have stories written about me that aren't true all the time. Only this time I'll be the one in charge of creating the story. I find I quite like the idea.'

Alexa gnawed on the inside of her lip in consternation. 'I still think we can find a way out of this if we try.'

'Fine. If you find one, you let me know. As long as it doesn't make things worse for my brother I'll be all over it.'

'And what if six months isn't long enough to convince everyone that this is real?'

'Six months will be plenty. But if you're worried you can just gaze at me adoringly from time to time.'

'That would only feed your ego.'

'Something I'm all for.' His gaze settled on her lips, and heat spiked deep inside her. Suddenly she was thinking about kissing him again and, as if he knew exactly where her mind had gone, his gaze lifted to hers, amusement highlighting the dark blue depths.

Embarrassed, and not a little disconcerted by the strength of her reaction to him, Alexa lifted her chin. 'It will be expected that we're seen together at some point, you know.'

'Perhaps.' His eyes were a hot and watchful brand as they locked with hers. 'But let's cross that bridge when we come to it, hmm?'

* * *

If Alexa had wondered over the course of the last two weeks how Prince Rafaele felt about their impending nuptials, all doubt evaporated when she caught sight of his grim expression at the end of the aisle.

He hated it.

Something Alexa would probably have been more aware of had they not delegated every aspect of the wedding planning to their respective assistants.

Not that she'd wanted to plan it. The thought of it had been so challenging she'd deliberately thrown herself into horrendously long working days so that she'd be too exhausted by the end of the day to think about anything at all, least of all the wedding.

The down side to having been so busy was that the time had seemed to rush by. And now she was about to trust her future to a man who liked to be in charge, and whom she hardly knew.

One she was incredibly attracted to.

The unwanted thought entered her head entirely without her permission. For two weeks she'd been trying to avoid thinking about the way he had kissed her and touched her and the way she had responded, but she hadn't been completely successful, her dreams often so erotic she had woken sweaty and embarrassingly aroused on more than one occasion.

Because sex with Prince Rafaele would be unforgettable.

And thinking that way would lead to trouble. They had struck a marriage bargain with each other for political purposes. It was nothing more than a marriage of convenience; the Prince might kiss like a dream but she couldn't have sex with him. Not only would it not serve any long-term purpose but she was very afraid that she'd like it too much. That she'd like *him* too much. And if he were to find her lacking... If he were to find her inadequate... A horrible queasiness settled in the pit of her stomach before she swallowed it down.

No. As tempting as the Prince was the key to making their temporary marriage work was to focus on her objectives—freedom to make her own marriage match in the future, as well as the restoration of political peace between their nations. The latter of which already seemed to be working.

The people of both Berenia and Santara had greeted the announcement of her impending marriage to the Prince with unmistakable enthusiasm, treating it as the love story of the age. That was thanks, mainly, to a photo that had been taken of the two of them dancing at the charity ball. In the photo the Prince was holding her far too close, the smile on his face shockingly sexual, while her own expression was one of stunned stupefaction. At least that was how it looked to her!

But their respective PR departments had loved the photo, adding it to their marriage announcement for the entire world to see.

Alexa eased out a steadying breath as she came to a halt in front of the Prince, her long white gown settling around her ankles in a rustle of silk. If ever there had been a stony-faced groom, he was it.

She swallowed the lump in her throat. If she'd been hoping for some other reaction from him, and maybe deep down she could admit that she had been, then she would have to get over it.

Gone was the devil-may-care seducer she had met at the Santarian Summer Palace just over two weeks ago. Gone was the charming rebel who didn't let anything bother him. This version of the Prince couldn't be more bothered if he was being swarmed by angry wasps, his face carved in stone, his muscles taut as if he were fighting the urge to run.

Join the club, she thought as the celebrant spoke the first words of the service.

As if in a dream state, Alexa barely followed the proceedings, her senses leaping with surprise when the Prince placed his hands on her shoulders and turned her towards him, his fingers sure and strong, his expression unreadable.

Before Alexa fully understood that they had reached the end of the service his head bent to hers, his lips covering her own in a searing kiss. She didn't mean to close her eyes at the contact but she did, and it only heightened the riot of sensations inside of her.

A tremor went through her as his fingertips brushed the nape of her neck in a feather-light caress and Alexa swayed, barely catching herself at the last moment before she completely melted against him.

Fortunately she was able to recover herself as the wedding guests clapped and whooped, and the *qanun* and *oud* struck up a lively tune as they proceeded back down the aisle.

Everyone seemed happy as they ate and danced and mingled during the lavish reception. Everyone except Alexa, who grew more and more miserable as the afternoon wore on. Prince Rafaele had behaved like a polite stranger during most of proceedings and Alexa couldn't wait for him to return to London.

Guilt and nerves ate away at her. Guilt that she had somehow caused this whole debacle with her wretched plan to find a temporary fiancé, and nerves because she had a strange premonition that her life would be changed for ever by marrying him.

Which, of course, it would be—but only temporarily.

And what was the shortest marriage on record? If it was two hours she'd surely beat it because she'd like nothing more than to pretend it hadn't happened at all and end it now.

Badly needing a distraction, she caught sight of King Jaeger, now dancing with his heavily pregnant wife, Queen Regan. Alexa had tried not to like the Queen when she'd first met her, but Regan's compassion and understanding of how she had felt to be jilted by the King had shone through from the start. It was embarrassing now how Alexa had become tearful when she'd first met the Queen, having had to sit through a dinner watching the man she'd had a teenage crush on stare at a woman he clearly adored.

It was strange watching them now because none of those old feelings she'd had for him seemed to exist any more. She could appreciate his good looks and strong masculine presence but she could no longer see herself by his side. As his wife. Instead she found herself comparing him to her new husband. They both had dark hair and similar eyes and they were both incredibly well built but, as suitable as the King had been as a marriage prospect, he had never drawn her gaze the way Prince Rafaele did.

Alerted by a tingling sensation along the back of her neck, Alexa's eyes cut across the room to find her new husband watching her closely, his face devoid of emotion. She couldn't hold the intensity of his gaze, her face flushed as she found herself admiring the cut of his suit that moulded perfectly to his wide shoulders and lean physique.

It was embarrassing how attractive she found him and the only saving grace was that he'd be returning to London some time in the evening. She couldn't wait for that to happen.

As if reading her desperation for distraction, the King of Santara and his wife approached her.

'May I have this dance, Princess Alexa?'

Alexa swallowed hard as she gazed at the man she had once thought she would marry. While the awareness of what might have been between them was gone, she was still embarrassed by how easily he had cast her aside.

'Please,' Regan encouraged when Alexa automatically turned to her for permission. 'The wedding was beautiful and I hope we can one day become friends as well as sisters-in-law.'

They were sisters-in-law *for now,* but not for ever. She was sure the Queen knew, because Rafaele had told her that he intended to explain the situation to his brother so that he could prepare for when their marriage ended. Alexa had only told Nasrin that their marriage was a sham, not wanting her father to know in case he tried to interfere with her decision.

Ignoring the curiosity of nearby guests as they took to the dance floor together, Alexa pinned what she hoped was a convincing smile to her lips.

'I hope you're having a good time,' King Jaeger murmured as they fell into an easy waltz.

'I am, thank you,' Alexa returned, keeping her misgivings about the wedding to herself. 'I only hope this isn't all for nothing at the end of the day.'

'I have a feeling it won't be,' the King responded enigmatically. 'Although I must confess my surprise in finding my rogue brother in the position of being forced down the aisle so neatly.'

'But you know how that came about,' Alexa said, her voice slightly husky as she gazed into blue eyes that were almost the exact shade as Rafe's, but which didn't make her breath catch at all when she looked into them. 'My father demanded it.'

'True,' he mused softly, a knowing glint in his eyes. 'But

not even our father could force Rafa to do something he didn't want to do if he *really* didn't want to do it.'

'Then he met his match in my father,' she said dryly.

'I wonder...' The King smiled. 'My brother is not his usual easy-going self today, and he didn't seem to try all that hard to get out of the wedding.'

As far as Alexa was concerned Rafe had definitely tried to get out of their wedding, and as to his lack of ease... well, that was easily explained. The man had been forced to get married. No doubt that would have wiped the smile off any confirmed bachelor's face.

'My dance, I believe.' Rafaele suddenly cut in, his eyes riveted to where her hand held the King's.

'I was just about to tell Alexa how beautiful she looks,' the King said smoothly. 'Don't you think she looks beautiful?'

'Extremely.' Rafe's eyes narrowed on his brother's, his tone anything but convincing. 'But perhaps if you devoted this much attention to your own wife she wouldn't appear so unhappy,' Rafe prompted lazily, his brow arched.

At that moment a joyous giggle rang out from across the room and they all turned to observe Regan, hand protectively over her baby bump, having a great time with a small group of guests.

'Yes, I can see she feels terrible,' the King drawled, his eyes just as mocking as Rafe's.

The tension between the two men, while not aggressive, was palpable, and again Alexa wondered at the state of their relationship. For two brothers who looked so much alike and who were so close in age they didn't seem overly bonded, the way she had been with Sol.

Alexa gave Rafe a curious look as King Jaeger strolled from the dance floor in the direction of his wife. 'What was that all about?'

'What was what all about?' He gave her a too-innocent look.

'You were rude.'

'Maybe I was jealous.'

'You? Jealous?' Alexa nearly snorted at the prospect. 'Have you ever been jealous before?'

'Not so far.'

'I didn't think so.'

'But then I've never married a woman who was once betrothed to my brother and who gazes adoringly at him every chance she gets. Are you sure nothing ever happened between the two of you?'

The coolness behind his question took Alexa by surprise. 'Of course not.' Her incredulous gaze met hostile blue. 'Your brother is an honourable man.'

'And I'm not?'

Sensing that his emotions were barely leashed beneath the facade of civility, Alexa moistened her lips. 'I didn't say that. But I was unaware that honour was so important to you.'

'It isn't.' The Prince gave her a benign smile that belied the tension emanating from his large frame. 'As you pointed out previously, I have very different priorities to my brother. That aside, I believe it's time for us to leave, dear wife.'

It took a moment for her mind to process his words but then she frowned. 'What do you mean, *us*?'

'Generally it denotes oneself and the person one happens to be speaking with.'

'Don't be smart,' she retorted. As far as she had understood, Rafe would head back to London alone, claiming that they would take a honeymoon later on, when time permitted. 'I'm not leaving with you. That was never part of the plan.'

'Alas no, but then nor was our actual marriage. But one must improvise.'

'I'm not big on improvising. And we agreed to delay our honeymoon so that we didn't have to have one.'

'Once the international press bought into our *love* story, I thought you'd realise that we would have to present a united front. You were the one who first mentioned that our people would want to see us together, if I remember correctly.'

'Yes, but I was projecting into the future. I can't leave with you now. I have people to see next week. Meetings to take.'

'It's not negotiable, Alexa. I'm not leaving here without you.'

The way he said her name sent a frisson of sensation skittering along her nerve-endings, flustering her. 'Why can't you stay here instead?'

The Prince arched a brow. 'Because it might be a bit hard to open my club from here next weekend—considering it's in Chelsea.'

'Oh.' She hadn't thought of that. 'Well, I need more time to think about this.'

'You have an hour.'

Feeling as if her life was spinning out of control again, Alexa tried to hold her ground. 'Maybe I can join you in a few days.'

'Fine. You do that. And while you're at it you can explain the delay to the press *and* your father, who happens to be watching us closely.'

Knowing she was defeated because she did not want to face her father right now, Alexa groaned. 'But I haven't packed.'

'Throw an overnight bag together. Anything else you need can be sent on.'

'How long do you expect me to be gone?'

'Allow for two weeks. That's the usual time allotted to a honeymoon, isn't it?'

'Honeymoon?'

Her startled gaze met his and something sizzled in the air between them, making it hard to breathe. The room seemed somehow oppressively hot and all Alexa could think about was that blisteringly short kiss at the altar. Her heartbeat picked up and she really wished she knew what he was thinking.

'Not a real honeymoon,' he drawled gruffly. 'Unless that's what you want, of course.'

For a moment Alexa nearly said yes, and the shock of that realisation was enough to have her vigorously shaking her head. 'No, no, it's not.' She hated how she sounded like a frightened rabbit, but it was exactly how she felt.

'I didn't think so.' He gave her a tight smile. 'Which is why we'll spend two weeks in my London apartment. I'll meet you at the palace airstrip in...' he checked his watch '...fifty minutes.'

Fifty minutes?

That was nowhere near long enough for her to work out how she was going to survive two weeks holed up in an apartment with a man who tempted her like no other, but who couldn't be more wrong for her.

CHAPTER FIVE

RAFE GREW MORE and more agitated the longer he had to wait on the tarmac for his new wife, his usual cool deserting him. Not that he had to wonder too hard to figure out why that was. He was married. A state he'd thought he'd never find himself in. And okay, it wasn't a real marriage—but it damn well felt like one, with the ceremony, the two hundred plus well-wishers and the stunning bride.

His heart had all but leapt into his throat when he'd first caught sight of Alexa holding on to her father's arm at the end of the aisle. Covered head to toe in a lace gown that had outlined every slim curve, her floor-length veil hiding her face, she had been a vision in white.

Over the last couple of weeks he'd told himself that he'd imagined how sensually alluring she was. Exaggerated how potent his response to her was. Then she'd walked towards him with a smooth, graceful stride and he'd known that he hadn't exaggerated any of it. If anything, he had underestimated her appeal.

A shocking realisation for a man who had decided long ago that he would never let himself be trapped into matrimony under any conditions and now found himself desperately attracted to his wife!

A wife he didn't want, but who he would neatly use to repay Jag for the debt he'd incurred when his brother had been forced to leave his studies and return to Santara to become king after their father had died. At the time Rafe knew the ins and outs of the palace like no one else and could have smoothed the way for his brother, but he'd been desperate to leave and make his own mark on the world and Jag had seen that.

He'd told him to leave, to go find himself, and so far he'd never found cause to call on Rafe to help out. Something that was a little galling, because he'd told Jag that should he ever need him he'd be there.

But Jag had never needed him. However, his brother *had* needed a way to repair the relationship between Santara and Berenia and Rafe had seized the opportunity to repay his debt of gratitude by marrying Alexa.

And he didn't regret it. He hated being in debt to anyone more than anything and doing this for his brother— for his country—would ease his conscience whenever his siblings got up in his face about the way he lived his life.

But that's not the only reason you married her, a sly voice reminded him.

It was a voice he'd ignored over the past two weeks, burying himself in his latest business endeavour to the point of exhaustion. Now, though…now it was hard to deny that perhaps he'd also been under the influence of a shocking sexual attraction when he'd decided to marry Alexa that had exceeded anything he'd experienced before. That, and a deep-seated need to keep her from Lord Richton.

And who's going to keep her from you?

Rafe exhaled roughly. Nobody would keep her from him because nobody would need to. He might want her in his bed but that didn't mean he'd follow through on it. Alexa was not a woman a man toyed with. Not only was she the future queen of Berenia, but she was ultimately looking for something long-term, something permanent, and the last thing he wanted was to sleep with her and give her the impression that he was the right man for her.

Because he was most definitely not that man.

A truth that bothered him, though why it should he couldn't fathom. He'd never wanted to be any woman's 'right' man. Ever. His life was just fine as it was, even if Alexa believed it to be 'hedonistic'.

He shook his head. A Buddhist monk probably had a more exciting life than he had of late. Even the Spanish supermodel hadn't inspired him enough to take her to his bed while they'd been dating.

But Alexa did. Alexa, with her potent combination of steel and sweetness. Alexa who he couldn't seem to get out of his head. Who lit a fire inside of him that made his body throb with need.

Alexa who he wasn't going to touch.

And no doubt she'd be happy with that decision if the horrified expression on her face when he'd raised her veil at the altar was anything to go by.

He exhaled a long breath and rechecked his watch. Realistically, he'd only been waiting on her for twenty minutes. It felt like twenty years.

And then finally she appeared from the side door of the palace, looking extremely tantalising in a casual pair of jeans and a lightweight jacket held closed with a zip that begged to be tugged downwards, the cool desert breeze teasing the long strands of her ponytail.

For some reason the tension inside his chest eased at the sight of her. Had he been worried she wouldn't show?

Irritated at the very idea, he scowled down at her. 'I hope you have a thicker jacket than that. March in London isn't exactly warm.'

Jewel-green eyes blinked up at him and he reminded

himself that this situation wasn't exactly her fault so he needed to calm down.

'I believe Nasrin packed one, yes.'

Her assistant, who stood behind her, nodded enthusiastically. 'I did, Your Highness. I also know that you stowed your laptop into your satchel before you left.' She gave Alexa a firm look. 'No matter who contacts you, your father specifically told me that you are on your honeymoon and therefore not to do any work.'

Alexa stiffened at the mention of their 'honeymoon' but then gave her assistant a warm smile. 'Duly noted.'

Nasrin made an unconvinced sound in the back of her throat, piquing Rafe's interest in their relationship. Alexa had a reputation for being cool and remote, and yet it was clear that she and this woman shared a strong connection that went beyond simple employee and employer. There weren't many things Rafe admired more than those in positions of power treating the people who served them with respect and kindness.

'Ready to leave?' he asked, aware that as he spoke her body went stiff with tension. Which irritated him even more. How were they going to convince anyone that their union was more than a marriage of convenience if she turned to stone every time he spoke to her?

Forcing his eyes away from her jeans-clad butt as she preceded him up the stairs, Rafe stopped to speak with his pilot while Alexa buckled herself into her seat. No doubt she wouldn't be impressed by his plane. He might be a prince, but he wasn't a king. He couldn't offer her anything that she didn't already have.

And why was he even thinking like this? Their marriage wasn't real. It wasn't even damned convenient when it came down to it. It wasn't anything. They were two people who were doing each other a favour. So why did something that wasn't supposed to be monumental feel as if it was?

The circular nature of his thoughts warred with the constant need to put his hands on her and did little to restore his usual good humour. He wasn't sure anything could.

Using work to distract himself, he opened his laptop to go over the latest specs on a building he'd just purchased in Scotland. It was a grand old edifice that had once been a cinema and his COO was urging him to tear it down rather than restore it because the cost would be exorbitant. There was something charming about it though and, while he was all about the bottom line, he had an inclination to go in the other direction this time.

He wondered what Alexa would make of it and then scowled at the thought. It wasn't as if he was going to ask her. He might have to live with her for the next two weeks but that didn't mean they had to interact. In fact the less they saw of each other the better. Because wanting her was driving him to distraction.

Perhaps he could discreetly settle her into a hotel, then he wouldn't have to see her at all. Which would work right up until the press got hold of the information and blew their whole 'love story' out of the water.

'Sorry.' She gave him a small smile. 'I feel sort of responsible for all of this honeymoon palaver, and I know you're not happy about it.'

'You're not responsible.'

'Well, at least you didn't try to make me feel better by pretending to be happy.' She gave a strained laugh. 'But I know you didn't want anything to change and it clearly has.'

'That was a bit short-sighted, given the monumental interest in our wedding.'

'Yes. It seems that my father was right about our marriage moving everyone's attention from problems to pleasure. Do you know they even have a mug and tea towels with our faces on it?'

'Quaint.' He noticed the purple smudges beneath her eyes that he hadn't seen before and wondered if she'd had as little sleep as he'd had over the past fortnight.

'I know. My people went all-out. I think after your brother ditched me no one thought I'd ever find anyone else to marry.'

At the mention of his brother Rafe was reminded of the way she'd gazed at Jag only hours earlier. It had appalled him to think that she might still have feelings for his brother, and he didn't like it.

'Why would anyone think that you wouldn't get married? You're the heir to the throne of Berenia.'

'Thanks for pointing out my most saleable quality.'

Her self-deprecating tone made him frown. 'That is not your most saleable quality.'

He'd say her lips were definitely high on the list. Along with her legs, and the keen intelligence that shone from those magnificent green eyes. 'My brother fell in love with someone else. That was hardly your fault.'

'Some saw it differently.'

Noting the way her shoulders had tensed, Rafe's eyes narrowed. 'Define "differently".'

'I can barely remember.' She waved her hand between them as if the whole thing was inconsequential. 'Something about me not being womanly enough to keep hold of him.'

Rafe made a rude noise in the back of his throat. 'I've never heard anything more ridiculous.'

Or wrong.

'Anyway.' She made another flicking gesture with her hand. 'I was thinking that if your apartment isn't big enough for the both of us, then I could stay in a hotel.'

Even though Rafe had come up with the same idea only

moments earlier, the fact that she would prefer a hotel to his home chafed. 'My apartment is big enough.'

'Still, I could—'

'It's big enough.'

'You didn't let me finish.'

'I didn't have to. How do you think it would look if I set my beautiful wife up in a hotel straight after our wedding?'

'I suppose.' She fidgeted with her phone so he knew there was more coming. 'And your staff? Will they think it strange when we have separate bedrooms?'

Rafe lazily leaned back in his seat, relaxing now that he knew what her angle was. 'Is that your way of telling me that sex is off the table, Alexa?'

As he expected, her eyes flashed and turned frosty. 'Of course sex is off the table. It was never actually on the table.'

'Really?'

Hot colour poured into her cheeks and he knew she was recalling every hungry kiss they'd shared, just as he was. 'That wasn't the impression I got.'

And no way would he let her paint it any other way.

'I'm sorry you got a different impression,' she said stiffly, refusing to meet his eye, 'but I'm not interested in meaningless sex.'

Meaningless sex?

He regarded her steadily. 'Who said it would be meaningless?'

She shifted in her seat, unwittingly drawing his gaze to her body. He could see the outline of her rounded breasts beneath the fitted jacket and his body clenched as he recalled how perfectly she'd fitted into the palm of his hand.

'What else could it be?' she said, bringing his eyes back to hers. 'And, regardless, it would only blur the lines between us. So there's no reason for us to become intimate.'

Her voice was matter of fact, her reasoning completely logical. So logical that he agreed with it. Unfortunately he didn't care. This thing between them pulled at his self-control and her ready denial of its existence only made him want to prove her wrong.

'I can think of at least one.' In fact right now he had about one hundred and one filtering through his brain. 'Pure, unadulterated pleasure.'

'Oh.' The soft catch in her voice fired his blood. It made him want to reach over and haul her out of her seat and into his.

As if reading him correctly her face flamed. 'I'm not that...*physical*...but, since you obviously are, I don't mind if you seek...*relief* elsewhere. I only ask that you be discreet about it.'

It took Rafe a moment to fully understand what she meant and then he didn't even try to hide his incredulity.

'You're giving me permission to cheat on you? What kind of wife does that?'

'The non-real variety. Obviously.'

'Princess, while I'd love to live up to this wild image you have of me as some sort of sexual deviant, not every relationship I have with a woman ends between the sheets. And, to answer your earlier question, I only have one full-time housekeeper, apart from my security personnel, and she won't ask any questions.'

'Good to know.'

What was good to know? That he didn't sleep with every woman he met, or that his housekeeper wouldn't care about their sleeping arrangements?

His mouth thinned. She was driving him crazy and when she coolly turned her attention to her phone he decided to drive her a little crazy in return. 'Alexa...' He waited for her eyes to reconnect with his before leaning toward her to whisper throatily. 'Sex between us wouldn't be meaningless at all. It would be mind-blowing.'

It was nearly midnight when the plane touched down in London and Rafe ushered Alexa into a waiting limousine.

She had spent most of the flight vacillating between being mortified that she'd told Rafe about the rumours pertaining to her lack of femininity and growing hot at the thought of what mind-blowing sex with him would feel like.

She knew better than to air her dirty laundry in public and what had she wanted him to say? That she *was* womanly enough to hold a man?

Wishing she could just curl up and sleep for the next two weeks, Alexa did her best to ignore the man beside her and take in what she could see of the city.

She'd been in London once before for a state dinner but she'd had no time to explore at all, flying in and out within twenty-four hours, due to work commitments.

It must have rained before they arrived because the streets were shiny and black, the twinkling lights outlining a world that was miles away from what she was used to.

In no time at all, it seemed, the big Mercedes pulled into the underground car park of an impressive plate glass ten-storey building.

Yawning, Alexa barely noticed the high-tech layout of the garage, or the impressive array of luxury cars parked in personalised bays.

She did, however, notice the state-of-the-art glass-encased lift that whisked them to the top floor and opened out into a polished marble foyer lined with a dark wood finish.

'The building is patrolled by Chase Security,' Rafe informed her, 'a high-level security firm, and all the windows are bulletproof. Two of your secret service detail will be arriving later on tonight. I've organised for them to have a lower level apartment while you're here. A concierge is on duty twenty-four-seven if you should need anything and I'm not here.'

He walked through to a living area with twelve-foot ceilings and enormous windows on three sides that gave an incredible view over the park and the city beyond. An ultra-modern monochrome chandelier hung from the high ceiling, perfectly setting off the sectional furniture that was both homely and state-of-the-art.

Even though she lived in a palace, the architectural elegance of Rafe's home took her breath away. 'It's beautiful,' she said reverently. 'Like a castle in the clouds.'

Glancing up from checking mail that had been neatly placed on a display table, Rafe gave her a mocking glance. 'The ceiling chains are in the bedroom.'

'Ceiling chains?'

'It's par for the course with being a *hedonist*. Isn't that the word you used?'

Alexa groaned as he threw that back in her face, but really, what did he expect her to think when he made so little effort to refute any of the wicked claims made about him? In fact, he'd basically told her they were all true!

'Are you saying I've got it wrong?'

His mouth twisted into a cynical line. 'I'm saying I had a good time in my twenties. Make of that what you will.'

Alexa thought about everything she'd read about him, and everything she knew to date. So far he didn't seem all that self-absorbed at all, and he *had* stopped kissing her in the library when she'd asked him to. In fact, he'd given her fair warning that he was going to do so, thereby giving her enough time to say no. Not that he'd given her fair warning the second time. The second time he'd taken her in his arms on the terrace she'd all but swooned at his feet.

'Here's the thing, Alexa.' His voice sounded all soft and growly. 'I like sex, but I like straight up bedroom sex. Sometimes I like shower sex or spa sex. I've even been known to enjoy table sex and floor sex. I leave kinky sex for those who enjoy it more.'

Knowing he was trying to shock her with his litany of sexual venues, Alexa ignored the jolt of pleasure from just hearing him say the word. 'Does that mean that the whips are in the bedroom too?'

Clearly surprised by her comeback, his mouth twitched. 'No.' Heading for the doorway, he gestured for her to follow him. 'I keep those in the safe.'

She couldn't help laughing, and it relieved some of the tension that had plagued her since she'd walked down the aisle towards him.

'I've asked Mrs Harrington to prepare one of the guest suites for your use down this hallway. If you want to use the pool or gymnasium they're on the lower level and the library is on the mezzanine above to your right.'

'I thought apartments were small,' Alexa said, admiring the artwork on the walls as she passed. 'You like the Impressionists?'

'I like all art as long as it's not a landscape. I prefer the real thing to a painting.'

'I feel the same.'

Alexa couldn't hold back a smile as she took in the gorgeous honey-toned bedroom with a view of glowing city lights that spread for miles. Her eyes darted to the ceiling with impish humour, but she wished she hadn't because now he was looking at her lips and she couldn't breathe properly.

Sexual awareness pulled at her insides, worse than it

had done all day, and the quiet of the apartment highlighted that for once it was just the two of them. Alone. Together.

As if feeling the same pull she did, Rafe stepped back. 'Your private bathroom is through the walk-in closet. Stevens will be up with your bags in a moment.'

Trying to steady her breathing so he didn't see how badly he affected her, Alexa dropped her handbag onto the king-sized bed that faced the wall of windows. 'I probably won't sleep tonight anyway. This view is incredible.'

'That's up to you. I intend to sleep very well. Goodnight, Alexa.'

Watching him leave through the reflection in the windows, Alexa let out a slow breath. She couldn't deny the effect Rafe had on her. Especially after he'd listed off places where he liked to have sex.

Good lord!

But being intimate with a man like the rebel Prince of Santara would be like driving a Formula One racing car on a suburban road.

Deadly at every turn, but, oh, so much fun.

And why was she even countenancing such a thought when she'd already made her position on intimacy clear? But she knew why, didn't she? She was attracted to him. Incredibly attracted and no logical reasoning or denial made a difference to how she felt.

And it was something she needed to work on. Because even knowing that he was the most unsuitable man on the planet, and that there was no chance she would ever imagine herself in love with him, she couldn't deny that just looking at him made her body crave something she had no experience to deal with.

At least not objectively. And she could not afford to fall into her old ways and get *emotional* over him. Because he certainly wouldn't get emotional over her. No one ever had and it hurt, knowing that men found it so easy to walk away from her.

And Prince Rafaele would definitely walk away from her; it was what he did with all women. It was why she had married him in the first place. She wanted him to walk away from her in the end.

Restless, she moved to stand in front of the tall windows, trying to figure out why she felt so unsettled.

Was it just the pomp and ceremony of the day? Was it exhaustion from lack of sleep? Or was it that tonight was her wedding night and she was spending it alone? Alone, overlooking a picturesque night sky in a beautiful room with a bed the size of a swimming pool, and an ache deep inside her that longed to be satisfied. An ache to have Rafe touch her again, kiss her again...

'Your Highness?'

A voice outside her door broke into thoughts that were rapidly spiralling out of control. Ushering the chauffeur into her room, she thanked him for delivering her luggage and immediately set out to find her nightwear. All she needed was a good night's sleep. She only hoped it didn't elude her yet again...

Fortunately it didn't and she woke feeling more refreshed than she had anticipated. After a quick shower she donned her yoga gear, stretched on her yoga mat until she felt all the kinks leave her body, then went in search of coffee.

Following one hallway to the next, she eventually found the kitchen, a beautiful room of shiny stainless steel and polished wood. The state-of-the-art coffee machine took almost as long to locate. It was set into the wall above the oven, and the various buttons and dials looked like they belonged on a flight panel rather than on a coffee machine.

Having only ever fixed herself a coffee from a small machine in her private suite, Alexa had no idea how it worked.

Still, how difficult could it be to operate? She opened a few cupboards until she located a mug and set it under the central cylinder that looked like it dispensed coffee.

Gnawing on the inside of her lip, she hoped that if she started pressing buttons she wouldn't blow the thing up.

Before she could decide which one to push, however, she felt Rafe's presence behind her.

'What are you doing?'

Alexa glanced over her shoulder to see her husband standing in the doorway. He was dressed for business in a pale blue fitted shirt buttoned all the way to the wide column of his tanned throat, and a royal blue silk tie that turned his eyes the same shade.

Beautiful. He was utterly beautiful and Alexa did her best to calm the spike in her heart rate.

'I'm studying your coffee machine and trying to figure out how not to break it,' she said, giving a tentative smile.

Probably the best thing going forward would be for them to become friends. Anything would be better than the sense of awkwardness she currently felt. 'You don't have an instruction manual, do you?'

His eyes narrowed even more as his gaze swept over her with cool indifference. 'What type of coffee do you want?'

'A soy latte. If it does that.'

'This thing could probably reboot NASA,' he growled, coming up behind her and reaching over her shoulder, stabbing his finger at the buttons. 'Let me show you how it works.'

He started going through the various options and Alexa tried to concentrate but his heat and clean woodsy scent were doing crazy things to her brain. The urge to turn her face into the crook of his neck and sniff it was incredibly

powerful and it took every lesson she'd ever learned in how
to be objective to prevent herself from actually doing so.

By the time she'd mastered the urge the lesson was over.

'Then you hit Start.'

Great, she hadn't learned a thing.

Moments later the machine hissed and gurgled and Rafe
handed her a perfectly made coffee.

Breathing the aroma deep into her lungs, Alexa groaned
gratefully, her sexual awareness of the man in front of her
immediately superseded by the need for caffeine. Which
lasted right up until she opened her eyes and saw his dark
gaze fixed on her mouth. Heat and desire swept through
her at a blinding rush but, as if he hadn't felt a thing in
return, he stepped back from her and fetched an espresso
cup from an overhead cupboard.

Seriously disturbed by how easily he made her want
him, Alexa racked her brain for something to say that
would ease the tension between them.

'So you're off to work then,' she said, silently cringing
at the obvious statement.

'It pays the bills.'

'And do you work at your nightclubs or an office?'

'Both.'

Okay, then. So he wasn't going to make this easy.

Unperturbed, Alexa leant against a glossy cabinet,
watching him reset the machine. 'You know I'd really love
to come to the opening of your club this Friday night. I've
never been to a nightclub before.'

'No.'

Alexa blinked with surprise at his curt tone. 'No?'

'That's what I said.'

'Why not?'

'You're too straight.'

'Too straight?' She scowled at him. 'What does that mean?'

'It means what it means,' he dismissed in a way that only ratcheted up her annoyance. 'And I have no intention of arguing with you about it. It's too early in the morning, for a start.'

'Then don't be obnoxious.'

'I'm not being obnoxious.' His brows drew down, matching the set of his mouth. 'You're not the clubbing type. If you want to do touristy things like shopping or going to the West End or the ballet, just let me know and I'll have Hannah arrange it.'

'Hannah?' She was completely miffed at his condescension. 'One of your old girlfriends?'

'She's my assistant.'

Oh, right. She remembered Nasrin mentioning Hannah now that she thought about it, but she'd been too incensed by his attitude to place her. 'I'm nowhere near as straight as you seem think I am,' she said, wondering what he would say if she told him about how she had gone behind her father's back to be with Stefano.

'Yes, you are.'

He retrieved his coffee and turned to face the kitchen windows as if that was the end of the discussion.

Infuriated, Alexa glared at his wide back. 'You're as immovable as my father,' she snapped, her temper spiking. 'And you think you know everything, just as he does.'

'Alexa—'

'Are you usually this grouchy or is it having me here in your space that's making you so unreasonable?'

'I'm not a morning person.'

'You don't say. Well, I am, and when you walked in before I thought maybe we could find some common ground between us, maybe even become friends, to make the next two weeks easier, but you're really making me rethink that strategy.'

Rafe let out a rough breath as if the very sight of her annoyed him. 'Good. It's best if we're not friends.'

Not having expected such a brutal response, Alexa blinked. 'Then what would you suggest?'

He paused, his blue eyes as stormy as the Atlantic as he stared at her. 'Nothing. I suggest nothing.'

Alexa's brows shot up. 'So you want me to come up with all the ideas?'

'No.' He pushed a lock of hair back from his forehead, clearly frustrated. 'I meant that we literally do nothing. This isn't a forever thing, Alexa. We're here because I mucked up and let chemistry get in the way of rational thinking. That won't happen again.'

'By chemistry you mean—'

'Sexual attraction. Biology.' His eyes pinned her to the spot and all she could think about was sex. Something hot and dark passed between them before he blinked, deliberately severing the connection. 'I'm referring to this thing between us that you'd like to pretend doesn't exist. Fortunately, it will fade soon enough. In the meantime I don't need to know if you're a morning person or a night person and I don't want to know if there is any common ground between us. If you want this to go easier you'll stay on your side of the bed—metaphorically speaking—and I'll stay on mine.'

Shaken by the harshness of his tone, and her own hurt response at how little he wanted to do with her, Alexa hid her emotions behind an arched brow. 'Okay, well, that does make it easier. Now I don't have to rack my brain trying to make small talk while I'm here. Thanks for the heads-up.'

'Alexa—'

'You know, if you ever get sick of women falling in love with you, just show them your grouchy side. It will cure them of any fantasies straight away.' She kept her tone deliberately light but she could tell by his frown that he wasn't buying it. Still, she didn't care. She was close to tears because, after their brief moment of camaraderie the night before, she'd thought he liked her, if only a little.

But that was what came from being too needy and she'd thought she'd learned that lesson a long time ago.

And suddenly she was assailed by a feeling of loneliness she hadn't felt since Sol had died, old feelings of inadequacy threatening to swamp her.

'Alexa—'

'Sorry, I have to go.' Knowing that her emotions were way too close to the surface and refusing to cry in front of another man who didn't want her, she quickly dumped the cold remains of her coffee in the sink and rinsed the mug. 'I'm all sweaty after my yoga workout. Thanks for the coffee. Have a nice day.'

Escaping down the hall, she headed for her bedroom, her ears straining to hear if he followed her. Of course he hadn't. Why would he?

She released a breath she told herself was relief, an ache in her chest she didn't want to acknowledge. What did she care if he didn't want to be friends? She didn't need his friendship either. She didn't need anything from him.

Grabbing her laptop from her satchel, she set it on the bed and typed in her passcode. Two weeks stretched before her as endless as two years, and she pulled up the files she'd been working on before the wedding.

If she did nothing else, these two weeks she could at least work. There was plenty of it, and she had to prove to her father that she could do this. And to herself. Besides, anything was better than this horrible hollow feeling of rejection inside her chest that she had never wanted to feel again.

CHAPTER SIX

A MAN'S HOME was usually his castle, but right now Rafe's castle—his 'castle in the clouds'—felt more like a prison. Only it wasn't a prison keeping him locked in; it was a prison keeping him locked out. This past week he'd found it safer staying at the office for as long as possible rather than risk returning home, where he might run into his delectable wife.

But even for a man who kept long hours, this routine was exhausting, especially since it was past midnight for the fourth night this week and he still wasn't home.

It was either stay away or be rude to Alexa again, as he had been that first morning. Finding her in tight-fitting yoga gear, frowning at his coffee machine like a cute disgruntled kitten, had nearly had him lifting her onto the counter, stepping between her legs and telling her that the only instruction she needed was in how to pleasure him.

Just thinking about it was enough to make his body burn. So instead he'd been rude and hurt her when he'd dismissed her invitation of friendship. And he hadn't liked hurting her. Hadn't liked dimming the light in her clear, green eyes.

Normally he was laid-back and calm. Normally he'd come home from a hard day at work and put on some rock music, maybe play a little jazz or classical Chopin depending on his mood. Sometimes he'd grab a cold beer from the fridge and turn on the football, catch up on some of the highlights. Other times, if he was tired after a night networking at one of his clubs, or being with a woman, he'd grab whatever Mrs Harrington had left for him in the fridge, wash it down with an accompanying Burgundy and head straight to bed.

Simple. Easy.

He rarely questioned his routine, and if he ever felt a little lonely, or restless, he hit the gym.

Now he found himself looking for signs of Alexa in his home. Like the sweater she'd left over the back of a chair last night, and the hairband she'd left in the kitchen the night before that. He probably owed her an apology for being so distant all week, but that would involve speaking to her and the last thing he wanted to do was to encourage her to want to be 'friends' again. Friends didn't want to tear the other person's clothes off at just the sight of them, so that was out of the question.

'We're here, sir,' Stevens said, alerting him to the fact that he was sitting in the back of the Mercedes and the engine wasn't even running.

'Great.'

He gave Stevens a curt nod and headed for his lift, thankful when he found his apartment shrouded in darkness because it meant that Alexa would be once again in bed.

Placing his computer bag on the sofa, he noticed a pair of socks sitting on the side table, along with an empty mug of herbal tea and a scattering of magazines.

Shaking his head, he wondered how he was supposed to forget she was living with him when she left tiny reminders of her presence lying around. Not to mention the sweet scent of her perfume that lingered in the air.

Gritting his teeth, he dumped her mug in the sink and her socks in the laundry before heading to his room.

Strangely, keeping people at a distance and compartmentalising his life had never been one of his issues before, but he had to admit that he was struggling with Alexa.

Nine days.

That was all he had left of her stay in his home. If he survived it with his sanity intact he'd deserve more than a gold star.

He'd deserve her.

Biting back an oath at the ridiculousness of that thought, he decided to ignore his hollow stomach and head for bed. God knew he didn't want to tempt fate and run into the woman in his kitchen again. Which was when he noticed a light glowing from beneath his library door.

Hoping Alexa had left the light on by mistake and wouldn't be inside, he was pulled up short when he opened the door to find her slumped over the antique desk in the corner.

With his heart in his mouth, he strode towards her, hoping with every breath in his body that there was nothing wrong with her.

'Alexa?'

He reached out and gently shook her shoulder, relieved beyond reason when she made a small snuffling sound and buried her face against her arm.

Thank God. She wasn't unconscious, or worse, and his heart rate steadied once more.

She looked angelic in sleep, her glorious hair piled on top of her head in a messy topknot. Rejecting his body's immediate reaction to the sight of her, he frowned as he took in the mountain of paperwork scattered over the desk.

Work, he realised as he studied the papers, remembering how her assistant had told her she wasn't to do any.

She must have printed the documents from the laptop that was on sleep mode beside her.

'Alexa?' He tried again to rouse her but she gave another grumpy little whimper and tried to flick him away. Presumably, since she was a morning person, she wouldn't be chirpy at being woken in the middle of the night.

He found he quite liked seeing her all rumpled and sleepy, and then cut the thought off at the knees.

'Alexa, you need to wake up.'

Coming to with a start, she blinked up at him, and it was all Rafe could do not to reach down and kiss the sleepy pout from her lips. To distract himself he jerked his glance in the direction of the papers spread around her. 'Have you been at this all day?'

'Oh, hello.' She yawned and stretched her arms above her head. 'Mostly. It took longer than I thought. I did go for a walk in Hyde Park, but I had to put the sightseeing I planned on hold— Oh, sorry, I didn't mean to bore you.' She glanced away from him and when she spoke next her tone was decidedly frosty, as if she'd recalled their last interaction and hated him. 'What time is it? No, don't answer that. I'll find out for myself.'

'It's after midnight. And you don't have to treat me like a villain.'

'I'm not,' she said coolly, stacking her papers together.

Rafe scowled. 'Have you been at this all night? You'll wear yourself out if this is the pace you keep in Berenia.'

'That's not your concern.'

'Okay.' He held his hands up in front of him. 'Will it help if I apologise for being a first-rate jerk the other morning?'

She glanced up at him from beneath long sooty lashes, and Rafe's jaw clenched against the punch of instant attraction.

'Perhaps.'

'Then I'm sorry. I wasn't in a great mood, but I don't want you to feel uncomfortable around me.'

'I don't. I've had work to do.'

Which brought him back to how tired she looked. 'Work you're not supposed to be doing.'

She shrugged. 'Someone has to do it or it won't get done.'

'Delegate.'

'It's not that simple. We need to hire new staff, and—'

'Duty called.'

'Yes. Something I would have thought you would understand even if you don't like it.'

'I understand it. I even lived it for a time, particularly when Jag was studying in the US. Unfortunately, I didn't live up to my father's expectations as a suitable fill-in.'

She blinked at his harsh tone. 'How could you not?'

Rafe's jaw hardened. 'I wasn't Jag.'

A slight frown marred her forehead, her eyes fixed on his as if she saw more than he had intended her to see. 'But that's—'

'Irrelevant.' He cut off her sympathetic response. He never talked about the past. Not even with his siblings. 'If the people of Santara should ever need me I would be there for them, but this isn't about me. This is about you needing to find balance.' He perched on the edge of the desk, his fingers itching to push back the strand of hair that curved over her cheek. 'I told you before that you need to say no more often.'

'I'm not good at no.' She gave him a brief look. 'I suppose that makes me the dutiful little mouse in your eyes but—'

'I should never have said that,' Rafe interjected. 'You're

dedicated and focused and that will make you a great queen, but you should stand up for yourself more.'

'Well, thanks. For the compliment.' She huffed out a breath. 'As to the rest... I do try to say no, but there's so much to learn. And it's so easy to make a mistake.'

'Mistakes are *how* we learn.'

'They're not how *I* want to learn.' She shook her head. 'They cost too much.'

Rafe frowned at the vehemence in her voice. 'You're speaking from experience.' And not a good one, he guessed.

'Yes, but we all make mistakes, don't we?' she replied defensively. 'Even you.'

'I don't deny it. Most of mine get splashed across the Internet. But I doubt you've ever made a mistake worth talking about.'

She narrowed her eyes and took the bait as he hoped she would. 'I told you the other morning that I'm not as straight as you think I am. I nearly caused a scandal once.'

Rafe raised an eyebrow. 'I doubt that.'

'You think me so boring?'

'I don't think you're boring at all.' He thought she was the most beguiling woman he'd ever met and, to his surprise, he wanted to know her secrets. Especially this one. 'Tell me about your scandal.'

Her lips twisted distastefully and for a moment he thought she'd tell him to mind his own business again.

'I was seventeen and naive.' She arched a brow as if daring him to mock her. 'He was Italian with nice arms and he worked in the stables.'

'Ah, I think I see where this is going,' he said, hoping he was wrong. 'Pray, continue.'

'It's not that ground-breaking, actually... He told me that he loved me and took me to bed. Then he went straight to my father and used my virginity as a bargaining chip so we'd be forced to get married.'

She was right; the story wasn't ground-breaking, just totally humiliating for the one who had been used so callously.

Knowing how bad it felt to be judged out of hand, he kept his tone as light as hers. 'I take it that your father didn't exactly jump for joy at the information and welcome him into the household with open arms.'

Alexa gave him a wry grin. 'I still don't know how much he paid Stefano to leave and never contact me again, but sometimes, when I'm feeling particularly low, I like to imagine that he put the country into debt because of it.'

Rafe laughed at her dryness, but it didn't stop him from wanting to shove this Stefano's teeth down his throat and bury him beneath the blazing sun with just his head showing, as his ancestors would have done.

'If you give me his full name I could find him and have the Chase brothers beat the cretin to a pulp.'

Unless he got to him first, of course.

'You'd do that for me?' She blinked at him in surprise, as if no one had suggested it before. 'Not even my father said that, and you're the ultimate heartbreaker. You leave women crying all the time.'

'That is not true,' he said curtly, for the first time wishing that his playboy reputation didn't exist. 'I only enter relationships with women who know that I won't fall in love with them, and I'm upfront and honest about that from the beginning. If they cry when it ends it's not because I duped them.'

Her green eyes grew thoughtful. 'How do you know you won't fall in love with them?'

'Because I don't need love. And I make sure to never confuse emotion with sex.'

She paused as if that information required some effort to digest. 'I need to be more like that. But at least Stefano taught me what to look out for when it comes to choosing a life partner. Or what *not* to look out for.'

'What he should have taught you was how good it can be between a man and a woman in bed.'

He saw her throat constrict at his words and suddenly his hands itched to touch her. That Italian idiot might not have been able to show her a good time, but now Rafe couldn't stop thinking about how much he wanted to replace her bad memories with good ones that he'd personally created.

Needing to stop himself from reaching for her and doing something he'd later regret, he pushed away from the desk. 'We should go to bed.'

Alexa blinked at him, her eyes as wide as a baby owl's. 'Together?'

The muscle in his jaw clenched tight as his brain easily conjured up an image of her naked on his sheets. Before he could figure out how to respond to that, a streak of hot, mortified colour scored along her cheekbones. 'Forget I said that. I'm clearly more tired than I thought.'

Wanting to defuse the situation, Rafe nodded. 'I get it. My club is opening tomorrow night and I could use a few hours myself.'

'Right.' She blinked up at him from beneath long silky lashes. 'About that. Am I still banned from your club?'

'Yes.' No way did he want her at one of his clubs, distracting him constantly.

'Won't that look strange?' she persisted. 'As your wife I would be expected to go to support you.'

'I don't need support.'

'Everyone needs support. But, regardless, the media

will expect to see me there. I take it you are having a media presence.'

'Only for a couple of hours. No one will know you're not there.'

She mulled that over and then tilted her chin up at a belligerent angle.

'I'd like to go.'

Not wanting to get into a debate with her when his brain and body were mutually stuck on images of her naked and wanting, Rafe sighed. 'Alexa—'

'You've just told me I should stand up for myself more. Not to take no for an answer.'

'I believe I said you should start saying no more often.'

'Something you're really good at. But it amounts to the same thing. Taking charge of my needs. And I'd like to see your club. So I'm taking charge.'

Rafe ran a hand through his hair, a frustrated growl leaving his throat. 'I didn't mean for you to start "taking charge" with me.'

Her sudden smile made his heart kick against his ribs.

'For some reason I feel safe with you.'

'The last thing I am is safe.' Especially with the visions currently going through his head. When she didn't respond, or back down as he'd hoped, he shook his head. 'Fine. I'll arrange a car to pick you up at ten.'

'Ten? Isn't that a bit late?'

'That's early by London standards. Nothing happens before then.'

'Ten. Okay, got it.' Her eyes sparkled like clean-cut emeralds, her happiness making his heartbeat quicken.

'If you need anything before then, or change your mind, I'll have Hannah on standby to help out.'

'I won't change my mind. And you won't regret this.'

She was almost vibrating with excitement. 'You won't even know I'm there. Promise.'

Rafe groaned silently at the enormous smile on her face. He should have left her asleep at the desk.

Pacing the upper floor office suite at Bound, Rafe watched on a bank of security monitors as guests continued to pour through the front door of the club, each one wide-eyed with delight as they took in the chrome and glass chandeliers and the Dalí-inspired decor.

'So far, so good,' Hannah, his assistant, ventured beside him. A pocket rocket, Hannah had the energy of a race-horse, which was probably why she hadn't quit on him like so many of his other EAs had done over the years.

Rafe grunted in acknowledgement. At this point he didn't much care about the success of the club. He just wanted to know where Alexa was.

'Oh, relax,' Hannah admonished as she saw him check his watch again. 'I organised Chase Security to travel in with her as well as her own security detail, as you in-structed. Between the lot of them, you'd think she was bringing the heads of state of fifty nations with her. But she should be here any minute.'

'Since when do I worry?' Rafe said, not bothering to hide his irritation.

Hannah's grin widened before she checked a message that popped up on her tablet. 'Since you got married, it seems. But I can see why you married her. We had a great time shopping. She's truly lovely. Not at all stuck-up, as one might expect from royalty, but then you're not stuck up, so I don't know why I thought she would be. And she looks incredible in her new dress. We had a lot of fun choosing it. Oh, I better go. The Duke and Duchess of Crenshore have arrived and I need to show them to their private table.'

Not hearing a word she'd said after 'new dress', Rafe's mind was now obsessed with exactly what this new dress would look like. Would her hair be up or down? He still had no idea how long it was. Another unwanted obsession he'd suddenly developed.

Glancing once more at the display showing the entrance, Rafe saw one of the Chase Security guards he'd organised to shadow Alexa walk through the door.

Not realising he was holding his breath, he waited for Alexa to appear and exhaled at seeing her.

Her hair was down. And it was long. Almost waist-length and as straight as an arrow.

Wearing a trench coat and stiletto heels, she looked regal and calm except for the glitter in her eyes that gave away her excitement as she scanned the foyer.

A similar feeling went through him now and he did his best to douse it. There was no reason he should be 'excited' that she was here. He'd agreed to let her come because he felt sorry for her, stuck in his apartment working. She worked too much, trying to prove herself, as he had once done. Only she was perfect as she was.

Stopping those thoughts dead in their tracks, he noted with satisfaction how her security detail scanned the crowd before allowing her to move further inside. It was guests only at the club tonight, and Rafe had personally checked over the list and given it to her team to cross-reference, but he didn't want to take any chances with her safety.

For some reason I feel safe with you.

A muscle ticked in his jaw. She'd been talking about taking charge of her professional needs, but his mind was still stuck on her 'taking charge' in a much more pleasurable capacity.

Cursing at the single track his mind had been on ever

since the Santarian charity ball, he refocused on making sure Alexa made it into his club without incident.

A member of his staff approached her, indicating that he would take her jacket, and Rafe's gut tightened as she slowly pulled at the belt, shrugging her shoulders so that the fabric slipped down her arms.

Rafe nearly choked on the air he'd just sucked into his lungs.

The dress she was wearing was black, tight and minimal in the extreme. It was as if the manufacturer had run out of fabric, shrugged and sewn it together anyway. Sheer gossamer tights covered legs that looked impossibly long in stiletto heels. Her waist looked tiny, her breasts full and voluptuous.

Nearby, men gave her covetous looks and Rafe found himself moving towards the lift that would take him to the ground floor before he'd even thought about it. She would cause a war in his club if he didn't immediately bundle her back into that coat.

'I feel so alive. Almost electric.' Alexa's eyes sparkled with pleasure when she spotted him. 'This place is fantastic. Dark and mysterious—it's as if something magical could happen around any corner. But it's also a touch romantic with the effect of the mauve and blue lighting on the wall murals. And the music—'

Hannah interrupted her excitement with a glass of champagne. 'It's French, of course. You look brilliant. That dress is perfect. Don't you think so, Rafe?'

'Perfect.'

Alexa raised a brow at his droll reply. He was going to have to pull himself together before he sank his hands into all that lustrous hair and said to hell with the club—they were going back to the apartment to have the kind of sex he was always reputed to have.

'Thanks to you, Hannah.' Alexa grinned happily. 'I had the most amazing afternoon.'

'My pleasure,' Hannah replied. 'I'll swap the office for Bond Street any day of the week.'

'Are you okay?' Alexa finally remembered he was present and frowned. 'You seem angry.'

'I'm not angry. But I suggest you don't bend over in that dress.'

'Is it too short? Hannah assured me that it wouldn't stand out in the crowd.'

Rafe gave Hannah a look that promised she'd be missing her bonus next Christmas. 'Hannah was wrong.'

'Okay, well... I think I see a fire I need to put out,' Hannah said tactfully. 'You two have fun.'

Alexa smoothed her hands down the slightly flared hem of her dress. 'It's no shorter than some of the other dresses being worn tonight. I have to confess I didn't think you'd mind, given the photos of some of the women I've seen you with.'

Yes, but none of those women had been his wife, and he had never even noticed if anyone had thrown them admiring glances. Now he couldn't stop noticing the men who cast covetous glances Alexa's way.

'Let's go to my table.'

That would be a safe place to stash her for a while. She could watch everything that happened from the third-floor balcony that overlooked two split-level dance floors before he sent her home.

She pressed in closely behind him, grabbing the sleeve of his shirt so she didn't lose him in the crowd. Rafe thought about placing her in front of him but there was only so much his control could handle, and having her pert derrière so close at hand just might tip him over the edge.

'I know I'm not familiar with nightclubs,' she said as he led her up the circular glass staircase, nodding to one of the ground staff monitoring the third floor, 'but I doubt there would ever be one out there to top this. You must be really proud.'

Exceptionally pleased by her praise, he smiled. 'I'm glad you like it.'

Reaching their destination, he ushered her into the velvet-upholstered circular sofa. Her slender legs were partially concealed by the small central table, but that left her cleavage and her wide, happy smile for him to focus on and that wasn't much better. Forget working out how much time they had left in days, he needed to work out how much time they had left in hours; it would at least give his mind something to do.

One hundred and ninety two.

Not helpful.

Trying to ignore how tense Rafe was wasn't easy, but by her second glass of champagne Alexa was managing it. Berenia didn't have anything like this and while she was used to being the centre of attention she'd never been completely comfortable with it. But here, in this club, she felt as if she could be anyone. She didn't feel as if she had to be the proper Crown Princess. She felt as if she could let her hair down. And she had. The feel of it against her bare back heightened her senses and made her feel so different from her usual self. So did the loud music flooding her body with its throbbing beat.

She glanced across at Rafe, who was speaking to someone who had stopped at their table and who was more interested in him than in her. This was his domain and she liked seeing him in it. She liked taking a back seat. Like this, she could just be any one of the women he took out with him. A woman he would later take home. To his bed.

Her gaze roamed his wide shoulders and silky dark hair. She'd always imagined that her dream man would be someone upstanding and good. Someone like his brother, whom she'd built her secret fantasies around, based on his chivalrous actions when she was younger. But really, the King of Santara, as handsome as he was, had never made her feel the way Rafe did. Never made her want to climb into his lap and straddle his hard thighs the way she wanted to do now.

As if she'd actually reached over and touched him, Rafe turned his head away from the man leaning on their booth seat, his smoky gaze connecting with hers as if he knew every one of her sinfully erotic thoughts. Instinctively, her eyes moved to his sensual mouth and the stubble that had grown in over the course of the day. In a black shirt, his hair falling in thick waves, he looked like a modern-day pirate.

Alexa casually picked up her champagne glass and tried to pretend that her heart wasn't racing. What would he say if she vocalised her desires? What would he say if she slid along the raspberry-coloured bench seat and whispered that she wanted to change their bargain? That she wanted sex with him whether it was meaningless or not.

'I see everyone agrees that this club is sensational,' she said as the man Rafe had been conversing with strolled away from their table. 'You must feel proud.'

'It takes an army of people to create something like this. It's not all my doing.'

'But it takes a visionary to conceive of it, and then someone to take the risk and actually execute it.'

He swallowed a mouthful of champagne and Alexa felt transfixed by the movement of his throat. She felt breathless and the cavernous room seemed to shrink as he sat there watching her with an intensity she wanted to interpret as sexual.

Because this man might be wrong for her on so many levels but that didn't stop her from wanting him. He was so easy to talk to, so easy to be with. It was sexy to be able to say something to a man and have him actually listen to her. And she did feel safe with him. Safe and sensual. Especially when he kissed her.

'Alexa, if you don't stop looking at me like that I'm likely to do something we'll both regret.'

His deep growly voice flowed through her body like hot caramel. 'Like what?'

His blue eyes turned as hot as a flame, his body going so still at her words she knew he was holding his breath. 'Like things you don't want to know about.'

Alexa's tongue slipped out to moisten her dry lips. 'Maybe I do.'

'You don't.' The blunt words were edged in steel and made all the insecurities left over from Stefano, and King Jaeger's, rejection come storming back to her. What was she doing? She wasn't some femme fatale! She was the woman that men walked away from.

But you already know he's going to walk away, a little voice reminded her. *It's why you chose him.*

Emboldened by that voice, her slinky dress and the hard, hot man beside her, Alexa decided she could either give into her inadequacies or throw caution to the wind and see what happened. With her heart in her mouth she embraced the latter, slowly crossing one leg over the other and gathering her hair in one hand to bring it forward over her shoulder. 'Why don't you let me be the judge of what I want? I'm not a child, Rafe.'

'I know you're not a child,' he bit out. 'Nobody looking at you in that dress could mistake you for one.'

'You don't like my dress?'

Before he could respond a laughing Hannah stopped by their table. 'Everything okay, boss?'

'Everything is fine, Hannah. You can officially clock off duty now and have a drink.'

'Oh, thank goodness.' She gave Alexa a wide smile. 'I've been desperate to hit the dance floor. Have you had a dance yet, Your Highness?'

'Please, just call me Alexa. A title seems so inappropriate tonight. Tonight I just want to have fun.'

'Then let's dance. Do you want to come, boss?'

'No.'

'Mind if I drag Alexa along?'

'Yes.'

But Alexa was already sliding from the booth seat. 'Don't listen to him, Hannah. I'd love to go dancing. It's what I'm here for.'

Hannah laughed. 'I like this one. Make sure you don't do anything to lose her.'

Weaving her way down the stairs, Alexa could feel Rafe's gaze on her the whole way but she refused to turn and glance back at him. Somehow she knew the steps to the timeless game he had started playing with her at the Summer Palace, which had stalled when her father had forced them to get married. Well, no one was forcing him to do anything now, and if he didn't want her she'd find someone else who did. After all, that had been the point of her initial mission—to buy herself some time to find a man she *did* want to marry.

Unfortunately, her mind seemed inconveniently stuck on one man right now. *Her Prince.*

'This club is going to be on everyone's list of where to

go for years,' Hannah stated, raising her voice above the upbeat music. 'I love my job!'

She waved her hands in the air, her enthusiasm catching, and Alexa found herself loosening up as she gave up any semblance of self-consciousness and moved her body in a way that felt sexy and liberating.

'So you like working for Rafe?' she asked.

'Oh, he's amazing. The best boss in the world. And I'm not just saying that because you're his wife—it's true. He's generous and disciplined and so kind. Last month he asked me to organise an all-expenses-paid holiday to the Caribbean for a month, along with six months off with full pay, for one of our accountants whose wife is ill. He's a dream boss.'

A dream boss? Hannah had just described her dream man. She certainly hadn't described someone Alexa had believed to be self-centred and hedonistic.

'You're a lucky woman to have captured him,' Hannah continued. 'I think a thousand women lay heartbroken in their beds on the day you married.'

'You can stop talking now, Hannah.'

Alexa turned at Rafe's droll tone to find him standing stock-still in front of her, the gyrating bodies of the other dancers surrounding him like caricatures in a stage play. She slowly dropped her arms from over her head, unable to take her eyes from his.

'I thought you didn't want to dance?' Hannah laughed.

'I don't.' Rafe's gaze slid down over Alexa's body with such searing heat she turned liquid inside. 'Go get a drink, Hannah. Your duty is done here.'

'I can see that.' Hannah grinned and melted into the surrounding dancers.

Alexa didn't notice Hannah disappear; she only had

eyes for Rafe, who was looking at her as a wolf might look at a helpless deer.

'I do like your dress. But I like you even more.'

'You do?'

His hands moved to the sides of her waist. 'Too much. I've been trying to avoid giving in to this all week, but you've defeated me.' His voice turned low and growly. 'But this won't just blur those lines between us, Princess, it will completely obliterate them.'

'I don't mind.'

A serious glint entered his dark eyes. 'And if it's another mistake?'

'Are you trying to warn me off you? I'm not that naive young girl any more, Rafe. I've grown up a lot since Stefano. I know this isn't about love, so if you're worried that I'll fall for you like every other woman, I won't.'

'That's not what I'm afraid of.'

'Then what are you afraid of?'

His hand came up to the side of her face, his fingers stroking through the heavy strands of her hair. They could have been alone for all the notice they took of the energetic dancers around them. 'I'm afraid I won't want to stop once I've had you. I'm afraid I want you too much.'

His words were thrilling, a balm to her wounded feminine soul. 'Then take me,' she whispered, moving a step closer so that her body was flush up against his. 'Take me and show me what pure, unadulterated pleasure feels like.'

A harsh curse left Rafe's mouth right before his lips crashed down over hers. It was like a match meeting a firecracker. Alexa's body caught alight, her mind empty of everything else but this moment. This man.

Too soon the kiss was over, Rafe lifting his head and tucking her in tightly against him. 'We can't stay here. We'll get arrested.'

All but dragging her from the dance floor, Rafe stopped briefly in front of her security detail before clamping his hand over hers and leading her along a series of narrow hallways until he opened a heavy door and ushered her through.

Glancing around, she realised they were in an underground garage beside a shiny black motorbike.

Rafe pulled out a leather jacket from beneath the seat and fed her arms into it. The jacket swamped her and smelled of him.

'What about you?' she asked when she noticed that there was only one.

'I'm hot enough.'

There were many responses she could make to that but she didn't have the experience or confidence to banter with him in that way.

Rafe pulled a helmet from the handlebars and turned back to her. One of his hands went to her hair and he breathed deeply. 'Your hair is beautiful.' He twisted the strands in his fist and brought her mouth to his in a fierce kiss that set her on fire all over again.

Alexa moaned softly as he released her.

'Home first,' he said, plunking the helmet on her head and buckling it.

Taking his hand, Alexa slid her legs over the back of the bike and settled on the seat, futilely tugging at her skirt. 'Ignore it and hang on tight,' Rafe instructed. 'I won't be going slowly.'

It was a rush to know that she affected him like this and she did what he asked, sliding her arms around his lean waist as the bike started to move.

CHAPTER SEVEN

THE RIDE HOME was as fast as he'd warned it would be. Alexa felt as if she'd just got used to the vibration of the engine between her legs and the thrill of being on a bike for the first time when he was zooming down the slope that led to his underground garage.

Moments later they were in the lift and heading skyward. Rafe watched her from across the small cubicle but didn't touch her. She used the time to catch her breath, her senses completely alert to his every breath.

Stepping out of the lift, Alexa smoothed her skirt and wondered what to do with her hands. Now that she was here, now that they were doing this, she felt a moment's hesitation.

'Alexa?'

Standing before her, all tall, dark and dangerously male, he made her heartbeat quicken. He was so beautiful,, his jaw clenched with the intensity of his arousal.

The knowledge was as intoxicating as it was scary because, for someone who always thought about the consequences of her actions, Alexa knew she hadn't thought this through completely. She also knew that she might never experience a feeling like this again and that she wanted this man. She wanted him more than was good for her.

'You still with me, princess?'

Rafe smoothed his hands over her shoulders, his touch electric. Alexa's eyes sought his and although she knew this would likely mean more to her than it would to him she couldn't bring herself to care. After she and Rafe ended their marriage she would always have this memory, this moment, and she shoved any remaining inhibitions and concerns aside and took the extra step needed to bring her into his arms.

'Yes,' she husked. 'I'm still with you.'

Taking her at her word Rafe took command, pressing her back against the door and eradicating the last of her doubts with an erotically charged kiss.

It was like a brand, a claim that said 'mine', and Alexa opened her mouth to the demand of his tongue. Her arms went around his neck to hold him close, her fingers buried in his hair as she pulled him closer.

'You smell like sugar and…leather,' he groaned, his lips working their way along her jawline as he swiftly stripped the jacket down her arms and let it drop to the floor.

Excitement poured through her at the hunger in his eyes, her legs suddenly giving out so that the only thing holding her up was his arms, banded around her waist.

He moved his hands to cup her bottom and Alexa moaned indistinctly into his mouth, her body craving his.

Needing to touch his skin, her fingers tugged at his shirt until she had it free, a frisson of desire racing through her as she stroked her fingers over lean male flesh.

Her touch unleashed something primal inside him because his mouth turned greedy and hot, his hard body pinning her to the door as his hands roamed, bringing her core up against his hot hard erection.

'Rafe?' Alexa wrenched her head back as everything inside her softened to yield to that hard male presence between her legs.

Swearing softly, he scooped her into his arms and carried her into his bedroom.

Momentarily breaking the kiss, he slid her body down his until she was standing in front of him. With sure, practised fingers he found the invisible zip in the side of her dress and deftly divested her of both her dress and her bra, holding her hands to the side so that he could look at her.

'You're beautiful,' he breathed, bringing one hand up to cup her breast while the other went to the back of her head to bring her mouth back up to his.

The kiss was fierce and sweet, the sensations of his fingers teasing her nipple sending sparks of need through her body that obliterated everything else except the man touching her.

'Oh, please...' She didn't know what she was begging him to do but when his mouth closed over the tip of her breast and he flicked her with his tongue she thought she might expire from pleasure. Shifting to her other breast, he let out a low chuckle at her soft pleas and then she felt the coolness of the mattress at her back as he lowered her onto it.

Aroused and aching, Alexa fumbled with the buttons on his shirt, desperate to expose his body to her view. Helping her, Rafe shrugged wide shoulders until the shirt slid down his back and her hands roved over his naked chest and back.

The sheer size and power of his corded body was breathtaking and even though part of her knew it was dangerous to want him this much she couldn't help it. She had no control over her body or her senses and she didn't want any. She was a willing captive to the fever raging through her body, and she would have flown into the centre of the sun if he had asked her to.

His lips returned to hers, commanding and potently

male, his fingers hot against the inside of her thighs as he swept them higher until he was cupping her through her panties.

A small whimper escaped her and she bit gently into the hard ball of his shoulder as his finger stroked and teased until she was a writhing mass of nerves and sensation.

'Rafe, please...'

Smiling against her neck, he nuzzled at her breast, flicking his tongue against the rigid peak at the same time as his fingers teased.

'Please what, my sweet?' He continued to stroke and torture as he slowly, so slowly, shifted the silk aside until finally he was touching her, his fingers finding and parting her flesh before plunging inside her hot, wet sheath.

Gripped in a fever of desire, Alexa wasn't sure who groaned the loudest and then she didn't care as Rafe expertly flicked a finger across the bundle of nerves nested at her apex and sent her spiralling into an earth-shattering orgasm that made her scream.

She must have lost consciousness because suddenly her panties were gone and Rafe had cupped her bottom and raised her to his lips, his tongue lapping at her and bringing her body to another mind-numbing climax.

Spent and gasping, she couldn't move as Rafe crawled back up her body, kissing every inch of skin he came into contact with.

'You,' Rafe growled, coming down over her with lethal male grace, 'are incredible.'

Alexa felt incredible but she wanted more. The space between her legs felt hollow and empty, her eyes widening as Rafe rose to his knees and unzipped his trousers. With bated breath she watched as he lowered the fabric down over his hips, his thick, gorgeous erection springing free.

Unaware that she'd licked her lips until he made a low growly sound, she pushed to a sitting position and ran her hands down over his heated torso, the dark hair on his chest soft like a wolf's pelt beneath her fingers. Moving downwards, she couldn't stop herself from reaching out to touch him. As she gripped him her eyes flew to his. He'd sunk his teeth into his lower lip, his eyes hooded as he watched her, and it made her more daring.

Stroking firmly, she felt one of his hands softly grip her hair and she hadn't even realised she'd brought her mouth closer to the swollen length of him until she felt him against her lips.

The earthy taste of him burst across her tongue, the flavour so deeply male. She opened her lips and took him into her mouth, a heady sense of power filling her when his fingers gripped harder in her hair and a groan tore from his throat.

Loving the silky hard length of him against her tongue, Alexa increased the pressure of her lips until she heard him swear, and then she was being pulled up and stretched out beneath him like a feast.

A thrill raced through her as he parted her thighs and looked down at her. Grabbing a condom from the side table drawer, he rolled it on and then braced himself with his hands either side of her face. Mesmerised, Alexa couldn't look away from his hungry gaze as he slowly pushed into her.

Something in the way he watched her almost tenderly made her unable to tear her eyes from his. Rafe must have felt the force of the connection too because his lips came down to claim hers once more as his body thrust hard, filling her and driving her to the heights of another pulse-pounding climax before he followed her over the edge on a hoarse cry of completion.

* * *

Waking up from what might actually have been the best sex of his life, Rafe glanced at the woman curled up in his arms, her dark hair spread out on his white sheets like a waterfall of black silk. She was asleep, her head nestled in the curve of his shoulder and her sweet breath warm against his chest.

Waiting for the usual need for space and privacy to overtake him, he was surprised when it didn't come. Instead he felt replete and relaxed, and more complete than he'd felt in forever.

Complete?

The alien concept entered his head then was gone just as quickly. Sex didn't make him feel complete. That wasn't what he was feeling. What he was feeling was... It was... He frowned. It was pure, unadulterated pleasure after a week of being tied up in the tightest sexual knots he'd ever experienced.

No woman had ever made him want so much or had satisfied him so fully.

Had he really thought he'd be able to ignore her, with the level of sexual chemistry they shared? Well, if he had, he couldn't now. Alexa had been responsive and giving and so sweet that just the memory of her hands and mouth on his body was turning him surprisingly hard again.

His hands stroked down over the silky skin of her arm, his fingers finding and twining with hers. She breathed out a sigh and relaxed more deeply against his side.

He remembered that she'd been up working late last night and was probably exhausted. She worked hard and took her job seriously. Which he supposed she had to. Just as seriously as he took his. When you had the amount of staff he had relying on you to provide their wages it was important to perform well. He supposed they were similar that way. Only he no longer sought the approval of others the way he suspected Alexa did. He'd given up on needing to please a long time ago. She would need to do that too once she became Queen or she'd work herself into the ground. But why was he thinking about Alexa's future?

Usually he didn't concern himself with a woman's life after sex. He'd already moved onto his next task or his next project. It didn't matter where he was, or who the woman was, Rafe always liked to be on the move, rarely staying still long enough to feel trapped. It came, he knew, from always having to toe the royal line when he was younger. From having a father who'd demanded that he behave a certain way, and then giving him grief if he missed the mark.

But why waste time thinking about things that weren't important when he had a warm naked woman he knew would be receptive to his advances if he were to wake her with a soft kiss on those delectable lips?

At least he assumed she'd be receptive. Every other woman he'd ever been with would be, but Alexa wasn't like every other woman. She didn't play the same games, acting coy to try to attract his attention, or turning girlish when she had it. Alexa was far too straightforward and earnest. But then she had no need to play games with him because they were already married. She already had his ring on her finger and he had hers on his.

He held his hand up to the moonlight that spilled in through the gap in the curtains. The room was too dark for him to see the gold, but he could just make out the dull shape of the band. When she'd first slipped it on his finger the weight had felt foreign and unwanted. Funny how it didn't feel like that any more.

It felt right and good.

Right and good?

Something stirred behind his breastbone, some unwanted emotion that caused his ribs to tighten around his chest.

As if sensing his unease, Alexa shifted her knee higher across his thigh. A shot of lust raced through him, a primitive hunger that bordered on need.

Not that he did need. Need had a serious edge of permanence about it. Want? Now want was something he understood. It came and went and put a smile on his face, and his body stirred at the way he *wanted* to wake Alexa now with a line of slow kisses starting at her slender shoulder and encompassing her whole body.

Shifting again, she made a cute little sleep sound that made him lose his train of thought.

He felt her body tense as she awoke and he gently gathered her closer, stroking his hand down the silky skin of her spine.

'Stay asleep, Princess,' he murmured, even though sleep was the last thing on his mind. 'I know you're tired.'

'Sleep?' She raised her head and blinked at him. 'I...' She looked flustered, her eyes uncertain in the dim light as she stared at his face, his chest.

Her tongue came out to lick her lips and before he was even aware that he'd made the decision he rolled her onto her back and kissed her.

After a split second of hesitation her arms went around his neck, her body rising to his.

Hunger ripped through him at the soft sound of pleasure she made when he stroked his tongue into her mouth, his body primed to take her immediately.

But he also wanted to savour her. He wanted to taste her body again, her sweetness.

Loving the way she clung to him, Rafe kissed his away across her face. First her cheeks and the soft skin below her ears, then her eyelids and her nose. Feeling her completely relax beneath him, he slowly moved down her body, laving her neck and licking at her collarbone.

Her gorgeous breasts pointed skyward, her nipples achingly beautiful, and he took first one and then the other into his mouth. Then he positioned her so that she was beneath him, her long legs moving restlessly on the outside of his own.

He used his knees to open her to the hard throb of his erection and he sank into her softness with unerring accuracy. She sobbed his name as he slowly filled her, sweat beading his forehead as her body took him in, her inner muscles gripping him tight.

'Alexa…' he groaned, remembering at the last minute that he wasn't wearing a condom. She arched beneath him, her lower body straining for his thrust.

Seriously perturbed at just how close he had come to forgetting protection, he reached into his side table and sheathed himself before thrusting back inside her tight body.

She came almost instantly, the hot pulsing sensation of her climax shattering his self-control in a maelstrom of pleasure.

Opening her eyes to find herself wrapped in Rafe's arms for the second time that morning, Alexa felt herself tense at the overwhelming vulnerability of being naked in his arms. Not because she regretted what they'd shared, but because she liked it a little too much. The feeling left her somehow defenceless, and her instinct was to pull back because, while she had anticipated the pleasure, she hadn't counted on the emotional connection she'd feel when he joined his body with hers. Only she was quite sure Rafe would have experienced no such thing in return.

Undoubtedly last night had been par for the course for a man of his experience, and she had to keep that front and centre in her mind at all times. Because while she had experienced something monumental in his bed, she knew she'd be alone in that line of thinking.

But it had been monumental. The way he had worshipped her body, the tender kisses he'd lavished on her, the powerful thrusts of his body... It had definitely been mind-blowing, but not in the way that he had meant it would be. It was mind-blowing in that it was so lovely. So beautiful. So everything.

Deeply asleep, he was sprawled on his side, one arm above his head, the other draped over her waist. Shifting slightly out from under his hold, Alexa took advantage of the moment to take her fill of him.

Naked, he was utterly superb. The swell of his biceps and muscled shoulders, the broad chest and trail of hair that bisected his flat belly, the lean line of his hip that made her want to put her lips on his skin again.

He'd lost none of his power or authority in sleep, but he did look more peaceful. More rested.

She thought about the things she had discovered about him the night before. His generosity with his employees, his strong work ethic and the way his employees treated him with such deference and respect. Hannah had sung his praises and not because he was a prince. She truly liked and admired him for the man that he was.

A man, Alexa was starting to suspect, was decent and kind, even though she doubted he'd admit to it. And why was that? Why did he hide that side of his nature? And why, if he wanted her so much, had he stayed away from her all week?

Was it out of deference to her wishes? Because he was afraid she'd fall in love with him? Or something else?

Whatever his reasons, Alexa accepted that she'd been very short-sighted in believing everything she'd read about him. And really she should have known better, but then almost everyone believed what had been written about him and he didn't help that by not defending himself.

Still, there was no doubting some of the stories. He was a notorious playboy, and he'd definitely been a rebel when he was younger—the story of him stealing his father's favourite sports car and cruising through the mountains with a girl, and another of him winning a dangerous cross-country horse race his father had forbidden him to enter, and the stories of his wild parties at the Summer Palace were the stuff of legend—but there was another side to him. A deeper side she longed to explore further.

Her eyes drifted to his mouth and her body flushed with remembered pleasure at all the ways he'd satisfied her throughout the night. He'd certainly delivered on his promise of unadulterated pleasure and in one night he'd completely obliterated her first bumbling sexual experience with the treacherous Stefano.

Recalling how easily she'd fallen under the Italian's spell all those years ago, even knowing that she was older now, still made her throat constrict with unwanted emotion.

The earlier vulnerability she'd felt on waking in Rafe's arms returned full force, along with the sense that she'd never felt such a soul-deep connection with another human being before.

And that was exactly the kind of thinking she needed to avoid at all costs.

Driven out of bed by the knowledge that she was at risk of history repeating itself and creating meaning where there was none, Alexa quietly made her way to her room and jumped in the shower.

Once there she groaned softly as the soapy cloth moved over the sensitive marks left behind by Rafe's love making. He'd been both tender and demanding during the night, and a smile curved her lips as she thought about the way one particular mark had been formed. Warning herself again not to get hung up on what had happened between them, she pulled on her kimono-style robe and went in search of a much-needed coffee.

Determined to figure out how to work the machine on her own this time, she'd just tried her fourth combination of buttons when she heard a deep chuckle behind her. 'For a smart woman, that machine seems to have defeated you.'

Alexa glanced over her shoulder to find six foot three of hot muscular man leaning against the doorframe watching her. He'd put on baggy sweatpants, the rest of him completely bare, his biceps bulging as he folded his arms across his chest, amusement shining from his sexy blue eyes.

She gave him a droll look, unable to stop her gaze from falling to his naked chest. 'For a man with a huge wardrobe, you seem to have forgotten your shirt.'

A sensual grin curved his mouth as he sauntered towards her. 'Why cover up what you like to look at so much?'

'So arrogant,' she accused, catching her breath when he wrapped his arms around her from behind and nuzzled her neck.

'Why didn't you wake me before you got up?' he murmured, his hot breath making her melt.

'I didn't want to disturb you,' she said. Nor had she wanted him to spot the panic that had galvanised her out of his arms.

His lips grazed her ear and he gave it a light nip. 'Next time you wake me, okay?'

'But you were sleeping so peacefully.'

'Wake me so I can kiss you good morning.'

Cupping her jaw, he turned her face so that he could demonstrate and Alexa sighed as she leant into him, a sharp pang darting through her as she wondered if he always insisted on morning kisses from his women.

Reluctantly breaking the kiss, he reached around her to change the coffee settings before pressing Start.

'Does this mean you haven't had coffee all week?' he asked, grinning down at her.

'No, it means your very helpful concierge has brought me one from the café next door every morning.'

He turned her in his arms and linked his arms around her lower back. 'Now you have me.'

The tender words made Alexa's heart beat faster. If she could stop time this second she would, with his strong arms enfolding her body and his hot gaze pinned to hers.

The tone signalled that her coffee was ready, and severed the connection between them. Alexa rubbed her hands over her arms and gripped the mug he handed her in both hands, inhaling the heavenly aroma with a sigh.

Rafe's fingers sifted through her hair, making the mass tumble down around her shoulders.

'This should never be restrained,' he murmured, winding it around his hand.

'It's not practical to wear it down.'

'Practical is boring.'

He dropped a kiss on her mouth before stepping back to grab his own coffee. Alexa watched the play of muscles over his back from beneath the sweep of her lashes, heat curling through her.

When he turned back and saw her a pulse of raw sexual energy arced between them. Watching his eyes darken, a thrill of excitement wound through her right before her stomach announced that it was empty, the loud rumble echoing off the polished angles of the cabinets.

Mortified, she clamped her hand over the offending area and gave him a startled look.

Rafe laughed. 'Aren't princesses allowed to make bodily noises?'

'Not in company.'

'Company?' His eyes narrowed. 'I'm not company.' He dropped his empty espresso cup in the sink and leant back against it, reaching for her and tugging her between his splayed legs. 'I'm your husband.' He massaged the nape of her neck and she moaned as she leant into his touch. 'And your lover. I get special privileges.'

She knew she liked the sound of his words more than was good for her but for some reason she couldn't bring herself to pull away. Being with a man like this was new and intoxicating, and somehow being with *this* man quadrupled the sensation.

'Like hearing my stomach growl?' she said dubiously.

'Like taking you out for breakfast. In fact, let's make it the whole day. We can start with this great place I know that does a mean English breakfast, and play tourist for the day. Go to those places you didn't get to during the week.'

'Really?' Her eyes sparkled like a child standing in front of Harrods' window display at Christmas. Then she remembered that she'd promised to email HR with the report she'd been working on the last few days. 'I would love that but I can't. I have work to finish up.'

'No, you don't. Not only do you need to rest, but it's Saturday.'

'Oh, so it is.' She grinned at him. 'I've lost track of time, and I *never* lose track of time.'

'You work too hard. And while I respect your dedication, you also need to know when to take time out for yourself.'

'And you're going to tell me that now is that time?' Not waiting for his reply and having thrown caution to the wind once already, she decided that she might as well go all-out. 'Okay, fine. The report I have to finish up isn't all that urgent and this...' she opened her eyes wide '...being here with you, is a rare treat. Will we go there on your bike?'

He laughed at the hopeful note in her voice. 'You liked the bike, huh?'

She gave him a wicked grin. 'I loved the bike. Especially when you did that corner thing where it dipped low.'

'The lean-in.' Setting his hands to her waist, he pulled her closer. 'I love that you love my bike.' He kissed her long and deep, making her body quicken.

Desire consumed her in a flame of need and she moaned, threading her fingers into his hair and flattening her body against his. Rafe made an indistinct sound that was somewhere between pain and pleasure, his hands on the sash of her robe. 'If this goes any further we won't make it out of the apartment.'

'Oh, then we have to stop.'

Stepping back, Alexa retied the sash on her kimono and smoothed her hair.

Rafe shook his head. 'Tossed aside for a hunk of metal. Nice to know.'

Alexa gave him a teasing smile. 'It is a really big hunk of metal, though...'

He reached for her to give her a punishing kiss but she danced out of the way, laughing as he threatened retribution for her impudence.

Breakfast was as large and decadent as he'd promised and afterwards Alexa didn't think she'd be able to eat for a week.

Rafe teased her for her measly attempt and hoovered

up her remaining eggs and spinach as if he hadn't just devoured a plate twice the size of hers.

The café he'd taken her to was warm and low-key, like she suspected he liked to live his life. Exactly the opposite to how she lived hers, which was all polished silver service and structured decorum.

Tossing money onto the table, Rafe took her hand and led her from the café as if they were just a normal London couple enjoying a springtime weekend on the town.

Throwing his leg over the big black bike, Rafe kicked the stand up and helped Alexa settle herself on the back, her body automatically moulding to his. He'd given her his leather jacket again and she curled her fingers into the over-long sleeves for extra warmth and tucked them against his stomach. The cool spring temperature wasn't so bad with the visor covering her, but she didn't really care about the cold anyway. She was just enjoying being with Rafe.

'Where to now?'

'I don't know. You decide,' she said, wrapping her arms around his waist as the bike moved off from the kerb.

Rafe was an exceptional driver, his movements smooth and confident as he navigated his way through the congested city streets. But then he was exceptional at most things. His business enterprises, his coffee-making—okay, that was mostly the machine, but still—his dancing, and most of all his love-making...

Hugging him tight, she stopped daydreaming and tuned into the world-famous landmarks that dotted the city. Rafe was clearly enjoying his new role as tour guide, but her attention was more on the man she was wrapped around than anything else.

Until the bike zipped past a relatively normal-looking building bursting with pedestrians and shoppers. Tapping him on the shoulder, Alexa indicated that she wanted him to stop and when she saw that it was a bustling market she clapped her hands with glee.

Ever since she was a young girl she'd been enthralled by the sights and scents of a busy market, loving the combination of old and new, and the anticipation that came with finding a hidden treasure. She still had the pair of lurid green sunglasses her father had once given in and purchased for her on a trip she had tagged along on and, much to Sol's disgust, she'd worn them constantly for months afterwards.

Rafe groaned good-naturedly when he realised how keen she was to explore, swapping their helmets for two caps and tucking her hair out of the way.

'Don't make eye contact with anyone and don't leave my side. I don't feel like getting into a fight.'

Alexa rolled her eyes. They might have left their security detail behind for the day but she'd never felt safer— or happier. Shelving that unsettling thought, she rolled her eyes. 'As if.'

'Sweetheart, with those exotic green eyes of yours I'm almost tempted to keep you indoors.'

Alexa grinned at him; she couldn't help it. 'Compliments like that will get you kissed.'

'In that case, you're not only beautiful inside and out, but when you slid down my stomach earlier and put your mouth on—'

'Rafe!' Knowing exactly what he was about to say, Alexa laughed and reached up to kiss him. His mouth immediately turned hungry and desire coursed through her with unnerving force.

Moaning into his mouth, she extricated herself from his arms and stepped back. Being with him like this, so relaxed and natural, had a freeing effect on her. It was as if all her fears and inhibitions had been washed away and she didn't have to worry about what the future might bring. It was just the two of them here and now.

'Come on.' She broke the kiss and hooked her arm through his. She'd stashed some pounds in her pocket on her way out of the apartment and she wanted to spend the lot.

Wandering past various vendors, Alexa soaked up the Reggae music and the delightful fragrance of the multi-cultural food on offer, stopping first to buy some exquisite chocolates and then to stand behind a crowd of onlookers to watch a curly-haired Australian juggler ply his trade.

Later, pleasantly exhausted and dressed in one of Rafe's shirts and a thick pair of socks, Alexa wandered into the kitchen to find Rafe putting the finishing touches to their evening meal.

'He cooks, he rides a motorbike *and* runs a multinational corporation.' She took a glass of Sauterne he held out for her. 'Is there anything you can't do?'

'Concentrate for any length of time when you're in the room.'

'I can live with that.' Alexa laughed because she was meant to, but a pang of longing she didn't expect to feel pierced her heart.

Careful, she warned herself. *You only have seven days left.*

'So what are we having?'

'Steak with pepper sauce, potatoes and salad.'

'Wow, now I'm even more impressed.'

Rafe smiled across the bench at Alexa, unsure if he'd ever enjoyed a woman's company as much as he was enjoying hers. She was bright, funny, beautiful… His eyes took in her clean face and laughing eyes. He liked being with her like this, relaxed, natural, just the two of them without any outside interruptions. And as much as he enjoyed making love with her, having her in his space filled him with a sense of wellbeing he would be hard pressed to explain. Maybe it was knowing that he could take her to bed any time he wanted. Because he did want to. All the time.

'I know that look,' she said huskily, her eyes growing heavy.

'You should.' Rafe told himself to pull it together before she accused him of having a one-track mind.

'So how is it you can cook?' she asked, reaching for a carrot stick.

Glad to be focusing on something else other than the way he was *feeling*, Rafe sliced vegetables and answered her question. 'When I moved to Cambridge I shared a house with a few other guys who could barely reheat beans. Since I had developed a penchant for fine dining, thanks to the palace chef, it was either learn to cook or starve.'

'I'm sure your brother would have provided a chef if you'd asked.'

'He would have, but I was determined to make my own way. Which I did. Partying, drinking, studying…playing darts. You do realise that your lover is a Cambridge darts champion?'

'Darts?' Alexa grinned. 'Be still my beating heart.'

Rafe arched a brow. 'Some respect, please. It's more difficult than it looks.'

Alexa grinned and sipped her wine. 'It sounds like fun. By contrast, I had private tutors and then I studied at Berenia University, surrounded by security.'

He looked up from chopping herbs for the vinaigrette. 'No partying for the future Queen?'

'No.' She gave a wistful sigh. 'I was accepted into an American university, actually. Sol helped me apply and then, when I got in, he managed to convince my father to let me study abroad, but then I made the mistake with...'

Rafe stopped chopping, noting the way the smile had died on her face. 'The Italian with the arms?' he prompted softly.

'Yes. Him. My father decided that I was too young. Too *vulnerable* to be that far away from home. He was probably right.'

'He wasn't right, Princess, and you need to stop feeling guilty about it. What happened wasn't your fault. You're entitled to make mistakes, and you have to live your life.'

'Yes, but I should have known better. I should have been prepared.'

Hearing the subtle anguish in her voice, Rafe reached over and took her chin gently in his hand. 'How could you? You were seventeen years old. I bet your father kept you under a tight leash when you were young—there, I see I'm right—so what previous experiences could you have had to prepare you for being conned by a man like that?'

She looked at him for so long he wondered if he had offended her when her lips twisted into a faint smile. 'Do you know, when I was in my teens I used to be a champion horsewoman and I always trusted my judgement. Then Stefano happened and *bam*—it's like I've second-guessed myself ever since. I've blamed myself for what happened for so long. Trying to be good and to do the right thing...' Her smile hit him like a sunbeam. 'Why did I never look at it the way you just did?'

Rafe leaned over and gave her a quick, deep kiss before handing her another carrot stick. 'Too hard on yourself, perhaps.'

'Maybe. It's something I've never been able to talk about with anyone else before.' She palmed her glass of wine and watched him cook. 'You're a good listener. And a good person, you know that?'

Rafe placed the steaks on the grill. 'Careful, I'll get a big head.'

'You don't like me saying that.' She tilted her head as she studied him. 'Why not?'

'I suppose I'm not used it. It wasn't something I heard growing up.'

'Your parents never told you that you were a good person?'

'My father and I never saw eye to eye. He told me he'd disown me if I didn't follow his rules.'

'But that's awful.'

'He was hard on all of us. We got used to it.' Rafe shrugged off her sympathy. He never let himself indulge in weak emotions like sympathy and need. 'Do you eat mushrooms?'

'Yes.' She frowned thoughtfully. 'I do remember hearing he was often upset with you, but you were always blamed for any issues that came up.'

Rafe laughed, turning the steaks. 'Often I deserved it.' He gave her his trademark smile, but somehow it felt false. 'I enjoyed riling my father by getting into scraps I shouldn't have.'

'At least he didn't actually follow through on the threat. I can't imagine how you would have felt if he'd actually disowned you.'

'I have no doubt that he would have, had he lived. Do you want your potatoes salted?'

'Yes, fine,' she dismissed with a wave of her hand. 'And your mother? She didn't tell you that you were a good person either?'

Wondering how the topic of conversation had turned from her to him so neatly, Rafe frowned. He had already told Alexa more about himself than he'd told anyone else and now he was flooded with memories he'd rather forget.

'My mother had her own problems,' he said tonelessly. 'Namely my father. They were always at each other's throats about something or other and I'm not sure she noticed any of us most of the time. She left when I was ten.'

He placed the steaks and potatoes on a plate and dressed the salad.

'Ten?'

He saw the sympathy on Alexa's face and his gut clenched. He still remembered waking up the morning after his mother had stolen out of the palace like a thief in the night, never to return. He'd come to terms with his childhood loss a long time ago. Come to terms with the fact that his mother lived the life of a recluse now, and rarely saw anyone.

'Did you see her often after she left?'

'No. She moved to Europe and Jag, Milena and I stayed in Santara. She didn't want us to go with her. She wanted a clean break, to be able to make a fresh start with her life.'

'But how could a mother do that?'

'Not all women are maternal, Princess.' He held two plates up with a flourish. 'Let's eat.'

Alexa was so shocked by Rafe's revelations about his childhood that she didn't know where to put the information.

According to stories she had heard about her own mother, she had been kind and compassionate, and Alexa would give anything to have memories of her, whereas Rafe sounded like he'd give anything *not* to have memories of his.

Her heart went out to him as a young boy stuck in a

volatile household. Hers hadn't been overly warm, her father often a distant figure, but she'd never doubted his love for her.

'But what about Milena and Jaeger?' she asked, following him to the table. 'Did it bring you closer to them?' Because she had always run to Sol when she'd felt down, and she missed him terribly now that he was gone.

'Yes and no. Milena was extremely young when our mother left and she needed a lot of support. Jag was away at boarding school.' He set their wine glasses on the table. 'I hope you're hungry.'

She was starving but she didn't care about food. 'Do you ever talk about it with Jag or Milena?' she prodded.

The look he gave her was one of surprise. 'Why would I do that? They have their lives, and I have mine.'

'It might be healthy,' she offered. 'How do you know they're not suffering in some way?'

She saw a muscle pulsing in his jaw as if she'd hit a nerve, his eyes suddenly remote. 'Jag and Milena both have my number if they need me. And you—' he said with silky emphasis '—do not need to concern yourself with any of this. I'm fine, Alexa. There's nothing missing from my life.'

What about love? she thought.

He didn't have love, but nor did he want it. As soon as the thought entered her mind a deep sense of misery filled her whole body. Misery for the boy whose parents had cared more about their own needs than those of their children. And misery at the wounds their behaviour had inflicted—inadvertent or otherwise. But at least now she had some understanding as to why he was the way he was.

Where she had always craved connection to others as a result of the lack of warmth in her own childhood—often to her personal detriment—Rafe had been let down by the very people who should have had his back, so he didn't let anyone close. He didn't try at all.

And she would do well to remember that because he didn't want that to change, and she'd be a fool to want it to be otherwise.

CHAPTER EIGHT

SOMETHING TICKLED HER ribs and Alexa swatted at it. 'Don't wake me.'

'I thought you were a morning person.'

She rolled over and groaned when she saw the clock. 'I am when I've managed to get some sleep.'

Rafe sat down on the bed beside her. 'I have coffee.'

'Coffee?' Alexa sprang up and blinked the sleep from her eyes. She breathed deeply and there it was, that delicious aroma.

Rafe laughed and handed her a mug. 'So predictable. But drink up. I have a surprise for you.'

'You do?'

'How do you feel about going on a road trip?'

'Don't you have to work?'

'Hannah's been nagging me about taking time off so I've cancelled my appointments for the next couple of days. If you need any further incentive, the road trip involves my bike.'

'It does?' Feeling helplessly happy and knowing it was dangerous to keep indulging in an emotion that had everything to do with the man creating it, Alexa shelved the voice in her head that said she was letting herself feel too much and nodded. 'Give me five minutes.'

Rafe laughed, leaning in to give her a lingering kiss. 'Now I really am jealous of my bike.'

A couple stretched into five days of exploring the English and Scottish countryside, as well as each other.

Rafe had taken her to Cambridge and the pub he'd frequented during his student days. From there they'd spent an afternoon climbing the ruggedly green Old Man of Coniston in the Lake District, before skipping over the border to explore Scotland. They'd stopped at Glasgow for a few nights where Rafe had checked out the nightclub scene and a couple of buildings he said he was thinking of investing in. One in particular, a grand old Art Deco cinema, Alexa had fallen in love with, totally on board with his vision of restoring it to its former glory rather than tearing it down.

Now they were by Loch Ness, standing under a cloudy sky and staring at the inky black waters of the lake.

'I've always wanted to see the monster,' Alexa said, her eyes searching for a tell-tale ripple or sign of an arched neck.

Rafe slipped his open coat around her body and hugged her closer against the sudden drop in the temperature. 'There is no monster.'

'Don't ruin the fun of it.' She burrowed even further into him against the cold. 'I've decided I'm going to do this every year.'

'Look for the Loch Ness monster?'

'No.' She jabbed him playfully. 'Take off for a week where no one knows who I am or where I am. I might even get my motorbike licence.'

'The Princess who rides?'

'Absolutely.'

She tilted her head up to gaze into his amused blue eyes. They stayed like that for what felt like an eternity, the connection between them so deep it took her breath away more than the scenery.

Suddenly feeling something damp on her face, Alexa shifted her gaze to the sky. 'Rafe! It's snowing!'

He smiled at her indulgently, stroking a flake from her cheek. 'So it is. Rare for this time of year, but damn cold enough!'

She started laughing and turned out of the circle of his arms to spread hers wide. 'I've never seen snow before. It's glorious.'

'You're glorious.' He pulled her back to him and crushed her lips beneath his until she forgot all about the snow.

When they finally parted to draw breath Rafe reached down to brush the wetness from her cheeks. 'Happy?'

Alexa could have melted into a contented puddle at the way he was looking at her. 'So happy.'

The following morning, their last on the road, Alexa relaxed in the quaint bedroom of a traditional English pub somewhere in a picturesque valley in the Yorkshire Dales.

It was dreamily quiet and she had woken to the faint sound of birds outside her window, and a crisp layer of snow covering the valley. Snuggled up in bed, she realised that she hadn't practised her normal yoga routine or thought about work all week, and she didn't even care. This trip with Rafe was a break from real life and she'd embraced it much more heartily than she would have thought possible.

Out here, they were just Mr and Mrs Nobody, taking a week off and travelling together. Last night the publican and his wife hadn't batted an eye as they'd pulled up late and asked if they had a room. A week ago Alexa would never have thought she would ever be in such a situation. She'd never thought she'd feel this magical, and all because she'd decided to 'take charge', as he'd suggested, and embraced uncertainty.

She could only imagine Nasrin's face when she told her how sexy the Prince really was. Or would she tell her? She'd certainly grown close to Nasrin over the last three years, but perhaps this experience was too private to share with anyone. Because she had no doubt that Nasrin would have her romantic hat on and interrogate her with a litany of questions about what had happened and how she felt about him. No doubt expecting Alexa to have fallen in love with him or something equally absurd.

Fortunately she wasn't at risk of that happening. She was having a good time with Rafe. A wonderful time, but that was all it was for both of them. The public might have bought their romantic love story but Alexa knew the truth, and this time she was determined to remain objective.

Wondering why she felt so unsettled all of a sudden, she nearly fell on the phone beside the bed as it started to ring. Out of habit she picked it up, checking the display before she realised that it was Rafe's phone and not her own.

Regan's name flashed across the screen and Alexa glanced at the bathroom door, where she could hear the shower running. She'd been too drowsy to join Rafe when he'd tried to cajole her into shower sex, promising to go in search of a soy latte for her as soon as he was out.

Regan's name flashed again and Alexa sat up, pulling Rafe's discarded T-shirt over her head to ward off the chill, and swiped the screen to answer the call. The Queen might be calling because of a family emergency and she didn't feel comfortable letting it go through to voicemail when she had the chance to answer it.

Delighted to hear her voice, Regan was keen to find out how Alexa was enjoying her time in England with Rafe and, before she knew it, Alexa found herself drawn in by the other woman's natural warmth. It was clear why the King had fallen in love with her. Even on the phone she was animated and sincere, so opposite to Alexa's own tendency to be closed down. Not that she'd been closed down this week. In fact the way she'd been with Rafe shocked the life out of her. Reminding her that she could be fun and relaxed when she wasn't so worried about the future, and how everyone perceived her.

Maybe a little bit of Rafe's capacity to let things go had rubbed off on her. Not that she'd go as far as he had in letting things go. Like letting go of his country, and his family.

'So I've organised a surprise birthday dinner for Jag in London tomorrow night,' Regan said in a hushed tone as if she half expected her husband to sneak up behind her. 'And I haven't heard yet if Rafe is coming. It's not that big a deal because I've booked the whole restaurant, but I'd really like to know. It would mean so much to Jag and me if you were both there.'

'Of course we'll be there,' Alexa said, not really thinking about the ramifications of that statement until she hung up and Rafe strolled out of the shower a couple of minutes later, a white towel draped around his lean hips, another draped around his shoulders, the tips of his hair glistening with wet drops from the shower.

'She lives.' He grinned at her. 'I was hoping you'd join me.'

'I was thinking about it,' she murmured, automatically opening her mouth for his kiss. 'But then Regan rang.'

Given that he'd said that he liked things just the way they were between him and his siblings, she wasn't sure how to tell him she'd accepted Regan's invitation. She would give anything to be able to go to another birthday dinner for Sol but she knew that Rafe didn't feel the same way about his family.

Rafe dropped the towel from around his shoulders, going still. 'Is everything okay?'

'Everything's fine. She told me she's throwing your brother a surprise birthday party tomorrow night and that you haven't RSVP'd.'

Rafe nuzzled a path down the side of her neck. 'I've been so distracted I forgot. I need to let her know that we're busy.'

Alexa braced her hands on the balls of his shoulders to shift him back.

'Are we busy?'

He frowned as she thwarted his attempt to rid her of his T-shirt. 'Yes. Tomorrow is our last night before you return to Berenia and I plan to make love with you the entire time.'

Their last night together? How had it come about so quickly? And how had she forgotten?

'Would you mind terribly if we had a slight change in plan?' she asked, arching her neck as he resumed his teasing kisses.

'How slight?'

'Well…' She winced, some sixth sense warning her that this might not go as well as she'd originally hoped. 'I sort of accepted Regan's invitation on your behalf.'

As predicted, Rafe drew back, frowning at her. 'How do you sort of accept an invitation?'

'You say yes.'

'Why would you do that?'

'Because it's a *really* nice idea, and she *really* wants you to be there. She said it would make Jag's night.'

Rafe shook his head, moving further away from her. 'I just saw my brother at our wedding two weeks ago, and then at the ball two weeks before that. I've seen him more this month than I did the whole of last year.'

'Surely that's all the more reason to go.' Sensing his physical and emotional withdrawal, and hating it, Alexa touched his arm. 'What are you afraid of?'

'Afraid of?' Rafe barked out a laugh. 'Fear isn't what's keeping me from wanting to go.'

'Then what is? Because it's important to make time for family.'

'Not all family members are best friends, Alexa.'

'I know. Which is why it's so vital to forge strong bonds. The more you see someone, the more you want to see them.'

Rafe gave her a look. 'Sometimes the opposite occurs.'

'It doesn't count with family because, as annoying as they can be, they're the only ones who will rush to your side when the chips are down.'

'I don't plan to let my chips go anywhere,' he drawled. 'Especially not down.'

Alexa returned his look of a moment ago and pushed a skein of her hair back behind her shoulders. Rafe's eyes darkened, the air between turning from frigid to molten in a matter of seconds.

'You did that deliberately,' he accused softly.

Dragging air into her lungs, Alexa blinked. 'Did what?'

'Doesn't matter. It won't work.'

Their eyes locked and then he vaulted off the bed, turning his back on her to stare out of the small window.

The morning had brightened and the sunlight drew shadows across his muscular shoulders and biceps, the white towel riding low on his lean hips. Alexa knew she had crossed a line in accepting the Queen's invitation on his behalf; she'd known it at the time, and she should never have done it. Not that she had expected his complete withdrawal or the hollow feeling inside her chest as if someone had carved out her heart and left an empty cavity behind.

'I'm sorry.' She moved towards him and placed her hand in the centre of his back, enthralled with the play of muscle that bunched beneath the surface of his skin at her touch. 'That was incredibly arrogant of me to impose my ideas of family onto you. I absolutely hate it when people think that they know better about my life than I do and I should have spoken to you first.'

Rafe swung around, his eyes full of an emotion that was somewhere between pain and anger, and she couldn't move. In the distance she heard the tread of someone's footsteps as they walked past their room and the sound of crockery clinking together, but all she could focus on was Rafe standing before her like a Greek God come to life.

He made a rough sound in the back of his throat and then his hands were in her hair, tugging her up onto her toes so that her lips were inches from his. 'How can I resist you when you look at me like this?' His voice was rough, his mouth hard and insistent when it met hers, his kiss eradicating everything else in the world for her but him. This man who gave new meaning to her life.

Alexa moaned, her mouth opening beneath his in an emotional onslaught of need that seemed never-ending, her hands clinging to his wide shoulders as if she might tumble over a cliff and be dashed against jagged rocks if she were to let him go.

Finally Rafe raised his head, leaning his forehead against hers, his breathing ragged.

'I'll go to my brother's party. This time. But, even though I know you mean well, I don't want you to ever interfere with my relationship with my family again. It is what it is, and I can't change that. I don't *want* to change that.'

'I hear you.' Alexa gulped in a few deep breaths to

steady her heartbeat. She did hear him and even though she might like to fix things for him that wasn't her role.

The following night Alexa smiled at Stevens as he opened her car door and waited for her to exit onto the damp London street.

An avant-garde restaurant loomed ahead, illuminated by a single bright light; the black door and grey brickwork looked as if it hid an illegal gin joint rather than a Michelin star restaurant.

Rafe's security team moved ahead of them, clearing the way and entering the building first.

Trying to lighten the mood between them that had shifted since she'd accepted Regan's invitation, Alexa chatted as if nothing was wrong.

'I've heard of this restaurant. The chef is some sort of food maestro. I read that he creates new recipes in a laboratory rather than a kitchen.'

'He's innovative,' Rafe agreed. 'And good at what he does.'

'Something you admire.'

'I admire lots of things.' His gaze slid down her body as the maître d' took her coat. 'Like you in that dress.'

Relieved that he no longer seemed upset with her, Alexa smiled. 'I believe you said that back at the apartment.'

'No, I nearly stripped it off you back in the apartment. Somehow I've convinced myself that anticipation will make the pleasure worth waiting for and didn't want to disappoint you by cancelling tonight.'

As usual the explosive chemistry that was never far below the surface when they were together ignited, stealing her breath.

'I'm glad you didn't cancel,' she murmured. 'I think it's going to be really special. And this dress deserved an

outing because I'll never be able to wear it in Berenia.'
Alexa adjusted the shoestring straps over her shoulders.
The dress was low-cut at the front, even more daring than
the one she'd worn to Bound, and it made her feel sexy
and confident—exactly how Rafe always made her feel.

Buoyed by a mixture of renewed happiness and lust,
Alexa glanced at him from beneath the sweep of her lashes.
'But I look forward to what anticipation looks like later on.'

'I can tell you what it will look like.' Rafe placed his
hand against the small of her back and leant close. 'A tenth
of a second.'

Alexa gave a husky laugh and suddenly she was plastered up against Rafe's hard body. She gasped at the unexpected contact and the doorman discreetly glanced at
his feet.

'Stay an extra week,' he said gruffly.

'What?'

'Don't leave tomorrow. It's too soon. Stay an extra
week. You can work from my place if you need to. I've
hardly scratched the surface of what I want to show you.'

Dazed by the forceful nature of his request, Alexa's
mind blanked of everything but him. She was sure there
were a hundred good reasons why she should say no, not
least because she wanted to stay with him in London a little
too much, but she couldn't utter any of them. 'I'd love to.'

'Good.' A satisfied smile curved his lips just before they
connected with hers for a brief searing kiss. 'Now let's go
and get tonight over with.'

Giddy with delight that Rafe wanted to be with her as
much as she wanted to be with him, Alexa floated through
the sliding steel door into a large room that had once been
an old warehouse. The designers had kept many of the
original features, including industrial lighting suspended
from black cables and exposed beams along the walls.

Long tables dressed with pristine white tablecloths and sparkling silverware filled the space, with a brushed metal bar running along the back wall.

Most of the guests seemed to already be present, about forty people standing in small groups holding champagne flutes and chatting animatedly.

A waiter in a white coat stopped in front of them, holding a tray full of coloured drinks.

'Mimosas,' Rafe murmured, obviously reading her perplexed expression correctly. 'Chilled juice and champagne. You might like it.'

Alexa accepted the pink drink, her eyes wide with appreciation at the sweet taste. 'I do like it.'

Rafe's eyes gleamed, but he had no chance to respond as Regan carefully crossed the room to greet them. She looked amazing in a gold three-quarter-length dress that cleverly hid her massive baby bump.

'I don't know much about pregnant ladies,' Rafe said, bending to kiss his sister-in-law on the cheek, 'but you look ready to pop.'

'Rafe!' Alexa admonished. 'You don't say that to a pregnant woman. You look amazing, Your Majesty. I hope I look as beautiful as you when I'm eight months pregnant.'

'Thanks. But please call me Regan.' Her eyes sparkled with merriment, her hand cradling her stomach. 'I'm not due for a month yet, but the sooner this little darling comes out the better. I feel like a hippopotamus.'

'My thoughts exactly,' Rafe deadpanned.

'I'll make him pay later,' Alexa promised. 'Where's the birthday boy?' She held out a silver-wrapped gift Rafe had organised earlier in the day.

'I'll take that,' Regan offered. 'And Jag is with a good friend who is plying him with some sort of whisky that was created in a cave five hundred leagues below the sea,

or some such. You should join them, Rafe, while I introduce Alexa to the other guests.'

'Love to.' Rafe gently touched Alexa's jaw. 'You okay
with that, Princess?'

Alexa's heart bumped behind her chest at the sweet endearment she'd come to love. 'Of course,' she said, watching as he walked away.

'Wow,' Milena said by way of a greeting as she stopped
beside Alexa. 'I never thought I'd see the day my brother
looked at a woman like that.' Quirky and exuberant in an
orange dress and bright blue stockings, she grinned de-
lightedly at Alexa. 'But it had to happen one day, right?'

Alexa knew she thought Rafe was in love with her, but
that was because Milena had no idea that they'd married
for political purposes. Alexa hated lying to her, but she
knew that the less people who knew their relationship was
staged the better.

'We're having a good time together,' Alexa supplied,
which was true enough. They were having a very good
time together. Or at least she was. She frowned a little as
she gazed over at Rafe, greeting the men beside the bar.
She was pretty sure Rafe was too. At least she knew he was
in the bedroom. Just as the thought formed in her head,
Rafe glanced back at her, his blue eyes finding hers with
unerring accuracy.

'Can you both excuse me?' Regan said. 'I need to remind the caterers about the cake.'

'I'll take care of Alexa,' Milena promised, snagging a
champagne flute from a passing waiter. 'You know my
brother can't stop looking at you,' she mused happily. 'And
whatever you've done to soften him, I'm glad.'

'Soften him?'

'Yeah, he actually listened to me the other day when I
called him to complain about the amount of security Jag

was insisting I have with me when I move to New York next week. He even promised to speak with him about it to see if he could reduce it.'

'He's worried you'll get taken advantage of. And there are a lot of toads out there,' Alexa said. 'Believe me, I know.'

'I suppose you're right,' Milena conceded. 'But I'm not thinking about that. I believe in destiny so whatever happens, happens. I'm just happy for my two brothers. One about to become a father, the other so in love he'd walk over hot coals for you. I still find it hard to believe, and I can't wait until you become Queen and Rafe has to walk two paces behind you at all times.' She gave Alexa an impish look. 'Given that he likes to always be in charge, I plan to tease him shamelessly about his subservient position every chance I get.'

Alexa knew that Milena meant well with her sisterly digs, but her comment struck a chord deep inside Alexa. In Berenia the spouses of a monarch didn't walk two paces behind; they walked ten paces behind.

And Rafe would never do it.

Moreover, she'd never ask him to do it.

And she'd like to be able to tell Milena that. Tell her that, actually, she didn't love Rafe at all. But even as the words formed in her mind she knew that not only could she not say them for reasons of confidentiality; but because they were no longer true.

She had gone and done the inconceivable and fallen in love with him, she realised with a sickening jolt. She didn't know when, or how, her feelings had changed, but she knew that they had, and the need to protect herself, to hide herself away from prying eyes threatened to overwhelm her.

She'd been so careful to keep their relationship in context. Tried so hard to remain objective and not to make more of their connection than was actually there, even embracing Rafe's ability to separate emotion and sex, and yet…at the end of the day she found him as utterly irresistible as most other women he'd dated. Because underneath that layer of sophistication and rebellious charm was a man who was caring and loyal and strong. A man who was worth keeping.

Her dream man.

Only she wasn't his dream woman. And she never would be because, although he clearly enjoyed spending time with her, he didn't want anything more from her. He didn't want that from any woman.

'Are you okay, Alexa?'

Milena placed a hand on her arm, her exotic eyes clouded with concern. 'You look a little dazed. Do you need to sit down? I hope it wasn't something I said. I know Rafe won't mind walking behind you. I should never have joked about that.'

Rafe was right, she thought with self-disgust; she really did need to work on her poker face if Milena had picked up on her distress so easily.

'I'm fine,' she automatically assured the other woman. 'I think this mimosa has gone to my head.'

'You need food,' Milena said. 'If I drink without eating I get lightheaded too. Let me find you some of the delicious canapés the waiters have been passing around.'

Alexa knew that an empty stomach was hardly enough to make her feel so dizzy. But realising she was in love with a man who would never love her back would do it.

She sucked in a deep breath. She was going to have to develop a new poker face and fast because this wasn't information she could ever reveal to Rafe. Everything would instantly change if she did. He'd see her as some lovesick fool like the women in his past who couldn't control their feelings for him. He might even withdraw from her like he had the day before, feel sorry for her, look at her with sympathy or, worse, worry that she would try to cling to him when it was time to end their marriage.

Right now she was his equal in and out of the bedroom. Right now they were having a good time, a wonderful time, but all she would have to do to ruin that would be to utter those three tiny little words and it would be gone. He'd probably send her home immediately, making up some excuse to avoid seeing her again. It would be awful.

And it was her fault. She'd become attached when she'd promised him that she wouldn't. When she'd promised *herself* that she wouldn't.

But she wasn't a dreamer in need of a fairy tale ending. She was a strong woman in charge of her own destiny.

Destiny.

There was that word again. And the irony of how her destiny had yet again interfered with her love life wasn't lost on her. Because even if Rafe did—by some miracle of the universe—have feelings for her it would never work out between them. While Stefano had wanted to marry her for who she was, Rafe *didn't* want to be married to her for who she was. He had made it clear on multiple occasions that he had no wish to return to Santara. That he hated all things to do with duty and royalty, so it stood to reason that he'd never want to move to Berenia. And while she could abdicate and pass the crown onto her cousin, it wasn't ideal because—

Abdicate?

Stumbling into a chair, Alexa threw her hands out to stop herself from falling when she was grabbed from behind and pulled up against a hard male body that sent tingles to her toes.

'Whoa.' Rafe reached for the half-empty champagne flute she'd nearly upended all over herself, grabbing it in time to prevent any of the pink contents from spilling. 'Careful, Princess.' He nuzzled her neck indulgently. 'You have a habit of spilling brightly coloured drinks all over yourself. At least this time you're not wearing white.'

Distracted by his lips against the tender skin of her neck, it took Alexa's dazed brain a moment to realise what he'd said. When it sank in she spun around in the circle of his arms and stared up at him.

'You?' Her gaze collided with his sparkling blue eyes as her brain rearranged the events of her past into a new world order. 'It was you. It was *always* you.'

Her heart lurched inside her chest and she didn't know whether to laugh or cry at the realisation that he had been the one to save her from embarrassment all those years ago, not his brother.

Her heart gripped tight inside her chest as she stared at his beautiful face. Him. It had always been him.

Destiny, whispered through her head again and she could have burst into tears on the spot. Because he wasn't her destiny at all. He wasn't her anything.

Bemused, Rafe cocked his head to the side as if he hadn't heard her right. 'Always me?'

'Yes.' How had she mistaken him for his brother all those years ago? How had she *not* known?

But then Rafe enjoyed playing the bad boy so much, how could she have ever thought that it would have been him? Who would have thought that the Rebel Prince would have possessed the empathy to prevent a young girl from embarrassing herself in front of a room full of dignitaries? But he'd always been that person deep down. It was why women fell over themselves to have a piece of him. Rafe was charming and debonair and handsome as the devil, but he possessed a deep sensitivity that eclipsed everything else. It was why his father's continual rejection had hurt him so much that the only way he'd been able to survive it was to pretend that it didn't hurt at all. It was why he reacted so strongly whenever he felt judged. He cared about those he loved, she realised, perhaps a little too much.

'Stop monopolising your new bride, Rafe,' Milena teased. 'She needs to eat!'

Feeling raw and exposed, Alexa gratefully accepted the small plate of canapés Milena offered. She knew her stomach wouldn't hold anything down, but at least nibbling at the food would give her enough time to develop an A-grade poker face.

Because she was going to need it to get through the rest of the night with her heart intact.

CHAPTER NINE

RAFE WATCHED ALEXA join his sister at the table, a slight frown pleating his brow. He would swear there was something up with her, but she wouldn't catch his eye so that he could be sure.

He'd taken her away this week on the spur of the moment and he'd enjoyed himself more than he'd thought possible. Being a loner, he usually couldn't wait to leave whoever he was with to get back to his own company, but that urge didn't seem to arise with Alexa.

He knew he liked her more than was wise, but he didn't seem to have any control over that. Looking at her, with her midnight-black hair catching the glints of the down lights and her perfect lips tilted into a smile, he wondered, not for the first time, at his total lack of control around this woman. Like asking her to stay an extra week because he didn't want her to leave.

She'd burrowed under his skin and although he was still waiting for the novelty factor to wear off, it wasn't happening. If anything, the more time he spent with her, the more he wanted to, which had never happened to him before.

Pleasure was pleasure but this... Being with her went beyond that and he'd be kidding himself if he tried to convince himself otherwise. He liked her both in and out of the bedroom. He liked her curiosity about the world, her dedication to her country, her loyalty to her people. He liked the way she teased him and challenged him and he loved that she shared his sense of adventure, and that she wanted to make the world a better place for everyone. Even him.

He'd been wrong to call her a doormat; she was far from a doormat. She was loyal and honourable and dedicated. They were all qualities he admired and tried to adhere to himself. He just wished her dedication was focused his way, rather than Berenia.

But then, if it was, what would he do with it? It wasn't as if he was looking for a permanent arrangement. They'd married with the express intention that it would end. She wanted it to end. And so did he.

Didn't he?

Well, of course he did. Alexa was as constrained by her royal duties as his brother was, giving her little choice as to how to live her life.

For a man committed to living his life with as few encumbrances as possible that would never work.

'You still thinking of ending things with Alexa in six months' time?'

Rafe gave his brother a blank stare. Jag had always had the uncanny knack of knowing what he was thinking. The fact that he'd been staring at Alexa for a full five minutes might have also given him away. 'Of course.'

'Okay.'

Jag joined him in watching Alexa chatting with the other women who had joined her and their sister at the table, sipping his glass of red.

'Okay? That's it?' He cut his brother a brooding glance. 'You're not even going to try and tell me I'm wrong? Not going to try and give me some brotherly advice?'

A smile threatened to break out on Jag's face. 'Would you like me to give you some brotherly advice?'

'No.' Rafe didn't need advice. Especially about his love life. And since when did he think of sleeping with a woman as his 'love life'?

'You sure?' Jag asked. 'You look a little torn.'

Did he? Well, hell. 'I'm not torn. Alexa is…she's great. But she's not looking for anything long-term and nor am I. You know that.'

'I know some things are bigger than we are,' Jag answered enigmatically. 'But the Rebel Prince and the future Queen of Berenia? It would never work, would it?'

'No, it wouldn't.' Rafe's expression turned grim. 'You know I can't toe the royal line if I don't agree with it.'

'That's always been one of your great strengths, Rafa. You speak your mind. Alexa would no doubt appreciate having someone like that in her corner when she starts her reign.'

'Father didn't.'

'No. But he was an ass.'

Rafe gave a short bark of laughter. 'Not to put too fine a point on it.'

Jag grinned, and suddenly it was as if they were teenagers again and racing each other across the sand in dune buggies.

'Remember that day in—'

'The mountains? Yeah. I beat you to the top that day.'

Jag scoffed. 'We'll call it even. But I definitely won the—'

'You wish,' Rafe cut in on a laugh. 'I've always been better than you at fencing.'

'Dream on, lover boy. I'll give you a rematch any time you're game. But I was talking about the yacht race around the sound.'

'A close call, I admit. But again, lucky.'

Jag laughed at the outrageous call. He'd always been the better yachtsman, while Rafe had excelled at dune racing.

He'd been wrong to dread tonight, Rafe realised with a jolt of clarity. Wrong to put so much distance between him and Jag over his guilty conscience because he had missed his brother. Missed his easy companionship.

'Listen, Jag...' he let out a slow breath '... I need to apologise for walking away all those years ago when you became King. I should have stayed to help with the transition.'

Jag gave him a look. 'There's nothing to apologise for. I wanted you to go. You'd lived under Father's iron rule for far too long. Staying would have stifled you even more.'

'Still—'

'It's okay, Rafa. We're—'

Whatever Jag had been about to say was cut off when his eyes turned as hard as stone. Seconds later he was striding across the room to where Regan leant against the back of a chair, one hand cradling her belly.

Noticing nothing out of place, Rafe followed, wondering at the tense set of his brother's shoulders.

'Goddamn it, Regan, I knew we shouldn't have come here tonight,' Jag said, steel lining every word, his hard gaze riveted to his wife.

'Don't swear,' Regan admonished. 'I got the all-clear to fly this weekend, remember?'

Sick with dread that his brother's seemingly solid relationship had gone the way of his parents', Rafe was about to step between them, as he had done with his parents many times during his youth, when Regan let out a low moan. 'How was I to know that my waters would break tonight?'

Her waters had broken?

Comprehension dawned on Rafe in a brutal rush.

'If something happens to you,' Jag ground out, his voice ragged with emotion, 'I'll never forgive myself.'

'Nothing will happen. I'm in labour. I'm not dying.'

'A month early!'

'Babies come early all the time. It's—' Her breath cut off as another contraction hit her. Jag swore and lifted her into his arms.

Acting purely on instinct, Rafe pulled his phone from his pocket, dialling the emergency services as his eyes searched for Alexa.

Before he'd located her, he felt her hand go into his, squeezing gently. 'What can I do?'

'What you are doing.' He brought her fingers to his lips, his worried eyes on his sister-in-law and brother. After organising emergency services he dialled another number, relieved when the call was answered on the first ring.

A ripple went through the room as the guests started to get wind of what was happening.

'The ambulance is two minutes away,' Rafe told his brother. 'And a friend of mine who is probably the best obstetrician in Britain will meet us at the emergency door of the hospital.'

'Thanks.' Jag swallowed hard, his eyes watering.

'She's going to be fine,' Rafe assured him. 'You focus on her. I'll take care of everything else.'

Two hours later, Rafe felt ragged as he waited for news, any news, that Regan was okay and the baby had been delivered safe and well. He'd never felt so helpless as he had at the sight of his powerful brother brought to his knees with worry.

This was why he wanted nothing to do with love. It churned you up inside and spat you out, battered, at the other end. It was such a stupid emotion. He had no idea why people actually sought this kind of thing out.

As if reading his thoughts, Alexa glanced at him from across the room. Two steps and she'd be in his arms and he'd feel one hundred times better, but he resisted the urge. He didn't want that. He didn't want to rely on someone else to make him happy.

But wasn't that already what had happened? All week he'd talked with her, laughed with her, held her in his arms and danced with her and that was exactly how he'd felt. Happy. Content. *Complete*.

Two of Chase's top security operatives stood to attention at the door of the waiting room, four more coordinating with Jag's special envoy outside the building and outside the delivery suite.

'I'm sure she's fine,' Alexa offered tentatively, a wary expression clouding her eyes. She was only trying to make him feel better so why wasn't he holding her? Comforting her? Taking comfort *from* her?

'Coffee.' Milena returned, bearing three steaming mugs. 'The café is closed at this time, so it's vending machine only, I'm afraid, but what can you do?'

'Alexa doesn't drink coffee at night,' he said absently.

'I will tonight,' she said, straightening to go to his sister. 'I think I'd drink anything right now. Thanks for thinking of it.'

'I needed to do something and since Sherlock here—' Milena gestured to the Chase security expert Rafe had asked to stay with her during the whole proceedings '—wouldn't let me go for a walk, or go find a decent café, that's it.'

The security operative's expression didn't change as he handed over a bag of snacks to Milena.

She took it begrudgingly. 'And snacks. Anyone want one?'

Remembering how much fun he'd had feeding Alexa chocolates they'd bought that day at the market, his eyes cut to hers. As if her mind had deviated down the same path, her eyes turned smoky.

Breathing hard, he deliberately turned to his sister before he pulled Alexa into an unlocked supply closet and rid himself of all this tension with something stronger than coffee.

When he glanced back, Alexa had her bottom lip between her teeth and was staring at the floor. Before he could go to her a nurse pushed through the glass door.

Rafe's heart rose to his mouth.

The nurse smiled. 'It's a girl,' she said. 'And mother and baby are both healthy and doing well.'

A noisy breath shuddered out of his lungs. His sister whooped with joy and Alexa had a hand on her heart.

'Can we see them?'

'Of course. Her Majesty asked for all of you to come through.'

Almost dazed at the notion that he was an uncle, Rafe followed his sister and wife into the delivery suite.

The room was quiet as they entered, Regan reclining in the bed while Jag held a small bundle wrapped in white. For a woman who had just given birth, Regan looked awfully good. Not that Rafe had ever seen a woman straight after giving birth before.

'Oh, my... She's adorable,' Milena cooed. 'Congratulations.'

Grinning from ear to ear, Jag handed the precious bundle to his sister.

'I'm so grateful, Rafe,' Regan said, her brown eyes tired but filled with joy. 'Your brother completely lost it in my hour of need. If you hadn't stepped up I probably would have given birth on the dessert trolley.'

Jag scoffed at the very idea and Rafe turned away from the loved-up couple—only to freeze when he saw Alexa.

At some point Milena had passed the newborn over to her and she had his niece cradled against her chest, an adoring expression on her face.

A tight fist wrapped around his heart and squeezed. For a moment he couldn't breathe. Her long hair had drifted over one shoulder, glossy and black, her face a mask of serenity. It was like the time he'd first set eyes on her, another bolt of lightning hitting him square between the eyes, followed quickly by the sure knowledge that he could look at this woman for the rest of his life and never grow tired of it.

'Do you want to hold her?'

Somehow, Alexa was in front of him. Rafe frowned. *For the rest of his life?*

He saw her eyes widen. 'You've gone pale. If you don't want to…'

'No.' He kept his gaze on the baby in her arms. 'I'll hold her.'

As if he was standing on the outside looking in, he took the baby and cradled her in his arms. She was so tiny. So dainty. This perfect little being that was both vulnerable and needy. Taking in the glow on both her parents' faces, he knew that she would always be loved. She'd never have cause to feel insecure or abandoned by those she needed the most.

What would it be like if this was his child? His and Alexa's?

Emotion, thick and unwelcome, clogged his throat. Those feelings he'd had for her earlier increased tenfold. Feelings he'd never had for a woman before. Previously, his life had always seemed so clear-cut. One thing had led on to another and he'd never questioned it. He'd just gone with it and cared little about the outcome. But he cared now, he realised. He cared very much.

Alexa had never felt more like running than she did right now. When she had passed the baby to Rafe all she'd thought about was how it would feel if that tiny angel belonged to both of them. The chilly expression on his face told her that he most definitely had not been thinking the same thing.

As a result the car ride back to the apartment had been quiet, as if they were both lost in their own thoughts. But it wasn't a happy quiet as it should have been after the safe arrival of a baby. It was fraught with unspoken emotions. It was as if all the closeness of the past week had fallen away as if it had never existed. And perhaps it hadn't outside her own imagination.

As soon as they arrived at the apartment Alexa didn't wait around to see what Rafe intended to do; instead she headed for the spare room she'd been allocated and pulled her suitcase out of the walk-in wardrobe.

'What are you doing?'

Heart thumping, Alexa turned and blinked at him. His eyes were unreadable as he took in her suitcase and the clothing in her hands.

'Packing.'

'It's nearly midnight.'

'I know.' She flashed him a bright smile. 'Your odd hours must have rubbed off on me.'

Intensely aware of him watching her, she kept her movements smooth and unruffled as she folded a shirt and placed it in the case.

'I thought you were staying an extra week.'

'I was but then I remembered that I have a number of

meetings booked in for Monday that I can't miss.' She knew she was rambling but she couldn't seem to take a breath deep enough to oxygenate her brain.

'Get your father to attend them.'

'I can't. I'm sorry. I didn't think it through enough when you asked me to stay earlier. How beautiful is your niece, though? I love the name, Jana. It really suits her.'

'Forget the baby,' he growled. 'And leave the damn clothes where they are.' His hands descended on her shoulders as he turned her to face him, his jaw tight. 'I need you, Alexa. I need to touch you. I need to make love to you.'

There was something in his eyes Alexa had never seen before. A depth of emotion she knew had come from experiencing anxiety about the unexpected birth of his niece. It had affected her too, making her want to find space so she could process everything. But she could no more deny Rafe than she could stop the cycles of the moon.

Gazing up at him, she let her eyes drift over the hard planes of his face. This was what happened, she reminded herself brokenly, when you opened yourself up to uncertainty. You got hurt.

Because she had to go. She had to return to Berenia and pick up the reins of her normal life. She had to get back to what she knew, not only because it was what they had agreed upon from the start, but because she would only be staying an extra week in the vain hope that Rafe's feelings for her would change.

And she wouldn't torture herself like that. Not a second time. And not with a man who already had too much of her heart, little did he know it.

'Stay.' He cupped her face in his hands.

Alexa's heart felt as if it had just cleaved in two at the look in his eyes, the anguish of her own emotions like a chokehold around her throat. She so desperately wanted to tell him how she felt, tell him that if he needed her she'd be his for ever, but fortunately he kissed her and she stopped thinking altogether. Stopped trying to make this into something that it wasn't and gave into the passion between them, winding her arms around his neck and holding him tight for the last time.

When he woke in the morning Rafe knew she was gone. There was an emptiness in the room, a silence in his apartment he hadn't felt since before she had arrived.

An icy feeling of disappointment entered his heart, followed by a hot rush of anger. Of course she had left like this. Stealing away in the middle of the night as if she'd never even been here. He'd known she'd wanted to go, and yet he'd asked her to stay anyway. No, *begged* her to stay. A futile exercise.

Thrusting back the covers, he pulled on his clothes and headed for the kitchen. She'd left a note. A pitiful piece of paper that thanked him for a wonderful week, asking him to call her if he needed her for anything.

As if he'd do that.

He might have had feelings for her last night, feelings that ran deeper than any he'd ever experienced before with any other woman, but that had only been because of the drama surrounding the birth of his niece. It had unlocked something inside him—some emotion that had made him think, for the barest second, that he was in fact in love with Alexa.

Thank God he hadn't told her that during the heat of their lovemaking during the night. Thank God he hadn't confused sex with emotion when that was all it had ever been.

Intense, yes. Controlling at times. But love…no. This wasn't love. This was white-hot fury that he'd allowed a woman to get under his skin and she'd walked out on him in the middle of the night.

Had she thought he couldn't handle seeing her leave? That he'd try and stop her?

He wouldn't have. Not a second time.

CHAPTER TEN

RAFE GLARED AT the pile of paperwork on his desk as if the fierceness of his stare might get it done without him having to actually do anything. The promise of spring had completely left London, and rain lashed the windows of his office as if some angry god were throwing spears from the sky.

Not that he cared. He wasn't planning to leave any time soon and when he did he'd just be going home to an empty apartment.

Still, the gloom of the exterior seemed to invade the office, casting a dim glow that not even the bright lights inside could drive away.

Another email pinged into his inbox just as Hannah knocked on his door. Knowing that his EA would be harder to ignore, he turned towards the door, his jaw clenching when instead of Hannah standing in his doorway it was Milena in a bright pink coat, her hair cut into an edgy long bob.

He'd successfully dodged his family prior to Jag flying Regan and his precious daughter, Princess Jana, home by explaining that he was coming down with something and hadn't wanted to infect the baby. Which had been true. He'd felt like death warmed up for the past eight days. But now his sister had caught up with him.

'I thought you had left for New York,' he said pleasantly, deciding that heading her off at the pass was his best game opener.

'I had some things to finish up in Oxford before I left.' She strolled closer and flopped down in the chair opposite his desk. 'Then Hannah staged an intervention so here I am.'

Rafe frowned. 'Hannah did what?'

'Staged an intervention.' Milena's eyes moved over his face with deliberate slowness. 'I have to confess I can see why she did. You look awful.'

'I haven't shaved for—' he couldn't remember '—a few days. That hardly constitutes awful.'

'You haven't slept for a few days either, if the circles beneath your eyes are anything to go by.'

'Forgot to moisturise.'

'Ha! What's up?' Her voice went soft, her gaze following suit. Rafe ground his teeth together.

'Work,' he intoned. 'Now, is there any other reason for your visit?'

'How's Alexa?'

She reached for the glass paperweight on his desk and started fiddling with it.

His eyes narrowed at her innocuous tone. 'Is this one of your trick questions?'

He hadn't spoken to Alexa since she'd walked out of his life and he couldn't be sure if Milena knew that or not.

'No, this is me trying to ease into the conversation without getting my head bitten off.' She gave a sigh. 'I know Alexa is back in Berenia. Jag told me.'

'Did he also tell you why?'

'He told me that your marriage wasn't all that it seemed, if that's what you mean.'

Rafe gave a harsh bark of laughter. 'Always the diplomat, our brother.' He ran a hand through his hair. 'Look, he's right. Alexa and I married for political reasons and, according to recent reports, it seems to be working. I'm considering it my good deed for Santara.'

'Sorry, I'm not buying it,' Milena said bluntly. 'I know you, Rafe. You didn't just marry her for political reasons. It was real. I was there. I saw you both say your vows to each other. I saw you kiss her at the altar.'

The last thing he wanted was to remember kissing Alexa and he turned back to his computer. 'It's done, Milena. In three thousand, four hundred and thirty-two hours we'll be divorced.'

'Oh, Rafe.'

Pushing out of his chair in frustration, Rafe glared at his sympathetic sister before stalking to the window. He angled himself against the window, wishing he was standing out there so that the icy blasts could numb the sudden pain in his chest.

'You really, really love her, don't you?' Milena prodded gently.

'If this is love you can have it,' he growled. 'Next time I accuse you of the same thing you can throw this back in my face.'

'I don't want to throw this back in your face. I want to help you fix it. But I think you're afraid.'

'Really?' He didn't try to keep the sneer from his voice. 'First Alexa, and now you. What exactly do you think I'm afraid of?'

'Feeling. Love.'

Rafe scoffed. 'Love doesn't exist.' Even if for a brief moment he had thought he'd felt it for Alexa. 'And if you go around thinking it does you'll experience a world of pain.'

'Like we did as kids? I was young when Mum left but I remember how upset you were. You punched a hole in the wall, remember? You broke two knuckles and had to have your hand bandaged for six weeks.'

'How do you know I punched the wall?'

'I saw you. And ever since then, it seems to me, you've closed your heart off to everyone around you. Including me and Jag.'

Rafe gave her a bleak look. 'I'm always there for you if you need me, you know that.'

'I do.' She touched his arm. 'But you won't let us be there for you when you need us.'

'That's because I don't need anyone.'

But the words rang hollow inside his heart. If he didn't need anyone why didn't he feel okay with Alexa leaving? Why did his life seem so colourless all of a sudden?

Rafe swore.

Milena smiled. 'I know love isn't a comfortable concept for you but she loves you too.'

'How would you know?'

'The same way I know you love her. It's the way you look at each other. Like the other person is the most perfect person in the world for you. Jag and Regan have the same thing going on, and I swear one day I want someone to look at me the way you two look at your wives.'

Fear made him want to snap at her and say it wasn't true but, unfortunately, what she said fitted. It explained the hard lump in his throat on the morning he'd woken to find Alexa gone, and the hollow feeling inside him every day since. It explained why for the first time in his adult life he didn't want to get out of bed in the morning and face the day.

Rafe let his head fall into his hands and acknowledged what he'd always known to be true. He loved his wife. He loved Alexa, and it wasn't going to go away.

He remembered noticing her at a formal function when

she had been a shy teenager on the verge of womanhood. Even then there had been something compelling about her that had held his attention. Something about her that had made him want to protect her.

But her loving him in return?

'I think you're forgetting that she left, Milena. If you love someone you don't walk out on them in the middle of the night.'

'Like our mother?' she asked softly. 'Alexa isn't our mother, Rafe. And who knows what would have happened if our father had gone after her? Maybe she would have come back and our life would have turned out very differently.'

'I don't know—'

'And you won't if you give up.'

Those words jolted something deep inside him. 'I don't give up.'

His sister's brow arched. 'So why haven't you asked her why she left instead of presuming that you already know the answer?'

Because he was petrified of stuffing things up and feeling like a fool. Because he was petrified of feeling even worse than he did now. If that was even possible.

'How did you get to be so smart?'

'Observing two thick-headed brothers my whole life.'

Rafe gave her a faint smile and palmed his keys. 'I owe you one,' he said, heading for the door.

'I know.' She grinned broadly. 'And I'll be sure to collect on it.'

Alexa flicked through the pages of notes Nasrin had printed out for her. She was up to page twenty of fifty so she really needed to get a wriggle on if she was going to at least know something of the details about the one hundred guests who would be attending tonight's trade dinner. Usually she would have done this already, but she couldn't seem to muster the enthusiasm for it right now.

She knew what was wrong. She'd been back in Berenia for just over a week and nothing felt right. Not that anyone would guess. She'd upped her game face and had been putting on a good front. Had been trying to convince herself that it was silly to feel bad about something that had only been temporary to begin with. Which was exactly what she'd said to Nasrin when she'd been confronted with her EA's crestfallen face.

'But I was sure it was going to work out,' Nasrin had moaned when she'd returned *sans* Rafe. 'The way you looked at each other at the wedding. *That* kiss.'

The way Alexa remembered it, Rafe had been horrified to see her walk down the aisle, and she'd been similarly placed—or rather displaced—so she had no idea what Nasrin was talking about.

It had taken half an hour of convincing, but finally Nasrin had gone quiet on the subject, or perhaps she'd gone quiet because she'd had no choice. Either way, Alexa had been relieved to not have to talk about Rafe.

Her father had naturally asked where her husband was and when he planned to move to Berenia, but Alexa had put him off too, turning the topic of the conversation to business to distract him, all the while knowing that she really needed to come clean about her marriage sooner rather than later.

And she would. She'd just needed another week or so to mourn in private before she closed the 'Rafe' chapter of her life. She supposed it had been cowardly to sneak out of his apartment while he'd been asleep, but at the time she hadn't cared. She'd just wanted it to be easy. And she'd left him a note. *Thanks for everything. Call if you need me.*

Of course he hadn't called; she hadn't expected that he would. And that was okay, because that was easier too.

'Are you ready, Your Highness?'

Alexa glanced at Nasrin and gave a silent groan. She was still on page twenty, the illness she'd been fighting since her return to Berenia making her feel dizzy at times. 'I haven't quite finished the notes you made. Is there anything in particular I should be aware of? Any topics of conversation I need to avoid?'

Nasrin rattled off a couple of things for her to consider but Alexa had to force herself to concentrate. Don't mention climate change to the Minister of the Russian Interior, and remember to congratulate the Ambassador of France on their latest election results, and absolutely steer clear of the Prince of Tongase because he would bend her ear back about export deals given half a chance.

Logging the details in her memory, Alexa gave her reflection a quick once-over. She'd opted for a simple navy blue sheath tonight and pinned her hair back into a tightly coiled bun.

Her image said that she meant business and she did. The time she'd spent with Rafe lazing around in bed or exploring the countryside was like a distant dream that had happened to someone else.

'The King and Queen of Santara sent a thank you card for Princess Jana's gift. They won't be attending tonight, but that was to be expected. The King hasn't left his wife's side since the birth.'

Alexa gave Nasrin a small smile. The last thing she wanted to hear about was how much the King of Santara cared about his Queen. 'And my father?'

'He's waiting for you in the south parlour. Are you sure you're up to this, Your Highness? You look a little pale.'

'I'm fine.'

She wasn't fine. She wanted to lie down in her bed and go to sleep. Maybe for one hundred years. Smiling at the irony of how her mind had turned to a fairy tale, she shook her head. She'd been awakened by her very own Prince Charming—literally—but he still hadn't wanted her in the end. He hadn't even attempted to contact her since she'd left. Not that she'd wanted him to. A clean break was much better.

Heading to the south parlour, she knocked quietly before entering and found her father leaning against the fireplace. His eyes scanned her and he scowled. 'You don't look well.'

Alexa grimaced. 'Thank you, Father. The same goes for you.' Her father had been fighting a head cold since she'd returned, probably what she was struggling with herself, and should have been in bed. 'I'm more than happy to attend tonight's dinner without you if you'd rather rest.'

'I can rest when I'm dead,' her father argued. 'And you should have support tonight. That husband of yours should be here.'

Alexa had been hoping he wouldn't bring up Rafe's absence again but…so be it.

She gave a faint smile at the memory of the last time Rafe had muttered those words. Sealing his fate in agreeing to marry her.

But she couldn't think about Rafe right now, not in that way; she'd probably start leaking tears all over the place and her father would guess how devastated she was. But maybe now was the time to mention the true nature of her relationship with Rafe. That way, her father wouldn't have a lot of time to grill her about it, and it would give him time to process the details before they met up next.

Taking the bull by the horns, Alexa perched on the chair opposite the fireplace. 'Before we head down the stairs there's something I need to tell you about Prince Rafaele and myself. And I want you to know from the outset that the whole idea was mine so any complaints or issues you have should be solely directed at me.'

To give him his due, her father listened patiently as she gave him the CliffsNotes version as to what had happened, leaving out the part where she had fallen hopelessly in love with her husband and how he didn't love her back. That he would never love her back. Her father didn't need to know everything.

But she told him the rest. She told him about her proposal, and Rafe turning her down; she told him how they had never meant to actually go through with the wedding, and the marriage bargain they'd worked out between them. She also told him that Rafe had turned out to be nothing like she'd expected, and that he was actually a decent, hard-working man who cared deeply about those he loved. 'And now I'm back,' she said, struggling to remain composed. 'And, as you can see, ready to resume my duties.'

'I see. So what happens now?' he asked, his frown revealing how unimpressed he was with her actions.

'Now we stay married for five more months, and then quietly go our separate ways.'

'You should have told me this earlier.'

'Would you have listened?'

Previously, Alexa would never have asked her father such an impertinent question, but he needed to know that she wasn't the same person she had been before she'd married Rafe. She'd grown up in Rafe's arms and she didn't want to go back to the way things had been before. With her ostensibly being a yes person to please her father.

'Perhaps not,' he conceded. 'But I'm listening now.' He straightened his cuffs. 'However, it is time we went down to the receiving line. Our guests will be arriving at any moment.

'Of course. But Father…' Alexa mulled over her next words. 'I know you don't feel that I'm able to do this job alone, but I'm going to prove you wrong. I will make a worthy Queen of Berenia in Sol's stead.'

Her father stopped and frowned at her. 'I've never thought you incapable of being anything but an incredible leader of our people. But this is a lonely job, Alexa. It will be harder for you to find a suitable spouse once you become Queen, and I don't want you to rule alone. It's too hard.'

Her father's lined face turned weary and Alexa's heart jumped in alarm. 'Father—'

'I'm fine. Just… I miss your mother. And never more so than when you are opposite me looking as beautiful as she once was.'

'But I never knew that was how you felt.'

A faint smile twisted her father's lips. 'Why do you think I never remarried? There was no one to replace her. And I didn't want that for you. Rightly or wrongly, I didn't want you or Sol to become so attached to anyone that losing them would make you feel this empty.'

'Hence the reason you changed our nannies and tutors so often,' she said, finally understanding the logic behind that decision.

'I wanted you both to become more resilient than I felt at the time. Stronger. But you were hurt by love anyway, and then we lost Sol. I felt like I had failed you both.'

'Father—'

'Let me finish.' He grimaced as if explaining such deeply emotional issues was akin to having his skin flayed from his body. 'I thought that if I could force you to make a practical match it would save you from unnecessary heartache in the future. I can see that I was gravely mistaken about that. But finding you a life match was never about your capability to do your job. I hope you believe that.'

Alexa's stomach clenched tight. 'I don't know what to say.'

'There is nothing to say. You should have a strong man by your side to support you. And I hoped that Prince Rafaele would be that man.'

So had she. Or at least she had come to think that way. But while he was a very strong and compassionate man, he wasn't *her* strong and compassionate man. He might never be anyone's, given his need for independence and freedom from obligation.

Which was all she knew. Obligation and duty. Would those dual requirements always have to take precedence over love?

A lump lodged in her throat, threatening to defeat her composure once more, and once more she pushed it back. 'Shall we go?'

'Yes. It is time.'

Three hours later Alexa knew that if she didn't sit down very soon she would likely fall down.

The head cold she'd been fighting made it hard to focus on the group currently discussing the merits of trade taxes and border control.

Offering to email one of their party some of the ideas her team had come up with on tax reform, Alexa made her excuses and was considering going to find a dark room to hole up in when her eyes snagged on a figure in black at the entrance to the ballroom.

Unable to believe that it was really Rafe, the hairs on the back of her neck rose when his eyes found her.

His expression was grim, his clothes as beautifully cut as they had been the night at the Children's Charity ball. But there was a wildness to him, and she realised that he hadn't shaved, giving him an even more dangerous edge than usual.

The guests he would have bowled over if they hadn't moved out of his way thought so too, their curious glances turning to wary alertness as they quickly moved out of his way.

Alexa only noticed them peripherally, her whole being focused entirely on Rafe.

He stopped directly in front of her, his frown darkening. 'Your hair is up.'

'Yes.' A wave of dizziness at having him standing in front of her made her instinctively reach out for him.

Rafe swore under his breath, taking hold of her elbow. 'And you're unwell.'

Shaking off her initial shock, Alexa cleared her throat, easing her arm out of his hold. 'Just a head cold. But you look…' Gorgeous. Commanding. And so desirable she wanted to throw herself into his arms and never let go. It seemed so unfair when she felt like death warmed up. 'Almost like your usual self.'

'I haven't been my usual self since we met, Princess,' he answered cryptically. 'That aside, I'm taking you out of here.'

Seriously rattled to have him here, Alexa shook her head. 'I can't leave yet. The speeches haven't happened.'

'Are you giving a speech?'

'No.'

'Then you're leaving.'

Alexa frowned. 'Rafe, you can't just turn up here and—'

'Prince Rafaele? So good of you to join us.'

Feeling a horrible sense of *déjà vu*, Alexa nearly groaned at the sound of her father's combative voice behind her, sure that he wouldn't back down now that he knew the truth of their marriage.

'You might not think that in a minute, Your Majesty,' Rafe answered. 'My wife is sick, and I'm taking her out of here.'

'Really?' King Ronan raised a brow. 'You've remembered that you have a wife, then?'

'I never forgot.' Rafe held her father's stare. 'Not even for a minute.'

Unable to decipher the silent code going on between the two men she was surprised to see her father nod his assent. 'Good. I told her she was not well. She needs to lie down.'

'I can make my own decisions,' Alexa said hotly, her voice low so as not to cause a scene.

'You can,' Rafe agreed. 'But we need to talk and I'd rather not do it in a room full of interested people.'

Suddenly aware that they were on the receiving end of about one hundred pairs of eyes, Alexa groaned. 'Okay, fine.'

Holding her head high, she started forward, her legs so shaky that she might have tripped over her skirts if Rafe hadn't caught her up in his arms without breaking stride.

'Put me down,' she urged. 'You're causing a scene.'

'Probably.' He gave her one of his devil-may-care grins. 'It is something I excel at, it seems.'

Alexa caught the surprised glance of the footman who scrambled to open a side door for them and just managed to resist burying her face against Rafe's neck.

'Which way are your rooms?' he asked gruffly.

'I'm not going to my room with you,' she said, knowing that if she did she really might throw herself at him. 'And I need you to put me down.'

Obliging her this time, he lowered her to the carpeted floor in one of the side rooms off the ballroom.

'Thank you.' She smoothed her hands down her dress, aware that she was in danger of placing meaning on his actions that probably didn't exist. 'What I need is to know what you're doing here. And why you look like you haven't had any sleep in a week.' Because this close, she could see that his eyes were not as bright as they usually were.

He grimaced. 'You and Milena should form a club. She thinks I look terrible as well.'

'I didn't say you looked terrible…but…why are you here, Rafe? What do you want?'

'Are you so desperate to get rid of me?' he asked softly.

No. She wasn't desperate to get rid of him. On the contrary she wanted him to stay. She wanted—

'Actually you have Milena to thank for my presence here tonight.'

'Oh.' A shaft of disappointment speared into her chest, bursting the little bubble of hope she'd been nursing that he'd come to Berenia for her. 'I'm not sure I understand. Does she need something from me?'

'No, Princess.' Rafe gave her a faint smile, his eyes so dark they were almost black. 'Milena doesn't want anything from you. She came to my office today and pointed out that I'm an idiot.'

'Rafe, I'm sure she didn't mean—'

'She did.' He took her face between his hands. 'Because she knows that I'm totally and utterly in love with you.'

Oh, God…

Alexa groaned softly. She knew Milena would have meant well, but she really wished the other woman hadn't interfered. 'I'm sorry she said that.' She shook her head, her hands trembling. 'She mentioned the same thing to me at Jag's party but I knew not to believe her. I knew—'

'You should have believed her.' Rafe placed a finger against her lips. 'Because she's right. I do love you.'

Alexa's eyes flew to his. 'How is that possible? At the

hospital, when I handed you Princess Jana, you looked at me as if you never wanted to see me again.'

'That was shock. When I saw you holding the baby all I could think about was how it would feel if Jana had been ours.'

'You did?' Her eyes turned watery because she felt so *emotional* hearing him say that. 'But you said you don't need love in your life.'

'I *didn't* want love in my life,' he corrected. 'Which is why I didn't go after you when you left. It was easier to let you go than to face how much I had come to need you. Especially since my mother left in the middle of the night and I woke the next morning to find her gone.'

'Oh, Rafe, I'm so sorry I reminded you of that. I didn't know what else to do. I was so afraid I'd blurt out how I felt and that you'd... It was cowardly.'

'I didn't exactly give you a lot of reasons to stay. I am now.' His hand smoothed over her jaw, tilting her face up to his. 'Tell me what you didn't want to blurt out last night.'

Alexa's smile was tremulous. 'That I love you, of course. That I think I've always loved you.'

Rafe crushed her lips beneath his, and for a moment all Alexa could do was cling to him. Then reality intruded with a thud.

'Rafe, wait...' Her voice shook and her knees threatened to give out as she eased back. 'This can't work. You know it can't. Your life is in London and I'm the future Queen, and unless I abdicate to my cousin I—'

'Abdicate?' Rafe took her face between his hands. 'Princess, nobody's abdicating. You're perfect for this role.'

'Then what are you suggesting? That we have a long-distance marriage?'

'Alexa, you're my wife. You're going to stay my wife,

and I'm going to be your husband and support you in any way that I can. In Berenia.'

'You'll move to Berenia?'

He gave her a wide smile. 'What can I say? I'm a glutton for punishment. But my life is no longer in London. It's wherever you are.'

'But your business, your clubs…'

'I can run my business from anywhere if I choose to but seriously, Alexa, you're not hearing me. If you want it, my life is with you and wherever you are.'

'If I want it?'

'Yes. Do you? Do you want to spend the rest of your life with me as much as I want to spend the rest of mine with you?'

'Yes.' Finally giving into the insane level of happiness welling up inside her, Alexa laughed. 'Yes, yes, yes.'

She let out a shriek as Rafe wrapped his arms around her and swung her into the air. 'Rafe, I love you so much it scares me.'

'Only because you haven't come to trust how I feel yet. But you will. I plan to tell you every day so that you'll never feel insecure about your self-worth ever again.'

'I can't quite believe this,' she said, holding him tight. 'You were supposed to be the most unsuitable man on the planet.'

Rafe eased back so that he could look down into her face. 'And now?'

'Now I never want to let you go.' Giddy with emotion, she reached up onto her toes to kiss him and then pulled back at the last minute. 'We shouldn't. You'll catch my cold.'

'Princess, I don't think you have a cold. Your nose isn't even red.'

'My nose doesn't have to be red to have a cold. But I

am sick. I feel dizzy sometimes and my stomach is unsettled a lot.'

'Have you seen a doctor?'

'No.'

'Then you should because I don't think you're ill. I think
you're pregnant.'

'No, I'm not. I…' Alexa's eyes widened incredulously;
her mind swung back to when her last period was due.
She was late but in her misery she hadn't even noticed.
'I can't be.'

'There were a couple of times I didn't put a condom
on right away.'

Alexa stared at him wide-eyed. 'Oh, God.' She clapped
her hand over her mouth. 'What will we do?'

Rafe gave her a half smile. 'We'll have a baby.'

'I mean, will you mind if it's true?'

'Absolutely not,' he said huskily. 'I need to catch up to
Jag, but…' His eyes grew wary. 'Do *you* want a baby?'

Knowing by the tense set of his shoulders that he was
no doubt remembering his own childhood, Alexa clasped
his face in her hands. 'If we have made a baby together
I'll be the happiest woman in the world. I love you. I want
to have your babies, and I intend to smother them in love
and attention for ever.'

Rafe gave her a slow grin. 'Then how about you take
me your room now, just in case I'm wrong. We can get to
work immediately.'

Alexa threw her arms around his neck. 'With pleasure.'

EPILOGUE

RAFE HADN'T BEEN WRONG. Exactly two hundred and seventy days after their wedding Zane and Tobias had been born. Now they were rambunctious one-year-olds.

'Milena, can you grab Jana and Zane before one or both of them climb into the fountain again?' Rafe asked, scooping his remaining twin up and tucking him under his arm in a football hold before he could think about joining his brother and cousin.

'On it!' Milena yelled, pretending to be a wicked witch as she ran after the two children, making them squeal with delight.

Seeing the fun his twin and older cousin were having, Tobias let rip a loud squeal of indignation.

'Looks like you have your hands full!' Jag laughed, burping one of his own newborn twins against his shoulder. 'Where's Alexa?'

'Grabbing a coffee with Nasrin while she checks in with her father. Okay, buddy.' Rafe swung Tobias to the ground and waited for his little legs to steady beneath him. 'Go pull some more of Aunty Milena's hair out. We don't like the colour right now anyway.'

Tobias let out a war whoop and took off as fast as his legs would carry him. Rafe gave a loud sigh of relief. 'This parenting gig is harder than tending to a room full of Berenians with a chip on their shoulder.'

'Well, he is half Berenian,' Jag observed, patting his daughter's back.

Rafe gave him a bemused glance. 'Lucky for you that they are. Thanks to me, everything has completely settled down between our nations now. The Berenians love me.'

'Yeah, right.' His brother grinned back. 'And, speaking of Berenia, how's the new business venture?'

'Great. The new university is so popular we have to build more student accommodation to cope with demand.'

'You don't miss the nightclub scene?'

Since moving to Berenia, Rafe had sold off most of his clubs, keeping a few that Hannah had stepped into running for him. He now worked on restoring old buildings and returning them to their former glory and loved it.

He'd also opened up to his sister and brother, forging a bond with them that was deeper than ever.

'Everything is great,' he said, and meaning it.

'And you wouldn't swap it, right?'

Knowing Jag shared his sentiments, Rafe shook his head. 'Not in a heartbeat.'

'Where are the twins?'

His wife's voice from behind had Rafe swinging around. 'Princess.' Immediately at ease with her by his side, Rafe drew her into his arms and kissed her. 'The twins are over by the fountain with Milena. How's your father?'

'Determined to reign until he's ninety.'

Rafe laughed, kissing her again. 'I'm okay with that. The more time I get you all to myself the happier I am.'

'You'll always have me to yourself,' she promised huskily.

Jag mumbled something about finding his own wife before heading inside, but Rafe only had eyes for Alexa.

Kissing her again, he felt her move against him and groaned softly against her lips. 'You know accepting your marriage proposal was the best bargain I ever made, don't you?'

'You didn't accept my proposal,' Alexa scoffed. 'My father forced you to marry me.'

'Did he?' Rafe gave her an enigmatic look he knew would drive her crazy.

'Yes.' She glared at him. 'He did, didn't he?'

Rafe's grin widened. 'Have you ever known me to do anything that I didn't want to do?'

'No.' Her green gaze narrowed menacingly. 'Are you saying you wanted to marry me back then?'

'Let's just say no other man was ever going to have you after the way you kissed me that night.'

'You mean the way you kissed me,' she huffed.

'Want to argue about it inside?' he asked suggestively.

Alexa glanced anxiously over at the twins. 'How long do you think we have before the boys need us again?'

Rafe grabbed her hand and tugged her towards the Summer Palace. 'Long enough for me to show you how much I love you.'

'Oh, good.' Alexa's grin made his heart catch. 'My favourite thing.'

* * * * *

MILLS & BOON

Coming next month

CINDERELLA'S ROYAL SEDUCTION
Dani Collins

"You're genuinely asking me to marry you. And if I do, you'll give me this hotel and spa, all the property and rights to the aquifer. Everything," she clarified.

"If you'll live in Verina with me and do what must be done to have my children, yes," he said with a dark smile.

She was still shaking her head at the outrageous proposition but found herself pressing her free hand to her middle, trying to still the flutters of wicked anticipation that teased her with imaginings of how those babies would get made.

She veered her mind from such thoughts.

"Why? I mean, why me?" She lifted her gaze to his, catching a flash of sensual memories reflected in the hot blue of his irises.

"I've already told you. I want you in my bed."

"And that's it? Your fly has spoken? That's the sum total of your motivation?"

His eyes narrowed, becoming flinty and enigmatic. "There are other reasons. I'll share them with you, but they can't leave this room."

That took her aback. "What if I don't want to carry your secrets?"

"You're going to carry my name and my children. Of course you'll keep my secrets. Would you like to tell me yours?" He regarded her over the rim of his glass as he sipped, as though waiting for her to tip her hand in some way.

She shrugged her confusion. "I'm not exactly mysterious," she dismissed. "The most interesting thing that's ever happened to me is happening right now. You realize how eccentric this sounds?"

"Eccentric or not, it's a good offer. You should accept it before I change my mind."

She snorted. "You're quite ruthless, aren't you?" She spoke conversationally but knew it as truth in her bones.

"I do what has to be done to get the results I want. You understand that sort of pragmatism, even if you've pointed your own efforts in dead-end directions. I look forward to seeing what you accomplish when you go after genuinely important goals."

"This is my home. It's important to me."

"Then claim it."

A choke of laughter came out of her. "Just like that? Accept your proposal and—" She glanced at the paperwork. "I'm not going to agree to anything before I've actually reviewed that offer."

"Due diligence is always a sensible action," he said with an ironic curl of his lip. He waved his glass toward the table, inviting her to sit and read.

Gingerly she lowered onto the sofa and set aside her whiskey.

Rhys kept his back to her, gaze fixed across the valley as he continued to sip his drink, saying nothing as she flipped pages.

His behavior was the sort of thing a dominant wolf would do to indicate how little the antics of the lesser pack affected him, but she was glad not to have his unsettling attention aimed directly at her as she compared the two contracts. Aside from the exchange of money on Maude's—and the fact that hers finalized on her wedding day—they were essentially the same.

"I want possession on our engagement. If I decide to accept your proposal," she bluffed, fully expecting him to tell her to go to hell.

"Done. On the condition we begin the making of our children on the day our engagement is announced." He turned, and his eyes were lit with the knowledge his agreement had taken her aback. "We'll keep the conception part as a handshake agreement. No need to write that down in black-and-white."

He brought her a pen. His hand was steady as he offered it. Hers trembled as she hesitantly took it.

"Are you completely serious?" she asked.

"Make the change. Sign it. I'll explain why I want you to marry me. You'll accept my proposal, and Cassiopeia's will be yours."

Continue reading
CINDERELLA'S ROYAL SEDUCTION
Dani Collins

Available next month
www.millsandboon.co.uk

COMING SOON!

We really hope you enjoyed reading this book. If you're looking for more romance, be sure to head to the shops when new books are available on

Thursday 9th January

To see which titles are coming soon, please visit

millsandboon.co.uk/nextmonth

MILLS & BOON

JOIN US ON SOCIAL MEDIA!

Stay up to date with our latest releases, author news and gossip, special offers and discounts, and all the behind-the-scenes action from Mills & Boon...

 millsandboon

 millsandboonuk

 millsandboon

It might just be true love...

MILLS & BOON

THE HEART OF ROMANCE

A ROMANCE FOR EVERY KIND OF READER

MODERN

Prepare to be swept off your feet by sophisticated, sexy and seductive heroes, in some of the world's most glamourous and romantic locations, where power and passion collide.
8 stories per month.

HISTORICAL

Escape with historical heroes from time gone by. Whether your passion is for wicked Regency Rakes, muscled Vikings or rugged Highlanders, awaken the romance of the past.
6 stories per month.

MEDICAL

Set your pulse racing with dedicated, delectable doctors in the high-pressure world of medicine, where emotions run high and passion, comfort and love are the best medicine.
6 stories per month.

True Love

Celebrate true love with tender stories of heartfelt romance, from the rush of falling in love to the joy a new baby can bring, and a focus on the emotional heart of a relationship.
8 stories per month.

Desire

Indulge in secrets and scandal, intense drama and plenty of sizzling hot action with powerful and passionate heroes who have it all: wealth, status, good looks…everything but the right woman.
6 stories per month.

HEROES

Experience all the excitement of a gripping thriller, with an intense romance at its heart. Resourceful, true-to-life women and strong, fearless men face danger and desire - a killer combination!
8 stories per month.

DARE

Sensual love stories featuring smart, sassy heroines you'd want as a best friend, and compelling intense heroes who are worthy of them.
4 stories per month.

To see which titles are coming soon, please visit

millsandboon.co.uk/nextmonth